Edgar Fawcett

**Olivia Delaplaine**

Edgar Fawcett

**Olivia Delaplaine**

ISBN/EAN: 9783337030537

Printed in Europe, USA, Canada, Australia, Japan

Cover: Foto ©Andreas Hilbeck / pixelio.de

More available books at **www.hansebooks.com**

# OLIVIA DELAPLAINE

## A Novel

BY

## EDGAR FAWCETT

AUTHOR OF "THE HOUSE AT HIGH BRIDGE," "SOCIAL SILHOUETTES,"
"TINKLING CYMBALS," "THE CONFESSIONS OF CLAUD," "AN
AMBITIOUS WOMAN," "RUTHERFORD," ETC.

BOSTON

TICKNOR AND COMPANY

211 Tremont Street

1888

To my Friend,

## J. V. PRICHARD,

I AFFECTIONATELY DEDICATE THIS CHRONICLE

OF

## CONTEMPORARY LIFE.

# OLIVIA DELAPLAINE.

## I.

THE funeral was over. Olivia had got home from
Greenwood about an hour ago. The house was still,
now, as the dead burden that had so lately been borne
from it. After a while the girl had stolen to a window
and looked out at the nude, creaking trees in Washington Square, and the black blotches made on the
pavements by the drying rain. May had come in raw
and petulant, this year; the morning had begun show-
ery and savage with gusts, but toward afternoon a
fitful sun had pierced transient fissures in the bluish
rolling clouds.

Olivia soon withdrew from the window and pulled
down its shade again, with a sense of having violated
one of the dreary formulas of usage on such occasions
by lifting it at all. Her sorrow, that would have
been anguish a few years ago, was now inseparable
from a grateful relief. For months her father had
suffered harshly; her own tireless nursing of him had
taught her to be more of a woman than her maidenly
blue eyes, the pink, fresh curves of her face and the
sunny floss of hair over her forehead at all plainly
showed; for Olivia had the kind of looks that a careless gazer can easily pronounce as commonplace as

they are pretty. It was only when you gave her a little observant heed that you saw how her youth had sweetly misrepresented her, and how her evident nineteen years or so had cast about the real womanly potency of her demeanor an undue girlish glamour.

She dropped into an easy-chair, after darkening the window at which she had committed her late rather reckless indiscretion; and just as she fell into the listless posture which the tufted seat induced, a lady appeared within the room.

The new-comer went straight to Olivia and took her hand. The girl scarcely moved, looking up at her companion with a sad, placid smile, and at the same time allowing her extended hand to be patted in the most softly sympathetic way.

"It was a dreadfully cold funeral, wasn't it?" Olivia said, with an intonation that seemed half to imply soliloquy.

"Cold?" returned the lady, who was her aunt, Mrs. Ottarson, the sister of her mother, dead years ago. "Of course it was cold, with all those stuck-up folks going to it! Gracious me! There wasn't one of 'em, Olivia, that went to Greenwood for any reason on earth except because *he* was a Van Rensselaer."

Olivia gave a little weary shake of the head. "I am a Van Rensselaer, too, Aunt Thyrza," she said, still smiling.

"Who said you wasn't?" cried the lady, clasping tighter the hand that she held and patting it with added zest. "That's just what I mean. But they didn't care a bit about it all. They only went because they're clannish, and thought it was respectable to flock round one of their own blood like that."

" Yes, I suppose you're right."

" I think *I* kind o' scared 'em," pursued Mrs. Ottarson, with her leaping staccato laugh that one might believe no solemnity short of her own burial could quite destroy. " I'm different from anybody they're accustomed to see. I ain't — what's the word? — swell. To be swell you've got to put on airs, and I never could do that. Whenever I tried I always felt as if somebody was giggling and making faces at me behind my back."

" I doubt if you ever did try," said Olivia. " It's altogether too artificial a part for any one to play who has your natural honesty."

" Oh, pooh! I ain't half the saint you seem to think me," said Mrs. Ottarson, putting her head sideways, and rolling her handsome black eyes at Olivia, in mock mutiny and challenge.

" If you *had* been a saint," Olivia answered, with the smile that has such a light of pathos in it when the face from which it gleams does not turn a whit less sombre, " I should not have liked you half as well as I do."

Mrs. Ottarson stooped and kissed her. " I'm glad, then, that I'm a sinner instead," she exclaimed jovially. And now she sat down beside Olivia, still retaining her hand.

One might think that aunt and niece had never been more dissimilar than these two. It would have seemed as absurd not to concede that Mrs. Ottarson was vulgar as to declare that the peony is not gaudy. She had a face as dark as a gypsy's, which had perhaps been seemly enough before it became touched by those merciless lines and wrinkles that might col-

lectively be termed one of Time's many war charts;
for alas! the old campaigner never shows himself
more destructive than when he uses the human
countenance for a map of his future hostile intentions! Mrs. Ottarson's figure, however, was admirably youthful. It seemed almost buxomly to refute
the fifty years which her swart, self-reliant, amiable
face asserted. She clad it in attire that clung to its
arches and slopes with a nice flexibility of adhesion.
She was what we must have pronounced a stylish
woman; she would have liked to be thought
"stylish;" she would never have held it the half-
vagabond word it has grown. To-day she wore
mourning for the husband of her dead sister; it
was jauntily patterned and shot through with furtive purples in the way of embellishment. It was
quite too ornamental to be called mourning at all;
but then Mrs. Ottarson placed a deep faith in ornament. All that was sterling about her lay somehow
beneath the surface. Continually misjudged as flip-
pant and superficial, she managed to keep healthfully
beating a heart of great tenderness and sincerity under
her befurbelowed bodices. It is not meant that those
who knew her well misunderstood her native kindness
and charity. Only the indifferent gaze failed to
detect either, and most certainly Olivia Van Rensselaer's was not of this tendency.

Olivia had always heard her late father mention
Mrs. Ottarson, if he mentioned her at all, with a
half-repressed sneer. A good many years of Houston Van Rensselaer's life with his daughter had
been lived abroad. The wide basement-house, with
its dormer windows, its spider-like iron stoop-trellises

and its antique Colonial doorway, had been visited by him four or five times during the past twelve or fifteen years. He brought Olivia across the ocean with him whenever such visits were paid to his native land. The little girl delighted in these trips; she held it rare fun to be taken to America, and the elm-trees and poplars verging South Washington Square would rise afterward through her retrospective visions of New York during the humdrum disciplines of her *pension* oversea. On such occasions Olivia was always permitted to see her aunt. She did not know then that Mrs. Ottarson kept a boarding-house somewhere up-town, and that the appearance of this lady at all in South Washington Square was solely a tribute paid by her punctilious parent to the memory of his deceased wife. He had loved that wife loyally; he was Houston Van Rensselaer, and when he had married her, a blooming girl of nineteen, all his relations had held up their hands at the odious and impolitic match. The bridegroom had not been of democratic views. He possessed many of those New World prejudices regarding "family" and "birth" which are at the present time a source of irony for European comment. He considered his stock exceedingly important; he had quite as much veneration for it as the aristocracies of transatlantic countries had ignorance of it. But he had, nevertheless, married a Miss Jenks. He had privately looked upon his marriage as a very imprudent and even ridiculous step. But he had taken the step because love, with a hymeneal torch grasped in its rosy hand, had too potently lured him toward what lay beyond. Miss Jenks had been poor. Her people

dwelt in Macdougal Street, only a step from the Van
Rensselaer home in which he had been reared as a
boy.  The Jenkses were a race which his own kindred
roundly affirmed to be of "low extraction."  If they
had had money it might have made a striking difference; for there is one point about our American patrician in which he may be relied upon never to differ
from that foreign model whereof he stands nearly
always the patient imitator: he is invariably ap-
peased by what he rates a misalliance when it is a
true *mariage d'argent.*  But the Jenkses were not
only poor; they were destitute of the least caste; the
father and his two daughters, in wholesome domestic
conspiracy, managed to make the combined profits of
carpentry and dressmaking yield them a fairly thrifty
income.  They had not even education, ran the wail
of the Auchinclosses and the Satterthwaites, both
families being near relatives of Mr. Van Rensselaer.
It was all quite too horrible.  "We shall not visit
her," rose the austere feminine chorus.  "We are
extremely sorry; but Houston has brought it upon
himself.  No, we shall not visit her."  And the
Auchinclosses and Satterthwaites did not.

Mr. Van Rensselaer had no intention that they
should — at least, not for a considerable time to
come.  He married his young wife in the quietest
way.  The wedding took place in the back parlor
of the little Macdougal Street house.  The season
was early June, and the windows were open, so
that you could see the interior of Mr. Abner Jenks's
carpenter-shop, which was reached by a short alley at
the side of the house proper.  But some big pink
roses were blowing in an intermediate court-yard

between walls of mellow brickwork that gleamed
richer because of the summer blue above it, and a
bird was singing from a cage not far away. The
blitheness of that bird's matins would not have led
you to dream that anything so dreadful was going on
a little distance below them as the nuptials of a true-
blooded Knickerbocker with the daughter of a carpenter. Inside it seemed a little sadder. Red-
handed, shining-faced and somewhat moist-eyed as
well, Abner Jenks stood watching his daughter.
Thyrza, the bride's sister, made no effort to keep
back her tears. She disapproved the marriage
quite as much from her point of view as did the
Auchinclosses and Satterthwaites from theirs; she
thought Houston Van Rensselaer a stiff, sour person,
and she trembled at the severities of tutelage to which
Rosalie must be hereafter subjected. For the rest,
Rosalie herself looked appositely contented. Her
awkward veil, her ill-fitting gown, and the general
air of commonness about her entire bridal gear, did
not prevent her from being, nevertheless, an extremely
lovely bride.

It was the smallest of weddings. No kin of
Houston Van Rensselaer's had been bidden to it;
he had merely asked his business-partner, Mr.
Spencer Delaplaine, to act as his best man. Mr.
Delaplaine was seven or eight years the senior
of his friend; he had then reached perhaps his
fortieth year, but Thyrza fancied that he must be
older, his aquiline face, his light, gray, shrewd eyes
and his spare, tall, neatly-garbed figure somehow
combined to express so much serene worldly experience. He observed the minister perform the cere-

mony with an air of composure that narrowly missed
betraying the disgust it concealed. This union
appeared to him a piece of the purest folly. The
banking-house of Delaplaine and Van Rensselaer
was still somewhat new in Wall Street. There was
every reason to fear that such an insane step might
be detrimental as regarded its future prosperity. Mr.
Delaplaine had always prided himself on being a personage of the highest position ; a short time ago he
had taken pleasure in the reflection that even his mercantile life was to be elevated by association with one
whose descent not only rivalled but surpassed his own.
And now Houston must go and do this headlong, sentimental thing! *He*, who could have walked connu-
bially up the aisle of Trinity Church or Grace Church
with Miss Van Peekskill, the heiress, worth three
hundred thousand, if a dime, in her own unrestricted
right!

Houston Van Rensselaer's first act, after marrying
Rosalie Jenks, was to separate her inflexibly from her
father and sister. He took her abroad within the next
fortnight, and remained there with her five good years.
His name still continued over the doorway of the
banking-house, which throve capably with Delaplaine
as its active working partner. People said that he
would never bring Mrs. Van Rensselaer back until he
had educated her so that she could hold her own as
veritable *grande dame* among those whom his matrimonial escapade had horrified. Meanwhile Abner
Jenks, the carpenter, died, and Thyrza, his other
daughter, married a worthless, plausible scamp named
Ottarson, who drank himself to death three years
later. But Mrs. Ottarson, full of pluck and energy,

succeeded in making herself the head of an establishment for boarders, and in securing thereby an easy, if
not a plethoric annuity.

When Mrs. Van Rensselaer returned to New York
with her husband, she bore the traces of a most telling
change. Her girlish loveliness had completely vanished; she was pale, tired-looking, timidly reserved,
and no more like her former merry, spontaneous self
than is a lily with its cut stalk kept in a vase for many
hours like the balmy-chaliced bloom that drank nur-
ture from its vital root. She had wedded into a
world that had chilled and wilted her. Houston Van
Rensselaer was still, in his stately, high-bred way, a
fond husband. But he had made her breathe the air
of perpetual disappointment, and she showed the
result with a pathetic plainness of disclosure.

Proudly and undemonstratively her husband waited
the acknowledgment of his return. He issued no
cards of invitation to the house in South Washington
Square. If he had done so the polite summons would
no doubt have been heeded. Curiosity could ill have
withstood the temptation of opportunity when it became a question of seeing how forceful had been the
alterative of those five educational years. But Houston Van Rensselaer merely said to Delaplaine, his
friend and partner: "They know that we are at home.
Let them come if they choose. Letitia Auchincloss
used to be a woman fond of talking about her duty.
As my elder sister, she *might* rank it her duty to call
upon my wife."

The Auchinclosses and the Satterthwaites met in
august council to consider this most exacting question.
The feminine head of either family had been a Van

Rensselaer; they were Houston's sisters, and each had been considered in the days of her virginity to have made a match that was notably brilliant. Letitia Auchincloss and Augusta Satterthwaite were women near of an age, and both were among the few undisputed leaders of social New York. The result of the council was that no unsolicited visit should be paid upon the wife of their brother. The *lèse majesté* of such a proceeding was not to be lightly esteemed.

But Thyrza Ottarson did not remain away from her sister. It was a meeting that Mrs. Ottarson never forgot; and years afterwards, when she and her niece became the good friends that we have already seen them, she described the meeting to Olivia in her volatile and colloquially homespun manner:

"There was your ma, my dear, and there was me. I can see it all just as plain this minute as if it was no more'n yesterday. Your pa'd met me in the hall, and gone into the libr'y down stairs. 'She expects you,' says your pa. 'She'll be down soon.' An' then I guess he saw I felt queer, so he said something 'bout seein' to the furnace, as it was growin' chilly, or some such kind o' humbugging thing as that, to get himself out of the room, and went. An' then I heard a step near the other door, and the door opened, and there was your ma. Well, as I told you, 'Livia, *I* stood an' *she* stood. It seemed's if the sight of her jus' scooped all the breath right out o' my chest. She was so altered that I felt like screechin' to her: 'You ain't *my* Rose; you can't be, and you ain't!' But I knew all the while that she was, and this made it harder to bear. They'd turned her into a high-toned, first-class lady; no mistake about that, 'Livia. But it had just pulled all the shine out of her eyes and all the pink out of her cheeks."

Houston Van Rensselaer took his wife to Europe again. Only one person knew in how haughty and disdainful a state of temper he had recrossed the ocean, and that person was his partner, Spencer Delaplaine. He had found out that the banking-house was in a finely flourishing condition ; there were unanticipated thousands placed to his credit. "I mean to show some of these American snobs here," he said to his single confidant, " how Parisian society will receive my wife."

"But, Houston," urged his partner, "you should remember that you didn't make the least formal announcement of your return."

"That has nothing to do with the affair," replied Van Rensselaer unpropitiatedly. "At least it has not so far as my blood relations are concerned."

"But your blood relations — " began Spencer Delaplaine.

"I understand," shot in the other, cutting him short, " New York isn't quite the universe *yet*, Spencer. The next time that I bring my wife back to her native country, I'll warrant you that the *de haut en bas* attitude will be hers to assume."

But Rosalie Van Rensselaer soon had crossed the Atlantic for the third and last time in her young and by no means cloudless life. Five more years were still allotted her, and these she passed amid fashion and luxury in Paris and various watering-places of Europe. She and her husband became much discussed both by foreigners and resident Americans. It undoubtedly reached the ears of the Auchinclosses and

the Satterthwaites that she had become a decided
somebody on the other side of the ocean.   They heard
of the balls and *fêtes* which she gave and attended; of
the royal patronage which lifted her several prominent
inches above her most aspiring countrywomen; of the
elegance and originality that marked her costumes; of
this or that princely Highness who had graced her
costly entertainments; and at last, suddenly, they
heard of her death.

She had died in giving birth to a daughter, the only
child she had borne during the ten years that had
succeeded her marriage.   Whatever grief Houston
Van Rensselaer may have felt, he shrouded from
publicity by the most guarded seclusion.   When he
once more took steamer for America little Olivia was
five years old.   His relations flocked to meet him,
then, with their sympathetic welcomings.   He received them courteously but frigidly.   But there was,
nevertheless, a distinct reconciliation.   Till Olivia had
reached her eighteenth year he had kept up a series of
occasional visits to New York, making Paris his real
place of abode.   It was affirmed that these trips were
taken purely for financial reasons; and then again
such reports were stoutly contradicted.   What did
Spencer Delaplaine want him for?   He had long ago
become a mere silent partner in the banking-house.
He still lived handsomely abroad, it was true; but the
business had gone on prospering under Delaplaine's
keen and able superintendence.

The last time that Van Rensselaer came home he
came a sick and death-threatened man.   It was then
that Olivia's aunt, Mrs. Ottarson, revealed how much
depth of humane goodness may co-exist with the

most disorderly syntax. Olivia had till now shrunk from her as from a personality offensively unpolished, and there was no dilettante daintiness, either, in Olivia's composition. Perhaps if there had been she would not, even now, have so indulgently overlooked all her aunt's glaring solecisms. As it was, to remember the dogged fortitude of Mrs. Ottarson's late ministrations at her father's bedside was to love her in spite of every barrier that breeding could interpose. Nature seemed to have dowered her with the sleepless eye, the unechoing step, the feathery touch and the clairvoyant perception of the instinctive nurse. Van Rensselaer had been subject to periods of intense pain; and as if by a satirical punishment wreaked upon his former pride, the woman whom he had professed himself while in health as hardly capable of enduring, now became the chief agent of alleviation for his physical torments. The dying man could not understand the wherefore of it all himself; but so it was; that very random bluntness of speech which had formerly set his teeth on edge in Thyrza Ottarson, touched his tingling nerves now with a cheery sincerity of intonation. When a sick-room has grown the ante-chamber of a certain dark king, it is wonderful how class-distinctions tend to shrivel away in its atmosphere; for the grim royalty that waits a new courtier somewhere off in the shadow beyond, appears to be throwing a continuous intangible sarcasm upon all grades of earthly rank. Through those weary weeks of self-forgetful surveillance the boarding establishment naturally missed its proprietress. Neglect took the place of attention, and several vacant rooms were the result. But on Olivia's remonstrance, Mrs.

Ottarson simply put an arm round her niece's neck, and said:

"Now, 'Livia, you jus' be still. I mean to stick right here, if every soul in the house leaves it. There's others in plenty, the minute I choose to advertise for 'em. La, sakes, yes! Besides, dear, it can't be very long, now, before we see *some* change in your poor pa, one way or another."

And it was not long. During their kinsman's illness the Auchinclosses, the Satterthwaites, and people whose relationship was much more distant than theirs, behaved duteously enough. And when all was over, and Brown, the corpulent sexton of Grace Church, came to conduct the funeral, which took place in the old Washington Square mansion, it was admirable to see what a throng pressed through the antique front doorway on that inclement May morning. There were the De Lancey Van Rensselaers, whom one knew on the instant by their red hair and freckles; and the Suydam Van Rensselaers, who all had arched noses which they held as though a breath from their family vault up at Spuytenduyvil had passed alarmingly near their nostrils; and the Brinkerhoff Van Rensselaers, who really were heads of their line but bore themselves with such jovial simplicity that they might have been Smiths from nowhere. All these, and many more, came to the funeral, but Olivia had been quite right in calling it cold. No one had seemed really to care. And why should any one have cared, for that matter? Even her father's late partner, Spencer Delaplaine, had only seen the dead man at intervals during a space of nearly thirty years. He had been markedly attentive all through the ill-

ness; he had called again and again personally to
inquire concerning the state of the invalid; he had
both sent and brought Olivia envelopes full of bank-
notes, which she had accepted as her father's and her
own rightful due, without a hint of more than dignified civility as she did so. He had struck the girl as
an elderly gentleman (for his age must have been
undoubtedly sixty) with just the loveless demeanor
and the dry, semi-ironical repose that you might have
expected from one who had passed so long a term of
preferred bachelorhood. It had evidently been preferred, Olivia told herself more than once during their
conversations together. He *was* a gentleman; you
could see that by a glance; and then, of course, he
had had, and he still had, a good deal of money, just
as her papa had had, and still had. There was a
smouldering memento of the beau in him, too; he
must have been gallant and winsome before he grew
so lean and gaunt, with those yellow, hard ridges, like
folds of parchment, just where the collar met his
throat, and that little limp of one spare leg, which he
said was his old foe, the gout. He had sent a superb
souvenir in the way of flowers that morning — lilies
and violets blended. Others had sent like tributes,
but none was half as beautiful as Mr. Delaplaine's.
Olivia mentioned this gift as she now sat with her
aunt in the still house and "talked it all over." The
weeks of certainty that her father's agony must end
in death had left her not only pardonably but most
explainably resigned; loss had come with an infinite
relief, and youth was already speeding, for this reason,
the merciful consolatory work which sooner or later
reaches all such pain.

"I whispered a few words of thanks to Mr. Dela-plaine this morning, Aunt Thyrza," she said, "for those lovely flowers. It seemed almost rude of me not to do so. But I somehow fancied he looked shocked that I should remember even to thank him at such a time."

"I guess he thought it was awful," replied Mrs. Ottarson. "I guess, 'Livia, that's he's a man who's always drilled himself by rule in ev'rything, whether it's been grief or business, and 's got his real feelings just about down to an oyster's. . . . My! to think how he's changed since your poor dear ma was mar-ried! I can see him then, just as *distinct!* He was pale and thin, even then — not my style o' man a bit; I always fancied a man with some flesh about him, and a look as if he eat his three square meals a day — *you* know what I mean?"

"Oh, yes," murmured Olivia. She had long since grown to translate Mrs. Ottarson's coarseness, fondly and forgivingly, into a more cultured idiom. The mental process was not difficult now; affection had indeed made it singularly facile.

"But, *my!*" continued her aunt, "he's so dried up, ain't he? He *was* 'ristocratic then, an' I guess a good many girls in the upper class where he's always moved must have took to him if he'd only wanted them to."

"I suppose he never did want them to," smiled Olivia, "and now he's lost every chance."

"Well, I should say so! Still, with his money I reckon there's some that just *would.* You can't tell. It's *such* a world! 'Livia, when I think that there's people in it as different as me and your aunt Letitia

Auchincloss, f'r instance, I can scarcely b'lieve what I
see!"

"You don't like Aunt Letitia," said Olivia, shaking
her head, dreamily, with another smile. "Well, neither do I."

"She was mad to-day," went on Mrs. Ottarson, with
a kind of sudden guttural tone and a significant tightening of the lips. "Oh, I could see she was, and so
was her sister — your aunt Augusta Satterthwaite.
They expected to go in the same carriage with you.
An' they would 'a gone if they hadn't seen you and I
stick so close together. They took the next carriage
the minute they saw I wasn't goin' to leave *you*. Oh,
that was *it!* They looked at you, but you didn't see
'em; you was cryin' under your veil, poor deary. But
*I* saw 'em. An' I jus' give your aunt Letitia *one*
*look*. She turned away, and nudged her sister after I
gave it." Here Mrs. Ottarson laughed with the glee
of scorn, but it was not a laugh that jarred upon
Olivia in the least; she knew too well the infinite
good in the heart it welled from. "W'y, Livvy, they
think me, those two aunts o' yours, reg'lar scum o' the
earth — yes, they do!"

"No, no; I hope not; I am sure not!" said Olivia,
reaching out a hand and clasping with it one of the
speaker's. She would doubtless have said more, but
just then a ring at the lower hall-door made herself
and her companion start a little.

"That's them, now, I guess," exclaimed Mrs. Ottarson, as she rose. "Or, no; p'haps it's *him*."

"They? He?" asked Olivia, also rising. "Whom
do you mean?"

"Your aunts, or else Mr. Delaplaine. They've got

to come back before long, you know; it wouldn't be
decent if they didn't?"

"It wouldn't be conventional," said Olivia; "I'm
afraid a good deal of decency means just that, with
certain people."

Mrs. Ottarson went out into the hall and leaned
over the banisters cautiously. "It's your two aunts,
dear," she at length informed her niece.

"I will see them up here," said Olivia. "Tell
Susan to show them up, please."

The big drawing-room in which Olivia stood as she
thus spoke was full of antiquated and cumbrous
effects. The heavy mahogany doors beamed like
glass; the marble-topped "centre-table," as it used to
be called, had the nether parts of dolphins for its
ornate legs, and bore upon its veiny slab a porphyry
card-receiver, and a large tarnished copy of Lord
Byron's poems. On the massively carved mantel rose
a basket of clammy-looking wax-flowers, with a glass
case over them, reconciled, as it might be said, to its
pedestal, by an ellipse of dense scarlet chenille. Still
farther above the fire-place hung one of those portraits
in oil which must always painfully remind the impressionable American of his immature country. The
ceiling was florid with execrable frescoes, and both
groined and corniced with ponderous gilded plaster-
work. Here and there you saw a rug, a stool, a fall
of decorative stuff, that betrayed the more modern
spirit of appointment. But as a rule the visits of the
Van Rensselaers to South Washington Square had
been temporary sojourns, with all their family splendor, as it were, left abroad to speedily lure them back
again. It would be hard to tell how many times

Houston Van Rensselaer had looked at the portrait over the fire-place and the case of wax-flowers just below it, and uttered "damnable!" But he somehow never actually had time to remove either. As it seemed to him, he was always either coming home to this country or going away from it. And then, finally, he had come home to die. It is so often just like that with the most diligent or dilatory of mortals. If the lists of the deeds, good or bad, that we have been intending to accomplish, could be put into our coffins after death, they might often make a scroll of somewhat uncouth bulk for the calculations of the undertaker.

"I'll run upstairs after I've told Susan that you'll see 'em here," said Mrs. Ottarson.

"No, no," swiftly objected Olivia, "I want you to stay with me, Aunt Thyrza."

"Stay with you, 'Livia! Mercy me! and be snubbed by 'em to their hearts' content? I guess not!"

Mrs. Ottarson was hurrying off. Olivia darted after. "Aunt Thyrza!" she exclaimed. The lady, hearing her reproachful voice, instantly turned and faced her. "How *could* you think I would let them do anything of that sort?" Olivia pursued, with an indignant little flash. "Stay! please stay!" she went on, with her tones promptly altered to pleading. "I —I shall feel so lonely with them just at this time, unless you are near!" She suddenly flung both arms about Mrs. Ottarson's neck, and let her soft young lips rest for a moment on her companion's cheek. "You've been so good! *Please* don't leave me now!"

"Very well," acquiesced Mrs. Ottarson. She gave

a laugh with an unwontedly hoarse note in it, as she returned her niece's kiss. "I'll stay, then, Liv, no matter *what* they do to me." She drew back and tossed her head defiantly; as she did so a faintly tearful light gleamed from her black eyes. "I'd put myself out a lot more'n that to do *you* a good turn!" she exclaimed. "But you must let me fight 'em if they try any o' their impudent nonsense over *me!*"

Olivia's acceding nod followed so rapidly that her aunt had only to turn again, partially descend the staircase, and meet Susan, the maid-servant, midway in her ascent.

"They have come to *gêner* me with their tiresome condolences," thought Olivia, standing, a sweet, mournful-robed figure, at the threshold of the old-fashioned drawing-room. "They have come to vex me with their expressions of stupid, insincere sympathy. How I wish it was all over and done with!"

But Olivia was mistaken. Her aunts had come to acquit themselves in quite a different way.

## II.

OLIVIA shook hands composedly with Mrs. Auchincloss and Mrs. Satterthwaite, as these two ladies presently entered the drawing-room where she awaited
them. Mrs. Ottarson stood a good deal in the background. But Olivia very soon veered about in the
direction of the latter, and said with a self-possession
assuredly rare in a girl of her years and her foreign
rearing :

"Let me present you to my aunt Thyrza, Mrs.
Auchincloss, and Mrs. Satterthwaite — my *other* aunt,
you know; my mother's sister."

There was a brief but dead silence as Mrs. Ottarson
came forward. Bows were exchanged, all three of
them as repressed and lifeless as salutations of this
purely ceremonial sort could be made. And then the
four sank into chairs, Mrs. Ottarson still keeping a
little in the background.

Mrs. Satterthwaite broke the pause that ensued.
She was a person qualified to break pauses; she had
the art of saying nothing when nothing was expected
to be said, and of delivering it with just the requisite
air of responsibility.

"This drawing-room has so familiar a look; has it
not, Letitia ? "

Mrs. Auchincloss lifted a pair of tortoise-shell eyeglasses by means of their long rectangular handle,
and held them to her eyes while she gazed all

about her with a kind of majestic finicality. She
had managed to avoid letting her cool gray eye,
however, light even for a second upon Mrs. Ottarson; and her sister had indeed done the same.

"Yes, yes, Augusta, very familiar. We used to
play here as children, you remember . . . here in
this very room."

"I was married in this room," said Mrs. Satterthwaite to Olivia. "And your poor papa, my dear,
was one of my groomsmen."

"I knew it was a very old house," murmured
Olivia, "but — " And then she stopped short,
coloring, very regretful of the inopportune speech.
But Mrs. Auchincloss and her sister were women
of the world trained to their finger-tips. They
swiftly saw that Olivia had lapsed into one of
those infelicitous phrases for which her youth must
supply the ready excuse.

"Ah, sister!" softly exclaimed Mrs. Auchincloss,
with just the dim smile of partial amusement that
seemed to suit the sober occasion, "Olivia is perfectly right. The house *is* very old, and we are
growing shockingly old as well."

Mrs. Satterthwaite nodded. She was never quite
as exquisitely receptive as her sister to all the nicest
requisitions of deportment; she had even said and
done rude things, it was avowed of her by her enemies, for so great a lady. Still, she answered with
just a shade less of amiability than she might have
shown, and with a touch of that rather cynical humor
for which she and the especial set in which she chose
to move were occasionally quoted:

"Dear Letitia, I think we've an advantage over the

house we were almost born in; we're not quite so much out of repair, don't you know?"

This little glint of wit struck Mrs. Auchincloss as ill-timed; she did not even pay it the notice of a smile.‾ But Olivia did, and quickly afterwards she said, glad to find a new theme of talk:

"The house *is* out of repair. If poor papa had lived a little longer he would have done a great deal for it, I am sure. That is, unless he had concluded to move farther up-town. For we meant to stay in New York this time."

"I think he would have concluded to move," said Mrs. Auchincloss, in her modulated, flute-like tones. "*South* Washington Square is no longer what it was."

"It is getting to be really dreadful, you know, my dear," said Mrs. Satterthwaite.

"Dreadful?" faltered Olivia, with an involuntary look at Mrs. Ottarson.

"It isn't as uppish as it was," declared Mrs. Ottarson, chiefly addressing her niece. She had no intention of remaining silent; silence, under any circumstances, had never stood high among either her virtues or her graces. "At least, that's what they tell me. You see, 'Livia, Thompson Street's close by, an' it's pretty much filled with colored folks; and then there's some other queer neighborhoods nearer still, and I guess some of 'em are really awful, 'specially after dark. And I see there's one or two lager-beer saloons an' billiard-halls crep' in on this very block. It's a shame, but it's so. The city *will* push up-town, what's best of it. W'y, *my!* it's funny to see how the respectable class *do* go gallopin' away from the lower end."

She finished this little series of remarks with a complete understanding that both of Olivia's guests would receive it chillingly. She was prepared for their drooped eyelids and the furtive glance that passed between them. They thought her beneath them; of course they did. She didn't care for that, though. She wasn't going to be "put down." She hadn't wanted to stay in the room; she had done so only on "'Livia's" account. But now that she *had* staid, she wouldn't sit with her tongue between her teeth, like a fool. She had never done it since she was born, and she guessed it was pretty late in the day for a woman of her age to begin.

"Ah, well," said Olivia, shaking her head regretfully, "I suppose that is the way with all large cities, Aunt Thyrza; they outgrow themselves and leave a kind of living past behind them. It is so with Paris, I'm sure. Still, what I hear about this being an undesirable quarter surprises me." (Here she looked at her two other kinswomen.) "I've been out so little since poor papa was first taken ill — and that, you know, was very soon after we got home."

"But you can't be attached to the house, can you, my dear Olivia?" said Mrs. Auchincloss, in her suave, cooing tones.

"You have really lived here so little," supplemented Mrs. Satterthwaite.

"But it — it somehow means New York to me," stammered Olivia. "When here I have not once lived anywhere else."

"Oh, never *you* mind, 'Livia," now broke in Mrs. Ottarson. "A person that's got your means can find

other houses just as comf'table and a good sight styl-
isher. I presume, ladies, you 'gree with me?"

The last sentence was lightly thrown, as it were, at
Mrs. Auchincloss and her sister. It cannot be said to
have taken them by surprise; very little had ever done
that. But it made them both decide rather rapidly
to show its deliverer a freezing disregard. ⸙ In all
the aristocratic circles of Christendom there are
women whom you could not more keenly insult
than by telling them they were not ladies; and yet
who unhesitatingly violate, in just this bloodless fashion, the sweet and sane laws on which they would base
half their own title to superior respect. ⸙

But in the case of Mrs. Auchincloss and Mrs. Satterthwaite the provocation to be crushingly uncivil
was not solely engendered by contact with a fellow-
creature held less cultured than themselves. I do
not deny their capability of dealing discountenance
for that and no more cogent reason. Still, they had
another greivance, just now, and one which had long
before loomed to them grimly formidable.

Their brother's marriage had always affected them
as a most execrable and even disgraceful proceeding.
They had been young wives when he had contracted
it; they had thought it a shame then and they had
continued to think it so ever since. Of course the
position Olivia's mother had secured abroad was pal-
liating to their distress; but the connection remained.
They could not exactly have defined to you just what
they meant by the "connection," now that Abner
Jenks was dead and the Macdougal Street carpenter-shop had vanished agreeably from its previous
detested site. They must have explained their pal-

pable antipathy to the surviving ignominy of the
whole affair by reference to Mrs. Ottarson. There
were no other Jenks relatives whom they knew of.
But they knew of her; they had forever kept her in
mind as a potential bugbear. She was a trial, so to
speak, that might befall them any day in the week,
any week in the month. They both stood before the
eyes of "society" in the colors of a magnificent
assumption. Naturally the misstep of their brother
was no social secret. But his madness had now become a matter of the past; his ill-born spouse was
dead; time had in a sense dimmed that blot on the
Van Rensselaer 'scutcheon. Meanwhile they rose *tout
en dehors* to the world in which they shone as rulers.
Every concomitant of their mundane lives had for
years helped to swell the prestige of their splendid
exclusiveness. Their husbands, their children, their
households, their servants, their entertainments, their
equipages, their gowns, their very bonnets and boots,
had all contributed honorably, effectively, enviably and
modishly to the brilliancy of their urban *élan*. And
yet that woman, who could declare herself a kind of
sister-in-law, was keeping a boarding-house in the
same town with themselves. They could not forget
her; she haunted them. Once she had got into the
papers through a lawsuit between herself and an
abusive, insolent lodger. They had read the accounts
of her prosecution with guilty dread; she was the roseleaf under their mattresses, and when one sleeps on
down, one probably pays the penalty of such nice
accommodation to a degree undreamed of by those
who stretch contented limbs on life's commoner
pallets of repose. We read of princesses and duch-

esses who pass their time in perfumed ease, without pausing to think now and then that our own so-named republican land can parallel these useless feminine types. Still there was a disparity between the sisters in their separate modes of asserting and preserving pre-eminence, and one worthy of the chronicler's record.

Mrs. Archibald Auchincloss had never prided herself on being a beauty. But now, when past middle life, she was tall, blonde, symmetrical, and of that visage and complexion to which the fading wear of time brings a false attractiveness. Those who had never met her when she was a plain young woman now took it for granted that she was a prettily dilapidated elderly one; for age became her, and its stealthy ravages left only what seemed the memento of a face that might easily have once been beautiful. It must be allowed that she grew old with an extreme gracefulness. She had married unexceptionably well even for a Van Rensselaer. Her husband was a lawyer of such prominence that his intimacy with a certain President now out of office had made his appointment to the Secretaryship of State seem at one time highly probable. As it was, he remained a personage of much distinction. He had never even joined any New York club but the Centennial, a club that assumed to be literary, artistic and intellectual, and to treat with great scorn the Metropolitan, the Gramercy and all other contemporaneous bodies of a like character. Mrs. Auchincloss had borne her husband two children, a son and a daughter, both still unmarried. She always declared that she was not by any means a fashionable woman; her church and her

church duties trenched too greatly on her time for
gay dissipations. And yet she kept upon her visiting-
book an eye of the closest attention. Her rigid con-
servatisms would have no concern with "new people."
It was for this reason that she had pleaded the
demands of her religion when asked to permit her
name to be placed among those of the lady patron-
esses of the Assembly balls. She could not endure
the idea of associating herself with the nobodies of
yesterday turned the nabobs of to-day. She went to
the Patriarchs and the Assemblies and the Cotillions,
with her *svelte* figure magnificently apparelled, and
her big, renowned pearls casting the lustre of delicate
illusion over a neck no worse for such adornment.
She took her daughter, Madeleine, to these and other
festivities, but it was somehow an accepted fact that
this young lady could not be made acquainted with
everybody. Of course no presentations were de-
clined; that would have been a piece of lamentable
manners; but there are variations of welcome, all the
way from one *à bras ouverts* to one of the lifted eyebrows and the pursed lips. In brief, Mrs. Auchincloss
was that rarity of rarities, a leader who maintained
supreme ascendency by refusing to lead.

Mrs. Satterthwaite lived in much greater splendor,
occupied a larger house, and having considerably more
wealth to spend, spent it with unrestricted extrava-
gance. Her husband, Bleecker Satterthwaite, was
one of the few thoroughly indolent men of fashion
whom the possession of from four to five millions
cannot succeed in making either a drunkard or a
gamester. Satterthwaite thought his brother-in-law,
Auchincloss, an unspeakable bore and prig. *He* did

not belong to the Centennial Club — not he; it was
quite too full of those seedy fellows like artists and
authors to please *his* taste. He was a member of the
Metropolitan and Gramercy (and devilish respectable
clubs he thought them, too!) besides the Jockey Club
and Coaching Club, in whose annual, slavishly Anglomaniacal parade he drove regularly each May. The
Satterthwaite progeny numbered five, three daughters
and two sons. Their great Fifth Avenue mansion
had been the scene of successive lavish and sumptuous entertainments ever since the eldest girl, Emmeline, had come out in society, and that was four
years ago. Each year they had given one ball, with
dinners and dances weeks before and after. It would
be impossible for any family to live in a greater whirl
of fashion. Even their youngest child, little Lulu,
aged ten, belonged to a dancing-class from which she
would return as late as nine o'clock in the evening,
laden with flowers and favors from her juvenile Germans. Mrs. Satterthwaite was a leader who led in
good earnest. She had no "church duties," like her
sister. She would have been horrified if you had
called her irreligious; she thought it abominable form
not to go to church as often as one could. As for
"new people," she accepted them unhesitatingly
whenever they were really *lancés* and went about to
places. If they were not, and did not go, and wanted
her to help them, she would have a talk with her husband on the subject and debate cold-bloodedly the
question of their wealth and the possibility of their
not casting disrepute on the Satterthwaite endorse-
ment. She was still young enough — or estimated
herself so — to dance at assemblages where there was

not too overwhelming a horde of fresh *débutantes*.
She was still held to be passably nice-looking, too,
and gossip had not spared her its covert innuendo
while never touching her with the unsheathed sting of
its accusation.  All in all, the two sisters mutually
disapproved of each other.  But it was a rather peaceful contest, in which either family joined and in which
the Auchinclosses gained a silent perpetual victory.
The Satterthwaites knew very well that they had a
remarkably good tone; but somehow the Auchinclosses, who gave no large balls, and one dinner party
to their five, had distinctively a better tone.  No open
enmity existed, and yet there was a certain bitter feeling on both sides.

As regarded this abhorred relationship of Mrs.
Ottarson's, however, they met on warmly congenial
grounds.  The sisters, in discussion together, had
called her "that horrible boarding-house woman" and
the fact that she had nursed their brother in his dying
hours had been to them a misery over which they
could mourn in faultlessly congenial unison.

"I presume, ladies, you agree with me," delivered
from so unpleasant a source as that of Mrs. Ottarson,
decided them in showing their most glacial unconcern.  They liked Olivia; they considered her excellent style for so young a girl, and were prepared to
help her and stand by her as one of their blood and
race.  They were deeply sorry that it had become
necessary to bear her a certain very miserable piece of
tidings.  They had concluded, however, that she
must be summarily though discreetly told, and therefore the presence of Mrs. Ottarson doubtless kindled
the animosity which surely needed no additional fuel.

Olivia saw the premeditated impertinence of their demeanor. She did not intend that it should hurt her aunt Thyrza by any prolonged sanction. "Oh, yes," she soon said, "I am certain that I can find other quarters, if this dear old house should prove unsatisfactory. Why should I not do so?"

Mrs. Auchincloss stole a glance at her sister. This kind of self-possession rang more like that of the typical American girl than of the *demoiselle* reared as Olivia had been among European surroundings. But they had yet to learn how American their niece had managed to keep herself, despite a life-time spent so largely abroad.

Mrs. Auchincloss coughed rather meaningly at this point. "My dear Olivia," she said, "you touch upon a matter that interests both your aunt Augusta and myself." Then she coughed again, lower than before, and proceeded: "I must say something to you now which would perhaps seem a little brusque unless — unless the full necessity of its disclosure were kept in mind. Your aunt Augusta and I have desired to speak with you — *alone*. We have thought it necessary to do so. We have —"

Here Mrs. Ottarson rose precipitately and bristlingly. "Alone, eh?" she broke forth. "W'y, there can't be the least objection to *that*. I'll retire, 'Livia." She was close at her niece's side now, and her cheeks had taken a little flush that matched the excited glittering of her eyes.

The next instant Olivia had risen too. She caught her aunt's arm and exhorted very persuasively: "I beg that you will remain! I prefer you to hear whatever is said."

"Olivia!" broke from the lips of her two other relatives, and not only in spontaneous exclamation, but with an inflection of equal dismay on the part of both.

"Mrs. Ottarson — Aunt Thyrza — would be sure to hear what you told me, whether you told it me alone or in her company. She is my dear friend, and I am more grateful to her than my heart can express." The girl stood with one arm about Mrs. Ottarson's waist now, and one hand clasping hers. In her black dress, and with her wistful face and bright hair, she made a picture of clinging tenderness and trust. But it was a picture that apparently failed to charm the two ladies who sat fronting it.

Mrs. Auchincloss never permitted herself to be angry. She looked upon the loss of one's temper as though it were something not wholly unlike the loss of one's conscience. She always smiled when she considered herself justified in showing indignation; it was part of her self-disciplining creed to do so; and besides a smile broke up and softened certain hard, tense-looking lines that *would* show themselves at periods of mental disturbance on either side of her slim, pink nose, slanting downward to the region of her thin and rather frosty lips.

"Either I am mistaken, my dear," she said, "or your gratitude is just now somewhat of a drawback to your civility." Here Mrs. Satterthwaite gave a little shrug of the shoulders and a satirical titter of laughter.

Mrs. Ottarson's face flushed deeper, till two spots of color bloomed quite richly in the olive dusk of either cheek; you saw what a comely young creature she must have been when her reprobate of a husband had fooled her into marrying him years ago.

"I guess you *are* mistaken," declared Mrs. Ottarson, gazing straight at the superb eldest daughter of the Van Rensselaer dynasty. "'Livia don't want to be uncivil, ma'am. But if you'll excuse my sayin' so, it looks a good deal more as if *you* wanted to be. I mean to *me*. You understand."

Mrs. Auchincloss fluttered her eyelids and turned with a gently despairing expression toward her sister, as much as to ask, "How shall I deal with this barbarian?"

But immediately afterward Mrs. Ottarson went on: "I'd ever so much rather leave this room. I haven't got any curiosity to hear what you ladies are a-goin' to say. But I'll stay if 'Livia wishes I should. I staid when her father was sick to death for jus' that reason — she wished me to. I hadn't got as good a right to nurse him, an' help him die easy, as you two very el'gant folks had. But somehow or other — I *must* say it — you wasn't on hand when you might 'a been. You're his blood, and I ain't; I s'pose I'm what you'd call no blood at all. But you didn't step up when the time came. You called, an' you sent calve's-foot jelly, an' grapes, an' things, and you looked mel'nc'olly when you heard how bad he was, an' said 'oh,' an' 'ah,' an' that was 'bout the whole o' what you did do. I s'pose you ladies know your duty; I ain't tellin' you what it ought to be. But *my* duty was near my dead sister's child, an' I just stuck there. An' if I stick there now 'cause she asks me, I'd thank you to remember that it *is* on that account an' no other. Our sp'eres, yours an' mine, are pretty wide apart. I do' want to move in yours any more 'n you want, I guess, to belong to mine. But I ain't to be *sat on*, for all that."

"Aunt Thyrza!" cried Olivia, at this point, with a very plain distress in her mien and voice, "it's of no use to be angry. Sit down here beside me." She put both arms about Mrs. Ottarson while she thus spoke, and pushed the lady into a chair near the one from which she herself had lately risen. Then she took a seat close at her side. "Nobody has thought of treating you rudely." Her blue eyes were swimming in tears now, as she turned toward her two visitors. "Aunt Letitia, Aunt Augusta," she went on, tremulously, "please blame me for everything. I know you didn't mean to show this dear, kind friend of mine the least impoliteness. I know . . ."

And then Olivia paused. Mrs. Auchincloss's face, in its serene austerity, smote her, for it had quite forgotten its formulated smile; and on the face of Mrs. Satterthwaite, plumper, a trifle redder than her sister's, and never without its claim to a kind of blemished but assertive charm, had appeared the signs of languid, sneering amusement.

"All this is really so very extraordinary," Mrs. Satterthwaite now laughed, touching her long gloves with either hand, as if to see that they were still blamelessly adjusted.

"Extraordinary?" echoed her sister, and speaking as if the words burnt her lips a little. "It is preposterous!"

In a certain way they were both quite right. If to be angry is to be wrong, Mrs. Ottarson had wretchedly committed herself. Mrs. Auchincloss had the power to defend her cause — if she could be conceived of as deigning to do so — by the announcement that she had taken the only admissible means of seeking a private talk with her niece. Mrs. Ottarson's attack was really the accumulated spleen of years — and not half or a quarter of it yet, either. She knew that these women had scorned her sister and loathed the tie which bound her to their brother. There had never been any circumstance relating to this Van Rensselaer marriage that had not wakened either her regret or her detestation, except one. That was Olivia. As she looked now into the girl's worried, moistened eyes, a thrill of repentance passed through her. "I *was* mad," she whispered. "I kind o' lost my head. She made me, 'Livia. I'll try not to again. But you better let me leave. I'll just wait f' you upstairs."

"No; stay," said Olivia, also whispering. There was something in the countenances of her two guests now that filled her with dread to remain alone beside them. It would not have been so at all times; she had inherent coolness, nerve, and courage, in ample share; but to-day her young soul had been brought downward into that valley of the shadow whose gloom must ever prove as keenly the repugnance of youth as it is sometimes the refuge and relief of age.

"My dear child," began Mrs. Auchincloss, with a *douceur* that seemed (as a witty Englishman once remarked of a contemporary's geniality) to be enamelled on iron, "we shall perhaps take a much wiser course, your aunt Augusta and I, if we say nothing whatever on the subject we had decided to discuss. For myself, Olivia, I confess that I have possibly been too hasty in alluding to it at all. And now let me ask your pardon for doing so." It somehow did not appear as if Mrs. Auchincloss were asking Olivia's pardon, or that of any one else, while she thus spoke; her last sen-

tence implied nothing but the most superficial ceremony of phrasing. "It *is* an important question; but
let it pass for the present."

Here Mrs. Satterthwaite rose, a little bustlingly and
imperiously, while her black draperies (in all respects
the kind of mourning which decorous millinery would
exact from a bereaved sister) disposed themselves to
advantage about her neat-moulded person.

"Yes," said that lady; "let it pass for the present.
We will come and see you some other time, my dear,
when you are less engaged with your rather explosive
acquaintance there."

"Augusta!" murmured Mrs. Auchincloss, with
great dignity, and a chiding intonation.

"I'm not an acquaintance, if you please," sped from
Mrs. Ottarson, even while Olivia was pressing her hand
as if in dumb entreaty to curb all irate repartee. "I'm
her mother's sister, an' quite as much her aunt as you
are. I'm a Jenks, or was, an' so was you a Van Rensselaer. You mustn't forget, though, that a Jenks once
*married* a Van Rensselaer. I dare say you'd like to,
ma'am, but you'll excuse me for remindin' you that
you mustn't. I ain't here as an acquaintance; I'm
here as a blood-relation, just as you are."

Mrs. Satterthwaite looked at Mrs. Ottarson with a
plain curl of the lip now. She had not her sister's
equipoise. She had lost her temper a good many times
in her life, and she lost it then.

"What an insupportable person you are!" she said,
with a drawl and a sneer. "You succeed in doing one
thing, and very successfully. You make me regret
more than I ever *have* regretted (and that is saying considerable) that a Jenks *did* marry a Van Rensselaer."

Olivia flung both arms round Mrs. Ottarson's neck.
"Don't — *don't* answer, Aunt Thyrza!" she cried supplicatingly. And Mrs. Ottarson did not.

"All right, 'Livia," she whispered. "Oh, pooh!
*she* don't rile me half as much as the other. I don't
mind spunk half as much as I do that s'castical, up-in-
the-clouds talk. I guess I can sit still; I *guess* I can;
I'll try, any way, for your sake. It'll be hard, but I'll
jus' grit my teeth an' try!"

Mrs. Auchincloss had now risen. Both ladies went
toward the door, as if in act of departure. Olivia
gave Mrs. Ottarson one final pressure of the hand, and
then rose herself.

"Are you going?" she said flurriedly. "You —
you spoke, Aunt Letitia, of — of something important. I — I hope it does not concern poor papa, in
any manner."

"My dear," said Mrs. Auchincloss, "it concerns only
yourself, now."

"Myself?" repeated Olivia. "How?"

Mrs. Auchincloss gave a sort of despairing sigh.
"We meant to put it all to you as gently as possible.
We meant, my dear, to tell you that we would always
be your helpers, your supporters, as far as we were
able. We only thought of mentioning it, on this most
sorrowful of days, because Mr. Delaplaine, your
father's late partner, urged and advised us to do so."

"I wouldn't say anything more, if I were you, just
now, Letitia," struck in Mrs. Satterthwaite, with a
haughty sidelong glance at Mrs. Ottarson, who still
remained seated.

Mrs. Ottarson had heard everything thus far. She
returned Mrs. Satterthwaite's glance with one that was

comically hostile, because she so instantly dropped her black, enkindled eyes after giving it, as if in forcedly penitent recollection of her promise to Olivia. And then she heard Mrs. Auchincloss continue speaking with her niece, but could make out nothing of what that lady said, for the reason that the latter spoke in so low a tone. The converse seemed to last quite a while; occasionally Mrs. Satterthwaite would put in a word, but her voice was equally inaudible.

Mrs. Ottarson made no attempt to listen. Her anger had died, as it always did die, rapidly. But her curiosity was now aflame. She sat wondering what this mysterious converse meant. But she would have lost a finger rather than show the slightest sign of anything but placid indifference to its progress or significance. ·

Presently the ladies withdrew from Olivia. Thus far she had not seen her niece's face; but now, as Mrs. Auchincloss and Mrs. Satterthwaite swept quietly across the threshold of the drawing-room, Olivia turned and hurried in her own direction.

In an instant she saw how terribly pale the girl had grown.

"'Livia!" she cried, starting up from her chair. "What is it? What have they said to you?"

But Olivia, too evidently, could not answer in the desired way. "Oh, Aunt Thyrza," she exclaimed, "it is too horrible!" And then with a white, forlorn, stricken look, she flung herself upon the breast of her companion, bursting into a torrent of woful sobs.

## III.

It was some little time before Olivia regained her self-control. Meanwhile Mrs. Ottarson had drawn her to a sofa and had used upon her arts of so volubly and naturally soothing a sort that if her wretchedness had not been severe as it was, the girl might have broken into laughter at some of the endearing diminutives by which she now heard herself addressed. When her tears had ceased to flow she sat with quivering underlip and stared straight before her. She seemed to be asking some silent question of the future's very silence. Mrs. Ottarson, stirred more by this mood than by the stormier one, at length showed her own suspenseful alarm.

"My sakes alive, 'Livia! if you don't jus' want to drive me clean out o' my seven senses you'll let me know what *is* the matter."

And then Olivia gave a start, turning again to her aunt, "I must have frightened you so, Aunt Thyrza," she said tremulously. "It was selfish of me. I should recollect how *your* nerves and strength have been tried far more than mine, with those many nights of watching."

"O, bosh," said Mrs. Ottarson, roughly intolerant of being over-valued. "I'm as strong as a horse, and never had a nerve in my life. Now do tell me what the trouble is. It's something those two said, of course."

"Yes," answered Olivia.

There was a little more silence, and then she impetuously cried: "Think of it, Aunt Thyrza! Papa has left nothing — or it's even less than that! Mr. Delaplaine had for years been warning him, they say, that he was over-spending his income. And finally his partner had written him a letter, very direct and plain, which brought us back to America for the last time. I recollect the letter. It came to us last August when we were at Zermatt. It made papa almost ill; his disease was beginning then, and he could no longer bear a shock without showing it. He said it was not the letter, but I always had my doubts. In October we crossed again, coming to this house as usual. There was a very long interview, I clearly recall, between Mr. Delaplaine and my father on the first evening after our arrival; but I am nearly sure there was no quarrel. Still a coldness, I think, sprang up between them from that time. And I suspected so little what the real difficulty was! Through three months or so, until he was taken ill, papa went very often to his office in Wall Street. Sometimes he would look miserably weary and disturbed when he came back. Everything was lost, Aunt Thyrza — *everything!* And I never dreamed he was in the midst of such misfortune. I believe this will be my chief sorrow hereafter — that he suffered so without my knowing it. Of course, just now, it almost takes my breath away to think of myself — of what I am going to do — of the little I actually *can* do. It has come so suddenly. They assure me there is nothing left — papa has spent it all. He kept over-drawing and over-drawing. He never had the least regard for money — I had often noticed

that in him. My aunts say that for years he continued
to answer Mr. Delaplaine in the most hopeful terms.
He had spent great sums while mamma was alive; he
had thrown thousands away. But he insisted that
the success of the banking-house would hereafter mend
his fortunes. Then he began to borrow of his partner.
All might have gone well, even then, if he had not
taken to gambling."

"Gambling?" echoed Mrs. Ottarson. Her idea
of a man who gambles was essentially a New York
one. She swiftly had a vision of personages with
dyed black moustaches and exorbitant gold watch-
chains, who haunted the stoops of certain semi-repu-
table hotels, who drove in "sulkies" behind fast
trotting-horses, who hung about the gilded bar-room
of the old St. Nicholas, on what was once central
Broadway, and who prowled at night to clandestine
gaming-dens in the gloom of Crosby Street and similar
uncanny purlieus, where they swindled credulous vic-
tims at poker or faro. "Gambling!" she repeated.
"Oh, no, 'Livia. It can't be true of your father,
dear! He was always too high-toned for *that* kind o'
thing!"

Olivia gave a dreary smile. "So many gentlemen
gamble abroad," she said, "and papa did it. It all
comes back to me now. I was with him for several
weeks, three years ago, at Monaco and Monte Carlo.
I never thought it even strange, then, that he should
play; hundreds of others played, his friends and acquaintances. But I realize now that it was a vice
with him." She drooped her head, for an instant, and
pressed both hands against her eyes. They were quite
tearless eyes when she again revealed them, but they

shone with a dry, hard light from her sweet, pale face.
"Oh, there is no use, Aunt Thyrza," she went on, "of
my disguising the truth to myself. Aunt Letitia and
Aunt Augusta came with a kindly enough motive.
You don't like them — neither do I. But they meant
to prepare me for the very worst as gently as they
could. Perhaps they'd have done it more gently still,
if you hadn't . . . But never mind. Don't think that
I blame you, for I do *not*. Mr. Delaplaine is coming
to see me this evening, and they would have me meet
him with some knowledge of what he would say. They
were quite right; give them their due, Aunt Thyrza."

"And he's a rich man, ain't he, 'Livia?"

"Oh, I suppose so. Papa is in his debt for I don't
know how much."

"Well, he won't mind that now, of course. He'll
make some proposal about . . . settling matters; of
course he will. He'll tell you just how things are,
and then — "

Olivia gave an interrupting laugh, so sharp and
bitter that it sounded like the travesty of mirth.
"And *then?*" she exclaimed. "What then, if you
please? This very house we are in belongs to him,
my aunts say. How can there be any settling of
matters? If he chooses to help me for a little while
until I've something to do for my own living, that is
his own affair. But to accept permanent help from
him — or from anybody!" Here Olivia rose, and a
great pride, at work in her young spirit, gave new
firmness to the line of her delicate lips. "As long as
my health lasts I shall never be a burden like that."
She shivered suddenly, as though a rush of cold air
had struck her, and looked to right and left with the

mixed bewilderment and rebellion of a bird that for
the first time finds itself caged. That new, captive
sense was upon her — that feeling of having been
abruptly tripped into a pitfall by destiny — which may
rouse just such an involuntary gesture of would-be
escape. "Oh," she burst forth, "how can I ever get
familiar with the change of it all! Aunt Thyrza, I
think I know something, now, of the way people feel
in an earthquake. The one support goes to pieces
that they've forgotten even to trust; trusting it has
grown like breathing. I never could conceive of myself as poor, somehow. I've pitied others often enough,
but there seemed always a great gulf between their
calamity and my secure state. Want and I seemed
not born to meet in this world. Ah, how differently
it has turned out!"

"If I only had a home fit for one like you are to come
to it!" Mrs. Ottarson sighed. "But I'm 'fraid things
would never suit you, 'Livia, up there to my boarding-
house." Here a very perturbed frown appeared on
the speaker's forehead. "La's a-mercy me! What
*can* you do for a livin', dear? You ain't handy at
your needle, much; besides, that's a dog's life. And
teachin'? Well, that isn't much better, I guess."

"That must be my fate, I suppose," said Olivia,
solemnly. "I shall have to teach. Some of those
fine relations of mine ought to assist me, there. If it
were only giving French lessons! I'm sure I could
do that; I know the language so thoroughly; it
would be strange if I didn't. Just before I left
boarding-school, one of the principal teachers said to
me that there was no difference between my accent
and that of the French pupils."

Never was the marvellous buoyancy of the youthful mind and heart more abundantly evidenced than now. Indeed, it would sometimes seem as if youth and health, when once fairly commingled, might make a talisman wherewith to resist the fiercest assaults of disaster. Already Olivia's eyes harbored a gleeful sparkle as she slipped back to the side of her aunt.

"I can't bear to hear you talk so!" cried the latter. "Th' idea, 'Livia, of *you* teachin'! W'y, the Auchinclosses and Satterthwaites, an' all the rest of 'em, ought to feel proud —— "

"I know what you're going to say," broke in Olivia, and not with the meekest of tones. "And I pray you'll not even suggest it."

"Well, then, there's Mr. Delaplaine, deary. He was always a friend o' your pa's, bein' his pardner. He ought to do something. Oh, I guess he will."

"I don't know what he will have it in his power to do, Aunt Thyrza."

"Oh, in these cases I dare say there's pretty much always some money sort o' layin' 'round. I mean something might be his takin's or your pa's leavin's, whichever way he chose to fix it."

Olivia looked at her aunt as though this rather curious view indicated a subtlety of monetary arrangement quite baffling to her own perceptions.

"If Mr. Delaplaine offered to *give* me any money," she said, "I should refuse it; for that would mean simply charity, and I will not live on anybody's charity except my own." She meant the words with such a splendid sincerity, then! Already the first unnerved and stunned sensation had passed, with her.

The world had not tamed her yet, and she even felt

at this early hour a faint thrill of that challenge to its
taming tendencies which few but the really strong
natures ever feel. Olivia had been thought a marvel
of determination and character while at school. It
was indeed strange to see how her American brain
and temperament told there. Not that she was unconventional. The niceties and elegancies, in her
case, had rather to be nourished than acquired. Her
poor dead mother may have been the daughter of a
carpenter, but she had died between costlier panellings
than Abner Jenks would have known how to con-
struct, and all the child's infancy had drifted through
experiences clement and soothing as the most faithful
attendance could make them. From whatever source
the money came — whether from the gaming-tables of
European watering-places or from the indulgent concession of Spencer Delaplaine's coffers, Olivia had
been reared by its magical assistance with as much
quiet fastidiousness as though she had been a little
princess of the blood.

But some hereditary trait of independence and self-
reliance had early revealed itself as her dower. At
the *pension* she was never like the other girls; she
would sometimes laughingly say to her teachers that
the lack of reserve and repose for which they chided
her was a result of certain influences exerted by her
first governess, who had been an American lady hotly
resenting an enforced expatriation. But this lady,
who adored her own country and never had enough
scorn to pour upon what she denounced as the shame-
ful restrictions and repressions brought to bear upon
all foreign damsels, could not have done more than
encourage and vivify in Olivia attributes which

merely waited the summons of her tuition and counsel. Those repeated visits to New York with her
father had strenuously influenced, as well, the mould-
ing of a personality destined for what alien censors
of etiquette esteemed over-assertive and even un-
maidenly. Olivia had always insisted upon the un-
manageable posture of having personal opinions. She
revolted against any compulsory retirement into back-
grounds. There had never been the least use in telling her that she spoke with too loud a tone, that she
was guilty of indecorous enthusiasms, that she violated
this or that *dictum* of recognized restraint. For
seven or eight years before her final trip to America
she had resented the slightest slur cast upon the
country which she exulted in calling her own. She
inflexibly championized the United States, and not
seldom with an ardor that roused enmity and dislike
in her classmates.

It would be hard to explain what this proclivity
meant if heredity were not really at the root of it.
Her father's distinct patriotism may have largely
helped its development. There is often a kind of odd
pathos in the love cherished for their native land by
exiled Americans who have deliberately concluded to
dwell elsewhere. Houston Van Rensselaer not seldom
talked in a loving strain about the superior government and institutions of "the other side" which his
close preferred proximity to the *Arc de Triomphe* or
to the Nelson monument in Trafalgar Square might
have caused a bloodless listener to condemn as rather
triflingly sentimental. No doubt Olivia, from the
most plastic periods of her childhood, had been impressed by just this inconsistent fervor of discourse.

But whether or no her father and the chronicled Europe-hating governess both proved, in a measure, strong incident forces upon her younger life, it is certain that her Americanism continued permanent and paramount. Altogether, she was by no means unpopular among her classmates. She had the gift of swaying them by her advice or suggestion, and just before she left for these shores, crowned with no mean academic honors, both instructors and co-disciples equally conceded of her that she bore the mental birth-mark of a vivid though perhaps dangerous originality.

She was a girl of whom those who knew her best, in her days of pupilage, and at the same time cared most for her welfare, would prophesy not a few of the future miseries that one's own error and weakness will engender. She had a monitory conscience enough; her moral atmosphere was visited by no misleading twilights; wrong was detestable to her from every abstract mode of regarding it. But there had been occasions in her brief life when the imp of the perverse had successfully prevailed with her. By escapades of mischievous audacity she had made the tranquil *pension* quake to its very centre; but these contumacious freaks had always ended in moods of passionate repentance, and in eager ascetic craving for punishment more rigorous than that which she received. "She has in her the stuff for a true *dévote*," would muse Madame Z——, her principal instructress, who was herself a fervent Catholic. "If she once gained the mastery over those wicked inclinations, there would be a penitential surrender of self that means just the right state of soul for the real zealot."

But Olivia lacked what is called the religious disposition. She would never have made an exemplary nun, any more than she would have made a confirmed scoffer. Reverence was as little a part of her being as impiety. The dubious and questioning bent of this remarkable century had not escaped her expanding intellect, since all the orthodoxy of her boarding-school encompassment had been constantly antagonized, so to speak, by long talks during vacations with her father, never a man to treat deferentially the "accepted" theologic codes. "I sometimes think, papa," Olivia had said to him during one of their conversations, "that I must have had a thoroughly evil person for an ancestor. He or she belonged either to mamma's people or to yours; I can't, of course, even speculate on that point. But I've had the conviction that there's some such reason for my occasional bad seizures."

Houston Van Rensselaer laughed at this theory as something prettily droll in a girl of sixteen. He had judged what his daughter had remorsefully confided to him as her *diablerie* to be the amusing compunction of an over-sensitive young casuist. He forgot how much her very mannerisms of speech had been borrowed from his own carelessly clever way of putting things, and he was wholly ignorant of how unconsciously but accurately she reproduced many of his indolent, daring views when once more reinstated among guardians whom these could not fail to shock.

"I've no doubt, my dear," he had answered, "that you could go back on both sides to all sorts of reprobates, male and female. But it's quite idle to think about that. When you get older, you'll wake up to the fact of how *bien élevée* you really are. Then it will be high time to weigh the advisability of never forsaking your present standard."

"But, papa, you don't understand," Olivia had objected. "I'm not speaking of what I've been taught. I mean a kind of headstrong wish, now and then, to do what I've been taught is awfully wrong."

Her father laughed away this protest as the merest *bagatelle* of hair-splitting scrupulosity. "Girls of your age," he told his daughter, " often get morbidly moral. It never does much harm, I suppose. It's like the stir of the sap in the virgin bud. They fancy themselves possible sinners because they begin to realize what a sinful world they've been born into. If a snow-flake, dropping from the sky into a dirty city, like this huge Paris we're in at present, could think and speak, I've no doubt it would express itself very much as you are doing now."

But Olivia was not at all satisfied with this light dismissal of her confession. She insisted on gauging her own faultiness at just what she estimated its true range of demerit. There were times when she grew to consider her acknowledged demon as a very tractable persecutor; he would lie so pleasantly dormant for days at a time. It was not that her wrong-doing ever greatly passed the bounds of roguery and pranksomeness, though it was not always exempt from the ire and spite of vengeful intention. What troubled Olivia about her own peccadilloes had far less to do with an exaggeration of their importance than with the fact that she committed them while clearly conscious of just what dagger-points of coming remorse she was sharpening for herself by the process. "There comes a kind of *vogue-la-galère* feeling with me," she once explained to a fellow-scholar. "I resist it, and then — well, then I don't resist it, and that's all. But I could if I wanted; there's always this painful *arrière pensée:* I could and I didn't."

"But do you really try with all your might and main, Olivia?" asked her companion, who was a tall, lithe, overgrown lily of an English girl, with a face like St. Cecilia's, and big brown, pleading eyes.

"I do — till the last moment," said Olivia dryly. "It's that last moment that makes me knock under," she added, with a rueful shake of the head, having borrowed unaware one of her father's pet phrases.

Absolute "young-ladyhood" dropped the mantle of dignity over her before she left the *pension*, and mischief of every sort became a diversion vetoed by pride. Olivia would now and then have a chilly little presentiment lest the vicious part of her composition were not so successfully tranquillized as it seemed. If the demon ever should rise again, he would have other weightier misdeeds to concern himself with than schoolgirlish capers. "Well," Olivia meditated once, not long after she had been graduated into freedom and leisure, "I can only hope that now I am old and grown-up, I shall be lucky enough to escape temptation. Without temptation as an assailant, it would be pretty hard for a girl like me, I should say, *not* to keep her self-respect unblemished."

Later on, this question of temptation assumed for her a strange and gloomy attractiveness. Her father had rarely exercised any heedful supervision over her reading. During the intervals of relaxation from study he had not precisely let her read what she chose, but he had been much less restrictive on this point than many less loving parents might have proved. And now, when her stay at the seminary was ended, he conceded a still wider latitude of choice. It was then that she found herself selecting books (whenever she could light on them) which dealt with the careers of those who had disappointed high expectations entertained by their friends and admirers, who had forsaken their own ideals of conduct either feebly or wantonly, who had fallen from grace, who had bartered for a mess of pottage the golden birthright allotted by circumstance. She incessantly put herself in the places of these unfortunate human failures. "How would *I* have behaved," she ceaselessly asked herself, "if I had been situated just as this or that character was ?"

The world that she was to dwell in, and that she hoped to shine in, spread before her like a delightful unventured country before a traveller who has just reached it along not a few wearisome preparatory leagues. She wanted to live her life duteously and nobly. She had said this again and again to her half-amused, half-admiring father during the last healthful months of his existence; she had said it more than once, while he lay ill in Washington Square, to the aunt whose unforeseen kindliness and fortitude had waked in her such a warmth of thankful love. Mrs. Ottarson had thought it just such a desire and resolve as a girl of her fine calibre would be visited by. But Olivia had not at all meant it in that way. She soon decided that her aunt Thyrza was incapable of following her lines of reflection and analysis. The fears

that she perpetually fostered regarding herself would
have seemed ludicrous to a nature at once as strong and
as simple as Mrs. Ottarson's. She would have thought
this whole matter of self-distrust quite as nonsensical
as Van Rensselaer had done; but she would have
lacked her brother-in-law's acumen and mental training
in the discussion of it.

And so, during those dreary days that preceded her
father's death, while she watched for the shadow that
had entered the still old house to gradually grow
blacker and more portentous, Olivia fell to brooding
upon all the chances which might await her of wisely,
honorably and capably husbanding what was truest,
sweetest and most wholesome in her own discerned
individuality. And it was now, when the dolorous
task which engaged her made this introspective office
take a more appropriate coloring, that she assured
herself how fecund were the opportunities within her
reach. She would be rich; she was what a good
many of her countrypeople would insist upon calling
an aristocrat by birth; she had been carefully educated; she could not fail of holding an influential
position. How would she use these rare advantages?
Ah, how preciously _could_ she use them! The types
already presented to her by Mrs. Auchincloss and
Mrs. Satterthwaite were despicable for their narrow-
ness and egotism. Would not she do more and be
more than these two servile devotees of sham and
arrogance had done and been?

The sudden blow that had fallen upon her produced
a disarray far stronger in meaning than that mere
ebullition of hopeful vivacity with which we have last
seen her rally under so distressing a threat. Mrs.

Ottarson's bluff and homely sympathies were welcome because of their invaluably genuine quality. But after an hour or two Olivia fled even from those, and locked herself in her own room upstairs, to try, as she told her aunt, if she could not get a little sleep before Mr. Delaplaine called upon her. She got no sleep, however, and courted none. She lay down, and the rest of body composed her quivering nerves, perhaps, while she grew almost unexplainably anxious to hear what her father's late partner would really have to say. Her aunts had told her that he felt the greatest hesitation about personally mentioning to her the subject of her dead parent's financial ruin. But it had somehow been one of the traditions of her childhood that he was an exceedingly able person. Her father had always led her to believe this, and her first thrill of irreverent disrespect for him had occurred during those meetings of theirs after the miserable days of death-bed anxiety had begun, when his frigid self-continence, his impenetrable stolidity had repelled and disillusioned her. Still, she now forlornly argued, he might come with the suggestion of some grateful and memorable expedient. Why not? He might have recognized that in spite of shattered patrimony, she was not one of those who would accept the tame conciliation, the galling peace-treaty of a proffered assistance. There might be likelihood that he would arrive equipped, as it were, with some proposition at once uncondescending and feasible.

"It will not be fair to let you remain here after to-night," Olivia told Mrs. Ottarson, while they were seated at dinner, that same evening, in the large, bleak dining-room below stairs.

"Oh, you jus' hush, 'Livia," retorted her aunt; "I'll stay 's long 's ever I want to; there! 'Taint a soul's business but mine; 'taint even yours."

"It's your boarders' business," murmured Olivia, looking round at three more family portraits, all of them with colorless faces that gleamed from a density of dark paint, and all bordered by tarnished gilt frames hardly a finger wide. "I hate to think of your goodness bringing any loss to you. I fear it has done so already. But, aunt," the girl went on, "I will promise, if you go to-morrow, to go with you. Yes, I will promise to go."

"An' stay?" faltered Mrs. Ottarson. Nothing could have given her greater delight, now that the tremendous change in her niece's prospects had presented itself, than to retain Olivia under her protection till death (or only marriage, perhaps) dissolved this desirable arrangement. "You don't mean to *stay*, do you, 'Livia?"

"For a little while," said the girl, smiling. "Until I can begin my fight with fortune, you know."

Her smile had the light of tears in it; at least, Mrs. Ottarson saw it thus. But she shrugged her plump shoulders, and tried to speak cheerfully. "Well, if you should go into any such fight, dear, an' get regular beat at it, y' know, there'll always be me, openin' my arms to take you in." . . . Here Mrs. Ottarson gave a most spirited start, dropping both knife and fork on her plate with a resonant clash. "W'y, 'Liv—i—a!" she slowly gasped, staring across the little round table at which they sat opposite one another. "Th' *idea* of my not thinkin' of 't 'fore now! Th' i—*dea!*"

"Well?" said Olivia. She perfectly understood that this violent yet unsolved consternation on her aunt's part meant no trivial fancy. A concept of moment must underlie it, or she would never have dedicated to it so asthmatic an intonation or so bewildered a grimace. "Well, Aunt Thyrza, what discovery have you made?"

"Discov'ry, 'Livia? W'y, it's just bursted on me! 'Xcuse the word 'bursted'; it isn't extra s'lect, I know; but I can't help it."

"I don't object to it," said Olivia. She felt confident enough that there was to be no groaning of a mountain over the birth of a mouse. She knew how unexplosively her friend could act when firmness and serenity were required of her, and she had the fullest certainty that no trifling disclosure, at this hour of her own mingled bereavement and perplexity, would be invested with idle pretensions. "But I should like to know," she proceeded, "why you are so immensely concerned without a minute's warning — really I should."

"Well, dear, you *shall* know." Mrs. Ottarson now spoke with an emphatic deliberation. "It's this. There's Ida Strang. You've often heard me talk 'bout Ida. 'Course you have."

"Ida Strang? Oh, yes. I've seen her, too, once or twice. She came here to speak with you about matters that related to — "

"My establishment," broke in Mrs. Ottarson. She looked round to see if the waitress had left the dining-room, and found that this was the case. If she and her niece had not been alone together, she would have preferred that Bridget should hear the word "estab-

lishment" instead of "boarding-house." But she
satisfied herself that Bridget was gone — a fact whose
weight had until now quite escaped her consideration.
"Or my boardin'-house, if you please," she added,
lightly, as if ashamed of her recent obvious feint.
"Yes, I rec'lect you *have* seen Ida. Well, as I've
told you, she's a kind of upper help, an' yet she holds
herself higher than any help I've got, by a *good* sight.
She 'tends to things I can't 'tend to. She sees that
the girls fix the rooms jus' so, an' she mends a little,
an' she keep an eye on the bed-clo'es an' piller-cases,
an' she stays in an' kind o' bosses things when I go t'
market, an' — oh, dear, 'Livia, I can't begin to 'numer-
ate *what* that girl *does* do. But mind, she ain't really
help, nor never was. Her folks are very genteel; they
live East; it ain't far from Boston. She always eats
her meals with me. She's been good as gold while
I've been away. She 'pears to suit splendid. Of
course the boarders 's missed my *deserts.* But they've
et what Ida an' Cook together could knock up f'r 'em,
an' no grumblin' that *I've* heard of. Oh, Ida 'd 'a
told me if there *had* been. An' now she's goin' to be
married. Yes, I got her letter yesterday. If 't
'a come 't any other time I'd 'a been in a fluster
'bout it. But *yesterday!* Why, *you* know! . . .
She'd first met him East. He's got a place here
in a clothin' store, ready-made, but first-class of its
kind. They're goin' to live in a flat, somewheres up-
town, an' . . . well, it all 'mounts to this — Ida's got
to go." Here the solemnity of Mrs. Ottarson's face
became tragic. "'Livia!" she exclaimed, in a voice
that rang with the deepest and truest feeling, "I'm
givin' Ida Strang twenty dollars a month. Of course

that means board, an' — well, I *was* goin' to speak
'bout her appetite, but now 's no time f' *that* kind o'
talk; *is* it? Still, *eat!* I never *did* see a girl that
*put away* like . . . But, oh, 'Livia, if any one had
told me this mornin' I should be makin' such a proposal t' *you*, I'd 'a laughed in their face f'r a fool o' the
first water. An' yet you say you *will* get your own
livin', an' you say — yes, you have said — that you
love y'r aunt Thyrzy, faults an' all, an' w'y isn't it
better t' come to me like that than t' go as gov'ness in
some stuck-up family that would chuckle behind your
back jus' t' see one o' *your* kind brought down. 'T
isn't bein' a servant, 'Livia, mind. Don't look like
that! — 's if you wanted t' scold me. I'll take it all
back if it bothers you. I'll — "

"You sha'n't take a word of it back, you darling!"
cried Olivia, as she sprang from her chair, rounded
the slight curve of the dining-table, and threw both
arms about her aunt's neck. "I'll go to you gladly
that way! I'll take Ida Strang's place with all my
heart. If you made me your servant, I shouldn't care,
so long as you paid me my wages for honest work!"

"'Livia! *Don't!* "

"Yes, I will! You know I'm proud, aunt, but I'd
hate myself if I dreamed of being proud to *you!* "
She kissed her aunt's olive cheek again and again, and
her tears began to flow as she did so, and no doubt
they mixed with Mrs. Ottarson's, which had surely
started too. "I'll meet Mr. Delaplaine (when he
comes this evening), oh, so bravely now! After all
you've done for papa and me, I should hate myself if
I thought there was the least shame in earning my
living in your house and at your side!"

Here Olivia drew backward from her aunt, who was still seated. She let a hand remain on either of that lady's shoulders. "Oh," cried the girl, with untold thankfulness in her breaking voice, "you've — you've taken *such* a load from me! I'll stay with you always! I'll be Ida Strang — I'll try very hard to be more — I — I *will*, truly!"

"Pooh!" cried Mrs. Ottarson, springing from her chair and snatching Olivia again to her breast. "'S if you, my dead sister's only child, couldn't be a million *times* more! I jus' *guess* you could!"

## IV.

Mr. Spencer Delaplaine made his appearance at about eight o'clock that same evening. Olivia was in perfect readiness to receive him. She looked pale as she entered the spacious, uncompanionable drawing-room, which had the doleful feature of somehow never seeming as if it were thoroughly lighted, no matter how many of the gas-jets in its cumbrous chandelier were made to shoot forth flame from the pinkish tulip-like shades. Perhaps the girl's black robe caused her to appear paler than she really was, but it brought out, at the same time, a cameo-like refinement of profile which might otherwise have eluded the more listless gaze. Mr. Delaplaine's gaze did not show any listless sign as he shook hands with her, gray and cold though his eye gleamed to the rather timid glance that now met it.

Olivia had her opening speech, as it were, prepared. She felt so reassured and placidly exultant since the recent conference with her aunt that possibly no real timidity possessed her; and certainly she revealed none, as she now said, sinking into a chair while her visitor reseated himself : —

"The flowers you sent this morning were very beautiful, Mr. Delaplaine! Poor papa always loved flowers. It was most kind and thoughtful of you to send him such charming ones."

Mr. Delaplaine had dropped his eyes toward the carpet. He gave a little husky cough, and then said : —

"Oh — ah — yes. I'm glad they pleased you. Those observances help, in their way, at such sad times."

"Indeed they do!" Olivia replied, with an earnestness abrupt as it was undisguised. "I hear that in New York some people dislike flowers at funerals. But I can't think why. Can you?"

He lifted his eyes again, and drew out a pair of gold-rimmed glasses, rubbing them with a white silk handkerchief before he put them on, and speaking before he had finished this brief preparatory process.

"Oh, people hate the humbug that is so apt to go with the custom."

"The humbug?" repeated Olivia, opening her blue eyes in a tender amazement.

"Yes. The crosses and wreaths and things that come from Heaven knows whom, and are sometimes almost an impudence, considering the comparative strangers who send them." He shifted in his seat, crossed his legs with a quick, nervous motion, and leaned backward a little. The glasses that now shone above his aquiline bend of nose became him; they gave him a more senile air, and yet one in perfect keeping with his high bald forehead, the little bushes of grayish hair at each temple, and the shoulders just stooping enough to show what a flexible, martial sort of figure they had once less weakly surmounted. "But of course," he went on, "you would not be apt to have any such experiences, Miss Olivia; you have met, naturally, so few New Yorkers."

"And they try to get into the good graces of people by sending flowers to their dead," murmured Olivia, musingly. "Well, if there were anything

sincere about such an attempt," she decided, with
a gentle little touch of positiveness, "I should say
that it was a very human and even lovely way of
expressing sympathy."

"But there lay the trouble," said Mr. Delaplaine,
with a crisp, smileless little laugh. "It was very
often quite the reverse of sincere. Some member of
a conspicuous New York family died — of a family
whose future kettledrums, dinners or balls certain
energetic strugglers wanted to attend, and lo, the
most costly floral emblems, with cards attached,
would appear on the day of the funeral. Such
offerings couldn't very well be returaed to the
senders, but being accepted, a kind of obligation
was accepted with them; and so, in many instances,
an abusive system of social pushing grew out of the
practice. Then somebody set the fashion of append-
ing to the death-notices in newspapers — 'It is particularly requested that no flowers be sent.' This
kind of a thing was of course a clincher. It effectually headed off the wariest tacticians. And then
came the droll part of the innovation."

"The droll part!" echoed Olivia, in sad surprise.

"Yes; everything .has its funny side, you know. I
recall several cases in which that little *addendum* was
made to the death-notice of relatives where very few
flowers would have been sent by anybody under any
circumstances; and yet there it was, staring you in
the face, just the same. They thought it the right
thing to do, and they did it. They wanted the inter-
ment to be *comme il faut.* After all, there's only a
slight step from wishing to live that way and to be
put into the grave so."

The cynic undercurrent in these words hurt Olivia.
"There's only the difference between life and death!"
she said.  "And that is such a wide one."

"It must be to you, at your age."

"I believe it is to everybody!" she affirmed most
seriously.

"Ah, that's because you're still young.  You
wouldn't be young and in good health if you didn't
cling to life."

Olivia made a negative gesture.  "I have seen old
people who clung to life," she said.

Mr. Delaplaine smiled.  "You mean they were
afraid," he answered, with a languid mutter.

"Awed, perhaps," she said, as if half assenting.

"Oh, it's the same thing.  They call it awe, but it's
only fear.  And fear takes many forms.  Religion is
often one of them."  He laughed his low yet sharp
laugh again, which was not unlike the faint tinkle
wrought by meeting metals.

"Not the right sort of religion!" exclaimed Olivia.

"The right sort?  My dear Miss Olivia, who that is
devout does not feel sure he possesses that?  It's an
affair of temperament and sentiment.  I'm not quarrelling with it wherever it exists.  I should as soon
think of quarrelling with the mercury in a thermom-
eter."  He began to smooth one of his knees with the
fingers of one hand, whose pink well-tended nails the
light struck, giving out from them dim, pearly flashes.
Everything about his person bespoke the most careful
nicety; his evening dress was the perfection of sub-
dued taste; his linen was spotless; he wore but one
ring, with an antique stone set in it, of far more value
than it looked.  "I take things as I find them," he

continued placidly, "and I find them best to endure
when they are taken that way." His composed face
underwent a slight change of expression, now; the
furtive blending of fatigue and satire seemed to die
from it and leave a deepened gravity behind. "I always did that with your poor father. But I grant,
now, that it might have been wiser if I had spoken
more plainly and harshly to him when he was so carelessly shutting his eyes to your future. . . . You
see, I assume that your aunts have made a certain
state of affairs more or less clear to you."

Olivia had dropped her head during these last two
or three sentences. But she raised it as the speaker's
collected voice died away.

"Yes," she answered, with a direct glance straight
at her companion. "They have told me that I
have nothing — that all has gone during papa's life-
time."

He nodded slowly and confirmingly while she
watched him. "Yes — that is but too true. I suppose it shocked you. But you seem to have borne it
with philosophy. I feared you would not. I'm glad
to see that you do."

She had astonished him, but he was not one to let
her perceive that. He sat observing her with much
intentness, now; she could not see how keen his
gray eyes were behind the lucid but obscuring lenses
they wore.

"It has been a great blow for me," she replied,
tremors coming into her voice but no hint of tears
ensuing. "I'm not over it yet; I shall feel it for
many a long day. And why should I not? It alters
my whole life; it changes me from an independent

being to an enslaved one. For poverty is slavery —
I'm quite old enough to have learned that."

"You're right," he said ; "and there's no slavery
so bitter as that which has once tasted freedom. . . .
I used rather direct speech to your father. Twice I
went over and saw him in Paris while you were at
your boarding-school. Each time I went prepared
for an altercation, and each time he welcomed me
so cordially and made me have such an agreeable
sojourn in the enchanting city that I sailed home
again feeling as if I'd left something behind me; I
suppose it was my scolding. Still, he heard from me
expressions of opinion regarding which he couldn't
have been greatly in doubt. But they never made
any difference with him. Of course he could not
have gone on borrowing much longer . . ."

"And he borrowed a great deal, did he not?" the
girl broke in here, with her cheeks turning paler.
Debt seemed to her something so onerous, dangerous, disgraceful.

"No; only a few thousands. I think there are
outstanding sums that will cover the whole liability
when his affairs are finally settled."

"Oh, I am very glad to hear that!" declared Olivia,
a bloom stealing back to her cheeks. The rich liquid
sparkle that secret excitement had lent her blue eyes
contrasted captivatingly with this damask tint; certain evenings in spring, when the first glitter of stars
tremulously begins above the rose-hued west, with
fresh winds fragrant from new leaves and grasses,
bear a lovely mystic analogy, in light and color, to
just such pure young faces as Olivia's now appeared.
"She's a wonderfully sweet-looking creature," Spencer

Delaplaine said to his own thoughts. "I have always held her to be so, but just now I feel more certain of it than ever."

"My poor child," he said aloud, "don't bother yourself about any indebtedness. Of course I made my loans with my eyes open . . ."

"But that is no excuse for me," struck in Olivia. "No excuse whatever."

"No excuse?" he repeated, leaning foward in his chair and playing with the slim gold cord of his eyeglasses. "I don't understand."

"The debt, I mean, is the same, if any should remain, after his affairs — as you yourself have put it — are finally settled."

"The debt is the same?" he once more repeated, and with undisguised bewilderment.

"Yes, I mean, it will be *my* debt. At least, I shall look on it so. I suppose the law would not, but that will be of no consequence to me. Whatever it turns out that papa owed you I shall continue to owe you."

He leaned back in his chair again. He was smiling, and the lines made by his lips at this moment had for Olivia an effect almost sardonically cruel.

"You!" he exclaimed. "*You!* Delightful!"

The girl felt herself crimsoning with annoyance. At the same time her spirit rose. "Ah," she softly cried, with a ring of rebuke in her tones that was womanlike enough to make, for at least that brief interval, her tender age seem incredible, "I cannot allow you, sir, to receive in sarcasm what I advance very seriously. If I am poor now I may not always be. To recognize the debt will not, I am well aware, be to discharge it. But I intend to discharge it if I can; I shall always bear in mind that I — I have inherited it."

He had ceased to smile. He had begun to rock the uppermost of his crossed legs in a deliberate manner that implied both diversion and condescension for the alert sensibilities of her who watched him. And his next words caused her to start and bite her lips, they so humiliatingly confirmed her expectations.

"Do you know, you simply fascinate me by your originality — your naturalness? That is rather a strong bit of enthusiasm for me, my dear Miss Olivia. I usually deal in the sober grays both of statement and emotion. I've never had many enthusiasms in my life — don't look indignant at me because I haven't. I couldn't help it. I must have been born on a foggy morning, when there was a raw, lazy east wind that didn't promise the slightest ray of sun for certainly twenty-four hours. But I'm not so benighted that I can't appreciate intensity in others. I said you were original, and I meant it. You're just the sort of daughter your father might have had; he was original in many ways; I remember once telling him that he was a free-thinking nonconformist in a shell of conventionalism. He frowned and didn't like it; so few of us like to hear anything that approaches being the real truth about ourselves. I've no doubt you will resent being told that you amuse me exceedingly. You can't see why you should. Of course you can't. If you did, my poor young lady, you wouldn't be half as amusing as you are. . . . You assert candidly and innocently that you have inherited your father's debt to me, whatever may prove its amount.

And you make this assertion only a very short time
after learning that you have not a dollar in the world.
Your confidence in the possibilities of your own opu-
lent future is what so particularly charms me. It has
the very dew of maidenhood upon it, if you'll pardon
such a poetic burst from an old fellow as steeped in
cold prose as I am. Some day, thirty or forty years
from now — when *you* are steeped in cold prose, too
— you'll be able to comprehend all this much better
than now."

Two bright spots were burning in Olivia's cheeks as
he ended, but otherwise she bore herself calmly.
"You turn what I have said into quiet ridicule,
Mr. Delaplaine," she responded. "It may seem to
you very entertaining; it is to me without the flavor
of comedy you detect in it. But I am not quite so
helpless, even now, as you judge me. I have a kind
friend in my aunt Thyrza, Mrs. Ottarson — indeed an
invaluable friend. I am going to begin at once earning my own living with her."

"Good heavens, my dear child! You can't mean
that you are going into that boarding-house they say
she keeps! And what on earth do you propose doing
there?"

"Getting honest employment."

He took off his glasses again and began to polish
them ruminatively. "Did the . . . er . . . the lady
herself propose this to you?"

"I induced her to propose it."

"Ah . . . indeed? And you intend to be a sort of
upper servant there? Is that the idea?"

"I should say it was. Except that Aunt Thyrza is
so fond of me as probably to become the most indul-

gent of mistresses.  But I sha'n't let her indulge me
too much; I shall constantly oppose that."

"But your other aunts . . . Mrs. Auchincloss and
Mrs. Satterthwaite?  They assure me they are willing . . ."

"To support me?  I have so understood.  It is
very kind of them.  But I prefer to support myself."

There was a silence.  Mr. Delaplaine readjusted his
glasses above the somewhat severe curve of his nose.
"You say that Mrs. Ottarson is your dear friend.
She has undoubtedly nursed your father in a very
capable way.  I surmise that she must have made a
most comforting associate for you in the sick-room,
and your having become fond of her is not at all
remarkable.  But, my child, to go and live with her is
quite a different thing.  It is worse than burying
yourself alive; for to bury oneself suggests at least
silence, and you will have about you, instead of
silence, a clatter of vulgarity which the American
boarding-house can alone perpetrate."

"Very possibly I shall.  But I shall be busy.  You
mind little troubles—*petites misères* like that—so
much less when you are busy."

She saw the icy smile edge his lips as he replied
loiteringly:  "What shall you do?  Darn towels?
Dole forth the tea and sugar?  Keep the mice out
of the strawberry jam?  Haggle with the grocer and
battle with the butcher?  You were simply not
brought up for such a life, and you may as well realize it now as a year from now—when retraction is
too late."

"Retraction?" said Olivia, lifting her brows.  "You

refer to my seeking the Auchincloss or Satterthwaite protection, after all." A dolorous little laugh fell from her, at this point. "There must be a good deal of haggling with the grocer and battling with the butcher before I do so."

"You don't like those ladies, then?"

"I don't like the plan of living with them!"

"It is not unusual in New York for people to try rather hard to cross their thresholds. How have they displeased you?"

"Not at all. I hope that we shall always be *bonnes connaissances*, but . . ."

"My dear, don't for an instant imagine that you will be," interrupted Mr. Delaplaine, lifting both hands for an instant and then letting them fall, "provided you sink so low as to live with that dreadful Mrs. Ottarson."

Olivia's eyes flashed. "You presume to tell me it is sinking low!" she began. "Now will you be kind enough to hear me tell *you* — "

"Nothing rude, I hope?" he again broke in. He was tranquillity itself; he could no more have become angry with her than with a June rose, bending and swaying in the wind, because one of its tiny thorns had made a spiteful lunge at his flesh. "I don't deserve to have you call me names, or anything of that sort. My dear young lady, I don't presume to tell you it is sinking low, or that Mrs. Ottarson is a dreadful person. I was merely making an imaginary quotation, as it were. I am positive that this is just what your aunts would say. Of course it is no concern of mine, except in so far as you are the child of an old friend."

"Forgive me if I misunderstood you," said Olivia, softening. "I know that Aunt Letitia and Aunt Augusta hold Mrs. Ottarson in great disfavor. She doesn't outwardly meet their approval, and so they never stop to consider what a heart of gold she has."

"Oh, I'm perfectly willing to admit that it's a heart of gold," he briskly returned. He had set himself to beating a little tattoo with the finger-tips of one hand on the marble-topped table near which he sat. "But hearts of gold have the misfortune to be invisible."

"Hers is not — at least not to me. I have seen it more than once for weeks past. She has shown it to me."

"Ah, Miss Olivia, are you entirely sure that it's eighteen carat? Pardon my atrocious flippancy. I sha'n't dare to go on if you wither me with another of those indignant looks that you gave me a little while ago. And you ought to be merciful; you ought to recollect how time has withered me already."

The banter in his voice was mockery itself to his listener; yet she felt it to be so discriminated, so modified, that her resentment of it could only make her appear ridiculous.

"Candidly," she said, "I would rather you would not go on, Mr. Delaplaine — in the strain you have adopted."

She saw his gray eyebrows elevate themselves over his luminous glasses. "Bless me! *what* strain? I've been admiring your championship of somebody you're fond of. I'm a good deal afraid of you when you look so tempestuous, but that doesn't prevent me from admiring you, all the same. We're very apt to be impressed that way by performances we're incapable of ourselves. I don't believe I've ever been so honestly angry as you just were, in all my life. I may have scowled and wanted to strike somebody; that's only the common, coarse style of procedure, with the raw Adam in it, the selfish personal thrill of retaliation. But your anger had a nice little touch of sublimity. If my nerves were a trifle stronger I should be tempted to beg that you would do it again ; for, upon my word, it's deucedly — I should say magnificently becoming!"

All this was delivered with so much measured, inscrutable repose of utterance that Olivia lost power to judge whether it were really meant for satire or sincerity. But if the latter, it stung her none the less keenly.

"It appears," she said, with the bitterness of unconcealed reproach, "that I must come back to my own country and undergo a great misfortune here, only to discover how lightly my unhappiness is looked upon. I am not sure whether you wish to jest with me or no." And now she rose, standing placid and sorrowful, in the large, cheerless room. "But it seems to me that you do wish to jest. This may be no more than your habitual mode of treating every subject in life, petty or the opposite. But it is not my mode, and this evening, of all others, I am averse to playing a part with which I have no sympathy. . . . Therefore you must excuse me for saying that I would rather not remain here with you any longer. Let us talk together, if you will, at some other time. You know what this day has been to me. . . . As for the course I shall take hereafter, I think I have fully explained that. I love Aunt Thyrza dearly, and I am going to live with her — you know on what terms."

He had risen by the time that she finished speaking. "So, I am dismissed," he said grimly.

She gave a slight smile, inclining her head with a grace that she did not dream of. "Only for to-night. I am tired — *distraite*, if you will. I . . ."

He took several steps toward her. As she raised her eyes to his face she discerned a new look upon it. His glasses dropped, and he caught them by their thin chain, swaying them to and fro while he now spoke.

"Olivia," he said, "I hope you're not too tired for one thing."

She stared at him questioningly, and he drew still nearer.

"Well?" she queried.

If he had been some one else she might have concluded that he was embarrassed; but embarrassment and he had no appreciable relations in the conception she had thus far formed of him.

"There's a means of saving yourself from stooping like this," he began. He still swung his glasses, and he glanced down at them fitfully while he continued to address her, scanning her face for an instant and then averting his gaze. "For it *is* stooping, and you'll be horribly sorry you did it. As for the means I mentioned — it's here; it's I, myself. I offer it."

She had not the faintest perception of his true meaning. "Thanks, no," she said. "You are kind to propose it. Please don't think me ungrateful. But I can't accept. I should be miserable if I did."

"You don't understand me," he replied, looking at her very steadily.

"Oh, yes, I do. It's to be your *protégée*, your —"

"Not at all, if you please. . . . Olivia, it's to be something much — much nearer than that." He took her hand, and she let him take it. She still had no idea what he meant. Her girlish thoughts had already swiftly shaped the question — "What can I be nearer to him than his *protégée* — than the daughter of his old partner, adopted by him?"

He still held her hand, fondling it. This revelation of tenderness in him was quite unforeseen to her; she had a qualm of self-rebuke for having pronounced him so thoroughly mundane and hardened.

"Ah!" she exclaimed, smiling. "You mean that I shall take in *your* household some such place as that which I have agreed to take in Aunt Thyrza's!"

He clasped her hand still tighter. "That isn't at all my meaning," he said.

"No?" she murmured, wonderingly. What could it be, then, if it was not that? He evidently wished to help her; it was unmistakable that he so wished. His eyes had almost an amiable light in their greenish-gray pupils; that indolent, derisive method of speaking had left him — that suggestion of being a person who treated life, death and the human soul as if they were a compound, yet forceless joke, a trinity of triviality.

"No," he said, seeming to echo her own monosyllable, while he watched the sweet, bold interrogation in her guileless eyes. "That is not my meaning. Can't you guess what it is?" His tones had become almost musical; they were so unlike those in which he was wont to speak, that for an instant the odd fancy crossed her as to the possibility of his having employed some whimsical trick of elocution. "Try to guess," he went on. "Try."

"But I have tried," she returned, shaking her head hopelessly.

"Try again," he persisted.

"Is he really making sport of me?" Olivia asked herself. The child is never quite dead, in a girl of her years, and for a little interval she was beset by that displeasure a child will feel when suspecting the presence of raillery in others. But no, she soon concluded; such a supposition was unjust; and then, almost immediately, she exclaimed: —

"I really am not equal to any more guessing, Mr. Delaplaine. You say that you would like me to be nearer than your *protégée*, and yet that you are not asking me to take any salaried position. . . ."

"Ah, it's a salaried position, in its way. There's a very handsome allowance attached to it. I shouldn't dream of supposing you'd take it, my dear, except for that saving clause, as it were. . . . I see that I shall have to blurt the truth right out. But it's wofully discouraging. . . ."

"What is discouraging?" asked Olivia. She looked alarmed, now; perhaps the first ray of real divination was entering her mind.

"That you should *not* guess without my telling you," he said. . . . And here he sought to retain her hand, while she made a little effort to draw it away. After that effort she let him keep it. Her eyes were full of doubt and her brow had clouded. She was not at all sure, yet; but it seemed to her as if each fresh minute rendered her more sure.

"How should this be discouraging?" she faltered.

"It makes me fear that you've no conception of me in the character I'd like to assume . . . as your husband, I mean, Olivia."

She snatched her hand away from him then, recoiling several paces.

"My husband — you!"

The words broke from her unawares. In another second she had regretted them, but it was too late for her to dispel the effect of repulsion, even of repugnance, which they must have produced.

"Am I so horribly old?" he asked. "A little past sixty? Is that so *very* old? It seems Methuselah-like to you, I don't doubt, because you are so young."

Olivia had drooped her head; her cheeks were burning so that they gave her actual pain. "You must forgive me," she stammered, "if — if I seemed to show you that I — I thought you *were* too — too old. It has taken me greatly by surprise. I — I was completely unprepared for it."

A little silence followed. To the girl it was truly agonizing. In all her life she had never known such crucial embarrassment as now. Spencer Delaplaine in a trice, as it were, had roused her pity where before he had evoked merely her tepid and indifferent distaste. He had in a manner bored her; he now promptly became interesting. It must be so frightful, Olivia had hurriedly told herself, to want to marry any one, and waken the mildly horrified sensations he had just wakened in her, simply because you asked the matrimonial question.

"Please do not think this proposal of mine," she heard him say, "the result of any suddenly-formed

resolve. It is very remote from being so, I assure
you. Ever since you came back for the last time —
and that is months ago — I have been sensible of a
. . . a deepening attachment. This sort of visitation
comes to only a few men as late in life as it has come
to me. I had reached an age when I was justified in
expecting that it would never come. What mortal
can have lived as long as I have lived without more
than one so-called affair of the heart? But I speak as
white truth, Olivia, as was ever spoken by human lips,
when I affirm that you are the first woman I ever saw
whom I longed to make my wife."

She raised her head and showed what seemed to
herself her blazing face. But it was only a face dyed
with a brilliance excitement had lit there, and fairer
now to him who saw it (fair as he had already silently
estimated it) than it had ever glowed before.

"You have paid me an honor," she said, catching
her breath, and putting one hand clingingly just above
her bosom, as women will do when they are in straits
of agitation. "I thank you for the honor. It springs,
I am sure, from the warmest generosity. I — I shall
never forget it — I shall never forget that you gave
me the privilege of declining it."

"Ah," he cried, with an imperious rigor in his voice
that made her start back from him alarmedly —
"there's not a trace of generosity about my conduct!"
He appeared to marvel, a second later, at his own
betrayal of something so intimately similar to passion;
he stood with a kind of self-astonished look in his
eyes and with a hand pressed against one temple, as
though he were asking himself in his own worldly-
wise vernacular what the devil he meant by such

queer behavior. And when next he spoke it was with all his old control.

"I had but one motive," he said, "in asking you to be my wife. I'm fond of you. I love you. I want to marry you for that reason, and for none other in the world."

Olivia clasped both hands together as she stood facing him. "I don't love *you !*" she exclaimed, using the naked fact because her poor disturbed wits could just then seize upon no other. "I don't love *you*, and I never could."

"I'm perfectly aware of that," he began, seeming to present himself before her, as the words fell from him, in precisely the same attitude of well-bred *aplomb* by which she had long since measured his individuality. "I don't expect you to love me. I'm not such a fool. But I —"

Here Olivia stopped him, with both uplifted hands. "No, no," she cried, beseechingly and yet forbiddingly.

Then a new thought appeared to strike her. But as it did so she plainly shuddered; and then, as if feeling that she had been rudely merciless in thus betraying aversion, she stretched forth one hand to him.

Instantly afterward, however, she withdrew her hand. He had meanwhile advanced toward her as if to clasp it. . . .

With precipitation, and with the sound of a repressed sob, she now turned from him, hurrying to the doorway and leaving him alone in the solemn, dull, ugly drawing-room.

He did not quit the house for some little time after

that.   He had folded his arms and was staring down at the uncouth scroll-work of the carpet. . . . But at last he roused himself and went downstairs to the lower hall, where he had left his hat and coat.

# V.

Olivia heard the front door clang as she stood in one of the upper rooms beside Mrs. Ottarson.

"There — he's gone!" she said.

"'Livia, you look so scared an' funny!" exclaimed her aunt. "For mercy's sake, what *did* happen?"

"I'll tell you," said Olivia. And with a burst of real hysterical laughter and a preliminary gasp or two, she began the narrative. . . .

Spencer Delaplaine walked quietly up-town from Washington Square. His gouty ailment had not discommoded him quite so much as usual, of late. Otherwise his health was nearly as good at a little past sixty as it had been all those years ago, when he stood beside his friend Houston Van Rensselaer in the little Macdougal Street house and saw him commit the absolutely tragical *faux pas* of marrying Rosalie Jenks. Delaplaine had always lived well, but with discretion. He used to say that if it were true every man at the age of forty was either a fool or his own physician, then he intended to take enough care of himself to prove an exceptional case: he would not be a fool, and he would be much too healthy for the need of his own medical services. Excess was not so distasteful to him as that the fine clarity of his common-sense forever taught him its peril. If he had been less selfish he might have ended disastrously as a drunkard, or met some like fate, born of his own trespassing indulgences; for he had many traits belonging to the confirmed voluptuary, yet did not possess the headlong and improvident ones too often uppermost in such a nature. The evil was with Delaplaine never sufficient for the day in such matters; he could not rid himself of the to-morrow, with its attendant prostration, inertia, penance. He had serenely calculated that just so much pleasure of a certain physical kind would be safe for him, and no more. Prudence reared her defensive paling at this boundary, and he never passed beyond it. The world accepted his reluctance as excellent decorum; it was in reality one of those valiant exhibitions of egotism which are lucky enough to lie within strict conventional limits.

He had always been an inordinately selfish man, and he had contrived never to let his selfishness transpire. Long ago he would have broken all connection with Houston Van Rensselaer if it would have repaid him to do so. But there was a magic of caste about "Delaplaine *and* Van Rensselaer" which mere "Delaplaine and Company" would never have been able to preserve. His own people, the Delaplaines, were all dead now, except a few cousins, whom he ignored as tiresome, and not of the class to which he belonged. He secretly laughed at there being any such class whatever in a republic whose very existence was a protest against all aristocratic principles. But what did he care for the inconsistencies and self-contradictions of the foolish throngs about him? His object was to ride securely on the topmost crest of the wave, success. He could not understand how any rational being could endorse any other system of philosophy. But he was by no means a shallow and unreflective

egotist; false, and indeed disrespectful, judgment of
his aims and tenets would spring from such a belief
regarding him. He had not only studied men thoroughly, and pronounced them for the most part fools,
with a sprinkling of intellectual zealots and enthusi-
asts; he had also studied books, guided by an early
education, fairly complete when we consider that he
had been graduated from such an institution as was
Columbia College nearly a half century ago. A member of fashionable clubs, a diner-out, a conceded supporter of social dignities and formalities, he had
nevertheless found not a little leisure — through entire
freedom from those vices that give the jaded palate,
the fatigued brain, or the rebuking digestion — to read
with zest, lucidity and mental satisfaction. He had
followed most carefully what is called the modern
movement in thought. He had marked many a pas-
sage in Mr. Herbert Spencer's great series of works;
he had become so interested in the purely mathemati-
cal portion of the "Psychology" that he had set himself to the study of higher mathematics in order that
no page of this wonderful work should remain dark to
him. He delighted in the hypothesis of Darwin and
its powerfully convincing deductions; he had no more
doubt that the intelligent ape was our primeval parent
than he had assurance as to the mythic origin of Adam
and Eve. He took regularly, and perused searchingly,
the *Popular Science Monthly*, and kept wary watch,
as well, upon the English *Nineteenth Century* and
*Fortnightly Review*. He prided himself upon being
an exact thinker, and abhorred metaphysics, which he
contemptuously classed with poetry as among the
solid stumbling-blocks to civilization.

The writings of Emerson impressed him, when in particular moods, but he always covertly resented the spells of that unique sorcerer, whom he looked on as "spoiled" by the influences of an overgrown imagination. He had been fascinated by the essays of so supreme an idealist and moralist, but rebelled against the very charm they exerted. "They're fine," he had once declared aloud, late at night, amid the silence of his library, after having yielded himself for an hour or so to the piercing qualities of their epigram; "but they're bricks without mortar; the ideas in them don't hang together. No wonder they've begotten so many gushing transcendentalists!"

Mentally furnished as he was with all that is best in the scientific discovery and speculation of this unparalleled century, he had still reaped from his voluntary and even fond studies nothing except the most barren materialism. The splendid standard of conduct pointed to by Herbert Spencer's priceless philosophy had not stirred in him a pulse of admiration. All that Huxley or Buckle or Lecky had taught him had been a deference to the brain-powers that could thus tear the husk of superstition and humbug from pregnant, irrefutable truth. It was all very well for a few men to live up to humanitarian theories, if so disposed. It was right; he admitted that it was right. But now, at sixty or thereabouts, he would probably have only ten or fifteen years more to live, and he meant to pass through those years in comfortable observance of accepted formulas. He had made a Will, bequeathing all his large fortune to well-known and trusted charities. That concession (surprising as it would prove for the poor cousins who had already

fixed expectant eyes upon his money) he was willing
to grant the enlightenment of the time. But there his
altruism stopped short. He was the kind of agnostic
who might have supplied unnumbered texts for denun-
ciators of reigning rationalism. The glorious future
possibilities that evolution offers to our race had failed
spiritually to move him. What has been called the
" new religion " struck him as being full of practical
wisdom apart from its exalted philanthropy. But he
still remained an unruffled idolater of self. He sometimes inwardly wondered that the men with whom he
talked in Wall Street or at the club did not guess of
what irresponsive marble he was made. He often
suspected that some of the women, least frivolous
and hollow, did guess; but then he usually chose, if
permissible, the company of women in whose fair
bosoms no hearts beat for the loftier ethical needs.
He had long ago assured himself that all except handsome women were repellent to him. Unless their
lineaments pleased him, their conversation irritated
him. It was different, of course, with great female
personages like Mrs. Auchincloss and Mrs. Satterthwaite. They were not merely women ; they were
majestic portresses at a palatial gateway ; give a
woman distinction, prerogative, and plainness or maturity can be endured in her. That was why marriage
had such a ghastly side to it ; two people swore at the
altar that they would calmly watch one another decay.
Delaplaine had congratulated himself again and again
that he had permanently escaped the making of so
foolish a vow. As it was, he had gone along through
this vale of tears, he felt inclined to think, at a very
prosperous pace, and he meant to take the rest of the

journey in equal comfort. He might have done a
great deal more good than he had done; but there
would have been the concomitant trouble in doing the
good — and that he chose to avoid. Besides, if he
spent his money that way, it would cease to roll up
like a gigantic pecuniary snowball. And he wanted it
so to roll up. There was far less of avarice in this desire than of inflexible ambition. Wealth meant such
domination, precedence, and supremacy nowadays;
the having it in great quantities implied a vast deal
more than the spending it in comparatively small
ones.

A blunder that above all others Delaplaine never
wanted to commit was the revelation of his own real
bloodless nature to those with whom he associated.
He had no friends, and desired none; he held all
friendship to be wrought of sentimentality — a mere
frangible air-bridge swung between the two massive
and calculable passions, hate and love. But he had
hosts of acquaintances, and these he was quite willing
to let believe him remarkably cold, though not abnor-
mally so. When they laughed at his astute or shrewd
sayings about men and things, it pleased him to have
them laugh. But the draughts of penetrative comment he drew for them must not be too bitter; he
liked at least a tincture of sunshine to blend with the
waters, so that they should not taste too acridly of
the dark earthy cistern whence they had been taken.
He liked to bear the reputation of a rather caustic wit,
but it did not at all suit him to rend that inner veil
which concealed his unrelenting pessimism, his contempt for the spirit of righteous law filmed over by
politic obedience to its letter, his inveterate distrust of

mortality at large, his innate faith as to the void noth-
ingness which lay behind our whole sublunar scheme.
He clung very stoutly to the outward seeming of daily
behavior. We were all mere puppets; the entire ter-
restrial proceeding was farcical as a Punchinello-show;
but, meanwhile, being in and of the show, he proposed that he should play there as one of those puppets which make a victorious bow to the spectators at
the fall of the pretty miniature curtain. Such arid
chaff as this he had reaped from contact with the most
fecund and stimulating minds of an epoch like the
present. They, the lineal heirs of Locke and Bacon,
of Spinoza and Comte, had taught him only the big-
otry of self-worship! But aggravating and pitiful as
it may sound, he had passed years of sleek contentment with his garner of scoff and lip-service, his har-
vest of despair and hypocrisy. "No one knows much
about me," he had more than once triumphantly meditated, "except that I am a flourishing banker, say
rather sharp things now and then, drop into my pew
at Grace Church every other Sunday or so, have the
*entrée* to all the best houses in town, and generally de-
port myself like a gentleman. If I live fifteen years
longer — and I ought to live twenty, considering the
care I've taken of myself — it will be going down
hill all that time. This infernal gout is sure to grow
worse as I grow older, and each attack nowadays, I
find, lays me up for a longer period. But what of
that? I shall have had more sweet juice from the
orange of life, and less of the harsh tang its rind can
mingle there, than nine-tenths of even the fortunate
fruit-gatherers. I'll go to my grave as one man out of
ten thousand goes — bah! it would be truer to say

twenty! My plot is bought in Woodlawn, and the
order for a handsome monument in the middle of it is
snugly appended to my charitable Will. All that remains for me, now, is to slide as gracefully and becom-
ingly out of the nonsensical worry and fluster as I've
acquitted myself respectably and commendably while
one of its participants."

So ran the reflections of this confident manipulator
with destiny, and so they continued to run, till a
special day, not long before the beginning of these
pages that faithfully expose them, brought him a
novel and unanticipated experience.

One name may stand for this experience. It was —
Olivia Van Rensselaer.

He had made jest, at first, of his own curious emo-
tional flutter. More than once, in former days, he
had seriously entertained the idea of marriage, but
had dismissed it before the least compromising step
had been taken. In one instance the lady had been
young, of radiant beauty, and the possessor of a copious fortune. If report spoke fact she had been devotedly attached to Spencer Delaplaine. But all this had
happened when he was just turning forty, and perhaps
as brilliantly eligible as any man in the metropolis.
He had cautiously reviewed the advantages and draw-
backs, then, of a union with so delectable a bride, and
had affirmed the latter to preponderate. It would all
be very distinguished and noteworthy, he concluded,
but it would most dictatorially interfere with the
comforts of bachelorhood. He could not see the use
in contracting new ties. Family ties, above all others,
were mere sugared pills. A so-called pleasant responsibility was none the less burdensome because you

tried to persuade yourself that you were not bowing your back under it. No; he would stay single. An eminent marriage would be of no consequence to a man like himself. Let the real strugglers mount on that kind of stepping-stone; he had gone up too high for the necessity of any such assistance.

Now, having met Olivia two or three times after her final return, and when the illness of his partner had made direct intercourse between himself and her a requisite occurrence, his own possible marriage dawned upon him in a totally new light. Since he had been fifty it had indeed not dawned upon him at all; it had been relegated to that limbo of unconcern where lay not a few abandoned projects in similar desuetude.

But the presence of Olivia, the light of her blue eyes, the appealing melody of her voice, the indefinable allurement of her chaste simplicity, had touched fibres in his being that he had long ago deemed either to be dead or never actually living. He had aired some grossly pungent opinions upon the love of the sexes, in former hours, when his tongue tripped more glib at smart *jeux d'esprit* than now; but he had never spoken half the contemptuous innuendo that slept hidden behind these open disparagements. Of all the calamities that could befall him he had failed to prophesy any positive seizure by a sentiment. But here, he soon realized, was malady of more poignant bane. If it did not closely resemble a passion, then all his past acute observation of his fellow creatures amounted to little. And at his age! Pah! it was clear burlesque!

To his keen dismay he found himself deriding it

with the laughter Mephistopheles might have inaudibly
bestowed on the infatuation of Faust. And yet, by
some puzzling enigma of circumstance, he enacted
both these rôles in the strangely unexpected drama.
It was in vain that he called upon all the grimmest
resources of a humor at no time genial. He likened
himself with no avail to a gouty and superannuated
Romeo. Self-scorn would not serve him. The sun in
Olivia's tresses beamed to him no less vividly; nor
did the elusive dimple in her roseleaf of a cheek obey
less flexibly her awaited smile.

He was in love at last — he, who had asserted love
to be a folly of the senses, rampant in youth and
extinct a decade or two after it. The very bodily
preservation in which he had exulted, now confronted
him as a jeering excuse for his fond transport; this
delightful malady would never have presumed to attack him, at his age, if he had not gone on judiciously
husbanding enough prime vitality for its maintenance.
There were two or three women in New York society
whom for some time it had amused him to make the
recipients of his loyal, though harmless gallantries.
Mrs. Satterthwaite was one of these. He would be
sure, a few years ago, either to seat himself in her
box at the opera during some portion of the evening,
or to hover near it if it were too full for entrance —
as those old boxes in the horseshoe of the Academy
of Music were easily rendered. At many a ball,
reception or dinner, he would exchange with her
words of gayety, gossip, or a certain sort of flirtation
in whose art he was the supplest of adepts, and she
was very far from inefficient. The world knew him
as one of Mrs. Satterthwaite's unfailing devotees; and

matrons of her years, even when they are the *châte-laines* of superb establishments and give banquets where the wines defy detraction, are rarely troubled by a plethora of devotees. After a rather prolonged battle with the new feelings that possessed him, Delaplaine determined to seek the advice of Mrs. Satterthwaite. He selected a particular evening when he was almost confident she would be at home, and he went early in order to anticipate other visitors. But almost the first ray that shot from her steely eyes weakened his resolution. And when her smile came, seeming to give her lips a cruel curl that he had never noticed until now, he abandoned his purpose altogether. How that smile would change into pitiless ironic laughter if she knew the truth! And what a fool he had been to dream of telling her! "I'll put the Atlantic between me and that girl!" he swore to himself, later in the evening. "This is just the season for the Riviera, and I've never seen half enough of it."

But he did not go to the Riviera. He stayed in New York, and felt the clutch of this astounding passion tighten about his heart, and so tell him that a heart was really there. His self-humiliation was, meanwhile, proportionate to his enchantment. During the interviews that he held with Olivia previous to that final meeting which has been described in detail, he battled silently against the impulse to disclose his secret, as though it involved rank disgrace. Like nearly all in whom love of self is paramount, he was acutely sensitive to ridicule. There is no doubt that he underwent severe suffering while he pictured the amazement, quickly succeeded by repulsion, which his amatory confession might cause. He mutely groaned beneath the curse of his gray hairs and wrinkles as perhaps few of his sex have ever groaned before. And here was just the girl to show him, with all the unvarnished frankness of maidenhood, how delicious an old fool he had made of himself!

Still, all this time his worldliness was counselling hope to him. Old as he was, he was not too old to marry a blooming young bride. Men had done it before, when their purses were as well-lined as his own. There was no young suitor in the field, either, and that counted for much. Then, if her father died (as die he must, said the doctors), she would be left to face the intelligence of his past ruinous disbursements. In her alarm, her bewilderment, why should she not grasp at the first strong hand of help proffered her? He found himself ardently wishing that she were a few years older, and that he yet cared for her as he did now. She would be sure not to hesitate then. No full-grown woman, who had outlived the early romantic quivers and illusions, ever did hesitate to marry where lay her best vantage of wealth and position. They were all alike; the lover with the languishing eyes and the slim bank account was sent off begging, and the plain-featured or elderly wooer with the fat income carried his point. Oh, yes, he had seen it work like this a hundred times. But Olivia was not a full-grown woman; there seemed to rise the dreaded impediment. That devilish romanticism which perpetually went with girls of her age might put up a barrier as powerful as if she were some demoiselle of the *sang azur* and he merely the American gentleman of means that he rated himself.

He had chosen to let his friend, Mrs. Satterthwaite, and her ultra-patrician sister, be the emissaries who should first impart the unpalatable tidings. That was unquestionably the neater plan. He would appear a little later — as we are aware that he did appear. He had not been at all sure that he would then make to Olivia the disclosure he longed to make. No palpitating lover of one-and-twenty could have been more uncertain as to the exact moment favorable for "speaking out" than this grizzly veteran of untold tact and duplicity. But the time had arrived when Olivia had announced to him her intention of earning her own livelihood — and with that abominable person, Mrs. Ottarson! He had met the girl's affirmation with a little rush of cynicism at first; that had been irreversible with him; he could no more have helped it than he could have helped his baldness or his attenuation. But afterward the chance for unreserved avowal had seemed to lie just here. It hardly appeared conceivable that Olivia would prefer paid servitude under Mrs. Ottarson to driving in her own carriage as Mrs. Spencer Delaplaine.

That she had treated him precisely as she had done he did not think at all surprising. It would have been highly improbable that such a girl should do anything else. A week — perhaps even a day — might change her mood, her point of view. Besides, that unutterable Mrs. Ottarson, with all her villanies against the Queen's English, was not quite dunce enough to advise the discountenancing of a match like this. And yet, who could tell? The woman might be one of those who read the *Weekly Wake-Me-Up*, or some similar harrowing sheet, where they printed stories of how Luella wedded the penniless young painter and

drew herself up to her full height, and smiled haughtily,
when his wealthy but wrinkled rival begged for her
lily hand.

He would not by any means retire from the contest.
He would simply silence his guns and watch the enemy's movements as best he might. Thus he decided,
that same evening, as he crossed the big, lonely, dusky
square, and moved up along the lower portion of
Fifth Avenue. It is always quiet here, with no rattle
of omnibus-wheels or jingle of car-bells. Delaplaine's
residence was not far away, in West Tenth Street.
He owned and occupied a rather spacious house there;
he had done so for years, not liking to dine regularly
at his club, bachelor though he was. There were too
few men of the very first grade, he had long ago made
up his mind, who lived in this way on our side of the
ocean. Besides, he dined out a great deal all through
the season, and he liked to return those dinners in
kind, with the mark on them of his own *ménage* and
his own *chef*. Occasionally he would give an evening
reception, at which every appointment was perfect,
with some reigning lady of fashion to welcome the
guests in his company. The year that Emmeline Satterthwaite came out he issued cards for a brilliant ball
in her honor — a signal of such profound civility to the
young lady's mamma and herself that envy seized the
weapon of gossip, as it so often does when it can find
one within reach. It asserted that "Of course the ball
was beautiful, and a success, and all that, but then one
couldn't refrain from asking whether it was *just* in the
*nicest* taste or no." Delaplaine and Mrs. Satterthwaite heard some of these affectionate hints, and
laughed together over them. The lady herself was

not at all bored, but not half so much amused as she
would have liked to be. She was too many rungs of
the social ladder above nearly all these jealous beings
to care for whatever spiteful pellets they might fling
from ambush. But the ball had conferred great joy
upon her for one conspicuous reason: the Auchinclosses had never had a like honor bestowed on their
Madeleine; and they would have thought it an unde-
niable honor. Severely as Letitia Auchincloss
"weeded" her list, she had never dreamed of supposing that her brother's partner could hold any but an
honorable place there.

Delaplaine ascended the soft-carpeted stairs of his
commodious home to-night, and felt what a rich frame
it would make for the living picture which he was
bent upon surrounding by it. And she was of the
Van Rensselaer blood, too. If he had believed in a
Providence, he would have been strongly inclined to
thank it for that agreeable fact. The entire mansion
was already most suitably prepared for the entrance of
a bride. The drawing-rooms were a nonpareil of elegance and comfort. The upper chambers, divided one
from another by silken *portières*, needed no fresh
grace of decoration. Costly paintings and engravings
lined every wall, for Delaplaine loved Art, as many
men of just his temperament do; he had purchased a
Bouguereau and a Gérôme, a Toulmouche and a De
Jonghe, and a little Meissonier at some huge price.
No Corot, however, was to be found in his dwelling;
he considered Corot a humbug, and Daubigny, Rous-
seau, Dupré, humbugs as well. They were quite too
idealistic to gratify him. He execrated artists who
strove to paint the unpaintable. There was enough

reality to put on canvas; why strive to put impossible dreams there?

His great tufted easy-chair was waiting for him in his library at the rear of the house, on its second story. The lamp of Japanese bronze on his reading-table beamed to him its old suave welcome behind a rosy shade. A genial flame writhed and sparkled from two burly logs on the low hearth, with its gleaming andirons and its glassy tilework. A valet was within easy call. To touch the little silver bell on the book-loaded table and summon him was no more difficult than to reach out a hand and take up the last copy of a noted English review, and find out what new American author it had vented its insular spleen upon.

"She would like all this," he said to himself, surveying the apartment, with its low book-cases, its precious bits of sculpture and bric-à-brac picked up abroad, its prostrate gorgeousness of Turkish rugs, its tapestries, its tasteful and luxurious air of faultless *bien être*. At the same time he recalled the exquisite arrangement of other rooms, visited perhaps but once a fortnight or still more seldom, yet always kept in the most irreproachable order by a body of trained servants. His entire establishment was an ornate monumental tribute to his own selfishness.

He lit a cigar. He never smoked more than two cigars during the twenty-four hours; one after dining and one a little before bed-time. As he sank into the big cushioned chair and puffed forth the first blue clouds from a Cuban tobacco imported by himself, he faintly repeated, half aloud, the reflection which had before been a silent one: —

"She would like all this."

He meant that she should not only like it, but marry to get it. He had not by any means done with Olivia Van Rensselaer yet. Indeed, the longer that he sat musing and smoking there in his library, the more convinced he felt that now the ice had been once fairly broken, the true line of action had begun.

Meanwhile, at this same hour, Olivia was saying, very earnestly yet sedately, to Mrs. Ottarson:—

"I don't think it possible that he really could *care* for me — an old man like that. Do you, Aunt Thyrza?"

"Oh, I s'pose so!" cried Mrs. Ottarson, in her galvanic style; "they sometimes do, 'Livia. But it's too awful to think of *you* goin' *that* way! Mercy sakes! I don't see how you kep' a straight face. *I* couldn't, 'f I'd been twenty years 'r so younger, and he'd said it to *me*."

"It would have been dreadful to laugh," answered Olivia. "It would have been insulting, you know."

"Oh, yes. Of course it would." . . . Mrs. Ottarson wore a meditative look for a moment. "'Livia," she presently murmured, all the celerity and levity gone from her tones, "I dare say there's plenty that would call it an el'gant thing f' you. There's mothers that would almost drag a girl o' theirs to the altar if she got such a chance o' goin' there. Oh, yes. I know this world, if any one does." Here she paused again, and a curious, drawn, perplexed, irritated look showed itself about the corners of her mouth. "I mus' say, 'Livia, that I *would* like t' see you his *widow*."

"Oh, Aunt Thyrza!"

"I'd like if you'd been all through the hateful part of it an' come to the part worth havin'."

"Oh, Aunt Thyrza," still pleaded the girl; "don't!"

"I can't help it when I think o' that sumpshus
house o' his there in Tenth Street, an' the carriage I've
seen him ridin' along the Fifth Av'nu' in. Nobody
dis'proves of 't more'n I do when 't comes to a girl
downright *sellin'* herself. No, *indeed!* But when I
think o' that carriage, 'Livia, with two men up on the
box in bottle-green liv'ry, and nobody inside but just
him, w'y, 't seems to me 't if some girl wasn't han-
kerin' partic'lar after *young* comp'ny, she might kind
o' jus' shut her eyes an' take the jump!"

Olivia broke into a laugh, but at the same time she
went up to her aunt and playfully put one hand over
the lady's mouth, as if to forbid further volubility in
at least a single direction.

"I'm not going to shut my eyes and take any such
jump," she exclaimed. "And I know very well that
you wouldn't either wish or advise it. . . . But what
I propose, with your permission, to do very soon,
Aunt Thyrza, is to move myself and my few possessions out of this house. Your people need you — I'm
certain of it. Before very long I hope to make them
feel as if they needed me too. I only hope I can get on
half as well there as Ida Strang did. It's just as if she
left you to give me a chance, but *I* shall never leave
you for any such reason as hers. I intend never to
marry, Aunt Thyrza, as long as I live. . . . Perhaps
we can manage to start for Twenty-Third Street by
to-morrow afternoon. Don't you believe it will be
possible? I want to go as soon as that. If my aunts
come again, or if *he* should come, I want them to find
me there with you. That will simply settle everything. Now let us try if we can't get away by to-
morrow!"

## VI.

They did try, and succeeded. That next day, with its hurry of packing, cost Olivia a good many pangs. But she consoled herself somewhat by thinking that possibly, if the day were less busy, she would have had time to suffer much more poignantly. Not the least of her trials came in the discharge of her French maid, a girl to whom she had become attached while abroad, and to whom the necessity of imparting full reasons for their sudden separation was trying enough. In the hasty collection of all those possessions to which she knew that she had a personal right, Olivia came inevitably upon not a few tokens that brimmed her eyes with filial tears. The bitter thought was already at work within her soul that the father she mourned had treated her with heedless cruelty. She strove against the distressing influences of such a reflection, however, and in a spirit of courage no less dutiful than pathetic, we have heard her tell Mrs. Ottarson that she believed it would form her chief sorrow hereafter, in thinking of her father, to recall how he must have suffered when monetary perplexities assailed him. But now, already, she could feel the impulse of reproach and blame cloud and mar for her the tender brightness of his memory. Her clear comprehension of moral obliquity, whenever and wherever met, compelled her to pass condemning judgment upon his actions. And she disliked to have his image in succeeding time rise before her with this blur across it of unconquerable resentment. It would be so unhappy a thing to go on seeking excuses for him, and perhaps never lighting on one that was truly adequate! . He had so long been her ideal of gentlemen that it was like putting out the sacred tripod-flames in a temple to discontinue accrediting him with virtue above the reach of condonation!

She had, as yet, no conception of how mordant were to be the changes in her life. Eager to avoid dependence where a girl of weaker parts would have almost thankfully grasped the chance of securing it, she had wholly miscalculated her own strength to enter among surroundings new in the sense of an unimagined novelty. The dismissal of her French maid was but a faintly unpleasant prelude to graver sacrifices. Stepping, the self-supposed heiress of a large property, down from a home which but yesterday she had looked on as inalienably her own, into a boarding-house full of people with whose types and characteristics she was entirely unacquainted and quickly prepared to disagree, meant a great deal more than fancy at its ablest flight could have informed her. It needed considerable effort for Mrs. Ottarson and herself to get away from the Washington Square residence, in the meaning of an absolute and final departure, before about half-past three o'clock that afternoon. But they accomplished the feat, and Olivia left with a certainty that she should find her baggage deposited at the abode of her aunt some time before she herself arrived there.

It was one of those thoroughly prosaic red-brick, high-stooped houses in the west portion of Twenty-

Third Street, between Seventh and Eighth Avenues, for which that momentous locality deserves anything but celebrating mention! There is probably no large city within the present ken of those versed in the topography of such progression, that has grown as un-picturesquely as New York has done. For years it increased the number of its streets with. an attention to quiet ugliness of outline that gave no promise of the lovely Central Park destined as a sort of metro-politan repentance for past misdeeds. From North River to East the hideous avenues have swept, one after another, across town. Smartness of exterior has now and then cropped out in the brown-stone front and the plate-glass window-pane, but except for the expression of a certain high-stepping, dapper gentility, there is not much relief from prevalent uncouthness anywhere between Waverley Place and Fifty-Seventh Street. Here the true architectural fire leaps into creditable blaze, and a half-suburban stroll up through Harlem, and even. beyond it, will easily make us ready to prophesy how beautiful, how imperial a city New York may one day become, when all the eyes that now mark the domain of its growing grandeur have long ago been sightless!

Mrs. Ottarson's boarding-house might just as well have been either of its next-door neighbors, for any outward individuality presented by it. But inside, it was probably cleaner than a good many of its fellow boarding-houses. Its proprietress endeavored to keep it so, and not without fair success. But the dinginess, the shabbiness, the wear and tear, the out-at-elbows and down-at-the-heel look of nearly everything, she would have found it hard enough to rectify. She had always managed to hold her own with her boarders, while never attempting to overawe them by the slightest assumption of undue majesty; it was extraordinary how skilfully she contrived to steer between austerity on the one hand and over-humility on the other. Such a position as hers it is not easy to assert and maintain; but she had done both for a number of years with excellent success. Her boarders were for the most part fond of her, and three or four of them had followed her to these ampler quarters from a narrow and much inferior house in Greenwich Avenue. Others were the result of her improved facilities of accommodation, and one or two of these latter she regarded with pride as the living evidence of her rise in the world. The day of her home-coming was indeed an eventful day for the boarders. Hearing that it was near and probable, they had " clubbed together," as they called the operation, and purchased a water-pitcher of sufficient splendor to glare down the' idea of its not being silver, though in reality but " warranted " plate — whatever that epithet may mean. Considering that every boarder in the house would most probably make use of this pitcher quite as often as Mrs. Ottarson would do, there was an apparent lack of self-forgetfulness in the nature of the gift that might wickedly have tempted a humorist. It was to be formally presented at the first dinner over which their returned landlady (who had so nobly devoted herself to the dying hours of an aristocratic brother-in-law) should hereafter preside.

"Here's your room, 'Livia," said Mrs. Ottarson, after she and her niece had ascended two flights of stairs together, and entered a well-furnished, thor-

oughly comfortable-looking chamber in the rear of the
house. "It's southern exposure, you know, an' there's
a fire-place f'r a fire whenever you want one. I'm so
glad, dear, that I can see my way to lettin' you have
it. It was Mr. Ab'nethy's an' I'm glad he went while
I was to your poor pa's. He's one o' *the mos'* tryin'
boarders, Mr. Ab'nethy, I've ever had since I've been
in this line o' livin'. *Towels!* He used seven a day!
He was English, an' had a tub that he flounced round
in so ev'ry mornin' it woke Miss Pank, who's got the
hall bedroom jus' next to this (you see, I've stuffed up
all the cracks o' the door), an' brought on her neural-
lerga that she gets bein' a gov'ness, poor thing; she
can only afford me eight dollars a week — though she
*pays* it ev'ry Saturday *so* reg'lar! An' then Ab'-
nethy's *airs!* Why, I pride myself on givin' hearty
breakfasts to 's many as wants 'em; but he called himself an inv'lid, an' yet he'd ring his bell 's late as 'leven
o'clock over-night to find out w'ether ther 'd be grid-
dle-cakes or not the next mornin'. An' *eggs!* W'y,
if an egg was too yeller to suit him he'd say 't was
green, an' if 't wasn't yeller enough he 'd say there
was the commencement of a chicken in it, an' . . ."

"Does Ida Strang have as large a room as this?"
asked Olivia, while she looked about her, unconsciously breaking in upon the details of Mr. Aber-
nethy's peculiarities.

"Oh, *about*," answered Mrs. Ottarson, suddenly, at
her wit's end for a beneficent and pacifying falsehood.
"Let's see . . . hers hasn't got jus' the same *closet*
'commodations, p'rhaps, but I guess yours an' hers
would pretty much tally. W'y do you ask *that*,
'Livia?"

"Oh, nothing," was the reply. This apartment struck Olivia as being rather beyond the deserts of her new position and prospective salary. But she knew so little concerning such matters; it was easy enough to deceive her.

Mrs. Ottarson meanwhile hurried on, with great hidden desire to change the subject: "You'll come to dinner, 'Livia? you needn't if you don't feel 'xactly *up* to it. You can have it here jus' 's well 's not. Now, do tell me w'ich you'd rather do."

"Oh, I'll appear at dinner," said Olivia. She glanced at her trunks, already deposited in the room. "I shall unpack a little, and then I shall be quite ready. Dinner is at six o'clock, isn't it?"

Mrs. Ottarson's boarders dined in the basement. When she first took possession of the house she had pondered the question of whether it would be preferable to have one large table in this room or small ones scattered about. The latter arrangement was more advisable from the standpoint of pure fashion, but there was a sociability in the former for which no amount of elegance could compensate. "Oh, it's *tonier* to have 'em — I allow *that*," Mrs. Ottarson had said of the small tables to a friend who counselled her adoption of them. "But I've been so 'customed, somehow, t' look on my boarders 's if they were friends an' relations. B'sides, I like to sit at the head o' my own table an' do the soup-helpin' an' the carvin'. There's something kind o' *human* about that; but I can't see as there is when the lady o' the house takes her victuals off somewheres alone an' leaves her boarders to sep'rate in comp'nies, one

table puttin' on airs. to the next an' another gos-
sipin' about 'em both."

There was not a single vacant seat at the long table
this evening, by a quarter past six o'clock. Such a
full attendance was rare in the extreme. Even young
Tredgett, who worked so hard "down town" and
would often appear as late as seven, or possibly a
quarter past, giving Ann and Bridget the trouble of
keeping three or four plates hot for him (and, it must
be added, now and then smelling of something very
like whiskey cocktails, in a manner that suggested
more pleasurable detaining causes than those of a
mercantile character) — even young Tredgett managed to be present on this highly memorable occasion.
Olivia had slipped into the place which Mrs. Ottarson
had provided, on her own right. The girl had supposed that her presence would hardly be more than
just noticed; but here she speedily found herself to
be quite wrong. This was the aristocratic niece at
whose father's death-bed their landlady had been
performing her ministrant offices. Only yesterday
morning the society column in the *New York As-
teroid* had mentioned his death, and added feelingly
that it would throw some of our first families into
mourning. Of course Olivia must not merely be
stared at, but pulled to pieces in a visual sense by
the little soulless corporation of the dinner-table.
She soon became sorry that she had not dined upstairs in her own room, after all. Still, the general
growing babble of conversation served her, before
long, like a friendly agent. If not forgotten by the
small community all about her, she was at least tem-
porarily ignored. She had asked her aunt to present

her to nobody for that evening, and Mrs. Ottarson, readily perceptive and congenial as to the motive of such request, had freely granted it. Meanwhile she listened, with sensations in which alarm had begun to play a stealthy part. Her aunt's errors and short-comings, both of grammar and taste, had weeks ago ceased to disconcert her; they were the mistakes of one whose heart was nobility and fidelity, however deep a few flaws of the surface might seem to a casual eye. But thus far her acquaintanceship with Mrs. Ottarson had stood for the girl's one encounter with meagre and feeble human culture. What she now listened to would not, under different circumstances, have proved uninteresting; she was naturally fond of watching various bents or oddities in the dispositions and temperaments of her fellows; to shrink from an attentive scrutiny of the unrefined lay wholly outside of her antipathies. She might have enjoyed listening and observing at present with the zest that all novelty of this description brings to a healthy and robust young mind, were it not for the furtive but insistent thought that she had undertaken to dwell among these people and accept them as her future companions and associates.

The talk had grown merrily jocose. A certain Mr. Spillington was speaking a good deal, by this time, and his pleasantries provoked great applausive mirth. He was one of the important boarders; he and his wife paid thirty-five dollars a week for a second-story room. He was a large, portly man, with nebulous, bulging, flaxen whiskers, and a prominent nose that shone with a waxy pinkness above his wide, ever-smiling lips. He held a position of superintendence in a noted Eighth Avenue dry-goods emporium, not far away. Some of the ladies who now sat at meat with him had received the honor of his most impressive civilities when "shopping" within his august radius. He had a little, pale, narrow-chested wife at his side, who thought him a prince of wits and a flower of manliness, and whom he could have taken in his arms and tossed like a baby without the least muscular effort. She pretended to be shocked at nearly everything he said, but kept her eyes incessantly rolling to left and right whenever he aired his humorous powers, for the evident purpose of ascertaining what risible havoc they created. Now and then she would exclaim, in a tenuous, piping treble: " Sam, *do* stop!" But there was a world of shy, covert pride in this remonstrance, which had become as habitual with the poor, devotedly uxorious lady as the sleepy trill of a sick bird to its more vigorous and songful mate.

" Oh, yes, we've been kicking up our heels here in a tremendous way while you've been gone, Mrs. Ottarson," Mr. Spillington was sonorously exclaiming. He had a bass voice of untold capacity, and he now made this organ felt in its full volume. "Drowle, don't you remember that night I got you so drunk on lager-beer that you opened one of the parlor windows and called in an organ-grinder to give us a Virginia-reel?"

This flight of invention was hailed with noisy laughter. The young gentleman thus daringly addressed would soon be ordained as a minister, and the scandalous fiction caused blushes to bathe his timid, beardless face.

" I guess I don't remember," he burst forth, with a

nervous titter, the moment that silence had been restored, " and I guess you don't, either."

This was not strong as repartee. Everybody saw
that Mr. Drowle was painfully embarrassed. Miss
Pank, the visiting governess, who sat next him, leaned
her head in his direction till one of her pendent front
curls (which it had been spitefully said of her that she
wore in defiance of the reigning mode because there
was a large amber wart on one of her cheeks, close to
the ear) almost dipped its hyacinthine end into the
gravy on her neighbor's plate.

" There's such a thing, *I* think, as carrying jokes a
little too far," whispered Miss Pank, and the soon-
to-be Reverend Mr. Drowle shot her a grateful glance
over one of his burning cheeks.

" Mercy sakes ! " now hurried Mrs. Ottarson ; " you
don't s'pose, Mr. Spillington, that I'm goin' to b'lieve
you left poor Mr. Drowle *'nough* beer to get intoxicated on ? Not you, sir ! I've seen you toss off too
many pitcherfuls to be gammoned that way."

There was a certain Mr. Struthers, who had given
a wild guffaw of delight at the end of Mr. Spillington's last speech, and he gave another wild guffaw
now. He was much pitted with small-pox, and had
beady black eyes and the slimmest of necks, with an
" Adam's-apple " that looked like a ligneous excres-
cence on a slender tree. Every time that he gave his
hilarious laugh, the " Adam's-apple " would take a
little upward bound, as though it were some sort of
curious machine for measuring the degrees of humor
reached by any occupant of Mrs. Ottarson's boarding-
house.

A plump, cherubic maiden, with a mouth like a

rosebud and two dimples looking like tiny bees that had come to sip honey from so tempting a flower, sat next to Mr. Struthers. This was his betrothed, Serena Sugby, the daughter of the well-known authoress, Aurelia Sugby, who detested the jocund Mr. Spillington, and prided herself on having more than once disastrously worsted him in a battle of tongues. Serena, a very lambkin of pranksomeness beside her dignified and almost funereal mother, lifted one fat little hand and began to slap her laughter-convulsed lover between his shoulder-blades.

"Serena!" remonstrated her mother, in severest undertone, "when will you learn the simplest rudiments of lady-like deportment?" And then, while Serena giggled penitently and smoothed her canary-colored bang, Mrs. Sugby exchanged a glance of mutual disgust across the table with her friend, Miss Pank.

"Oh, yes, yes," continued Mr. Spillington, ruminative and incorrigible; "we've had some famous old times, Mrs. Ottarson, while we've been running the house ourselves. I suppose I'd better not say anything about the surprise-party we gave Mrs. Sugby, one night, in her own room."

"Sam, *do* stop!" twittered his wife, rolling her eyes to this side and that, as if determined on seeing just who appreciatively laughed and who did not.

Mrs. Aurelia Sugby stiffened herself. She abominated Mr. Spillington, but she had always regarded him as a person to be "put down" without much difficulty. She was the well-known Aurelia Sugby, author of "Beryline, the Babe of Sorrow;" "Bertha, or the Bride of an Afternoon;" "Teresa, the Type-

writing Girl," and many other fictional works of an
astounding popularity, as the editors of the weekly
journals in which they had run serially for the delight
of innumerable avid readers, could plainly testify.
She bore no resemblance whatever to her blonde,
mettlesome little daughter. She was dark, emaci-
ated, with a lantern jaw and a thin-lipped, disputa-
tious mouth. She had a great opinion of herself.
The editor of the *New York Fireside Friend* had
made a contract with her to furnish him two continued stories a year, one sprightly sketch (" with
plenty of love in it") every week, and a fortnightly
poem " thrown in," for a remarkably handsome annual
sum. The poem was to be as much as possible like
that piece of lyrical work which she had once written,
and made such an immense hit by writing, entitled
" Only the Baby's Empty Shoe." She had followed
up this classic stroke of success by " Only a Mother's
Tear," " Only a Cradle Void," and " Only a Wee
White Sock;" but somehow none of these latter cre-
ations had achieved the wide vogue of the first. Her
verse was said to touch the popular heart, and like
certain other verse of the same reputed efficacy, it was
quite remorseless in rhyming " sound " with " brown,"
or " slumber " with " under." But the popular heart
had beaten no less responsively to it on that account.

Bold Mr. Spillington was not to be dismayed. In
previous conflicts with Mrs. Sugby he had always preserved his temper, which is considerably more than she
had done. For this reason, if for no other, he had
believed himself repeatedly to have been the victor.
He now said, with his broadest smile, looking at Mrs.
Ottarson:

"Oh, it was a very fine affair — very, indeed. It was a masquerade."

Up darted Mr. Struthers's "Adam's-apple," and a roar left his lips, followed by a choking sound. His *fiancée*, forgetful of all past injunctions, gleefully lifted her clenched rosy fist, and pounded him five or six times on the back, as though the performance were great sport, and at the same time a matter of distinct duty. Her mother was too absorbed for the usual admonitory " Serena! " this time. She was indeed bent upon the overthrow of the audacious Mr. Spillington.

" Ah ? " she said, with a sepulchral blandness. " A masquerade in my apartment, sir ? And, pray, what *sort* of a masquerade? "

This was precisely the opportunity by which Mr. Spillington's diabolic fun-poking was balefully stimulated. As he prepared to answer, Mrs. Ottarson struck in, with joviality, but with a vocal note of seriousness also : —

" Now jus' look here, Sam Spillington (you limb, you!), stop this tomfool'ry ! Try your nonsense on somebody that enjoys it. Do 's I tell you ! "

" Mrs. Sugby seemed to enjoy it very much," asserted Mr. Spillington, as he gave one of his big, vapory whiskers a swift twirling stroke. " That is, if you mean our surprise-masquerade. The costumes were all so well-chosen. You've heard of Charles Dickens parties, of course. This was an Aurelia J. Sugby party. We all dressed like characters from our esteemed friend's favorite works of fiction. Struthers, there, he went as Del Monte, the heavy Spanish villain in . . . what *is* the name of that most exciting romance? And Drowle, poor fellow, he was Claribel,

the Sewing-Machine Girl. His figure was just slender
enough to suit the female get-up, and then we curled
his hair, and parted it in the middle, so that. . . ."

But Mr. Spillington's voice was now drowned by
tumultuous peals of laughter. Olivia sat and wondered what they had heard to plunge them in such
ecstasies of mirth. She felt, on her own side, merely
the discordant condemnation of one who sees the
shafts fly from an insolent personality, reckless how
deep they pierce. She had not been prepossessed by
Mrs. Aurelia Sugby; few people ever were. But she
now became conscious of a kind of sympathy with that
lady's grimness and acidity, as the latter, having waited
for a pause in the prevailing clamor, somewhat
hoarsely said:

"You exhibit, sir, a most exact familiarity with my
published works, truly!"

"Oh, yes," exclaimed Mr. Spillington, with that
temerity by which the over-indulged humorist will tell
how dizzying an elixir applause can brew him, "I assure you, madam, that I read the *Blood-and-Thunder
Gazette* every Saturday night."

"Sam, *do* stop!" bleated his wife. . . . But her rolling eyes could now detect few signs of amusement on
the various faces they swept. Mr. Spillington, like all
jokers who serve the capricious approval of the minute, had for once over-shot his mark. His last sally
had fallen pointlessly flat. Mrs. Sugby's admiring
readers were not in the minority this evening. It was
well enough playfully to antagonize her, but to hurl
scorn at her luminous talent was quite another posture.
Even Mr. Struthers, oblivious of his guffaw, refrained
from a smile, and if the up-springing of his " Adam's-

apple" was to be calculated on as an indication of Mr. Spillington's triumph or defeat, its fixity now conveyed but a single sombre meaning.

Mrs. Sugby's field of attack was ready for the marshalling of her forces. She made no delay; her sober eyes kindled with an uncompromising spark, and the smile that touched her lips had the gleam in it of a naked blade.

"I do not write for the journal you have mentioned, sir," she said, amid the silence which had ensued. "I haven't ever even perused that periodical, as I'm aware of. I presume you find time to do so, sir, but if you'll allow me to express myself free on that point, I think it would be much more suitable if you perused, instead, a book on the manners of good society."

"How scorchingly sarcastic!" whispered Miss Pank to Mr. Drowle, as a stillness followed these inimical words.

Mr. Spillington did not appear to think so, however. "Are *you* the author of such a book, madam?" he inquired. "I didn't know you went into good society." Here he gave a voluminous cough, and added, as soon as its accompanying throat spasm would permit: "That is . . . a . . . of course, in your *writings*, I *should* say. I supposed you confined yourself mostly to low life."

Even the amiable Serena had by this time become incensed. "Low life!" she exclaimed, looking at her mother, as though shocked by a charge so grievous. "Why, ma, your Coralie Talbot Montmorency in 'Bertha, or the Bride of an Afternoon,' is one of the greatest heiresses in England."

"My dear," said her mother, throwing a glance of

untold contumely upon Mr. Spillington, "the gentleman doesn't read my works. He hasn't time. He's
too busy among the *other* man-milliners and counter-
jumpers at Bigsbee and Company's, in Eighth
Avenue."

Abusiveness could hardly go further than this. But
so far Mrs. Sugby had, nevertheless, won the day.
The suppressed murmur that greeted her bludgeon-
flinging sentence was one chiefly of approbation. She
had defended her intellectual offspring, the treasured
produce of her brain-labor. More than one lady or
gentleman present had flushed over the perils of Beryline or of Bertha.

But Mrs. Ottarson here dashed in between the com-
batants. She showed herself the most belligerent of
peace-makers. Her black eyes flashed savagely at Mr.
Spillington. "You're served jus' right!" she cried.
"You began it all, an' you've only got your dues."
Then to Mrs. Sugby: "But don't *you* say 'nother
word, ma'am. We've had 'nough wranglin', I *guess*,
for *one* evening." Then, finally, to both: "If either
of you *does* begin again, *I'll* up 'n leave the room, an'
take my niece, here, along with me. A pretty piece
of goin's-on for *my* first night home and *her* first 'pear-
ance 't my table! "

Olivia, coloring, bit her lip. This allusion to herself
fired in her a new pride, and made an inward voice
sound to her, as if saying that she had no place among
men and women stamped with such coarseness as she
had already witnessed here. But self-reproach quickly
overcame that impetuous little secret vaunt; it seemed
like disloyalty to the aunt who had saved her from a
far worse indignity — that of becoming a pensioner, a

dependent, a recipient of doled-out alms from others.
The greater and worthier pride in her sped to destroy
the lesser and meaner one.

But still she remained keenly discomforted. It
rushed through her anxious mind, while the battle between Mrs. Sugby and Mr. Spillington threatened at
any instant to break the bounds of their landlady's au-
thoritative reprimand :

" How can I endure living among people like this ?
Are not their world and my world thousands of miles
apart ? What would poor papa say if he could know
now that I have drifted into these surroundings ? And
how can I bear myself among them ? Even if I go
on, with as much bravery and control as I can possibly
muster, shall I not in the end make the dreariest failure of it all ? "

Meanwhile, whether betokening an enforced armistice, or only the ominous calm that precedes a more
desperate engagement, there had fallen over.the entire
dinner-table that lull which is so much more significant
when it comes after the flurry and turmoil of a heated
skirmish.

## VII.

But Mrs. Ottarson had carried her point. With a
rather embarrassed giggle, which bespoke coercive
surrender, Mr. Spillington subsided beneath the last
scathing *coup de grace* of Mrs. Sugby. A buzz of talk
now succeeded, from whose complex web could no
doubt have been unravelled many different opinions
concerning the recent passage-at-arms. But the general decision went against Mr. Spillington.

"Your husband will have to apologize to Mrs.
Sugby," said a certain Mrs. Disosway, who sat next to
the wife of Mr. Spillington and now addressed that
lady. Mrs. Disosway abhorred the late assailant of
the celebrated authoress; he was always cracking his
inane jokes at somebody's expense; he had once presumed to crack one of them at hers. She was a sort
of concert-singer and had been an operatic prima
donna before that, and he had asked her, one day,
when she spoke with fervor of how deep and fond
were her hopes of heaven, whether she expected to
meet her lost voice there. This was a view of celes-
tial benignancy which Mrs. Disosway had not felt at
all inclined to take. She did not by any means regard
her vocal proficiency in the light of a departed bless-
ing. She was a stout, sallow woman, with an apocry-
phal look about the lustrous black of her fancifully disposed tresses, and a pair of eyebrows that had the
appearance of having been ruthlessly burnt off at their

roots, leaving only two pale, smoke-colored arches to contrast with the copious *coiffure* above them. She was undoubtedly very decayed and artificial to contemplate, and it did not require much imagination on the part of any one who carefully observed her to decide that perhaps an organ of the most worn and precarious quality might lie below her tallowy and sagging lips.

"My husband will have to apologize?" appealed Mrs. Spillington, with her wan face drawn into lines of the most incredulous disdain. "Dear me! I'd like to know why!"

"Oh, I'll tell you why," retorted Mrs. Disosway, grandly, "if you really *would* like to know. He spoke *most* insultingly to Mrs. Sugby."

"Pshaw!" fumed Mrs. Spillington. "I guess you don't know my Sam, if you think he'd bemean himself like that, when it was only a joke, and she understood it was only one. . . . And to insinuate that my Sam was a man-milliner and a counter-jumper! *She* might better apologize!"

"She didn't insinuate it at all," said Mrs. Disosway. "She stated it, in just so many words, Mrs. Spillington."

"Yes, she *did*," struck in a gentleman with a dense fall of long iron-gray hair that surged quite unparted from a bloodless face, and who sat on Mrs. Disosway's other side. He was a spiritualist, and his ardent faith in the materializations wrought by Katy Conroy, the last mediumistic idol of the hour, had been smitten by the jeers of Mr. Spillington. "It seems to *me*, ma'am, begging your pardon, that I never saw anybody as well *laid out* as your husband was a few minutes ago. And you may tell him that, with my compliments."

Mrs. Spillington showed two rows of large and not flawless teeth, which her small, wilted face, with its unhealthy tints, did not make less unfortunate as the kind of disclosure brought about by her bantering and twitting smile.

"Oh, I guess I won't tell my Sam anything with your compliments, Mr. Smear. If there's any talk about laying anybody out you might recollect what quick work he once made with your ghosts and spirits and things."

Mrs. Disosway and Mr. Smear put their heads together in low laughter of vast irony. "Quick work!" whispered Mrs. Disosway in the large ear of her companion, with its big cartilaginous flange, that kept the torrent of gray locks from breaking bounds and inundating the clean-shorn, bluish cheek. "Oh, to think, Mr. Smear, of that midget trifling so with the great truths of Eliphalet K. Tomlinson and Cynthia Jarvis Duryea, as *we* know them! Isn't it *too* pitiful?"

Mr. Smear looked as if he thought it was quite too pitiful. Mrs. Disosway had "assisted" at several *séances* held by both the just-named mediums, in Mr. Smear's company, and she had also heard Mrs. Cynthia Jarvis Duryea in a trance-lecture. The ex-prima-donna thought it really unfortunate that Mr. Smear, on such occasions, should wear that gray shawl, fastened at one shoulder by that tarnished-looking buckle, instead of the more conventional overcoat. Still, his acquaintance had been a source of *such* comfort to her! Had he not been the means of opening her soul to the marvels of spiritualism and of bringing her into contact with her deceased second husband? The late Mr. Disosway had not, it is true, proved a model spouse; still, communications from him in a dark room under conditions of a truly awful solemnity, had cast an idealizing glamour over the hard fact of his having conducted himself like a reprobate for several years previous to his entrance into the summer land.

But Mr. Spillington, like all persons who volunteer amusement of a mercilessly disrespectful kind, had secured adherents and supporters. There were toes under Mrs. Ottarson's mahogany, this evening, on which the coltish hoof of his so-termed humor had not yet trodden. Hence a certain share of the loquacious bustle that now prevailed was not adverse to him; it excused him on the ground of "not meaning anything but his fun, you know," and of "only wanting to wake us all up."

Mrs. Ottarson, having laid the tempest, tried to diffuse forgetfulness of its ended rage. Of necessity, her efforts were restricted to a minor audience, and it is possible that overheard semi-tones of criticism might have spurred the quieted contestants into a fresh duel of wits, had not the arrival of dessert brought with it the time for presenting that fond testimonial of the silver-plated pitcher which was to terminate this exceptional repast.

It was a most unsuitable hour for such presentation. Mr. Spillington, as the only inmate of the boarding house who possessed the least oratoric talent, had been chosen to offer the gift, with some kind of apt accompanying speech. Meanwhile the pitcher itself had been placed in charge of a Mrs. Tingle, a little wiry lady, with a tiny pair of glasses forever on her tiny

near-sighted eyes, and a gown that always looked as
if it were about actually to touch the floor, but never
did so, swinging nimbly clear of any such contact
with an oscillation that suggested unforsaken crino-
line. Mrs. Tingle had a passion for economy, and it
was agony for her to hear of any article having been
purchased at a dime lower than she could herself
obtain it elsewhere. Hence, when the question of the
pitcher arose, she sturdily fought against its being
procured up-town. She knew a shop in Maiden Lane
where you could get plated ware so cheap that it was
a positive sin not to go there. She had got *her* own
water-pitcher there; you could see it engirt with
bric-à-brac on the adjustable bedstead in her apartment, when that harmless incarnation of domestic
hypocrisy was trying to pass itself off as the most
undeceitful of side-boards. She had carried her point,
and a pitcher almost the duplicate of her own had
been found in Maiden Lane. As the servants were
beginning to pass round the oranges, Mr. Spillington
made a sign to her, and she slipped away from the
table, hurrying upstairs. She had been a good deal
flustered by the late disturbance, thinking it in horrible taste on both sides, but having a partisan feeling
of indulgence for Mr. Spillington, whom she considered such a "comical, funning gentleman," and
"the life of the house." When she had regained her
seat, with a very tell-tale bulge in the shawl that she
had thrown over her slim shoulders, Mrs. Ottarson,
whose attention had been roused by her unwonted
proceedings, would probably have addressed her concerning them, if Mr. Spillington, sensationally clearing
his throat, had not now risen.

He commenced an address to Mrs. Ottarson, in
which rhetoric was called upon for her most flowery
and prismatic tributes. He spoke of their landlady's
beaming visage having dawned once more upon the
expectant gaze of her boarders like a long-clouded
sun through envious but relenting vapors. He compared her genial spirits to the blandness of a spring
morning, and her matronly charms of person to the
mellow richness of a midsummer afternoon. At this
stage in the complimentary harangue, his wife's eyes
rolled from one face to another with a magnificent
pride in the sonorous periods of her lord. Once or
twice the poor little lady's lips moved as though she
were about to utter her time-honored remonstrance of
" Sam, *do* stop ! " But she was saved from the dire
unfitness of such ejaculation by an opportune access
of common-sense, and went on rolling her eyes instead
of indulging in the old playful comment. And now
Mr. Spillington waxed still more picturesque, blending
pathos with his florid imageries. Mrs. Ottarson, the
well-beloved custodian of their daily comforts, had
gracefully, and almost at a moment's notice, exchanged
the horn of hospitable plenty, whose contents had been
so freely poured upon these, her admiring friends
for the . . . for the (he cleared his throat a great
deal just here, as even the noblest orators will occasionally do when they find themselves in the presence
of a dangerously inexact metaphor) for the . . . ahem!
sombre apparel of the sick-nurse, and the . . . er . . .
gloom of the . . . er . . . chamber of . . . er . . .
dissolution. " Death " seemed a rather strong word
to use before Olivia, and " dissolution " answered decidedly better. And then Mr. Spillington turned

toward Mrs. Tingle, who was only a short distance away from him, and who instantly handed up the pitcher she had been concealing, which was passed onward until it reached the spokesman's grasp.

"Accept, my dear Mrs. Ottarson," he now said, lifting the pitcher in both hands as though he were about to consecrate it by some impressive ceremonial, "this insufficient and yet warmly affectionate proof of our . . ."

But here occurred a sudden most unforeseen interruption. It was made by Mrs. Tingle. She probably meant to whisper, but what she accomplished was nearer to a plaintive scream.

"Oh, dear!" she broke forth, "I've made a mistake. I'm so near-sighted, and — and my room was dim. Yes, I — I've made a mistake."

Mr. Spillington, with the pitcher still raised aloft in an attitude that seemed to him particularly fine as an idea and was majestic enough to be called sacerdotal as a performance, here turned somewhat scowlingly to the agitated speaker.

"A mistake?" he said, in low, gruff voice. "What do you mean, ma'am?" Seeing that every eye was now turned upon her, Mrs. Tingle palpably shivered. She drooped her eyes, and then raised them again with an expression of acute despair. "The pitcher,' she gasped. "*Don't!* It — it isn't *it.*"

"Isn't *it*?" cried several voices in amazed concert.

"No," stammered Mrs. Tingle. Agitation always produced in her the painful effect of completely depressing her lower lip, till it dropped below her under teeth in flaccid limpness. "I mean it's the *wrong pitcher!* It's — it's my old one, and not her new one! Oh, I'm *so* sorry."

There was a momentary silence, and then came a roar of laughter. But all the while Mr. Spillington preserved his consequential posture, and when calm was restored he said severely to Mrs. Tingle : "Oh, very well, madam. Then your blunder will compel me to present this pitcher, so to speak, by proxy for the other — that's all. . . . Be sure," he added, while he now gave the piece of plated ware into Mrs. Ottarson's outstretched hands, "that you don't allow yourself to be bamboozled out of the pitcher that really belongs to you." And then they all roared again — except Aurelia Sugby, and a very few others. Mrs. Sugby would not have done more than smile now, no matter what had been the terms of her acquaintance-ship with Mr. Spillington ; for slang was deeply distressing to her, whenever and wherever lighted on, and she rejoiced in making her newsboys, her boot-blacks, her street waifs and even her thieves and des-peradoes talk with an elegance and correctness of diction that might stingingly reproach certain other contemporary novelists for their over-realistic methods.

Olivia, when it was all over, and she had left the dinner-table for that most pleasurable privacy which her own room afforded, felt as if she had been violat-ing the requisitions of retirement due her deep mourn-ing, and had witnessed a theatrical display in the teeth of opposite inclinations. An environment like this, as she clearly realized, must hereafter bristle with vexatious trials. But she meant to be most brave, and to hide as well as she possibly could from her aunt's detection the very effort of fortitude that she exerted. On next meeting Mrs. Ottarson, she per-mitted no semblance of complaint or of adverse criticism to evidence the weightsome discouragement that oppressed her. And the next few days of residence in Twenty-Third Street had the effect of brightening her gloomy outlook. Inexperience prevented her from comprehending how light, and in a manner nominal, were the duties assigned her. She soon discovered herself possessed of a far more liberal leisure than she supposed would be at all compatible with her new position. But the tact of Mrs. Ottarson in concealing just to what real extent Ida Strang's discontinued employments had been made like those of a comparative sinecure, quite evaded Olivia's untrained discernment. She failed to suspect that very little in the way of household aid was asked of her, and that this very little had been dexterously adapted to her novitiate as a bread-winner.

Still, the people whom she must now not merely meet and know, but meet and know on conditions of thorough equality, incessantly dealt her wounds as sharp as they were unconscious. No high-strung daintiness had to do with her inward revolt against them. It was simply, as she more than once told her own thoughts, that she felt *déclassée* and ill at ease among them. In education she was the superior of most of them, and where others were as mentally cultured as herself, their errors from the line of mannerly usage to which she had conformed for so long without even recognizing her own implanted acquiescence, were a source of continual aversion. She began to perceive that there were innumerable deviations from the code of good breeding with which she had never before met the rough-and-ready means of acquainting her own antipathies. She had had until now no lucid idea of how many different ways there were of not being a gentleman or a gentlewoman.

That she should have gone to live with Mrs. Ottarson had struck her other two aunts, when they first heard of it, as an act grossly unpardonable. Olivia had found time to write each of the ladies a civil little note, saying that she had preferred this course to any other which might be recommended. Mrs. Satterthwaite, a half-hour after receiving the news that her brother's child would become a species of upper servant in a boarding-house, jumped into her carriage, accompanied by her eldest daughter, Emmeline, and had herself driven to the home of her sister, Mrs. Auchincloss. The latter received her kindred with a mournful smile; she was holding in her hand her own letter from Olivia, recently received. And then, a little later, while the sisters were lamenting together, Madeleine Auchincloss came into the room and joined her cousin, Emmeline.

These two young ladies cordially disliked one another. Though they were nearly of the same age, Emmeline had been out four seasons and Madeleine only two. Madeleine was jealous of her cousin for being the sort of personally attractive girl who would have shone as an indubitable belle even if she were not a Satterthwaite; whereas Madeleine, with her thinnish figure and dark, small-featured face, would never have shone the least in the world as a belle if she had not been an Auchincloss besides. Emmeline was large, and had been irreverently called (perhaps from the springy, mercurial style of her walk and of her step in the dance) "bouncing." But she had the low, broad brow, the lustrous eyes, the brilliant smile,

and the full, deep bosom of a young Roman girl.
Men were sure to flock about her wherever she went,
and her cold, daring, imperious air both fascinated
and repelled. She thought Madeleine "slow," prud-
ish and affected, just as Miss Auchincloss thought her
"fast," romping and indecorous. But Emmeline was
jealous of her cousin for the atmosphere of extreme
propriety and selectness always floating about her like
some rare scent impossible to secure. The Satterthwaite name was talismanic in society, but the
Auchincloss name was a degree or two more so, and
Madeleine appeared forever to be covertly pluming
herself on this delicate yet distinct grade of ascendency. Emmeline always had a sense of being objected
to when in her cousin's company, and at such times
Madeleine felt that her own placid *bienséance* was an
object of intangible satire. Since they had been little
girls together, these relations, influenced only by their
respective ages, had endured between them, and it
was safe to assert that they would be modified or
destroyed by no fresh force but that resulting from
the future rise or fall which marriage would effect for
either. Madeleine had long ago resolved never to
marry unless she gave her slender, milky little hand
to a man of much greater wealth than her own and a
position quite on a level with that of the Auchinclosses. Emmeline had resolved to marry as well as
she could; but she had reached that cooler state of
matrimonial exploration when the loftier peaks begin
to loom a trifle insurmountable and the lesser ones
offer chances consolatory if not inspiriting.

"You are looking so very well," said Madeleine to
her cousin, in the calm, smooth voice which was

almost a counterfeit of her mother's, and while the
two elder ladies were holding converse but a short
distance away. "You always manage to keep your
fine color, my dear; don't you?"

Emmeline had never cared to have her color remarked; Madeleine knew it, and the other was well
aware that Madeleine did know it. Miss Satterthwaite
put her handsome, firm-throated head a little on one
side, and answered with a note or two of laughter:
"I don't manage; good health manages for me. It's
a source of immense vanity to me, my perfect health;
I'm always enchanted to be complimented on it . . .
Do you still have your wretched headaches, my dear
Lina?"

"We are so quiet now, since poor uncle's death,"
said Madeleine, with a faint, flickering smile. "That
makes a difference with me, don't you know? . . . By
the way, Lily Ten Eyck told me that she saw you
out, somewhere, quite recently . . . where was it?
She also told me *that* . . . but I forget."

Emmeline shook her head in serene negation. "Saw
*me!* Why, there's nothing going on so late as this,
you know. Lily is always imagining things. Besides,
uncle's death has the same effect on *us*, naturally, as
on *your* family. Of course, there are still dinners.
But we refuse them, just as you do."

"I remember, now," said Madeleine, with dove-like
gentleness. "It was at the new exhibition of the
Academy of Design; it was last night, I believe."

Emmeline started, and laughed somewhat nervously.
"Was Lily Ten Eyck there?" she flurriedly ques-
tioned. Then growing composed again, she continued:
"I went, but mamma did not."

"Ah! you *went?*" said Madeleine. Those three quiet words conveyed a volume of soft reproach. She had had no more regard for her dead uncle than for any one whose demise had lately been chronicled in the newspapers; but "a death in the family" meant a sacred obligation to refrain from everything that resembled festivity — and especially when that death concerned a Van Rensselaer, for which name (notwithstanding the misalliance that had begotten her cousin Olivia) she entertained deep reverence.

"Yes, I went," declared Emmeline, with a sudden show of that *empire sur soi-même* for which she had already become noted among friends and foes. "Mamma did not go, however."

"Surely not!" murmured Madeleine.

"The Plunketts took me," said Emmeline, thoroughly composed now.

"The . . . Plunketts?" queried Madeleine, with a sudden titter. "Excuse me, but it's *such* an odd name!" And she tittered again.

"Yes," said Emmeline, "it is, rather, isn't it? They're very nice people; you wouldn't be likely to know them, however . . . they're fond of art and books and such matters." (Emmeline had probably read twenty books herself in the past four years, and those were novels of a not very elevated type.)

"I have met people of that sort," said Madeleine, a little stiffly. "They didn't have extraordinary names, as far as I can recollect, but I found them very nice, notwithstanding. They were all men, though. Papa brought them from the Centennial Club."

Here Emmeline laughed a little.

"Oh, you mean the club that papa thinks so dreadfully rowdy?"

"Rowdy?" echoed Madeleine. "Did your father really say that?"

"Why, yes, my dear; I heard him say it to *your* father's face. Wasn't it perfectly atrocious of him?"

"Papa thinks *his* club, the Metropolitan, full of the most objectionable members," Madeleine now said.

"Oh, I suppose that's true enough," answered Emmeline; "but then you know, my dear, they're not shabby and Bohemian members, like painters and writers."

"Are the Plunketts shabby and Bohemian?" asked Madeleine, in her very sweetest tones.

"Oh, no . . . The eldest son, Arthur Plunkett, goes out sometimes in society. I dare say you have seen him."

"Never, to my knowledge," said Madeleine coldly. A vague, self-conscious touch about her cousin's reply had made her wonder if there could be any chance of Emmeline taking up, at a future day, with some such person as this Arthur Plunkett. "And you are very good friends, you and he?" she added.

"Passably good friends. His mother has quiet little dinners, that rest one after the big whirl of things."

"Oh, I see," said Madeleine, leaning her small head, with its bands of glossy dark hair, a little backward, and giving to her upper lip the faintest curl. "You mean that they are people at the outskirts who are trying to push themselves farther in. I think it is so very good of you to treat such people civilly. I confess that I never can."

"Ah, my dear," returned Emmeline, looking pen-sively down at the smart freshness of her semi-mourning apparel; "I am afraid it will never do for you and me to hold ourselves so much above the outsiders hereafter."

"Hereafter?" questioned Madeleine, with the curl of her lip increasing. "Why, pray, what *do* you mean?"

"Oh, I refer to this absurd action on Cousin Olivia's part. Of course you've learned of it, as your mother has been notified."

And just then Mrs. Auchincloss was heard, softly exclaiming: "It seems as if that unpleasant woman *must* have tempted her to do it. And yet Olivia writes that she does it of her own free will."

"Very well, then," retorted Mrs. Satterthwaite, with the clear nip of spite in her accent; "Olivia shall take the consequences as far as Bleecker and myself and the children are concerned. I know it's wretched form to disown your relations; but we are not going to follow the girl *there.* If she comes to us, that is another matter."

"I suppose we ought to remember who she is," said Mrs. Auchincloss, with a musing shake of the head.

"It appears to me, Aunt Letitia," exclaimed Emme-line, "that she has taken pains to remind us she's the niece of Mrs. Ottarson."

"Yes, I know, my dear," responded Mrs. Auchin-closs, who thought her sister's eldest daughter shock-ingly forward, even for a girl in her fourth season, and gave almost daily thanks that her Madeleine had not that curt American way; "but blood is blood, and we, who come from a very old and honorable race, cannot afford to forget this."

"I don't forget it," said Emmeline, tossing her prettily bonneted head. "But Olivia's behavior makes me very sorry indeed that Uncle Houston forgot it a good many years ago."

Mrs. Auchincloss gave her sister a look that seemed to say: "Shall you not rebuke this unmannerly pertness?"

But Mrs. Satterthwaite did not rebuke it. She merely remarked, with a careless glance in her daughter's direction: "Oh, that's one of the ancient bygones, Em. There's no use of raking it up nowadays."

"I'm not, mamma," said Emmeline. "It's Olivia who is raking it up — and very disagreeably, I should say. . . ."

"What a loud, rude, *married* style that girl, Emmeline, has!" declared Mrs. Auchincloss, after the Satterthwaites had departed. "We must *always* bear in mind, Madeleine, that as a *family* we are entirely *ourselves,* and quite distinctly, separated from all other branches of it."

"Of course, mamma," assented Madeleine, who had heard this kind of pronunciamiento, in various modes of utterance, almost from her cradle. "But do you think of going to *see* Olivia, really, after the way she has conducted herself? Do you actually think of going to see her, mamma, in *that house?*"

Mrs. Auchincloss heaved a sigh. "My dear Madeleine," she answered, "I have not yet clearly made up my mind. I must consult with your father. There are duties in life which we must not shirk. Olivia is very young. If I do go it will be an ordeal. Perhaps I ought to go. I will reflect, and as I said, I

will talk it all over with your father. His advice will
of course be precious to me, as it always is. In any
case, we will not jump to conclusions, after the style
of the Satterthwaites."

Madeleine went up to her mother and kissed her on
one of her chilly little cheeks as if she were going
through some long-revered domestic rite. "You will
certainly do what is proper, mamma," she said; "you
never fail to do that."

"Thank you, my dear," replied Mrs. Auchincloss,
accepting the kiss, but not returning it. . . .

Three or four evenings later, Mrs. Satterthwaite, in
her showy and almost gorgeous Fifth Avenue drawing-room was the recipient of a visit from her old and
valued friend, Mr. Spencer Delaplaine.

"How good of you!" she said, as she shook hands
with him. "You needn't tell me that your horrid
gout is worse. I know about its being so."

Delaplaine made a sad little motion. "I suppose
you saw me limp as I came in," he answered.

"Oh, not that. Snydam Desbrosses told you'd
spoken of it at the club the other evening. I was so
sorry for you! Take a more comfortable chair —
do!"

"No, thanks. This is a Sleepy Hollow for comfort.
All your chairs always are. I *am* a trifle under the
weather." He looked about him, as if some other
occupant of the great room might be discoverable
amid its rich assortment of sofas, *fauteuils* and
screens. He rubbed a hand against one of his knees
as he went on speaking. "Yes, my devil has broken
loose again. But the doctor is doing everything to
quiet him. You stare at me as if you thought I ought

to be home in bed. Well, I shan't attempt to contradict you if that *is* your opinion."

"Pshaw, I've seen you when you looked better," said Mrs. Satterthwaite, who did not recall ever having seen him when he looked worse. "But you're not seriously ill. It's very plain to me that you're not, Spencer."

"Not yet," he returned grimly. "As it is," he went on, fixing a regard upon her that she, who knew him so well, instantly knew to betoken some matter of moment, "I should not have ventured out at all this evening."

"Perhaps you're right there, inhospitable though it may sound in me. I never recollect such a ghastly May; do you?"

"Oh, there's never any May in this country. I thought you'd learned that long ago."

"We occasionally get a few hours of sunshine, though, and a wind not altogether easterly. I've known nice days when the Coaching Club paraded, for instance."

"Yes — which it didn't deserve to have. Providence should conspire, every year, with the American Eagle to drench it through for being such a piece of Anglomaniacal brummagem."

"Oh, don't!" Mrs. Satterthwaite pleaded; "you make me think of what *might* have happened to my Emmeline. She was invited to go next Thursday in Tom Forsythe's coach. She was to have the box seat, poor girl!"

"And isn't she going?"

"Oh, dear, no. Houston was her own blood-uncle, you know. One must draw a line somewhere, as I

told Em.   And that reminds me, Spencer — Have you
*heard* of Olivia's delightful caper?"

"You mean her going to live with her maternal
aunt?"

"'Maternal aunt' has a highly misleading sound,"
said Mrs. Satterthwaite, with a bitter smile.   "It puts
that dire Mrs. Ottarson in quite too respectable a
light."   She looked extremely wrathful now; she
bit her lip, folded her arms for a few seconds, and
leaned back in her chair, watching her companion
between half-shut eyelids.   "Olivia is old enough to
know better, and *my* side of the family, from Bleecker
to little Lulu, shall give her to understand that we
think so.   Why, Letitia and I both said to her the
day we told her about the state of her father's affairs,
that our homes would be hers from now till she married!   And then to prefer that woman's house!   And
they say that a foreign education has a refining influence!   My Elaine, you remember, was crazy to go
abroad with Lucy Van Ness when she was sent there
to school a few years ago.   I'm glad enough, now, that
I kept her at home."

There was a silence.   Delaplaine was slowly smooth-
ing his lame knee again.   His keen gray eyes were
downcast while he did so, but he now lifted them to
Mrs. Satterthwaite's face as he said:

"It was about Olivia that I came here to speak
with you.   Indeed, if it had not been for her I would
not have come, I can assure you; for I am ill — very
ill, and at this moment —"

He paused abruptly.   He had grown strangely pale,
and his lips twitched as if from some fierce attack of
pain.   Mrs. Satterthwaite sprang to her feet in sharp
alarm.

## VIII.

"No, no; it is nothing," he said, in answer to her anxious look. Already, during a few seconds, his cheeks had won a less ghastly tint, and the signs of distress had fled from his mouth and eyes. "I'm better. . . . The doctor warned me I might have one or two visitations like these — confound them! I ought not to have come out to-night; my hateful malady must be nursed for some little time, or it will get beyond the powers of nursing." He took her hand, pressing it, and watching her solicitous face with a smile that was nearer to being tender than any like expression she had seen there more than once or twice in all her long acquaintance with him. "Sit down again, I beg, and listen to me. I've something that I want to tell you."

She obeyed him, but wheeled her chair closer to his before she again seated herself. "I knew you had some important thing to say," she answered, leaning forward and fixing her gaze upon him very earnestly. "I somehow saw it in your face when I first met you."

"I didn't know I carried my heart on my sleeve like that."

"Your heart! you haven't — I mean you've always tried to make people believe you hadn't one."

He set his lips rather sourly together, and shook his gray head. "I sha'n't have one long, if this gout concludes to fly to it. . . . But that doesn't concern the present question."

"Well, and pray what *is* the present question? It's so odd, don't you know, my good friend, to find you very deeply interested in *any*."

He made a gesture of mock sober contradiction, and began to put on his eyeglasses. "That kind of talk, when I have been interested in you for a century!"

"A century! How scorching of you!"

"Not to a woman like yourself — a woman who has managed to have so pretty a quarrel with time that she couldn't grow old if she tried."

"Oh, I like that much better. You pass a sly powder-puff across my wrinkles."

"I haven't yet perceived them. You manage to hide them till their existence, like that of your faults, becomes a myth to your many admirers."

She laughed. This dexterity of compliment was a kind of balm to her, as it is to all women of her age, and her persistence in the evasion of life's larger and stronger appeals. "But what is your great secret? I'm dying of curiosity to learn it."

He looked once more about the room, with its shadowy corners, where the gloss of satin tapestry or the drowsy lustre of bronzes, or the pale gleam of marble, was to be richly glimpsed. "Where is everybody to-night?" he inquired.

"Oh, don't be afraid of listeners. Emmeline and Elaine have gone to a sewing-class. Very dreadful of them, isn't it, *considering?* But they would go, and I only hope there isn't the least bit of a German afterward. The Schenectadys, who chaperoned them, vowed it was to be nothing but tea and conversa-

tion. . . . Bleecker's playing cards at the club, I suppose. He usually is, at this hour — if he isn't doing
worse. And as for young Aspinwall — well, he's got
his latch-key at last, after fighting his father about it
all winter, and I don't know where *he* is; I dare say
he's smoking cigarettes in the *café* at Delmonico's,
instead of studying for his next Columbia examina-
tion, which takes place rather soon. . . . Peyster, the
dear stupid boy, and Lulu, the strange little vixen,
are both asleep in bed. Lulu danced herself almost
sick this afternoon at a child's affair the Stuyvesant
Smiths gave; she begged so hard that I let her go;
for how can a child like that be expected to feel sad
about the death of an uncle whom she's scarcely
seen? . . . There, Spencer, you have a full account
of just how the entire family are occupied at present,
so far as I'm able to inform you. . . . Come, let me
hear your secret."

"It will surprise you very much," he said, slowly
and with an unwonted air of implicitly meaning each
word. "Perhaps you'll be inclined to ask yourself
whether this last illness of mine hasn't put me a little
out of my head."

"It's a very wise and prudent head," she replied;
" at least I've always found it so."

"Ah, what if I should tell you that I had lost it —
or that it had been turned?" Their eyes met, and he
went on: "I tried to stop Olivia from going to live at
her aunt Ottarson's the other day. I tried to stop her
by asking her to come and live with me. . . . As my
wife, I mean."

"Ah!" exclaimed Mrs. Satterthwaite, looking as if
she were powerless to speak another word.

"She would not come," Delaplaine pursued, staring straight before him, now. "But I think she can be prevailed upon to come. I think you can help me in prevailing upon her. You've always stood my friend, as I've stood yours. I am afraid I can't act for myself very capably during the next week or so. . . ." There was a pause, and as yet Mrs. Satterthwaite did not seem to have recovered from her amazement; her startled eyes were riveted upon Delaplaine's visage, while about the corners of her mouth lurked an incredulous expression that seemed to belie the consternation above it; she looked, indeed, as though she were prepared at a moment's warning to be informed that this whole queer bit of tidings meant nothing less trivial than a mere humorous deception.

"I want you to help me, if you will," Delaplaine soon continued, "I am nearly sure that you can, and importantly, too. I don't mean that you can quicken or even touch in the girl any impulse of sentiment. But if you speak with discretion you may appeal to her reason — yes, her reason alone, Augusta. I despair of your doing anything else. For that matter, how can I fitly use the word 'despair,' which signifies an ended hope? And I have never had a ray of hope. You must understand that."

"Despair? . . . . hope?" she exclaimed. "Good heavens, Spencer Delaplaine! Do you actually mean that you, at your time of life, *care* for the girl in *that* way?"

"I mean that I am in love with her," he responded. And then, after having spoken these few words in what sounded to their listener like a voice borrowed from another being (she had been so long accustomed

to the lambent play of his ironies over almost every
conceivable subject!) he employed a tone much more
familiar to her, and added, with the tart, laconic, gelid
phrasing that she had heard hundreds of times before:
"Yes, I'm downright in love at last. It's sad but it's
true. I'm in love,—gray hair, baldness, wrinkles,
worldly experience, sixty odd years and gout, all
included."

She was about to break into a laugh as he thus terminated his droll confession. But something re-
strained her from doing so. She was to a great
extent a scoffer like himself. If he had been almost
anybody else among the many men whom she knew,
and had made an admission at once so unexpected
and so incongruous, she would not have spared him
the mischievous cut-and-thrust of her amusement. But
as it was, she contented herself with this quiet answer,
while she stretched forth one hand until it rested
lightly yet decisively on his arm:

"I'll help you — of course, I will, in any manner
that you think best. Just tell me how you would
like me to act, and I will promise faithfully to follow
your instructions."

Meanwhile it shot through her brain: What a god-
send for Olivia, and what a happy stroke for *us!*
She changes "Van Rensselaer" for "Delaplaine"—
not at all a bad change. And she changes that horrible boarding-house for an establishment any woman in
the country might be proud of. She *shall* marry him,
if I've the power to show her how great a fool she
would be in refusing him! . . .

Mrs. Auchincloss had meanwhile consulted with her
husband on the question of paying a visit to Olivia in

the foolish retreat which that rash young girl had chosen. She had permitted Madeleine and her brother, Chichester, to be present at the discussion, and had selected the hour of dessert for commencing it, after the coffee had been served and the butler had been dismissed.

It was one of those evenings when the Auchinclosses dined *en famille.* They had so solid and profound a respect for one another that occasions like the present, happening two or three times every week, were looked upon as refreshing and priceless relaxations from the ritualistic worry of social duty. The whole Auchincloss family might be said to accept every event of life either in this light or in no other that was worth the smallest real consideration. They moved all four of them (a most august quadrilateral!), in the sole unswerving and punctilious groove of duty. Mr. Archibald Auchincloss, as head of the great house and a lawyer of unimpeachable standing, had long ago secured the reputation of making duty his inflexible watchword. How, as a lawyer of any standing whatever, he had managed to reconcile his ideals with his practical operations, is a question which melts away from the art of the annalist into that reverend obscurity known as this gentleman's well-ordered and irreproachable conscience. But he effected such a truce without the least apparent difficulty. Of his wife's dutiful proclivities we have already enjoyed a glimpse. Madeleine, their only daughter, bowed to her own private little *lar* of duty with the calm fervor of a nun to her crucifix. Chichester, who was not very much older than his cousin, Aspinwall Satterthwaite, had long been a pride and a gladness to both his parents. He had gone to Harvard, not Columbia, and had been graduated three or four from the head of his class. You could not have induced him to sit and smoke cigarettes in the *café* of Delmonico's, after the fashion of his cousin. For that matter, he never smoked at all, secretly detesting the practice, in common with his father. He was now one of the most creditable disciples of the Columbia Law School, and looked forward with eager joy to being made at some future time a member of that unsullied legal house, Chichester, Auchincloss and Gibbes. There were some people who thought the heir of the Auchincloss family an insupportable young prig; his cousin, Aspinwall, was one of these; the latter always puffed his cigarette-smoke a little more recklessly through his nose, and assumed a larger amount of swagger, profanity and piercing knowledge of the whole vain and worthless female sex, whenever Chichester and he encountered one another. In consequence Chichester would speak of his cousin with shudders, at home, as the very worst type of "dude" — the "dude" that rolls a vicious eyeball toward unlawful pleasures. Aspinwall, on the other hand, would mention lazily to his father having met "that confounded young ass of a Chichester," and having ached to kick him. Either young kinsman doubtless exaggerated the faults of the other, but it is possible that a great deal of pertinent and veracious criticism lurked beneath their mutual disesteem.

"Of course Olivia has done a miserably foolish thing," Mrs. Auchincloss now said, looking across the table at her husband's clean-shorn, statuesque face, with its big, curvilinear nose and its square-molded jaw.

"But the great point is that we *might* pardon it because of her youth."

"Yes," said Mr. Auchincloss, as though he were thinking of the *pros* and *cons* in some professional "case." "Youth certainly is an excuse for such acts of rashness. It may not have occurred to Olivia how direct a slur she was casting upon you and her Aunt Augusta, since you had both expressed your willingness to protect her."

Chichester coughed deliberately. "I can't undertand," he said, "how she is less to be blamed for the affront because she is still under twenty years old. *I* would not have done any such thing as that when I was nineteen, and I am sure Madeleine would not, either."

"*We* have had peculiar advantages of home-training," said Madeleine, in her precise, demure way. "*We* have been taught what duty means, Chichey, thanks to mamma and papa."

"My dear child!" said Mrs. Auchincloss, giving Madeleine the most benign of motherly smiles. And then she glanced at her husband, as if to say: "What a rich reward we are reaping for our parental devotions of the past?"

"Even duty has its limitations, however," remarked Chichester, very much as though he were stating that the square of the hypothenuse of a right-angled triangle was equal to the sum of the squares of its other two sides.

"True, my son," applauded his father. "But to err generously from the restrictions of a dutiful standard is often to show a humane and . . . a . . . er . . . commendable mercy." He gave forth this platitude as though it were a bit of wisdom ripe with the meditation of years.

"Oh, certainly, sir," acknowledged Chichester, who considered his father one of the leading minds of the time. "I suppose mamma means to forgive Olivia and go to see her in those objectionable surroundings. I don't think I could do so, under the circumstances; but then I do not lay claim to mamma's truly Christian spirit."

He looked, while speaking these words with his orderly, measured manner of saying everything, as though he possessed no spirit whatever except one of a *petit maître* in all the conventionalisms (not to name the bigotries) of polite conduct. He still had a boyish appearance, with only those pimply premonitions on lips and chin which betoken the coming virile growth there; but his face was in every feature a living reproduction of his father's, notwithstanding its immature expression.

And surely there was no one beneath the visiting moon whom he would have preferred to resemble more than this very father, upon whose countenance he sometimes gazed as though it were a magic mirror, showing him his own future physiognomy improved by mellowing manhood. Being entirely satisfied with himself, Chichester was no less satisfied with his father. He could not perceive how any career could be more delightfully distinguished than that of Mr. Archibald Auchincloss. To marry aristocratically, to acquire fortune and reputation at the bar, to accept fashion and patronize talent, to avoid all vulgar extremes, and never to leave one conservative strong-hold until you could slip safely from it into another

capable of protecting you against the horrid pest of
the unorthodox and the radical; having done things
like these, or going on brilliantly doing them from
year to year, was Chichester Auchincloss's idea of a
noble and profitable life. It all meant "duty" to
him, and there was no more sacred word than that in
his gilt-edged dictionary, from which a great deal of
naughty verbiage had been exiled.

His mother's Christian spirit triumphed in its angelic desire to pardon Olivia. Mrs. Auchincloss was
indeed on the point of ordering her carriage, two or
three days later, and having herself driven to the
abominated doorway of Mrs. Ottarson, when her
sister Augusta appeared, brimming with the most
unexpected news.

"I hope, my dear Letitia," said Mrs. Satterthwaite,
after she had made her first astonishing announcement,
"that you will keep this a profound secret even from
Archibald."

"Oh, certainly," agreed Mrs. Auchincloss. It had
speedily become her intention, however, to tell her
husband all about it; and Mrs. Satterthwaite, proud
of Delaplaine's intimacy with herself, privately wanted
Mr. Auchincloss as well as his wife to know of the
confidence the banker had reposed in her. For
Spencer Delaplaine held just that unassailable place
in society toward which the Auchinclosses loved to
show homage. He had been a person of importance
when hundreds of the present regnant dignitaries were
struggling to mass together the dollars which had
paid for their subsequent "positions." Mrs. Auchincloss remembered him as one of the leading beaux,
more than twenty years back, at the old Fourteenth

Street Delmonico Assemblies, or, a little more recently, at those most enjoyable " Cheap and Hungry " dancing classes, in Dodworth's Hall, on Fifth Avenue and Twenty-Sixth Street. Of course a Delaplaine was not a Van Rensselaer — no, nor even a Ten Eyck, nor yet a Van Peekskill. She even recollected hearing, a long time ago, when there had been some talk of Spencer Delaplaine going into partnership with her brother, that there had never existed any family of that name to speak of, and that this gentleman (the ambitious, clever, and moderately well-off) only deserved to rank as the first of his line. But years and events had so multiplied since then! No one ever presumed to hint, at this late hour, that the wealthy proprietor, dwelling in West Tenth Street so luxuriously and entertaining with so much blended grace and discrimination, was not born to the rare and fine name which he now held. It is notably true of New York that some of her present social leaders are those whose early youth was a strife to win what they now wear as if it were hereditary ermine.

"This would make an admirable match for Olivia — admirable ? " Mrs. Auchincloss now proceeded, as it were, to muse aloud. "There is no drawback but age . . . none whatever."

"I should call that more of a drawback for *him*," said Mrs. Satterthwaite, with the cold, hard, loud-voiced manner to which her sister objected as being painfully underbred and which she thought on the increase, lately, because Augusta *would* choose her friends from among so many new people. "Very few men of his age decide to marry at all; still fewer, when they are also men of much means. As he offers to make a handsome settlement on Olivia, I should say that she has everything her own way — or nearly so — provided she takes him."

. Mrs. Auchincloss drooped her eyes.

"I hate to invest anything so . . . so holy as mar riage, Augusta, with views like these."

Mrs. Satterthwaite gave a stealthy smile of amuse ment; she knew her sister so well! "Oh," she said, primly, "then you think it's our duty to dissuade Olivia from the marriage?"

The other lady started. "Dissuade Olivia?" she faltered. "Oh, no! I — I mean, my dear sister, that it would not be fair to the girl if we did not let her clearly see all the . . . er . . . the mere worldly advantages which would result from such a marriage. And I am nearly sure that Archibald will sanction this mode of regarding the matter, when — "

"Oh, but you mustn't *tell* Archibald," struck in Mrs. Satterthwaite.

"Ah . . . yes; I remember."

"And now, my dear Letitia," Mrs. Satterthwaite went on, "since you have these feelings, and since mine agree with them, we had best pay Olivia a visit. I think we shall somehow be safer if we go together; there's no telling about the barbaric be havior of that Ottarson woman; it may break out at any moment."

"We will not ask for her," said Mrs. Auchincloss, "and perhaps by this means we shall be able to get it through her head that we do not wish to see her."

They went that very day, and saw only Olivia. As they drove together to the Twenty-Third Street boarding-house, Mrs. Satterthwaite informed her sister of Delaplaine's illness. He had not left his home for some little time, now. The doctors did not yet think it a dangerous attack, but it might become dangerous at very short notice.

"It will be advisable, I think, to tell Olivia this," said Mrs. Auchincloss meditatively.

They did tell her. After Olivia appeared before them, entering the shabby parlor, with its air of being lounged in, romped in and generally both used and abused, they met her with no rebukes whatever. They sat and talked quietly with her in tones that she could not help feeling were like music beside the shrill and harsh organs of speech to which she had been listening of late. While they thus spoke, a smell of cookery, pungent as the broiling pork-chop or the browning potato can render it, filled all the lower portion of the house; for it chanced to be lunch-time at Mrs. Ottarson's, and as we know, her meals were expected to feed many mouths. As Olivia now observed her aunts, it was to remark what figures of elegance and distinction they both looked; that smell from below-stairs had somehow accentuated their own delicate aroma of gentility. The boarders were descending to luncheon from their various upper rooms, and presently the peacock-like voice of Mrs. Spillington was heard, as if it called from the middle of the outside staircase to some one above:

"*Oh!* . . . I presume I must have left my red worsted shawl laying across the back of your rocking-chair. *Will* you just bring it down when you come, please?"

Mrs. Auchincloss and Mrs. Satterthwaite seemed

like two ladies who had never worn red worsted
shawls in their lives and had never been called upon,
for that matter, to inflict their nerves with the kinds
of people who do wear them. It was of course easier
to talk with Olivia on the subject of Mr. Delaplaine's
offer now that it had been made to the girl in person a
few days before. But, notwithstanding this fact, it
was still by no means easy. Olivia soon flushed and
grew sadly embarrassed.

" I — I would so much rather not speak about that
affair," she said, biting her lips. " I told Mr. Delaplaine that it — it wouldn't be possible." She now
looked from one to the other of her aunts, with her
eyes widening a little and a wave of surprise beginning to sweep over her face. " Oh," she exclaimed,
putting her hands together with what had half the
semblance of a tender supplication, " if you've thought
that you could *persuade* me to take any such step as
this, I beg that you will at once receive my positive
answer. It is no, no; it's a hundred noes, if you like,"
with a roguishly obstinate sparkle showing in her blue
eyes, which were then beaming above cheeks that
shame had hurriedly reddened.

The two sisters exchanged glances.

" My dear," said Mrs. Auchincloss, with her suave,
*traînante* voice, " I think Mr. Delaplaine should make
you very happy as his wife. Very happy, indeed."

" Very ? " iterated Mrs. Satterthwaite more briskly.
"Pray don't suppose that he is thought to be an *old
man*, here in New York society. He has always
lived a most exemplary life; he has taken great
care of himself; and now, when men of half his age
find themselves broken down, he is full of youth —

absolute youth." The recollection that this belauded lad of sixty was just now a severe sufferer from gout had wholly escaped the speaker, who went energetically on : "And then, my dear, his exquisite little palace in West Tenth Street, and the perfect air of everything connected with it! Ah! what a charming frame for so pretty a picture as yourself!"

"But there is another side — a far more . . . more *moral* side to the question," now exclaimed Mrs. Auchincloss, "which your Aunt Augusta, my dear, seems to overlook."

Olivia burst out laughing. "A moral side!" she ejaculated, and then her face quickly grew serious again, as though she had heard something it were sacrilege to make light of. "I don't see how such a mere buying-and-selling marriage as this," she said, "can possibly be spoken of as having a moral side."

Mrs. Auchincloss grew a little pinker in each cheek, and her small head moved somewhat farther back on the support of her slender neck. "Oh, my *dear!*" she reproached offendedly. "As if I could recommend what you call a buying-and-selling marriage! No, indeed, Olivia! I was thinking of the really beautiful protection which he would bestow on you, now that your poor father is gone, and you are left so unexpectedly without a home of your own. And then his having been your papa's friend and partner — that gives the whole matter so engaging a little touch of romance!"

"I see no touch of romance," said Olivia, as her mouth hardened. "I see no touch at all except a commercial one."

"My dear!" cried Mrs. Auchincloss.

"I'm sorry to shock you, Aunt Letitia, but that is the only view I can take of the whole proposition. I saw a good deal of this kind of marrying while I was abroad — or rather I heard of a good deal. But I never became in the least used to it, I assure you. And I must also state, if you've no objection, that you are the first person whom I have ever heard make even the faintest attempt to invest it with anything resembling sentiment."

Mrs. Auchincloss was about to offer some reply, but Mrs. Satterthwaite spoke before she had time.

"Mr. Delaplaine," said the latter lady, "hasn't expected you to look at it from any sentimental point of view. He instructed me to say that he would very gladly settle three hundred thousand dollars on you, Olivia, the day that you and he are married."

This monetary disclosure affected the girl like a piece of sheer brutality. . . . Her two aunts left her, that afternoon, without having accomplished the least satisfactory results.

It was only a few hours later that Mrs. Ottarson keenly irritated Olivia by a speech in which her niece failed to recognize just the desired amount of sympathetic repugnance for this anomalous marriage.

"Upon my word, Aunt Thyrza," cried the girl, almost flaring up at her prized friend and kinswoman, "I'm half tempted to believe that you *don't* think Mrs. Auchincloss and Mrs. Satterthwaite ought to be ashamed of themselves to endorse such a proceeding!"

"Well," came the answer, given with uncharacteristic delay, "I can't really say, 'Livia, that they're t' blame '*t all*. You see, they know jus' how splendid you'd be fixed, deary, 'f you *did* consent, and —— "

Olivia hurried from the room, in high annoyance. It made her feel so alone and deserted by everybody, when even her Aunt Thyrza began to share these prosaically hard-grained opinions. Still, she knew that in *her* case only the warmest personal love inspired them. There was, at least, comforting afterthought in this reflection. Aunt Thyrza was incapable of any save affectionate motives toward her.

It was about eleven o'clock that same evening, and just as Olivia was on the verge of retiring for the night, that she sought Mrs. Ottarson once more. She held a note in her hand, hastily written by Mrs. Satterthwaite, and despatched thither by a messenger.

"He — he is very ill," she stammered. "They fear he is dying. Isn't it dreadful? And so sudden! Neither of my aunts even spoke of his being ill while they were here this afternoon."

"Who on earth do you mean, 'Livia?" asked Mrs. Ottarson, staring at her niece. "Who's *he?*"

"Mr. Delaplaine," answered Olivia, showing the note she had just received. "Think of it! The doctors say there is hardly more than a hope for his life. He may not live even two days longer?"

## IX.

Olivia's aunts had purposely refrained from mentioning to her the illness of Mr. Delaplaine. They
had decided that such information could carry with it
no force of inducement. Besides gout was such a
volatile sort of complaint; it pounced upon you to-day
and darted away from you to-morrow. In a short
time Mr. Delaplaine might be well, and able to continue whatever work they, the coadjutors in his cause,
might successfully have started.

But Olivia's reception of their advances had been
worse than merely unfavorable. She would not marry
her late father's partner, as she bluntly but rather
picturesquely said, though he should promise to clothe
her in cloth-of-gold and to hang her all over with
diamonds. Mrs. Auchincloss's most dexterous quib-
bles and jesuitries were effete as implements for un-
dermining a prejudice like Olivia's, founded upon
youth, health and nature, and similar to the enclasping
outgrowth of all three. As for Mrs. Satterthwaite,
she left the house considerably more hopeful than her
sister.

"Only give *him* another chance or two," she said,
with an oracular nod, as the carriage rolled away,
through that section of Twenty-Third Street where
the boarding-houses are, so to speak, epidemic. "He's
an extremely attractive man, is Spencer, and I don't

believe many girls could resist him, even at his present age, if he really made up his mind that they must
surrender."

"I knew you always thought him remarkably fascinating," replied Mrs. Auchincloss. There had been
those bitter little breezes of scandal in other days, and
perhaps the elder lady had now made some stealthy
allusion to the fact of their having once blown. Still,
if this were the case, she gave her very insinuation a
sort of non-committal harmlessness by immediately
adding : "But don't you think he *can* plead his own
cause in a little while? Is this last attack so serious a
one, after all?"

"I am afraid it's the worst he has ever had," said
Mrs. Satterthwaite, "and he has had two or three
rather bad ones. I sent to his house early this morning to inquire how he was, and the answer came that
he had passed a painful night."

That evening at dinner the Satterthwaite family
freely discussed Mr. Delaplaine's offer of marriage to
Olivia. Mrs. Satterthwaite had neither the conscience
nor the temperament of one who keeps a secret well;
she had found herself unable to refrain from "just telling Emmeline," after holding a rather long talk with her
husband on the subject of their friend's infatuation.
Emmeline had soon afterward found her sister, Elaine,
and with a little scream of excitement had seized the
latter by each of her shoulders, exclaiming : "Oh, *such*
a piece of news! Mamma says I musn't breathe it
yet; but I can't help letting *you* know what it is.
Elly . . . " And after that, in a very short time,
nearly the whole Satterthwaite household proper had
become aware of it, and before the dinner-hour this

same day one of the French maids had succinctly and exhaustively conveyed it to one of the footmen.

The Satterthwaites always talked in the most unrestricted manner before their servants. "Oh, d— it," Bleecker Satterthwaite had once said, with that mixture of a yawn and a sneer which his son Aspinwall had tried zealously to imitate ever since the great territory of dudedom had found in him one of its most loyal denizens, "if our servants like listening, let them listen. It's about the only real pastime they have — that and pilfering the sherry or the cigars. There are certain acts of mischief that I expect from a servant in my employ; but what I can not and will not stand is their having the impudence to allow me to find them out."

Sentiments of this kind had more than once wakened a disgusted shudder in Archibald Auchincloss; but then between the large-nosed, judicial, moralistic lawyer and his red-haired, red-moustached, jaunty, world-worn, devil-may-care brother-in-law lay a big, tossing channel of uncongeniality.

The Satterthwaite dinner had nearly reached its completion, but the two youngest members of the family, Peyster, aged twelve, and Lulu, aged ten, had been detained by the gayeties of an afternoon dancing-class, and had not yet appeared. Their continued absence had just been referred to by their mother; and Elaine, who would have been pretty in a placid, creamy style if her eyes had not had so much languid superciliousness in them, had drawlingly said:

"It's a perfect luxury to have those two children away. I always dread the evenings when we dine alone and they don't have to stay upstairs."

"You'd better hurry, then, El," said her father, reaching out for an olive, "Lulu will be coming down for good and sending you to the background, as sure as you're born."

"I declare," pouted Elaine, "it makes one nervous the way you and mamma are forever talking marriage to us girls. Doesn't it *you*, Em?"

"No; not a bit," said Emmeline, cracking an almond too thoroughly, and then hunting for its edible fragments amid the chaos of tawny shells on her plate. "If the worst comes to the worst I can always *get somebody.* So can you, Elly. Marriage is a good deal like the German, *I* find. No girl, if she plays her cards right, need go home from a ball without a partner. There's always somebody you can hint to at the very last minute, even if you've snubbed him for twenty evenings before, and who'll be willing to dance with you if you only hint hard enough. *My* last minute hasn't come, though, when it's a question of marrying. And if it *had* . . . why, look at Olivia."

Aspinwall here giggled. He sat superb in evening-dress, with collar so high that you could scarcely imagine his wearing it without much physical pain, and so glossy and stiff-looking that it appeared to be made from some new material, like a snow-white tin.

"'Pon my word, Em," scoffed her brother, "I like your conceit. I wonder what Spencer Delaplaine would say if he heard you underrate him like that. For my part, I don't see how Olivia could do much better — or how any girl could."

"Neither do I," declared Elaine, who prided herself on regarding marriage with a freezing philosophy in whose air the most hardy spray of sentiment needs must perish. "And *what* an idiot she'll be if she doesn't take him!"

"There's only one objection to it all," mused Emmeline, as she cracked another almond.

"What is that?" said her mother, a little sharply. If any one in their most undomestic of domestic circles ever became guilty of stupid sentimentality it was sure to be Emmeline. But the daughter of Mrs. Satterthwaite agreeably disappointed her, this time, as she now went on, between her spasms of squirrel-like munching.

"I don't know why, but there's always something about a *young* widow that isn't precisely good style. Yes, young widows are somehow vulgar. Their mourning is so apt to give them a fast look."

Elaine replied with a recognizing nod. "I understand that feeling," she said; "I've had it myself about young widows, without just being able to explain it."

"Oh, *children!*" cried Mrs. Satterthwaite, throwing back her head in laughter. "What will you say next?"

"I shouldn't be surprised," said Mr. Satterthwaite, "if Delaplaine lived twenty years yet. He can count on his fingers every cocktail he ever drank before dinner, no doubt; and *he* never drew into his lungs those vile cigarettes that Aspy's killing himself with."

"It's a pleasant way of dying," smiled Aspinwall, above the pale acclivity of collar.

"Oh, of course Olivia *will*," exclaimed Elaine, as though the improbability of a permanently negative side of the question had just struck her in a fresh convincing light. "Common-sense will come to her rescue."

"She hasn't much common-sense," said Emmeline.
"Just see how she behaved in going—."

"Em!" broke in her mother chidingly; and Emmeline stopped short.

There was, after all, a *rien ne ça plus* to the topics which the Satterthwaites aired before their servants. They did not desire that quite everything should be heedlessly spoken of. It was well enough that their majestic, white-cravatted butler and his decorous, white-cravatted assistant should hear them say gossipy, daring, heartless, or even ill-bred things; but it was wholly another affair that these functionaries should learn a syllable from their employers' own lips about that horrible Mrs. Ottarson. The Satterthwaites certainly lived with a quiet commingled ease and splendor which few of the " new people " whom Mrs. Auchincloss tabooed could effectually have imitated, even in these days of plentiful upholsterers and eager caterers. Their money was very probably at the root of all their tastefulness, but they had the art of spending it, somehow, as if it were drawn from no brand-new pocket-book. And yet there was the tone of a certain hard, crude Americanism about their household which might have taxed the severest condemnation of foreign critics. They lived in the midst of beautiful statues, tapestries and pictures; they ate off glittering silver and costly china; on every side of them was refinement, grace, elegance, dignity; and yet as personalities, characters, human beings, they all seemed to delight in a sort of mechanical, dispassionate, semi-wooden indifference. Almost the only thing which any of them appeared to do with much real earnestness was to ridicule the people forming his or

her acquaintance. It should not be forgotten however, that out-of-door sports roused them. Tobog-
ganing and skating at Tuxedo during the recent
winter had pricked the younger members of the
family into a positive enthusiasm. The girls would
sometimes drive their father out while in town, and
at Newport they incessantly drove with merely a
coachman at the rear of the vehicle. Down to little
Lulu they were all devotedly fond of horseflesh.
Aspinwall was a noted polo-player, and his younger
brother, Peyster, only twelve years old, longed for
that hour when the paternal veto should be withdrawn from a clipped pony and a mallet.

Lulu and Peyster came into the room soon afterward, and were at once rather tartly reprimanded by
their mother for being so late home from the dancing-
class. They need not have stayed so long, ran the
maternal expostulation; they knew perfectly well the
hour for dinner, and that to-day was one of their days
to dine with the family. Mamma announced that she
had a great mind, as it was, to make them both dine
upstairs.

Meanwhile the two men-servants were waiting on
them, there in the big, stately, ornate dining-room,
as if they had been a little prince and princess. Peyster was an awkward, sluggish-looking boy, with a
pair of salient, fan-shaped ears; but Lulu had a
bewitching, elfin little face that seemed to be set
within the centre of a golden cloud of hair as the
disc of the sunflower is set midmost its yellow
leaves.

"I know it was dreadfully wrong of us to stay so
late," Lulu said, taking a cautious spoonful of the hot

soup which had just been handed her; "but oh, I *was*
having such a glorious time!"

"Now, she kep' me," blurted Peyster, who swal-
lowed his soup like a young ploughboy, and with
whom the word "now" was ubiquitous in his discourse, like the "γαρ" of Homeric text. "Now, I
wanted to come sooner. Ask Françoise if I didn't.
Now, it ain't fair to blame *me*. Is it, Lulu."

"Oh, how tiresome you are, Peystey!" exclaimed
Lulu, with the manner of a girl twice her years. Emmeline, Elaine and their parents exchanged glances as
the quaint, old-young little creature continued:
"*Please* have the goodness to let me explain to
mamma."

"Go ahead," sanctioned Peyster, stolidly, putting
the point of his spoon into his mouth, although he
had been told a hundred times that he must not commit this illicit act.

The whole family, including young Peyster, thought
little Lulu capital fun. Her precocity was a source of
endless entertainment to them, but their feelings appeared definitely to stop just there. They never
petted Lulu, or showed her the least spark of tenderness. But then tenderness, or the slightest exhibition
of anything that resembled it, had no place whatever
among any of their home relationships. None of them
ever seemed to have time enough for a revelation of
brotherly, sisterly, or even conjugal fondness, provided
he or she had the faintest desire to indulge it. They
all appeared to be rather fairly pleased with one another, not to be by any means bored with one another,
to like one another's society moderately well when nothing of a more exciting quality offered; and there it

stopped. Affection was a word of obsolete meaning
with them. Emmeline had given signs of possessing
a certain warmth and sensibility that corresponded to
it, but long ago these had been discountenanced and
slighted by her kindred.

"You see, mamma," re-commenced Lulu, "I had a
perfectly splendid partner for the German — Charlton
Van Dam. He is awfully old, you know — he's four-
teen and a half, and he *never* dances with any girl
under eleven ; he makes a point of it. To-day everybody was surprised when he asked *me.* And we
danced second couple — Beekman Van Horn led,
and oh, it was all just *too* lovely! I was taken out
twelve times. Carrie Livingston, who danced next us
with Willie Winthrop, said ten. But she told a story,
and she knew she told it. She was jealous of Charlty
— Oh, what *do* you think? He *asked* me to *call* him
*Charlty!* I laughed, and I said: 'Oh, no, sir; I
guess I won't do anything so bold as *that.*' And he
said, ' What makes you think it bold ? ' And I said,
' Why, *you* seemed to think it so the other day when
you snubbed Lily Van Vechten for calling you
*Charlty.*' And he got just as red as ever he could
get, and says he, ' Lily Van Vechten and Miss Lulu
Satterthwaite are two very different persons.' And
oh, during the German he was just *too* sweet, and I
*had* to wait till it was over, because if I hadn't I
know he'd have been angry, and would never have
asked me again."

"All of which I think a rather lame excuse, Lulu,"
said her mother. "It's getting worse and worse, the
way that children like you imitate the manners of
their elders. I don't know where it *will* stop. If

Charlty Van Dam is a conceited little boy (and his
mother told me a few days ago that he was getting
so conceited she didn't know what to do with him)
that is no reason why you shouldn't find plenty of
other partners."

"Now, I always get partners," here asserted Peyster, having finished his soup and begun to attack
his fish. "And (now) I don't beg for 'em, either.
Only (now) I fight shy of the old girls that put on
fearful airs, and (now) think themselves to be such
mighty big swells."

"Oh, Peystey's contented with any sort of trash!"
exclaimed Lulu, tossing her head, with its fleece of
nebulous gold, in fine disdain.

They all laughed at this, and Elaine said, soon afterward, in her frigidly critical way, to her little sister:
"Lulu, you're thinking of these matters quite too
soon. They'll give you heartburnings enough when
you get older." She turned to her mother : "Mamma, you *must* make that child go to bed earlier and
have less excitement. She's dark rings round her
eyes at this moment."

"Perhaps they're engagement rings ; coming events
cast their shadows before," said Aspinwall, who prided
himself on smartness of this nature, and had won, by
reason of it, the repute of being witty among a little
band of rosebud maidens whom it plunged into giggling ecstasies.

"So much excitement is killing to the child," said
Emmeline, but in a lazy tone, as if she rather thought
her statement open to contradiction.

"I'm no longer a child," bristled Lulu, quite haughtily. "*Some* girls of my age are children, it's true.

But I'm extremely advanced; I heard mamma say so to Mrs. Arcularius, the other day at school, and of course it's true; everybody thinks it of me. I don't know how many times I've been complimented on it during the past few months."

"Lord Scarletcoat says that he hasn't seen any children since he has been in America," said Elaine, "and I'm almost inclined to think he's right."

Lulu made a wry face. "I should like to have Lord Scarletcoat presented to *me*," she said, with that look as of a wise little fairy which so often overspread her features. "*I* could show him a great many children. Poor Peystey, there, for instance. Why, I sometimes think Peystey doesn't know enough to come in when it rains."

"You *know* enough," said her father, "but I think that in most cases you'd rather stay out and have the fun of getting wet."

"That depends on who staid out *with* me," murmured Lulu, drooping her eyes and shaking her nimbus-clad head. "If it were only Charlty Van Dam I think I could stand a good deal of wetting, papa, and not feel it."

This created more laughter, in which Mrs. Satterthwaite did not join; for just a minute or two previous a note had been brought her, which she was now intently reading. Her face presently wore a most troubled look as she said across the table to her husband:

"Delaplaine's a good deal worse."

"You don't mean it," was the answer. "Seriously ill?"

"They're afraid so."

" Who writes ? "

" That young Adrian — his secretary, or valet, or whatever he calls him. Don't you remember whom I mean ? "

" No ; but that's of no consequence. What *is* it that he writes ? "

" He sends word, at Delaplaine's dictation, that pneumonia is feared, and a bad night is expected — much worse than last night was."

"Pneumonia, and at Mr. Delaplaine's age?" broke in Lulu, as if she spoke to her own thoughts. " That certainly is serious."

There was irresistible comedy in these grave words as the tiny child uttered them, and they were quickly answered by a burst of laughter to which possibly the servants contributed their involuntary share.

" Lulu ! " exclaimed Emmeline. " I declare there's something about you positively uncanny, at times. You make me afraid of you, with that queer-looking little face of yours under its fluffy hair — as if you knew ten times more than you've any business to know."

The little face looked, indeed, as if some feverish, unwholesome influence might be at work in the frail body below it. Two touches of color nearly always burned vivid in its cheeks, and its hazel eyes had constantly that dry sparkle which betokens in a child of Lulu's years an overplus of perilous mental activity. There are some children to whom surroundings of continual gayety are like the effects of a daily nervine. Mrs. Satterthwaite would have been offended and wounded if any one had told her that she was bringing up her little daughter with the most imprudent disregard of a nervous system curiously sensitive and an intellect exceptionally premature. She was really not bringing up Lulu at all, but letting the clever, wayward, brightly-gifted creature breathe just the luxurious, fashionable atmosphere on which Emmeline and Elaine had flourished well enough in their juvenile days. Often for a full twenty-four hours she would not even see Lulu at all. But she had perfect trust in the French *bonne* who was appointed to guard the child. Of course Françoise would instantly notify her if there should be anything the matter with Lulu. But Françoise never brought any ill-reports of a sanitary kind. Sometimes the nurse would come to her with sad tales of Lulu's rebellion and contumacy. Then a maternal scolding would occur, severe or light, as the derelict behavior demanded. But no bodily ailment was ever spoken of, and Mrs. Arcularius, principal of the very select school where Lulu had lately been enrolled as a pupil, had no accounts to render except of the dear pet's highly amusing speeches and her occasional mischievous proclivities. Mrs. Arcularius was that kind of school-disciplinarian who never bored the parents of her scholars (especially when they were persons of great social importance like the Satterthwaites) by depressing tales about either the moral or physical condition of their offspring. She was a lady who had long ago found this course of action militant against her widely-conceded vogue as a successful instructress of aristocratic younger New York.

A short time after dinner, that same evening, and while her husband was smoking a cigar and playing a game of billiards downstairs in the billiard-room with

his son, Aspinwall, Mrs. Satterthwaite, cloaked and
bonneted, sought her easy-going lord, and said:

"Bleecker, I'm going to see Delaplaine. I suppose
there's no impropriety in it, as he's so ill. But of
course you can go too, if you like."

"Thanks, Augusta. I don't think I *will* go." He
stood with his cigar between two fingers and his back
against the billiard-table, while Aspinwall, who was
bored at being interrupted in the game, had dropped,
with a simulation of dreary exhaustion, upon one of
the lounges that lined the apartment. "I've an engagement at half-past nine and" (he took out his
watch, giving it a glance) "it's not long from that
time now."

"Oh, very well," said Mrs. Satterthwaite. She did
not ask what the engagement was. She had expected
to find her husband unwilling to go with her. If he
had expressed a desire to do so she would have been
somewhat annoyed. She had no concern whatever
with his engagements. He might go or come as he
chose. He was the father of her children, but she
had never loved him as a wife should love a husband.
She had married him because he was Bleecker Satterthwaite and a "catch." The engagement to which
he had referred might or might not concern an infi-
delity. It caused her no thrill of jealousy to think on
this unsavory conjugal subject. She did not want to
*gêner* herself with Bleecker's private affairs. Every
man had them, and so long as he kept himself out of a
*scandal publique* she was perfectly contented that he
should follow in the beaten footsteps of all the other
men who resembled him.

She entered her *coupé* a little later, and had herself

driven to the house of Spencer Delaplaine. In a short
time after crossing the threshold of the Tenth Street
house, she stood at Delaplaine's bedside. The sick
man received her with a cordial clasp of the hand.
He looked ill; his face was nearly colorless.

"It's you, Augusta?" he faintly said. "How good
of you to come!"

"Not good at all, my friend," said Mrs. Satterthwaite. "And so you're not as well as when we last
saw each other?"

"No. The fact is I'm pretty ill. Dr. Clancey and
Dr. Robeson have just been here together. I don't
think they're at all sure that I am going to pull
through. It's this right lung now, with the other
threatened."

Mrs. Satterthwaite had by this time seated herself
near the bed. "You must not dream of giving up,"
she exclaimed. "There is so much in that — not giving up. Have you a nurse?"

"Adrian has gone to fetch a nurse. Meanwhile
I've one of my servants; she's there in the next room.
But I want to speak with you before Adrian comes
back."

Mrs. Satterthwaite had a chilled, nervous feeling,
now. She dreaded lest she should be made the
recipient of something funereally moribund, and she
was not at all the sort of woman to whom any confidence of this character would be endurable even on
grounds of charity.

To be intimate with Spencer Delaplaine while a
flourishing and popular millionaire was a decidedly
different position from that of sitting at his bedside
and hearing him breathe forth some farewell charge

that would have about it the very odor of the grave. She had never precisely believed Delaplaine's story that this handsome young Adrian was no closer to him than being the son of a distant relative who had died as a clerk in his employ; it might prove (why not?) a horrible little history that would bring the two into much nearer relations. Besides Augusta Satterthwaite was not the woman to "put herself out" in any way whatever for a friend. If it came to a question of whether or no she cared to have friends at all, she might, under cover of secrecy, have confessed to you that successful, accomplished or fascinating acquaintances continually stood for her in the place of them. She was prepared to make no amicable sacrifices, and she demanded none from others. What so many critics have condemned as the superficiality of social life pleased and satisfied her. She wanted nothing truer or deeper. Nor did she wish it to appear, after the way of her sister, that she wanted anything truer or deeper. In her callous worldliness, at least she was not hypocritical. She now keenly regretted having come this evening. It might turn out a visit with odiously compromising results; for she could not in decency refuse to grant him almost whatever he might ask, provided he asked it as a dying man. There were things one might hate most heartily to do, but having the courage to risk its getting abroad that one had refused them was challenging a still stronger disinclination.

"What is it you would like to say, Spencer,'" she asked, and without the least ring in her voice of the selfish anxiety she felt.

He was silent for some time, staring, as it seemed,

at one of the rare engravings which lined the walls of
his charmingly tasteful chamber.  A clock on the
velvet-draped mantel ticked audibly in the stillness,
and shaped, with its brisk, sharp vibrations, imaginary
words of foreboding to her who sat and waited there
at the bedside.  Her relief was excessive when she at
length heard Delaplaine answer:

"I want to speak to you about . . . Olivia."

"Olivia?" she repeated, trying not to let him see
how glad that one name had made her.  There were
no unpleasant revelations that he could utter concerning her niece; she was well enough aware of his in-
ability here.  But he might say, on the other hand,
what it would prove very welcome to learn.  He
might say that he had altered his will (or had had one
drawn up for the first time) in favor of his old partner's only child.  Then Olivia would perhaps discontinue casting shame upon her father's people by
dwelling with that horrid aunt on her mother's side,
and the abused Van Rensselaer standard would be
reared again from the dust.

"Yes," Delaplaine went on, very slowly at first.
"You've seen her by this time, I suppose, and you've
done as well as you could."

"Oh, yes; I've done my best."

"Well, what *was* your best?"

"I'm sorry to tell you it was a failure."

"Failure?"  He gave a low laugh as he repeated
the word.  But the rattle that went with this laugh
showed the congested state of his lungs, and set him
coughing in a wheezy, senile, though not violent
way.  "She wouldn't marry me, eh?" he at length
went on.  "I thought not — I feared not.  She

hushed you right up, I suppose, and wouldn't hear of it."

"Yes."

"She grew angry, eh?"

"Yes—and it became plain, also, that she was deeply wounded. Finally, she refused to listen, and I thought she would be rude enough to leave the room. No doubt she would have done so, too, if the whole question of the marriage had not been abandoned."

Another silence now followed, and Mrs. Satterthwaite began to assure herself that her friend had no dying act of beneficence to perform toward Olivia. He had merely wanted a report of his ambassadress's proceedings. As for his dying at all, now that his watcher had become more used to the dim light in which his face had first dawned upon her, she began to have solid doubts of any such demise. Of course pneumonia must go hard with one of his years. But then, on the other hand, why should there not be an excellent chance that he might recover—and marry her niece yet? Meanwhile it was very nice to reflect that on his recovery he would certainly bear in mind her own friendly endeavor, not to speak of visits like the present one. (Twenty horse-power could not have dragged her near him if it had been anything catching, like typhoid or scarlet fever; but then he need never dream of this.) Possibly, at the opening of next season, he might give a ball for Elaine, just as he had given one for Emmeline. And in that case how very fit and *chic* it would look for Elaine to receive at the side of her young cousin, Mrs. Spencer Delaplaine, *née* Van Rensselaer!

She had time for these musings amid the pause

which had followed her last sentence addressed to the invalid. But they did not require many seconds. The pleasurable tingle of the egotist takes no longer than the philanthropist's most heroic one.

"If I *should* get well, Augusta," the sick man presently said, "I should want to have that girl for my wife, just the same."

Mrs. Satterthwaite bowed. "So I should imagine," she acceded.

"But I have been thinking. . . ." Here he came to a dead stop, letting his voice fall suddenly.

"You mean that you may not get well? Oh, don't allow your mind to brood upon that subject in the least. I must say that so far you've disappointed me very agreeably. You don't seem to be half as ill as I first thought you."

A sparkle crept into his dull eyes as he fixed them on her over-bending face.

"Suppose she were to come here and . . . and bid me good-bye. Her father's old friend, you know. I don't believe she'd refuse it, do you?"

"Refuse it? No; how could she? You mean. . ."

"Oh, I mean a genuine death-bed farewell. Don't fancy that I don't. I admit I'm not yet past hope, but that doesn't prevent me from being very sick — very sick indeed — with internal gout and pneumonia in complication. . . . Well, now, suppose Olivia came here to-morrow and found me a little worse . . . we'll say not exactly dying yet, but nearer to it than I am to-night, and . . . and a proposition were made to her . . .?"

"A proposition? Yes? Well? What proposition?"

The sparkle in those gray eyes of his, which she had so often seen lit by the crafty, algid humor peculiar to the man, grew more keen now as he murmured :

" A proposition of marriage."

" Marriage ? "

He stared up at her from the white pillow.  " Can't you guess, Augusta, what I'm driving at ? " he said.

" No," she answered, with a blank look.

" Then I'll tell you." . . . And long before she left him he had given her a thorough explanation. Once or twice she repressed a shudder while she listened, for it all struck her as not merely novel, but even ghastly as well.

## X.

THE note which Olivia received that same evening
had been written by Mrs. Satterthwaite herself at the
residence of Delaplaine. It conveyed the tidings that
the latter was exceedingly ill, but it bore no request
that Olivia should pay a visit on the friend of her
dead father.

The next morning, however, by about eleven o'clock,
came a second note. As Olivia read this the blood
rushed to her face and her eyes filled with tears.

It also was written by Mrs. Satterthwaite, and ran
as follows:

No. — West Tenth Street,
May —, 188—.

MY DEAR OLIVIA : I have just been holding a very sad
talk with poor Mr. Delaplaine. The doctors think there is still
less hope of his living now, as the pneumonic symptoms are
worse instead of better. This morning he has been in great
pain, and yet he would hold a few words with me, and they
have been words which have had you for their subject. Mr.
Delaplaine feels that his end has almost come. He had made a
will several years ago, leaving all his fortune to charities of various kinds. But now he has determined to alter the will in your
favor. He says that there is no earthly reason why he should
not do this act of helpfulness to the child of his oldest and
dearest friend. His few distant relations will not suffer from
the change of the plan, for in any case they would not have
received a dollar of his money. Mr. Delaplaine begs that you
will come to him, at the above address, by two o'clock this
afternoon. I will be here to meet you. My dear child, although I am losing a devoted friend in Spencer Delaplaine, I

cannot but congratulate you because of the immense windfall
of good luck that promises to become yours. My loss will be
your gain, but is it not thus in all the events of life? Pray do
not refuse to come. But I know that I need not make this
petition of you, Olivia, since your natural humanity will not
permit you to remain away.

Your loving aunt,

AUGUSTA SATTERTHWAITE.

Mrs. Satterthwaite had seen one of the attending
physicians privately just before she wrote this note to
her niece. Dr. Clancey was a man of extraordinary
medical position, and he gave an opinion of Delaplaine's case as unhesitating as it was discouraging.
He apprehended a failure of the heart in his patient,
though the lungs might resist even the severe congestion burdening them. They were remarkably strong
lungs, but the diagnosis revealed a cardiac weakness
from which it might be difficult for the patient to
rally. Two sinking turns had already occurred; there
was reason to believe that the patient would not resist
a third. Mr. Delaplaine had held a conversation with
his lawyer between ten and eleven that morning, in
obstinate contradiction to the orders of his physicians.
No bad result had yet shown itself, but now at any
moment the invalid might again collapse. His tenac-
ity was admirable, but he had already trifled with it
most recklessly.

"If he is conscious at two o'clock," said Mrs. Satterthwaite, "he will, I know, desire to see Miss Van
Rensselaer, the daughter of my brother, his former
partner, whose recent death you are of course aware
of."

Dr. Clancey gravely nodded. "He will see the

young lady, or any one except his nurse, Mrs. Satterthwaite," was the answer, "at his own imminent danger."

Soon after this, Mrs. Satterthwaite wrote to her sister, imperatively urging that she should come at once to West Tenth Street. Mrs. Auchincloss obeyed the summons. The two sisters met in Delaplaine's exquisite lower drawing-room.

" My dear Letitia," began Mrs. Satterthwaite," I fear you *may* think that I have been behaving imprudently."

" Imprudently, Augusta?" As Mrs. Auchincloss thus spoke she shook her head in apparent deprecation and looked down at the black-gloved hands which she had folded in her lap.

Mrs. Satterthwaite gave a little agitated preliminary cough, and then softly plunged into the subject. " Spencer Delaplaine, my dear, sent for me last evening. We had a long talk together. He is possessed with the idea of settling all his money upon Olivia."

Mrs. Auchincloss abruptly started up. " Upon Olivia!" she exclaimed. " Before he dies? He is then so sure of death?"

" Not so perfectly sure."

The eyes of the two sisters met. Mrs. Auchincloss perceived that something was being withheld from her. But she made no reply; she waited, with her most composed expression, for some further announcement. At last it came.

" He is bent upon asking Olivia to marry him — to have the ceremony performed at once. But . . . " Here Mrs. Satterthwaite averted her eyes, and bit her lips very worriedly. " Well, Letitia, he does not wish that Olivia, when she comes, should know there is any chance whatever of his recovery."

Mrs. Auchincloss started again. "And pray on what account, Augusta? Does he . . . ?" The lady rose, with a fluttered, appalled air, and then reseated herself. "You can't mean that he wants to — to *trick* the girl into marrying him!"

Mrs. Satterthwaite threw up both hands toward the ceiling, and lifted her eyes at the same time. "That is what I have been so terribly afraid of, Letitia!" And then the sisters looked at one another quite steadily again. Each had her own special kind of worldliness, of artificiality, perhaps of real evil as well. But each also had her own method of conceal-ment. If, just at present, there were to be anything culpable done, no such neat policy could be adopted, the younger sister had reasoned with herself, as that of a mutual masquerade. If Letitia chose to approve the whole odd business and lend a hand to its further-ing, let her take the cue offered. And so Mrs. Satter-thwaite, with the skill of one adroit in all such tactics, offered the cue.

"It would be perfectly fearful, would it not," she now went on, "if he should conclude to *get well* after such a marriage? I suppose he has a kind of hope that he will; and loving Olivia, as he undoubtedly does, he wants to . . . to . . . (dear me, Letitia! how *shall* I express it?) to give himself the . . . benefit of . . . "

"I see," Mrs. Auchincloss here interrupted the speaker, in the midst of this intentional stumbling. "You spoke a minute ago, sister, of his concluding to get well. People do not usually accomplish such ends

as that by their own volition. . . . And you say that
the doctors give him up?"

"Yes."

"Still, he *may* live?"

"Oh, it wouldn't by any means be a miracle if he
did."

"I see," again murmured Mrs. Auchincloss, gazing
fixedly at the floor; "I see."

Her sister felt that she saw—and very lucidly, by
this time. It looked as if she were going to slip into
the little plot that should raise, if it were successful,
her niece out of pauperism and dependence. Her
next words, Mrs. Satterthwaite knew, would decide
what part she would take—whether one of non-com-
pliance or of coöperation. And her next words did so
decide, as they fell with lingering delay from her lips
—those lips that could press together their pink rims
with such untold prudishness when occasion made it
seem desirable.

"My dear Augusta, I think that if Mr. Delaplaine
chooses to believe there is a hope for him, in spite of
all that the doctors have said, it is quite his affair and
not ours. Naturally the intelligence of any one so ill
as he is must be weakened. I should advise that we
grant . . . his little . . . stipulation, or . . . er . . .
request, regarding Olivia being told there is . . . er . . .
*any* chance of his recovery. Humor him in this . . .
why not? And as for Olivia herself, I only hope that
she may see the spiritual sweetness in such an act as
that which he shall ask of her, besides the more . . .
er . . . more material aspect it will present."

Augusta Satterthwaite rose from her chair with a
short nod. "I hope so," she said, with cold laconism.

It was very pleasing to secure her sister as a confederate in this proposed little enterprise, but she could not help a pang or two of aggravation at Letitia when the latter threw on her puritanic, not to say hypocritic, mantle, and began mincing about in it; for she had long ago assured herself that Letitia was never so apt to do this as when she was on bad terms with her own vaunted conscience.

"The great point is here," Mrs. Satterthwaite now went coolly on, in matter-of-fact tones that contrasted noticeably with her former perturbed and insecure ones; "Will Olivia consent to such a marriage? You and I, Letitia, have already had rather full proof of just how obstinate she can be."

"Yes — *indeed*, yes!"

"But the girl, I think, has her fair share both of pity and gratitude. These must be appealed to. She must *see* Delaplaine. I shall make a point of that; we both must. If anything *should* be said afterward, you know, we must have it in our power to vindicate ourselves thoroughly."

"Oh, thoroughly." struck in Mrs. Auchincloss. Both sisters at length understood exactly how to conduct themselves to one another; their rôles were to be those of the most blameless apparent innocence. And now Mrs. Auchincloss continued : "We want to stand hereafter, if anything *should* happen, in the very clearest colors before that girl. For she is hasty-tempered (we've seen that) and she would not hesitate to bring an accusation of some sort against us, embarrassing enough, however undeserved."

The masquerade, as Mrs. Satterthwaite now realized, was being most skilfully conducted on the part of her sister. She, in turn, proceeded to enact her own due share of it.

"Yes, Letitia; we cannot be too mindful of how delicate a position we will occupy. If Olivia *should* consent to this marriage, and if *he should* get better after it, the girl will of course pour blame on *us* for not having distressed poor Delaplaine by making her aware of one little remote probability that he might get well."

"And yet," answered Mrs. Auchincloss, with a dainty upward gesture of the black-gloved hands, "at least *there*, Augusta, we shall be justified in using actual deceit. We need not let Olivia know that *we* ever knew of that remote little probability . . . Still, her consent to the marriage looks very uncertain, I should say." Here the lady grew visibly excited, as she drew forth a tiny crystal vinaigrette and placed it at either thin pink nostril. "Oh, no, no," she proceeded, with sidelong dips of the head toward her restorative salts till the sprays of jet on her black mourning bonnet sensitively tinkled, "I'm sure she'll never do it. Don't depend on her, Augusta. She would simply fly from the house in amazement if we made her any such proposition. And I doubt if she will even come here, unless you ask her in the most cautious way."

"I've done that. I did not mention in my note that Delaplaine desired to do anything except alter his will in her favor. Oh, she will come; it would be despicable in her if she remained away at the hour I appointed — two o'clock this afternoon. She certainly could not refuse to stand at the bedside of a dying man — and that man so old and prized a friend of her father."

"No . . . as you have put your request she will of course accede to it. But this change in the will . . . has it been made already ? "

"I think so. His lawyer was with him for some time this morning — and against his two doctors' positive orders."

"The will *is* no doubt altered, then," said Mrs. Auchincloss. She was inwardly very much exercised about the whole affair. Had she been too reckless in her late tacit little compact ? Ought she not to have waited and discussed the advisability of it with her reverenced Archibald ? And yet could she do more than fancy that this oracle of tranquil wisdom would fail to commend the course she had taken ? Such a marriage as this one for Olivia might savor of sensationalism and of theatric coarseness. But then, how ameliorating it might prove to the girl's future !

Singular enough was the diversity between these two sisters when their congeniality was also fairly regarded. Both were astute, both lacking in that guidance of disinterested principle which makes the honor and creditable hope of all human progression. Both were selfish women, enswathed in superciliousness, degraded by ambitions of shallow and idle reach. And yet a gulf separated them, since Mrs. Auchincloss's paltry ideal of conduct was to worship some perfectly meretricious god that she named good-taste, and the *morale* of Mrs. Satterthwaite was to worship an ideal, just as paltry, of temporal eminence, and glittering though tawdry power. Neither woman had the least vital valuation of abstract right; neither would have scrupled to sell her finer self-respect for that mess of pottage which the unsoiled spirit defines

by mere external and circumstantial acquirement.
But the elder sister wanted her mess of pottage in
a silver dish, with a cover that hid from all prying
glances the homely quality of the viand; while the
younger sister, willing enough that it should be set
before her in earthenware, clung to the desire of having it brought by a liveried domestic and in a frescoed
dining-hall. They were both snobs to their finger-tips,
but one was the scandal-fearing and one the scandal-
daring snob. Mrs. Auchincloss dreaded to risk a
speck of odium upon her scarf-skin of respectability;
Mrs. Satterthwaite jauntily snapped her fingers at the
infliction of any such petty soilure, so long as she
maintained the gracious prerogative of going everywhere, knowing everybody, and of putting everywhere that she went and everybody whom she knew
in the rose-tinted light of concession rather than of
recipiency. All things considered, Mrs. Satterthwaite
undeniably had the best hand in the cheap, trifling,
fleeting game. To place the parallel much lower, it
is the reprobate with a vestige or two of decency who
picks a pocket under conditions of smaller individual
gusto.

At two o'clock that afternoon Olivia punctually appeared. She disliked coming with as much strength
as that by which she had felt herself urged to come.

There had been no evading the necessity of presenting herself at Delaplaine's side; she would have
despised her own shadow for months afterwards if
she had refused so simple a boon. But the bequest of
his fortune to her on the part of her father's old friend
— that had placed her in a kind of dizzying dilemma.
Her pride revolted at once; for was it not a deed of

charity which she would have refused without hesitation if the donor's hand had been a living and not a
dying one? But self-rebuke struck an immediate
blow at such pride, and bade her hold at its rightful
worth the kindliness, beneficence and devotion of so
magnificent a legacy. Perhaps the enthusiastic gratu-
lations of Mrs. Ottarson had not a little to do with
the final calming of her bewildered mind, which had
almost lost the power to think coherently amid the
rush of unaccustomed thoughts that besieged its faculties.

"'Livia!" quivered her aunt, in a voice between
laughing and weeping, "I 'clare t' goodness it jus'
*can't* be true! It can't be, an' *'tain't!* I'm dreamin';
I've got one o' those spells o' dreamin' I sometimes
get from layin' flat on my back . . . Oh, no, I ain't,
though! It's all true 's it *can* be!"

And here the benignant if unsyntactical being
caught Olivia to her breast and kissed her. "Of
course it's awful to think of him dyin' so sudden;
but then, as your Aunt Satterthwaite says in her
letter (an' the Lord knows she's 'cute 'nough 'bout
all *such* things!) it's an ill-wind, deary . . . or something kind o' like that. 'T seems a reg'lar sin to
laugh, don't it? An' 't seems a sin to cry 's well,
seein' 't I cry on'y from joy, jus' 's I laugh . . . Oh,
my *sakes!* To think o' you havin' w'at you was born
and brought up to, after all! . . ."

Generalities now gave place to particulars, and in a
trice Mrs. Ottarson was viewing the whole recent
event with practical vision. "I s'pose 't won't be
very pleasant to go all alone. I wish I could be
there too, an' kind o' stay somewheres round so 's

you knew I was near while he kep' you talkin' in the
sick-room. You've just *come* from so much sufferin',
Liv, it don't seem right you should see any more, f'r
ever so long; does it! W'at you goin' to wear? I'd
put on, 'f I was you, the black dress with the ruffles
up the sleeves; it suits you to a jiffy . . . an' then,
you know, if the room's warm you can slip your
sacque off, an' even if the old gent'man *is* goin' fast
't won't make him go any quicker 'f he sees you
lookin' 's pretty 's possible."

Olivia wore the dress with the ruffled sleeves, but,
as it turned out, she slipped off her sacque, with Mrs.
Satterthwaite's assistance, very soon after she had entered the house. She felt excited, and knew that her
cheeks were glowing hotter as her aunt kissed her;
but she did not know how sparklingly blue her eyes
had become. She was not even aware that she had
shaped the question "How is Mr. Delaplaine?" until
Mrs. Satterthwaite answered it by saying:

"He's easier now, and ready to speak with you."

Then Olivia looked full into her aunt's eyes. "It's
a great kindness on his part, Aunt Augusta," she said
a little brokenly. "I—I hardly know how I ought
to receive it—or whether I—I ought to receive it at
all."

Mrs. Satterthwaite put her hand on Olivia's shoulder. "Receive it all, Olivia!" she softly exclaimed.

Just then a young man entered the room. It was
Adrian, of whom we have heard mention before.
During four or five years he had held a subordinate
position in Delaplaine's household, not exactly explainable as to the question of its being secretaryship
or servantship. His full name was Adrian Etherege.

He sometimes would spend an hour or two with Delaplaine at the bank. He lived here in the West Tenth
Street house, and had a room beyond any of the servants' rooms in appointment and preference of loca-
tion. He could not have been more than twenty years
old; perhaps he was still younger, though there was a
certain mature look about his large, velvety brown
eyes. They were feminine eyes, and his extremely
slender and graceful figure, just tall enough to surpass
that óf most women, made an imaginative observer
regret the unpicturesque limitations of our modern
male costume; for Adrian Etherege, this boyish young
beauty, with his smooth, oval face just touched about
its upper lip by the downy growth of a blond moustache, and with the clustering mass of yellow curls
lying negligent and too profuse above a broad, sculpt-
urally white forehead, would have acquitted himself so
admirably as a page of earlier romantic times! What
gave him the appearance of being perhaps a little
older than twenty years, was a pensive expression
that instantly revealed itself when you squarely confronted the lovely delicacy of his countenance.

Olivia was at once won by him as he paused before
Mrs. Satterthwaite. It swiftly struck her that he was
one of the most beautiful youths whom she had ever
seen. His dress, quite out of the prevailing fashion
and yet as modestly inconspicuous as any garb of
to-day could well be cut or worn, heightened the
sweet, adolescent charm of his bearing. It darted
through Olivia's mind, in spite of her anxiety and
perplexity, "What a wonderfully winning and fascinating presence he has!" But he roused in her only
the delight we bestow upon some thrifty and splendid

plant, with its knots of bloom lifted clear and perfect to the view. He caused her almost to forget the melancholy mission on which she had entered this abode of her dead father's friend, while she heard him address Mrs. Satterthwaite in these few, low-toned words:

"Mr. Delaplaine wishes to know if the young lady is here yet."

"Yes," answered Mrs. Satterthwaite. She turned away from the speaker and put a hand on either of Olivia's arms, while she scanned the girl's flushed face. "You *are* ready to go up and see Mr. Delaplaine now, are you not?" she asked.

"Yes," said Olivia. Her gaze wandered to the young man while she thus replied. It seemed as if she made her reply to him rather than to her aunt. A moment afterward, having transiently fixed his superb brown eyes upon Olivia's face, he passed from the room.

"Who is he?" quickly whispered Olivia, her look following him as he receded.

"His name is Etherege — Adrian Etherege," responded Mrs. Satterthwaite.

"Adrian Etherege," Olivia repeated. "How handsome he is! What a charming face he has! It makes me think of faces in pictures that I saw somewhere abroad . . . in Dresden, Venice, Florence, somewhere among the galleries I used now and then to visit with poor papa."

"Isn't he just *too* enchanting," cried Mrs. Satterthwaite. "I'm so glad to hear some one say he is, for I've thought so a perfect age . . . I've only seen him once or twice before," she went on self-correctively.

"Mr. Delaplaine has now and then sent him with a message to me since . . . since he engaged him about three or four years ago. He lives here, you know — he's a sort of servant."

"A servant — he?" murmured Olivia.

"Yes. A *sort* of servant. . . . You wouldn't believe it, would you? Neither would I at first. But he's educated; he's not a real servant."

"I should suppose not."

Mrs. Satterthwaite laughed. "You've fallen in love with Adrian. So have I. He's adorable. And yet Mr. Delaplaine thinks him dull and rather stupid. But men don't see with our eyes, do they? I'm so glad you're *éprise* with Adrian, poor little fellow . . . But we mustn't talk of him. We must talk of doing what he told us to do."

"Going up to . . . to see Mr. Delaplaine," faltered Olivia.

"Yes. You're not afraid to go, are you?"

Olivia drew backward a few steps. "Afraid?" she repeated. "No. But this great act of kindness he wants me to benefit by. . . . *That* makes me almost afraid."

Mrs. Satterthwaite was looking steadily into her eyes. "You know, Olivia, that he was in love with you before he was taken ill. You know that. He told you so."

"Yes . . . he told me that he wanted me to marry him."

"He told you that he was in love with you," persisted her aunt. "Yes, he did, Olivia. And we — your Aunt Augusta and I — assured you of it afterward."

" Well . . . yes," replied Olivia.

" Now, my dear girl," suddenly broke forth Mrs.
Satterthwaite, " he wants you to accept this great
favor at his hands."

" I know.  You wrote me."

" But I did not write you *all.*"

" Not all?"

" No.  He has changed his will.  The lawyer was
here this morning.  But there . . . well, there is
something else."

" Something else?"

" Yes.  Don't look so startled.  How can I tell you
if you look so startled? . . . He is dying you know."

" I do know.  You wrote me that."

" But, my dear girl, there was something I did not
write you."

" No?" said Olivia, with a child's innocence of surprise.  " What was it?"

Mrs. Satterthwaite shrugged her square, firm shoulders (so different from the drooping, fragile shoulders
of her sister, Mrs. Auchincloss) and half turned away.
" You shall soon know, my dear.  *He* will tell you.
It's . . . it's something he will want you to do."
Suddenly Mrs. Satterthwaite veered about and caught
both Olivia's hands in both her own.  " I won't tell
you, my dear.  It's a dying request of his.  Remember that."

" A dying request?" Olivia said, in a dazed way.
She felt as if some weird trap were about to be sprung
upon her.  She had always distrusted these two aristocratic aunts of hers.  Now one of them seemed to
her brimming with guile and stratagem.  She silently
regretted that she had not allowed the staunch and

incorruptible Mrs. Ottarson to accompany her hither, as that doughty lady had proposed, if not insisted.

"A dying request?" she repeated. "Tell me what it is."

But Mrs. Satterthwaite went up to the girl and put one of her arms within her own, drawing her resolutely and determinedly toward the door. "Now, don't be frightened," Mrs. Satterthwaite admonished. "You've nothing on earth to be frightened about . . . Come . . . What· he asks of you, my dear, you can refuse or accept, just as you choose."

Olivia allowed herself to be led. The staircase in the outer hall was broad enough for them to ascend it two abreast. When they had reached the second hall and paused before a closed door, the first that they met, Mrs. Satterthwaite said:

"Now go in. You'll find him very gentle and sweet. And, recollect — he's dying."

The next moment Mrs. Satterthwaite opened the door before which they both stood. She pushed Olivia into the chamber. Then she closed the door, leaving her niece alone with the sick man who was himself alone amid an artificial gloom, waiting for her, having dismissed every attendant. Whatever was the communication which he desired to impart, he had made up his mind that it should be for one pair of ears only.

Olivia, seeing the bed and the dim face outlined against its pillows, drew quietly forward.

"Olivia," called a faint voice. "Is that you?"

"Yes, Mr. Delaplaine."

"Come, nearer."

She went nearer. He stretched out his hand, and

she took it, standing at his bedside. She looked down at his face. It seemed wan and drawn and changed to her.

"Olivia," said the sick man, "you have come to me like the dear, good girl that you are. . . . They say I can't last very many hours longer."

"I hope it isn't true, Mr. Delaplaine."

"I know you hope that, Olivia. But if I really must go, I've arranged that you shall have all I leave behind me. I've arranged it. Did they tell you?"

"They said you had done me this goodness," she answered. "But" . . . And then she paused, while the hand that he clasped trembled and he felt it tremble . . . "are there no others, Mr. Delaplaine, whom . . . ?"

"No others — no," he interrupted her, with a feverish, peevish ring in his husky voice. "But there are others — relations of mine whom I don't care for — whom I've helped now and then, but not even seen since I was a man of forty or thereabouts, and these might dispute my will." He paused, and gasped a little for breath, with a rattling in his throat that made Olivia's heart throb for pity. "Now, Olivia," he presently resumed, speaking with difficulty, "I want to make your claim sure. Sure, do you understand?"

"Yes . . . I understand."

She felt his fingers grow tenser about the hand that still lay within his own. "No, you don't understand. There's only one sure way of making all their future litigation useless. Only one sure way."

He closed his eyes and drew a long, stertorous breath, still clasping her hand.

She watched him. She did not know just what to answer, except to ask him concerning the avoidant way to which he had alluded. So, presently, she said: "What is that way, Mr. Delaplaine?"

He unclosed his eyes and fixed them upon her attentive face. "By marrying you here, inside the next hour. You'll only be my wife for a little while . . . I'll die soon afterward. I'll—there, don't try to drag your hand away like that. Listen!"

She let her hand stay in the clasp of his. But if the room had not been so dusky he could have seen what a pallor had overswept her face.

"I—I will listen," she managed to answer: "but I —I can't do what you ask."

He raised himself in bed, taking her hand, now, in both his own. A new effect of light showed her how haggard he was. "Olivia," he cried hoarsely, "do this for me! No—not for me—for yourself! It isn't only that I love you—it's far more—it's that they'll try to take the money away from you if you won't consent! Don't be foolish, Olivia. You'll be my wife only for—for a few hours. But . . ."

"No! no! no!" she cried, dragging her hand away from both his clinging hands. She stood for a moment, watching him as he sank back upon the pillows. "No! no! no!" she repeated. And then, with her heart beating so that it seemed almost as if it would leap out of her breast, she hurried toward the door of the dim chamber, opened it, and fled into the hall beyond.

## XI.

The day on which Olivia made that unsuspicious little pilgrimage to Delaplaine's abode proved the first by which the reigning May had asserted her somewhat slender right even to be called vernal. A sharpness yet lingered in the breeze, but it was at least southerly — strong concession from so bad-tempered a month as this had shown itself — and you could easily imagine over what radiant wavelets it swept while it passed northward through the narrows into New York Bay. Fifth Avenue looked cheerful enough almost to deserve the name of a handsome thoroughfare, since its miles of deplorable brown-stone spruceness are never so far from being a shock to artistic nerves as when they cumbrously scowl at us through a merry golden veil of sunshine.

The Satterthwaites' house was of that usual sulky sobriety in the way of design which its locality loves to perpetuate for ill-starred future generations, and which, if the best speech of architecture may be called eloquence, might well deserve the name of platitude. But this large family-mansion, with its two windows on one side of the high stoop and one window on the other, was of brick, with stone copings, and had been decoratively and improvingly touched by a clever architect after the Satterthwaites purchased it. Being on a corner, it ran a good distance down along the transverse street, and showed glimpses of lace and

silken tapestries, of statuary and of other costly orna-
mentation within, from its two large embayed windows
and its many other smaller ones.

To a young man, of calm, dark, serene face and
rather foreign air, who had just ascended the stoop
and pulled the bronze door-bell, it seemed a strikingly
brilliant sort of residence. Though an American by
birth, he had not been in this country for over ten
years, and many changes were now evident to him in
the great city which he had last observed as a boy of
sixteen or thereabout. The footman who presently
admitted him into a marbled and richly upholstered
hall, was like a living memento of Parisian sojourns;
the new-comer had seen in Paris just such clean-shorn,
intelligent, quick-moving fellows, among the *salons*,
the best cafés. About ten minutes afterwards, while
he sat with Emmeline and Elaine Satterthwaite in the
grand gilded drawing-rooms, he expressed a similar
opinion regarding New York itself.

" It all has grown to wear a more foreign look," he
said, in his even, composed, unassertive voice, which
somehow always carried the latent suggestion of his
being ready to weigh most carefully and respectfully
any opposite opinion that you, on your part, might
care to advance against his own. " At least all that I
have yet seen of the huge town."

" We don't see much change," replied Emmeline,
looking at her sister for a moment; " do we, Elly? I
suppose that is because we hardly ever give it a
thought; we've become so used to it, you know."

" Yes," Elaine struck in, at this point, " you must
remember, Jasper, that it will very soon be four years
since we all met you in London." Here the younger

sister cast down her eyes and sighed. She had been told that the broad, creamy-white effect of her drooped eyelids at such times became her quite effectively. "How often Em and I have thought about the lovely way in which you treated us!"

"I?" exclaimed the young man, surprisedly looking at her with his dark, sweet, serious eyes. And then came his throaty, mellow, English-sounding laugh. "I have no idea, Elaine, really, in what my loveliness consisted."

"Oh, Elly means that you devoted yourself to us in a more than cousinly manner during those pleasant London days of latter May and early June!" answered Emmeline. "You took us everywhere — to the National Gallery, the Kensington Museum, the British Museum, the Grosvenor Gallery, the Tower, the 'Zoo,' Madame Tussaud's, Richmond, Greenwich, Windsor . . . where Jasper, did you *not* take us?"

"And now, " hurried Elaine, as if she were determined not to be out-done in the grace of gratitude by her elder sister, "you've come to New York at so dull a season that we have no means of repaying you for all that past kindness. There's never anything going on now in New York; and besides, as you see, we're in mourning."

"In mourning?" repeated their guest, with that nice, prompt sympathy of tone which was all the more welcome because it partook of his intrinsic spontaneity and naturalness. He never appeared to be other than he really was; his perfect breeding bespoke some chivalrous origin to which the everyday skin-deep civilities bore little true resemblance; no kindly words ever escaped him without making his

listener somehow feel that they would not have been
uttered at all if they had had to be delivered hypo-
critically.

"Our uncle, Mr. Houston Van Rensselaer, died a
few days ago," said Emmeline. "We never knew
him well, but then of course it can't be forgotten
that he was mamma's own brother."

"You remember Uncle Houston, don't you, Jasper?" said Elaine. "He crossed over to London
from Paris, that spring, with his daughter."

"One very warm Sunday we all went together to
Hampton Court," said Emmeline. "Don't you remember *now*?"

"Yes, yes, indeed!" suddenly declared the young
man, as though memory had not until that instant
obeyed his call. "And Mr. Van Rensselaer had such
a sweet little daughter, with big blue eyes. Pray,
what has become of *her*?"

"She is here," answered Emmeline, stealing a fleet
look at Elaine.

"Ah? You mean that she is stopping here with
you in this house?" asked the young man.

"Oh, no — Em only means that she's here in New
York," hastened Elaine, "She's . . . staying with
. . . er . . . some *other* relations of hers."

"Indeed?" said their guest. "I shall get you to
give me her address, if you will be so good. I should
like to see her again. She promised to become a most
delightful creature; I shouldn't like to miss my opportunity of finding out whether the bud belied the rose.
But of course I don't mean that I should think of paying her a visit for a long time yet."

It is difficult to say which of his two hearers re-

garded with more profound disgust the idea of his
going to see Olivia Van Rensselaer at all in her
present highly plebeian abode.  He was their cousin,
though several times removed, and if he had not been
Jasper Massereene — or some one of equal notability
— they would perhaps have shown a very limited concern for the relationship.  As it was, they held his
visit to be impressively complimentary.  Even in
London he had not shone to them in the colors of
a compatriot, but in those of an Englishman whose
American birth was but dimly recollected, as if it had
been some sort of early juvenile escapade.

He had left Cambridge with high honors; he was
handsome, singularly amiable, and endowed with an
address of the most gentleman-like fascination.
"Mamma and papa" had been so proud and glad
to meet him, and then it was easy to see that he
had friends everywhere in the best London circles.
Mr. Bleecker Satterthwaite's first cousin had been his
mother; she had married his father, Trevor Massereene, in New York, and it had been regarded as a
very advantageous match.  The young lady was a
beauty, and a belle in society.  Trevor Massereene
was a near relative of the Earl of Meath, and had
come to New York, years ago, to enter a banking-
house of greater importance than that of Delaplaine
& Van Rensselaer.  He had acquired a fortune and
afterward married one, the Satterthwaite estate being
divided between Bleecker and his cousin, with a superb share for each. · When his father had become a
widower he had retired from Wall Street and taken
his only child, Jasper, to live with him in England.
The Earl of Meath had cordially received his kinsman,

and at his father's death young Jasper, with a really
great inheritance, had found himself by no means
neglected or ignored.

He had come to America, after his long residence
in England, with uncertain views as to how long he
should remain here. He had passionately loved his
mother, and she had died in New York. This formed
a certain reason, rooted in sentiment, why he should
wish to see once more the city of her birth and death.
But there were other reasons for his coming. He
had been a sincere student of many questions which
he believed that this transatlantic trip could, perhaps,
render more clear to him. He was a young man who
could intellectually repress himself with so ready an
adaptability that he possessed scores of acquaintances
quite unconscious of any striking trait in him apart
from that of his being a good fellow of the most con-
vivial proficiences. But he never with intention shut
to one acquaintance particular doors or windows of
his individuality, and opened them to others. This
process, which went on with him as often as he bade
farewell to Tom, spoke a greeting word to Dick, or
shook hands with Harry, was no less undeliberate
than it was authentic. He had, in marked degree,
the social gift, the rapid insight that measures and
gauges character, the power to enjoy various phases
of human society for what they were, apart from what
they had failed in becoming. He was a student of his
fellow-creatures, a philosopher who not seldom gazed
upon the world with eyes of melancholy astonishment.
But only those who knew him best ever perceived in
him this occult spiritual distress, and even they found
it to be transitory as a piece of gloomy emotion; for

Masscreene did not have it in him to repine; his was that order of optimism which sees a line of light at the verge of the stormiest horizon, and deafens itself to all the grumbles of thunder that may lurk below. You could never have persuaded him that life was not worth living, though he fairly and unflinchingly faced every modern reason which the scientific pessimists presented for its being altogether vain and futile. He could not with justice have been called other than agnostic, and yet that kind of grisly mental twilight which the consistent agnostic usually prides himself upon preserving, was lighted, in the case of Massereene, as one might easily imagine, by more than a single lonely trembling star.

So long as it was a question of seeking to explain the universe, he tried to possess his soul in patience; but his hopes and dreams that all was well, and that humanity would hereafter confront the explanation of its worst agony — these were like white birds that incessantly hovered about him, while making with the tender palpitations of their wings a harmony that drowned many harsher noises. Cheerfulness always flung its rose-light over his bearing and converse; but there was something more than mere cheerfulness in this, the companionable and gregarious part of the man's nature; it bore a closer resemblance to charity, expending and diffusing choice possessions with the freedom of copious alms. "I don't believe you have an enemy in the world, Jasper," one of his English friends had said to him once. And he had replied, with a little start and a troubled frown on his thoughtful face: "I hope that I don't deserve an enemy. I'd rather have ten than feel that I deserved one."

He did not specially admire either Emmeline Satterthwaite or her sister, Elaine. They both affected him
repellingly by their hardness, just as certain landscapes
did in painting, ingenious though he might have found
not a few of their minor details. But notwithstanding
that he had brought here a number of letters, the Satterthwaite family made a first appeal to him through
the memory of his dead mother, whose maiden name
they bore. Emmeline and Elaine, on the other hand,
considered him a most adorable young gentleman.
They had learned from their father just how many
thousands combined to form his annual income; they
had duly weighed the fact of his being an earl's near
relative; they had observed his good looks, his manly
and tastefully-garbed shape, his polished manners, his
unfailing geniality. To meet him again like this, quite
unexpectedly in their own drawing-rooms, produced
for them both a mild, pleasing shock. And then had
come the exasperating reflection that the lateness of
the season and their own mourning-attire stood in the
way of their having him accompany them among fashionable metropolitan gayeties. It would have been
such a *grand coup* to have entered drawing-rooms at his
side — to have had it transpire that he was their kinsman, and yet the cousin of a distinguished nobleman
as well! The Auchinclosses would have felt it. It
was something that would have pierced Madeleine's
haughty little soul with envy! Ah! did not they
know? If there was anything on earth that could
make Madeleine, with her prodigious veneration for
herself and her parents and her priggish brother, bend
that slim neck of hers cringingly, it was proximity to
the British peerage! . . . Jasper Massereene had mean-

while no shadow of suspicion what thoughts were passing through the minds of his two young hostesses as he said, in response to a second lament on Emmeline's part that New York was at present so "dreadfully quiet": "I didn't care much for going to dances and five o'clock teas, I assure you. One has so many of those across the water. I merely wanted to look about me and observe how the town has really altered since I last saw it. And then I thought something of going into the West. Now there's Chicago, for example. I want to see that. I hear it has become so enormous and so handsome."

Emmeline broke into a mocking laugh, which Elaine echoed. "Oh, don't think of going to Chicago!" exclaimed the latter. "Nobody *ever* does, except on business."

"Well," smiled Massereene, "I shall go on business. I want to make a business of observation."

"But it won't interest you," said Emmeline. "There's nothing in the world to see there. All those Western cities are so tiresome. The Rocky Mountains are probably stupendous, and that sort of thing; but our entire West is fearfully monotonous and full of semi-barbarians. We always pity people who are obliged to go out into those half-civilized regions. If it were not for the Englishmen who land here with a wild desire to shoot buffaloes, we would never bother ourselves that such dreary stretches of country exist."

Emmeline spoke with an arrogance of which she was completely unconscious. She represented a class of New Yorkers who hold our splendid American interior in a contempt as unjust as it is ridiculous.

Only the foreigner who enters New York for the first time and associates with the cliques and clans that base all their noteworthiness upon a smart imitation of habits, deportment, verbal accent, and personal vesture practised reverentially three thousand miles eastward, can appreciate how much typical partisanship this young lady had just exhibited.

"I don't want to shoot buffaloes," said Massereene; "but I confess that I entertain respect of the most substantial kind for anything that resembles a prairie."

"Oh," comically wailed Elaine, "that is the way all you Englishmen feel as soon as you get over here."

"Please don't call *me* an Englishman," Massereene admonished. "I'm a born American, you know. I've never forgotten it; I should be sorry to do so, for I'm proud of it."

"Oh, of course," assented Emmeline, with a shrug of her solid, symmetrical shoulders. "It's all very well for you to *say* that — you, who've been through Cambridge, and go wherever you please in London, and can take the steamer home again as soon as you're thoroughly bored here." She looked incredulously at Elaine, who returned her look in the same way; and then both the girls laughed in concert, as though they understood very well what an easy bit of harmless posing it was for such an adopted Englishman as this to air a little dainty patriotism.

But Massereene at once answered, in a voice which he had lowered and otherwise changed, and which instantly made both his hearers comprehend his extreme earnestness as clearly as if he had used no small amount of ardor and emphasis.

"All that I say I mean. And I regard this country,

not England, as my real home. I've no right to do
otherwise, and if I had the right I should not possess
the inclination. I'm a good deal of a traveller; I've
been in many other lands; during those three years or
so since I last met you young ladies, I've seen a large
part of the Orient, besides some rather out-of-the-way
places in Europe; and I come to America — to these
United States, in fact — with a belief that I shall be
less disappointed here than I have ever been elsewhere,
and that I shall find more true civilization, more healthy
national greatness, than all my former experiences will
be able to offer me."

He spoke these words with so much gentle serenity
that they quite lost the form of disagreement and contradiction, while retaining the significance of each.
Possibly Elaine failed to perceive either their full drift
or force; for almost immediately after he had ended
she broke in, with much lightness : " I begin to think
that nothing makes one such a good American as to
dwell outside of one's country."

"Wait till you've been here a few months, Jasper,"
said Emmeline.

"I hope to wait that long," replied Massereene, with
the implication (as often was noticeable in some of
his most placid speeches) of meaning more than he
said.

"Oh," suddenly cried Elaine, as her brother Aspinwall now entered the room; " here's a young gentleman
who would be very glad to change New York with you
for London! . . . Aspy, I hope you haven't forgotten
our cousin, Jasper Massereene."

Forgotten Jasper Massereene! Elaine might as well
have asked her brother if he had forgotten the Houses

of Parliament or the Thames Embankment. He was indeed a mere boy then, though it *was* only three years ago. But during that London May had first budded in his soul the eager desire to be what he had since unfalterably and inflexibly become — a dude. The very word had not then shaped its quaint monosyllable out of that etymologic mist whence it has so phantasmally drifted to us, but it now expresses to perfection, nevertheless, just what Master Aspinwall Satterthwaite found himself yearning to become. Masscreene was wholly unconscious of the secret reverence with which the young New Yorker watched every fresh pair of trousers, coat, or waistcoat in which he appeared. He dressed, like most Londoners of his age and position, somewhat smartly and carefully. But to Aspinwall he was the silent preacher of a new and precious creed. The unnumbered refinements, delights, intoxications of dress were now for the first time revealed to this noble-minded boy's expanding intellect. Aspinwall had since bloomed forth as the kind of young gentleman who is considerably more exercised about the spotlessness of his gloves than of his moral character, and who would humiliate himself to an amazing degree rather than wear a hat which had not come out of Piccadilly. He shook hands with Massereene, actually daring to pass upon the latter's clothes a rapid mental criticism, and not a thoroughly favorable one at that. So does the past perish, and the influence of memory and tradition grow even as the dust that we sprinkle upon the wind ! Still, success and achievement have their stimulating retrospections. "By Jove," thought Aspinwall, while he buttoned one of his gloves, "the man isn't as well dressed as I am !" And poor Massereene, equally ignorant of either this most virile creature's former worship or his present alienation, looked as amiable as usual, and tried to crush a doubt lest his visit on the Satterthwaites that afternoon might not prove a trifle fatiguing.

" Where are you going, Aspy ? " Emmeline presently asked of her brother, who carried his hat besides wearing his gloves. " Or have you just come in ? "

" I'm going to see the coaches parade," returned Aspinwall; and before he could add something sullenly regretful about his father's coach (for reasons explainable on the ground of family bereavement) not being to-day in the general line of the forthcoming procession, Elaine rather excitedly said :

" Oh, let us all go. It's only a few streets from here, Jasper — Madison Square, you know."

" I recollect Madison Square very well," said Massereene.

" It's our apology for not having a Hyde Park," said Aspinwall, sitting forward in his chair, stooping a good deal, and knocking the but of a phenomenal silver-studded stick that he carried against the knuckles of one gloved hand. " It will seem a pretty small affair to you, Jasper, after the big London show."

" Well, never mind whether it does or not," exclaimed Emmeline. " You'll go, won't you, Jasper, if Elly and I run upstairs and put on our bonnets ? "

" I'll go with pleasure," said Massereene.

Aspinwall had been right. It did seem a pretty small affair, this New York apeing of a custom so essentially English. A short walk brought himself and the Satterthwaite party into the neighborhood of the Brunswick Hotel, that establishment which began by

appropriating to its uses a private residence and then
absorbed other contiguous ones, until it now looms
from the corner of Twenty-Sixth Street and Fifth
Avenue as a curiously ill-proportioned and many-
windowed pile, shorn of all dignity by its irregular
roofage. Massereene and his companions reached the
great gathered throng of people a trifle too late.
Eleven coaches paraded that day, and their place of
rendezvous had been the east side of Madison Square,
opposite that row of mansions which is perhaps the
most advantageously and salubriously situated of any
in our narrow and building-crowded metropolis. One
or two of the coaches had now passed the hotel, and
the rest were slowly following, amid the continuous
mellow clamor of horns made by some of their various
occupants. The small, well-trained horses, four at each
vehicle, stepped along with a brisk yet suppressed
energy. They seemed to be conscious of the rainbow
burdens that they drew, for the coaches themselves
were severally tinted blue, green, red, and yellow, in
chromatic disdain of all sombre panelling, and the ladies
and gentlemen who had climbed up to their accommodating summits were clad in costumes of a most unconventional gayety. The gentlemen wore "white hats,"
with a few dusky exceptions, and many of them were
apparelled in pearl-hued coats with large gaudy nose-
gays bulging from the lapels of these. The ladies, as
next day's papers recorded of them, wore robes of
" mouse-colored brocade," " white silk trimmed with
flowered foulard," " crushed strawberry satin," and
numberless other stuffs quite as costly and modish. . . .
Massereene watched it all, and through his mind, as
he did so, may have slipped the silent, instinctive com-

ment : " *C'est magnifique, mais ce n'est pas la guerre.*"

It was certainly, in a limited way, magnificent ; and yet to him who had seen, season after season, the far more diverting and spectacular exhibition of Hyde Park, with such superior amplitude of local surrounding and a multiplicity of coaches which put this pitiable eleven into humble numerical shade, it seemed like the most meagre attempted repetition of memorial grandeurs. It was English, and yet it was somehow not English enough to be authentic. He felt a kind of pained shame as he continued to look upon it ; the very expressions of the men and women who sat upon the coaches were in many cases not those which he would have desired to see on the faces of his country-people. They were often smiling enough, but they were daintily arrogant and even childishly pretentious as well. Perhaps they had been that in London, too ; but he had not thought of it there. It had possibly suited England ; it smote him like the most unrepublican of discords now and here. Emmeline and Elaine and Aspinwall were delivering their keenly interesting remarks at his side, but he scarcely realized the sense of what they spoke ; he was thinking whether such a proceeding as the present one were not a shame and a folly to be regretted and denounced.

" There's Minnie Saltonstall," Elaine was saying. " Did you *ever* see such an unbecoming hat ? . . . And Lou Rivington's feather, Em — *do* look ! . . . Oh, dear, this is the first time for an age that *we* haven't been in the coaching-parade, too. . . . Aspy, stop trying to make Jenny Hudsonbank see you. . . . Just think ! I was to have worn my pink silk, new from

Worth, and papa had filled his coach with such a jolly lot of people after we'd been invited to go on the others. . . . Look at Sadie Van Tassel; she got the box-seat, after all, on the Van Courtlandt coach, didn't she?"

"Don't speak so loudly, Elly," remonstrated Emmeline. "Recollect where we are. People are hearing you."

These people, whether they heard or did not hear, appeared to Massereene as un-English in the extreme. They had, for the most part, none of that stolid recipient quiescence which usually marks the British looker-on during any such distinctly patrician manifestation. They either stared greedily at the whole performance, as though it were in all respects novel to them, or they contemplated it with sinister grades of expression that varied from smouldering sarcasm to overt hostility. But the latter sign was, after all, not frequent, nor was the locality one to call it forth. A good deal of socialism may lurk among the beer-saloons of the Bowery and its contiguous streets; but Fifth Avenue, in the jocund sunshine of a May afternoon, is rather too blithe a place for such grim pedestrians as these to choose it. Massereene soon caught, however, some grunted sounds of disgust not far away from him, and on turning saw that a massive-framed Irishman, with a ruffianly look about his very soiled face, had just addressed a mate nearly as clumsy and unkempt as himself.

"Jim," said the man, with a broad, red, snarling sort of grin, "is them fellers lords, d'ye think?"

"They luk 's if they wus," growled Jim, under a

clotted auburn moustache, while he scratched one
bristly jowl with dirt-caked nails.

His comrade gave a bitter, gruff, contemptuous
laugh. "*American* lords and ladies — dooks and
duchusses?" he exclaimed, so shrilly that perhaps
a score or so of people heard him. "They ain't the
genooine make, not quite, but they're warranted to
wear, so they are, almost ez good. Come along, Jim."
And he drew his friend away, with another scoffing
laugh. "It's a queer kind o' country, this Ameriky,
annyhow. It's alwus a-screamin' out that it's freer
nur any other, an' it screams this so loud that half
the fools in the wurld is gettin' to believe it."

The man's voice died into distance, but the meaning
of what he had said stayed frettingly with Massereene
for some minutes afterward. Then he shook off the
little chill, as of omen, that it gave him — the presentiment that his own hopes and expectations might
not be satisfied and confirmed. And meanwhile he
heard Emmeline's voice at his side, murmuring rather
petulantly: "What are those dreadful men saying? I
do think they ought to have dividing-lines, or something of that sort, at times like this. One has no idea
whom one is being jostled against."

This had for Massereene a decidedly "West End"
sound. But he made no reply, and watched the entire procession out, feeling rather bored at having to
do so, as not a single person on any of the coaches
chanced to be known to him. Now and then he fancied that he had seen one of the men in some London
drawing-room, or perhaps in some restaurant like the
Hotel Bristol or the *Café Royal* in Regent Street.
But he was never quite sure — the huge English

capital is so huge, and human countenances, during all occurrences of the daily routine, so rush there upon the vision. It was a relief to find the parade ended and to meet, as they at length did, Mr. Bleecker Satterthwaite, strolling along with a flower in his buttonhole and the general demeanor of a man for whom life offers no requisition more of a *chose obligatoire* than whist, billiards or coach-driving.

Satterthwaite was apparently very glad to meet Massereene. "My dear boy," he said, "it's a devilish shame that you couldn't have seen something of all this fun. "I'd have crowded you in at the last minute on top of my coach — yes, I would, no matter how the girls and the men fussed and fumed about it. And I was to have such a jolly load . . . I suppose the girls have told you. Houston Van Rensselaer's dead — my wife's brother, you know. Decency's decency . . . but I never really knew the man; he was forever living abroad; he hated it here. . . . Well, Jasper, old boy, I'm awfully glad to see you." He put one hand caressingly on Massereene's shoulder as they all walked together up toward the Satterthwaite residence. "I was sure you'd come over at last. You look just the same, except that you're a trifle stouter."

"I've gained a little in weight," said Massereene.

This very ordinary remark struck Bleecker Satterthwaite as something especially apt and neat. Almost any remark that Massereene could have made would thus have appealed to his kinsman. The father of Emmeline and Elaine was delighted to have seen his daughters in this wholly unexpected company. He had already swept his eyes over the *personnel* of

Masscreene, and let his paternal soul swiftly whisper
to him that he was a possible son-in-law of surpassing
value.   Jasper had nearly always met precisely this
kind of parental welcome.   He was so notoriously
wealthy, he had such a presentable, reputable, attractive mien.   Manœuvring English mammas of the
highest position — wives of county grandees, baronets,
and even noblemen — had long ago forgiven him the
drawback of his American birth in recalling that he
was rich, handsome, a *parti*, and that he shared the
blood of the Earl of Meath.

Satterthwaite patted him on the shoulder and jo-
cosely said : " My dear Jasper, don't you mind a few
more pounds or so of weight.   You can stand them.
You're tall enough ; they don't take away from your
good looks.   It's deuced pleasant, old fellow, to see
that you haven't forgotten us.   This is a bad season
— infernally bad season for New York.   But I'll
write you down at the Metropolitan and Gramercy
clubs.   I'll have you made a six-months' visitor at
both, if you'll agree to stay here as long as that."

" Thanks," said Masscreene.   " I shall certainly stop
here as long as six months."

When Bleecker Satterthwaite had reconducted him
into the Fifth Avenue mansion, and Emmeline, Elaine,
Aspinwall and the head of the house himself had all
gathered about him with a profusion of conversational
hospitality, he began to feel the utter coldness and
worldliness of this family as he had never felt it before.   They had no subject to discuss except *banalité*
of the dreariest kind.   Emmeline was a little different
from the others ; her mind seemed now and then of an
opposite order ; but her promises of a more interesting

development soon faded. Masscreene was about taking his leave, having courteously refused an invitation to remain and dine, when Mrs. Satterthwaite made her appearance.

She greeted him warmly. But she appeared to forget him a moment afterward, and turned toward her husband and daughters.

"I have *such* news for you all," she exclaimed, sinking into a chair and beginning to untie her bonnet-strings rather agitatedly.

Everybody except Massereene gave a concerned start. "I do hope it's nothing bad about Delaplaine," said her husband.

"Mamma!" exclaimed Emmeline, rising and coming forward to where her mother sat. "Is he dead?"

"Oh, yes," followed Elaine, rising too, and remembering that her anxiety (such as it was) had "Cousin Jasper" for an observer. "You do mean that Mr. Delaplaine is dead; don't you, mamma?"

"No," replied Mrs. Satterthwaite, as she removed the bonnet. "I mean something much . . . well, much stranger than that."

## XII.

Before Olivia had taken more than twenty paces, on having closed the door of the sick man's room, she met somebody who soon addressed her dazed senses as her aunt, Mrs. Satterthwaite. And yet the girl's mind was in so flurried a state that she did not even recognize, at first, the person who accosted her.

"Olivia," queried her aunt, "what has happened to make you look so dreadfully disturbed, my dear?"

Mrs. Satterthwaite knew perfectly well what had happened. She caught both of her niece's hands and held them tightly while she scanned the delicate, alarmed, bewildered face of their possessor.

"I have had a great shock," Olivia said, drawing a deep breath. Then she gave a little sigh, followed by a quick, distressful glance. "Did you have any idea that he — he was going to speak like that?" she asked.

"Like that?" repeated Mrs. Satterthwaite, as her niece broke away from her. "Why, what do you mean? What has he said?"

"Forgive me, Aunt Augusta!" now fell from Olivia. She was pierced by an abrupt self-reproach for having done her aunt an injustice. "Of course you did not know; how should you know? Mr. Delaplaine has asked me to marry him — *me!* On his death-bed, too! Think of it!"

Mrs. Satterthwaite had thought a great deal more about it than her poor young kinswoman remotely

imagined. She now threw open the door of an apartment next to that from which Olivia had just fled.
"Come in here, my dear," she murmured, and they
entered together. She had not been quite sure of her
forthcoming policy until now, and now she suddenly
felt herself to be quite sure. There was a large, comfortable, tufted lounge in the chamber, and as Olivia
sank into one corner of this her aunt sank at her side.
"I will be very frank with you," Mrs. Satterthwaite
now went on. "I will confess to you that I had
suspected something of this sort would take place."

"Mr. Delaplaine told you, then —?"

"He could make the matter plain to me without
precisely telling . . . do you not understand? And
now pray let me know just what passed between you."

Olivia clasped her hands together in her lap, lowered
her eyes, and gave a clear if somewhat hesitating
account of all that had taken place. When she finished, her aunt allowed quite a marked interval of
silence to ensue. And then she said, very measuredly
and reflectively:

"My dear, it seems to me a most noble action on
his part. And if you were to do as he requests, no
one could reasonably blame you. Marriage, Olivia, is
a very sacred relation; there should be love on both
sides; it is folly to affirm there should *not* be. But
this proposed marriage is an affair outside of all ordinary considerations. It is — or it would be, my dear
— a marriage of duty. I don't only mean duty to
your dead father's old friend; I mean duty to your
dead father himself."

"Aunt Augusta! what are you saying?"

"The truth, Olivia — or at least, the truth as I feel

it and see it. Mr. Delaplaine cannot live. He wishes
to save you endless trouble and vexation in the retaining of that inheritance which he has left you after he
is gone. He told you this—you admit he did. Perhaps you shrink from taking such a step because you
believe it would be so hollow a mockery. But I can't
agree with you on that point; I'm older than you,
and I've had a great deal more experience than you
can possibly have had, and I am convinced that the
whole proceeding (if you *should* consent to it) would
rank among the tenderest and sweetest concessions
that a young girl like yourself could make . . . My
dear girl, it isn't as if you were marrying an old man
for his money!"

Olivia nodded her head with positiveness here.
"Yes, it is," she exclaimed. "It isn't anything else.
I would be marrying an old man on his death-bed for
his money. Just that; you can't make it different
from that; I'm sure that you can't."

"Let us see if I cannot, Olivia. He was the most
faithful and devoted friend your father ever had. By
leaving you his fortune he confers upon you a benefit
which you may most honorably accept. But he has
relatives; and then, most probably, the members of
those charitable associations to which he had bequeathed so much, having learned long ago of his
intended bequests, would array themselves against the
administration of a will that had been changed a short
time before his death. . . . All such distressing results as these, a marriage like the one which Mr.
Delaplaine proposes would swiftly and forever prevent. . . . Are you following me, my dear Olivia? You
somehow look as if you were not . . . as if you . . ."

"Oh, I hear every word that you say?" exclaimed Olivia, rising from the lounge and beginning to pace the floor with drooped head and with hands joined behind her back. Mrs. Satterthwaite remained seated, watching her as she thus unexpectedly deported herself.

"This promises well," thought the astute lady. She kept silent now, waiting for her niece to speak again.

"If I *did* do it I can't help but feel certain that I would act with a — a mean, grasping selfishness." Olivia said nothing more for some little time, though she still continued her nervous walk from end to end of the apartment. She was thinking of her life at Mrs. Ottarson's — of the odd, coarse, uncongenial people whom she was forced to meet there — of how the changed conditions of her days had begun to affect her with an incessant erosive and unconquerable discontent. She was thinking of brief moods which had recently visited her when she had told herself that it would perhaps have been wiser, more judicious, to have entered, even on terms of genteel dependence, into the household of either the Auchinclosses or the Satterthwaites. There she might have had her moments of chagrin, irritation, humiliation, but at least she would have been among persons who knew the *convenances*, who were not continually reminding her that she came of gentlefolk and they did not.

"You say, Aunt Augusta, that it would be a tender and sweet concession on my part. It wouldn't be at all that, for if I *were* to consent I should have only the realization that I had done so on my own account, and not Mr. Delaplaine's."

"That would not prevent the good consequences of what you *did* do, my dear."

"Good consequences!" As she repeated her aunt's words, Olivia paused directly in front of Mrs. Satterthwaite, and looked down at this lady with eyes full of suppressed fire. "And what would he know or care when he was dead?"

"It might make him die easier."

Olivia nodded once or twice, gnawing her lips. Her face appeared to have aged within the last few minutes; she had never seemed less maid-like and more womanly than now, while her features were influenced by traces of the severest trouble. "That is perhaps true enough," she exclaimed, beginning her restive walk again. "But *my* motive! I can't deceive myself by not admitting that I would be marrying him for no other reason than the money he has settled upon me. If he wanted me to marry him simply as an act of benevolence, or a — a tribute of sentiment before he died, would I hesitate for one instant in my refusal?"

"Then you do hesitate now, my dear?" asked Mrs. Satterthwaite.

The calm question, falling in modulated tones from this wiliest and most strategic of women, dealt Olivia a kind of sting.

"I — I do not *want* to hesitate!" she stammered, knotting her hands together.

"My darling, you want to think it over all alone by yourself," said Mrs. Satterthwaite, rising, going up to her, and kissing her on one check. "And you shall do so. . . . There, I will leave you for ten or fifteen minutes. Your aunt Letitia was to be here this afternoon; perhaps she has arrived. . . . And, Olivia, love, remember that you will be taking a step of which we

both approve. . . . Candidly, my dear, I believe that if
you do *not* take it you will feel pangs of conscience
hereafter."

"Especially if his relatives carry a successful lawsuit against me," said Olivia, with a swift irony that
was quite unwonted in her, and showed how sharp a
secret moral revolt had begun against the temptation
that had latterly assailed her.

Mrs. Satterthwaite patted her on the shoulder. She
understood, with her worldly shrewdness, that this
bitter sentence, so filled with feverish self-reproach,
had its practical promise of surrender. "You argue
foolishly, Olivia," she murmured. "If your stay at
Mrs. Ottarson's has fatigued you, and you feel yourself unsuited for its . . . peculiar requirements, that is
no reason —— "

"But I have not said that it fatigued me," broke in
Olivia, with a querulous, perturbed, self-contradictory
look straight into her aunt's composed eyes.

"I grant that you have not, my dear. . . . We will
let that pass. . . . But you must not assert to your own
mind that the impulse would be a selfish one. You
behave more heroically than you now perceive."

"Heroically! Aunt Augusta!"

"Yes, yes. I use the word in no careless way. It
would all be a very fine and admirable service for you
to perform. Your nice sense of right will make that
plain to you hereafter. . . . There, now, my dear, I
will leave you to think it over, as I said." At this
point Mrs. Satterthwaite glided toward the door which
led into the outer hall. "Pray wait here until I return. If you decide that your consent is impossible,
*please* don't think that either your Aunt Letitia or I

will attempt to use with you the least strenuous persuasion. Oh, no, indeed. Everything will be left entirely with yourself — with your well-known regard for your poor lost father — and with your own interpretation of duty toward the truest and most faithful friend whom that father ever knew."

She passed at once from the room after thus speaking. "It's *in* the girl to consent," she rapidly assured her own thoughts. "That awful woman, with her boarding-house *entourage*, has had just the effect I hoped for. And advice will do the rest — or else I'm immensely wrong in my whole estimate."

Olivia, left alone, dropped into a chair and stared at the floor. She had been slightly affected by her aunt's train of argument. There was no moral reason why she should marry Spencer Delaplaine. She did not owe it to her dead father; she did not owe it to her father's dying friend. The oath of marriage was too holy a one to be taken except because her heart willed that she should swear it. If Delaplaine had been a man whom she had loved, this deathbed union would have its complete justification, and its romantic sanctity as well. But he was not such a man, and to marry him would be, under existing circumstances, a sacrifice unsupported by rational requirement. Her father would never have asked her to make it; it must mean so much to a girl of the least sensitiveness, the least sensibility

"And yet" her musing continued, "I stop to brood over the matter. I don't refuse, once and for all, to give it a further minute of consideration. Why is this?"

She met and faced the exact solution   It was be-

cause she would. reap material benefit by becoming
Spencer Delaplaine's wife. She was far too honest a
custodian of her own mind and heart not to insist
upon flouting all duplicity with either. There lay the
nude, unflattering truth. To allow this marriage
would be to soil her own purity, to debase her ideal,
no matter what Mrs. Satterthwaite might urge in
refutation.

But desire pushed its claim against the monitions of
honor. Those past boarding-school days came back
vividly to Olivia now. She recalled the sudden self-
abandonment that would almost seem to thrust her
over the brink of some misdeed. . . . Was it not the
same at this moment? Did she not feel that old malign force at work?— the insubordinate obstinacy of
spirit —the reaching out after a boon forbidden her
by order, law, propriety, whatever name was held
fittest to bestow on the opposing stress? Yet she
might resist if she chose. It had always been thus in
former days, when comparative trifles were brought
into question ; and now, when the trial was of larger
moment and stronger meaning, she also might resist if
so inclined.

But, instead, she began to ask herself whether men
and women would be liable to call such a marriage on
her part a sordid and cold-blooded one. True, it would
be almost like standing at the side of a coffin, and becoming the bride of the corpse ; and yet, when everything was known, as everything must be at length
known, society would doubtless take the same view of
her conduct as that of Mrs. Satterthwaite.

And then — the subsequent gain ! Could she shut
her eyes to that ? All the freedom and independence

of a married woman would be hers, to go whither she
pleased, to do a hundred things that in an unwedded
member of her sex would fall under the head of pre-
sumption or immodesty. The fortune bequeathed her
would be safe from litigious attacks. Olivia knew
very little about the methods of legal administration
in any country, but it was not hard for her to assume
with confidence that as the wife of Delaplaine her
title of heirship would prove unassailable. And what
good might she accomplish with her fortune! She
had often declared to herself, during the latter years of
her girlhood, that the one most cogent means of securing earthly happiness was in the vigilant and careful
discharge of charitable offices. Once possessed of
wealth, she would never find contentment in such idle
pre-eminence as that which her father's two sisters
were now enjoying. Not she! It was no sophistry
that wrought tricksy spells upon her here. She was
willing to admit her own selfishness in yielding at all
to the voice that lured and enticed. But this was the
generous and high-minded side, so to speak, of that
very selfishness. Had she not again and again meditated upon the good that she might do with the money
of which her orphanage would, as she once so firmly
trusted, make her the mistress? In the stillness and
suspense of her father's last hours thoughts like these
had often come to her. It had never been among her
musings, for some strange reason, to dream, as other
girls were forever doing, of a possible gallant, gracious
and irreproachable husband. A curious, delicate, vir-
ginal fierceness had risen within her the moment she
let her brain ponder that probability. What we have
heard her tell Mrs. Ottarson on the subject of never

meaning to marry, had been spoken straight from the maidenly innocence of her own chaste, candid, foolishly devout conviction.

And now it looked very much as if she would indeed marry — though after a fashion startlingly different from that to which her former protestations had borne reference. . . . She had for some little time ceased to pace the floor of the apartment. She had thrown herself into a half-reclining posture upon the lounge when Mrs. Satterthwaite softly opened the door and passed into the room.

"My dear," said this lady, drawing quite close to her, "I have seen your Aunt Letitia, who advises . . ."

"Well," broke in Olivia, lifting up her head and showing how pale her face was, "what does Aunt Letitia advise?"

"That you do not trouble yourself any further regarding this matter. If your mind is not made up yet . . . or if you still feel that you had best not consent . . ."

Olivia rose, here, with suddenness. "My mind is made up," she said, "and I do consent."

"My dear child!"

"Yes, I consent. Neither you nor Aunt Letitia could ever persuade me that I am doing right — that I am doing what poor papa would sanction — that I am serving any one's true interests except my own." . . . She paused, just here, and the feeblest and saddest of laughs made at her lips a sound that seemed only formed to die there as drearily as it did die. "But I am resolved. You may let Mr. Delaplaine know, whenever you choose, that I am . . . ready."

During the next half-hour or so Olivia felt herself beset by a fright that quickened her pulses and more than once sent shivers through her frame. But her determination had been taken. She moved nervously about the room, hardly aware that she did not still remain seated. She knew that her aunt Augusta had gone away again to superintend certain preparations. She was waiting. Sometimes her heart galloped so wildly that she believed herself on the verge of breaking down altogether and of rushing out to find Mrs. Satterthwaite and avow her disability, her change of mood, her withdrawal of everything that she had lately affirmed.

But no such hysterical act really resulted from her perturbation. She did not herself realize how strong was the new desire that filled and ruled her. Unable to do more than despise it, she still perversely clung to the idea of its gratification. Her choice was made. . . . When Mrs. Satterthwaite re-entered the room it did not seem to Olivia as if she had been away, this last time, longer than five minutes at the utmost.

Mrs. Auchincloss, on the present occasion, followed closely behind her sister. She kissed her niece and pressed the girl's hand; a sense of duty was everywhere manifest in her behavior. You could see it, too, in the lines of her lips, the angle at which she held her nose, the very management of her eyelids.

"There is something truly beautiful in your having consented, my dear," she whispered to Olivia.

"I don't think there is anything beautiful in it at all, Aunt Letitia," was the reply, given with a blunt promptitude which bespoke more self-possession than Olivia's kindled eyes and pale, twitching lips other-

wise evidenced. " But if the affair is really to be gone
through with, I — I, should like it begun — yes, and
ended — as soon as possible."

Mrs. Auchincloss still retained Olivia's hand ; she
softly patted it with her other disengaged hand, now.
" I have heard," she said, " that you insist upon sepa-
rating from your proposed step any . . . er . . . com-
passionate or . . . er . . . duteous impulse. But I
*know* that this exists in you; your Aunt Augusta
knows it as well. We both . . ."

Here Mrs. Satterthwaite gave a little dry cough of
pronounced impatience. She saw that Olivia's condition was more excited than when she had last quitted
the chamber. The girl looked in no mood to endure
much discussion of her resolve. How was it certain
that Mrs. Auchincloss's efforts to moralize character-
istically on the subject might not result in some sort of
impetuous and disastrous recoil ? Besides, Delaplaine's
malady had assumed still more fatal symptoms. It
was by no means a surety that he would last until
morning. What was to be done had best be quickly
done. And so Mrs. Satterthwaite translated her admonitory cough, as it were, by at once saying : —

" Letitia, I really think we should lose no time."

Olivia drew her hand away from the caressing clasp
of her elder aunt with a vehemence of movement that
admitted no misinterpretation.

" Yes," she exclaimed, " do not let us lose any time.
It might turn out very badly for me if I did so."

The irony in that final sentence could not fail to
affect its hearers. It caused them to exchange a look.
It made Mrs. Auchincloss pretend that she was grievously surprised ; it sent from the eyes of Mrs. Satter-

thwaite the glance that seemed to say: "Don't disturb her any more than she is disturbed now. Leave good alone. Don't you see that she may break down if we are not careful!"

The apartment of Delaplaine, as Olivia, between her two aunts, entered it a little while afterward, was considerably less dim than when she had hurried thence hardly an hour ago. Two or three figures stood near the bed, and one of these, from its clerical attire, left no doubt that it was the minister summoned to perform the wedding ceremony. Delaplaine lay with open eyes and an expression of suffering on his hueless face. But he smiled faintly as his gaze rested upon Olivia. Mrs. Satterthwaite gently pushed her niece to the edge of the bed. An extreme stillness reigned in the apartment.

Olivia heard her own heart beat as the sick man stretched out his hand and slowly clasped hers. She let him draw it toward him. Her head grew a little dizzy then, and she feared that she might fall. But soon this most tormenting sensation passed, and she perceived that the gentleman in the clerical dress was close beside her. He looked down at Delaplaine, who was breathing somewhat heavily now, and whose eyes would close for a few seconds, quickly to re-open and seek the face of Olivia, with a sharp relief that had the meaning of "Ah! you are still there!" and with a sudden tightening of his feverish fingers about the girl's palm. And in response to the clergyman's mute inquiry, Delaplaine nodded a very faint affirmative.

The large, soft hand of the clergyman fell upon his and Olivia's where they lay joined. And then a low, rich voice broke the silence, repeating the Episcopal wedding service. . . . To Olivia it all had a dream-like unreality and rapidity. The ring had been slipped on her finger, and the last words of the sacred ritual were being uttered, when she became aware that Delaplaine's breathing was louder and more difficult than it had yet sounded. "If he should die before we are fully married!" swept through her mind. . . . A little later her aunts drew her away; he seemed in great pain, and she heard him moan, "My side! my side!" as if the chief agony were there.

Both her aunts kissed her, and then she let them lead her from the room

"Will he live much longer?" she asked in low and trembling tones.

Mrs. Satterthwaite spoke: "The doctors think not."

"I — I wish to go, now," said Olivia. "I will of course come to-morrow, and send this evening from Aunt Thyrza's to find out how he is. But I would prefer to go, now."

She saw amazement depict itself on Mrs. Auchincloss's face. Mrs. Satterthwaite raised both hands and shook her head in energetic negative. The latter immediately spoke, saying:

"Go now, Olivia! Why, my *dear*, of what *can* you be thinking? "And then Mrs. Auchincloss: "Go *now*, Olivia!"

They had all three just entered the same room whence Olivia had passed in their company only a short while since. The girl stood in the centre of this room, after thus being unexpectedly addressed, and let her eyes wander from the countenance of one companion to that of the other.

"I don't understand you at all," she faltered, "why can I not go now? I have done what you required me to do. I—I have married him. He is very ill; he is going to die." Here she paused. The pain of remorse was already at work in her. She had been quite certain the remorse would come. In other times, after she had yielded, and doggedly committed the very fault which she recognized as a fault, she had always foreseen the stabs of conscience to which, as it were, she had both rashly and deliberately committed herself. But the remorse, like the culpability, had been of so different kind, then! A tremulous nervous weakness, a gloom of spirits, a shrinking from the arraignments of her own mortified and incensed moral obligations, had commenced to play fatal havoc with her inward peace. She felt none of the calmer reaction that with many natures would succeed fulfilment of a purpose conceived in turmoil of soul and executed as the means to a self-serving attainment.

"You can't expect me to stay here," she at length continued, with a wistful though petulant ring in her voice, "until . . . until *it* happens. It may not happen for hours yet—perhaps not for a day or two longer."

Mrs. Auchincloss drew near to her and laid a light but firm touch on her arm. "Olivia," this model of all the higher and better duties now exclaimed, "do you not see that your present part is to behave as if it might not happen at all?"

"As if . . . it . . . might not happen at all?" she repeated brokenly. "No; I don't see that I should so behave, Aunt Letitia. At least not to *you*."

"Your aunt is right, my dear," said Mrs. Satterthwaite. "Remember, you are a wife now."

"Yes . . . I am his wife. . . . And I shall soon be his widow."

Mrs. Auchincloss gave her sister a despairing glance. " But, Olivia, you are not his widow *yet.*"

"No," was the answer. She looked down at the wedding-ring on her finger. " Not yet. Well? And if I am not?"

Mrs. Auchincloss was about to speak, at this point, but Mrs. Satterthwaite silenced her by a gesture half imploring and half commanding.

"Your proper place, then, is *here*—here in this house. Don't you see that it is? . . . Word will be sent to Mrs. Ottarson, if you wish. Change of attire, my dear, and all that, will be attended to. But you ought not to leave this house . . . you must not leave it."

The door of the room had been left ajar. At this moment the graceful and handsome youth whom Olivia had seen not long ago, and whose name she had learned to be Adrian Etherege, crossed the threshold. He went at once to Mrs. Satterthwaite and said, in his clear, soft, winning voice:

" Mr. Delaplaine is suffering very much, but he has asked to see you."

"I will go to him," was the lady's ready answer. She made a step or two toward the door, and then turned, addressing Olivia:

" You will remain here till I come back, my dear? You will remain with your Aunt Letitia?"

Olivia made no answer. She had fixed her eyes upon Adrian Etherege. As if possessed by a sudden idea, she approached the young man, standing close at his side before he himself seemed to be aware of what she had done.

"Tell me," she said, "do *you* think that Mr. Delaplaine will live through the night?"

He whom she thus questioned gave a start. His large, luminous brown eyes lost all their gentleness, for an instant, as they met Olivia's. A hardness, a bitterness, for which she was totally unprepared, seized and altered his charming visage. . . . And then the change vanished as swiftly as it had come. . . . It had already passed when he responded, in a voice full of respectful courtesy:

"I can't tell you how long Mr. Delaplaine may live. But I do not believe he is dying *now* at all. He is very ill, but I have every hope that he will recover."

"Recover?" murmured Olivia. . . . She shot a wild look at either of her two kinswomen. Both of them avoided it.

"Recover?" she again said . . . In another minute the room had begun to whirl about with her. She knew that she was staggering as she tried to find her seat. One of her aunts — she could not tell which one — helped her to find it.

"You are ill, my dear," she heard a voice say. She could not make out to whom the voice belonged, her brain seemed in such a tumult.

"Recover?" she murmured once more, though unaware that for the third time this word had left her quivering lips.

## XIII.

THE faintness that had assailed Olivia soon left her. When she sat up and looked about her once more with a clear gaze, Adrian Etherege had quitted the room. Her first words were spoken to Mrs. Satterthwaite. "Do you believe this to be true?" she asked. "You mean what Adrian just said?" she replied. "Yes; that is precisely what I do mean." Mrs. Satterthwaite had gone toward the door, and her hand was already on its knob. A request from Spencer Delaplaine at such an hour was not to be disregarded. "Positively, my dear," she said, "I do *not* believe it to be true. This young man, perhaps, finds it hard to realize that death has actually come. . . . There, I must leave you. Remain with your Aunt Letitia . . . promise me that you will."

Olivia made no answer, and Mrs. Satterthwaite quitted the room with a furtive and telling signal to her sister. The latter understood perfectly; she was enjoined to repress all tendency on their niece's part in the direction of escape. And Mrs. Auchincloss was prepared to oppose that course in Olivia with quite as much vigor as any which Mrs. Satterthwaite could have drawn upon.

Olivia had seated herself now. She was very pale, but her former excitement had apparently quite vanished. Mrs. Auchincloss took a seat on the lounge at her side.

"Have you such a horror, then, of Mr. Delaplaine's recovery, my dear?" asked her aunt.

"Why should I not have?" she answered in a voice that rang firm and steady, but held a new hollow note, like the emanation from some great hidden dread or anxiety. "If I thought he would get well, Aunt Letitia," she went on, "I am almost certain that I would kill myself."

"Olivia! What *are* you saying?"

"I would either kill myself or else hide from *him* —somewhere, miles and miles distant—where he would not dream of finding me." She gave a slight, dolorous laugh here. "But he *would* find me, would he not, in these days of telegraphs, detectives, and newspapers, if he only searched enough?"

"My child!"

"Oh, the very thought is so terrible! It has given me a kind of benumbed feeling. I was merely fluttered and *distraite* before, thinking of how coldly calculating a thing I had done! But now this seems like a vague threat of punishment." She drew herself up, and a smile flashed along her lips. "I am too absurd, however, am I not? There is no chance— none at all. That young man, Adrian Etherege, gave me such a shock! I wish he had not spoken as he did; I fancy I shall detest the very sight of him after this, handsome though he is."

Mrs. Auchincloss felt chilled into silence. This abhorrence that was ready to steep itself in the blackest tide of tragedy, frightened and amazed her. She was unused to such robustness of emotion; she had held it in polite and dainty scorn all through her life. A surge of regret swept over her that she — *she*, Letitia

Auchincloss, a woman of race and breeding and the most haughtily exclusive habit — should thus have encountered the risk of being connected with anything so sensational, so "newspaperish," as the headlong despair at which her niece's behavior hinted. After a while she falteringly managed to say, while Olivia sat with eyes riveted on the floor and her lips tightly locked together:

"You will not for a moment imagine, my dear, that *I* have had the least desire to make you act otherwise than as a dutiful daughter of your poor papa. I was *quite* without knowledge, on the other hand, Olivia, that you entertained such repugnance toward Mr. Delaplaine. . . . And, indeed, if I had supposed —"

"I entertain no repugnance toward him," Olivia trenchantly broke in, lifting her head and showing how much trouble blent with her strange composure. "But to — to *really be his wife!* " She put her hands up to her face, covering it from sight. Her aunt watched her, while a faint tremor shook her frame. "Do not let us talk of that subject, please," she continued, letting her hands fall again into her lap. . . . "You wish me to remain here, you and Aunt Augusta. You think it best that I should stay over-night. . . . Well, I will do so. But I must send for Aunt Thyrza — for Mrs. Ottarson. You don't like her, either of you, I know. But I must send for her, all the same. She will come to me as soon as she gets my note. . . . Where can I write it? a bit of paper and a pencil are all that I want. I must write it at once." She rose as she finished speaking, and looked about the room. She saw a desk in one corner, hastened toward it, and perceived that writing-paper was placed there, with pen and ink.

She seated herself before the desk, and began a note to her aunt with extraordinary swiftness. Mrs. Auchincloss, from her place on the lounge, gazed with lifted eye-glasses at this hurried proceeding. "If that horrible woman is to be sent for," she reflected, "I had best go." It struck this lady very much as if she might be instrumental in having sown the wind to reap a hurricane. She had always borne herself as a placid idolatress of conventionalism, and now, when there was even a dim omen of her flawless respectability being put into any peril, she desired to lift her nice skirts clear of the least soilure.

"There," said Olivia, having finished, sealed, and directed her note. "I have made it short, but Aunt Thyrza will understand that I want her." She rose, and again glanced about the apartment in search of a bell. She saw one and went to it. As she rang it she proceeded, still in the same collected voice that she had used of late: "I must have the note sent without delay. Some servant will be found to take it, of course."

"I suppose so, Olivia," said Mrs. Auchincloss. "How you do cling to that lady, my dear!"

"I cling to her because she is the only real friend whom I now have on earth!"

Mrs. Auchincloss rose from the lounge with a pained look. "Are not your Aunt Augusta and I your friends, my dear?"

"I hope so," said Olivia, with an unmerciful frankness. "But you are not — pardon me for expressing just what I mean at such a time — you are not the same to me as Aunt Thyrza is. I want her near me now, and I must either have her here or else go to her."

Mrs. Auchincloss sighed. "Then you agree to stay until she comes?"

"Yes."

"Very well. Please do not expect me to meet her; that is all."

"I don't expect it, or even wish it."

Mrs. Auchincloss sighed again and walked toward the door. Just as she did so it was opened, and her sister once more appeared.

Olivia, on seeing her, instantly said: "Well? . . . what is the news?"

Mrs. Satterthwaite eyed her niece with much assumed gravity. "Mr. Delaplaine is very weak, my dear," she answered, "and failing fast."

"Ah!" said Olivia, drawing a deep breath. "Then that young man — Adrian Etherege — was wrong?"

"I fear he was," returned Mrs. Satterthwaite.

"Augusta!" here exclaimed Mrs. Auchincloss, in tones of great distress, "I — I am most wretchedly agitated by what Olivia has been saying. I — I feel myself to have been thoroughly misunderstood. I had no conception that she shrank with such loathing from the possibility of Mr. Delaplaine's recovery. She has written to Mrs. Ottarson, and insists upon having her note at once sent to that . . . person. And she has spoken words which have *more* than shocked me — words, I mean, relative to her course of conduct in the — the event of Mr. Delaplaine's *not* dying. She has mentioned *suicide*, Augusta — yes, really! . . . It is all too dreadful! I must not stay here and listen to such language any longer; it has made me truly *ill*. I — I shall go at once. I should never have consented to this marriage — *never!*

— if I had known our niece had entered into it with such extremely worldly intentions."

Mrs. Satterthwaite surveyed her plaintive sister tranquilly enough. "You are scared out of your wits and want to play traitor to me," she told her own thoughts.

But aloud she said: "Very well, Letitia. Leave me to speak with Olivia alone." And Mrs. Auchincloss, with a most aggrieved shake of the head and a deprecating elevation of both hands, passed from the chamber.

"My dear," said Mrs. Satterthwaite to Olivia, as soon as they two were alone together, "what folly is all this?" The girl gave no answer, and she presently went on with harsh directness: "It certainly has not the advantage of being in good taste."

"Good taste," murmured Olivia, with a laugh full of forlorn mockery. "I should say not. No more has the act I've been guilty of."

"No one sees guilt in it except yourself. Come, Olivia, be sensible. I haven't a doubt that you've been shocking your poor Aunt Letitia half to death. Fortunately it is not quite so easy to shock *me*. What you have done, my dear, you have done. Retrogression is too late, now. You were not forced to take the course you did take. I have a very clear recollection of my own words to you just before your decision was made — of how I advised that you should not trouble yourself any further regarding this matter. But you chose to do otherwise. As for Mr. Delaplaine's condition, you can't say I deceived you the least in *that*. I thought him fatally ill then, and I think him fatally ill now. . . . Really, Olivia, if you talked about suicide, and that sort of thing, with your Aunt Letitia, you did so without the faintest provocation. I have no doubt whatever that he will have ceased to live in twenty-four hours' time."

Olivia felt those latter sentences nerve and cheer her beyond expression. A little while ago she would hotly have resented such a charge as that she could, under any conceivable circumstances, have rejoiced in the tidings of a fellow-creature's imminent death. "In twenty-four hours' time," she softly repeated. That was the only answer she made, or thought of making. How comforting to have the distance between oneself and so calamitous a doom widen! If Mrs. Satterthwaite had insulted her, now, she would hardly have minded it from one who came the emissary of such courage-bringing news.

As it was, Mrs. Satterthwaite continued in no conciliatory tones: "You wish Mrs. Ottarson here. You have a letter in your hand which you wish despatched to her."

"Yes."

'At this moment a knock was heard. Mrs. Satterthwaite turned and opened the door. A servant stood outside, having come in answer to Olivia's summons.

"I rang," Olivia now went on. "I wish this letter sent immediately to the address written on it." She handed the envelope to Mrs. Satterthwaite, who in turn gave it to the servant.

"Let it be taken as quickly as possible," Mrs. Satterthwaite said. After the servant had gone she turned to Olivia, reclosing the door.

"You see, your letter is sent. But now that Mrs.

Ottarson is coming here, I prefer to absent myself —
at least until to-morrow. You agree, do you not, to
stop here over night?"

"It . . . it will be so strange!" Olivia answered,
with uneasy hesitancy.

"But it will be best; it will be right. This is your
home now. You will claim it if he dies; you must
not desert it while he lives. . . . And, Olivia, bear in
mind that you have contracted no *secret* marriage. It
is sudden, hasty; but it must promptly be published
to the world for all that. I will see that it is printed
in all the morning newspapers. People will talk, gossip; that is to be expected. You are a Van Rensselaer, and no one with your name and position can do
anything of this sort without causing a perfect fer-
ment of remark. But we have nothing to conceal.
This is not the first time that such a ceremony as a
death-bed marriage has taken place. . . . And now,
promise me that you will preserve the propriety of the
thing, my dear, and spend the night — as Mrs. Spencer
Delaplaine should — in the house of your husband."

Olivia's response was somewhat slow in coming, but
at length it came: "Yes," she finally acquiesced; "I
promise."

"That is the suitable way to speak, my dear — and
to feel, as well. Orders shall be given the servants to
accommodate you perfectly. They know what has
happened. As for changes of clothing, Mrs. Ottarson will, no doubt, capably assist you there. . . . My
dear Olivia, you have only to behave with discretion
for a few hours longer. Afterward you will be you
own mistress. You understand; I am sure that you
*do* understand."

"Yes, I understand," the girl replied. "You may trust me."

Mrs. Satterthwaite had left the house in Tenth Street by the time (a good hour later) that Mrs. Ottarson arrived there. Olivia received the latter in that same apartment which she had entered and had never once quitted since leaving her funereal bridal-chamber, not far away.

The meeting was, on Olivia's side, a passionate one. The moment that she and Mrs. Ottarson were together, with a shut and locked door between themselves and the outer hall, every sign of tranquillity died from the girl, and she surrendered herself to an outburst of tears and moans, while both arms clung about her aunt's plumply accommodating neck.

"I wrote you that I was married — *married*, Aunt Thyrza! And I *am* — it's true! Oh, I've so much to tell you! You don't know anything yet. It seems now as if *I couldn't* have done it — as though some one else must have done it, not I! . . . But do not blame me till you hear everything — till you hear just how and why it happened."

"I won't, 'Livia," replied Mrs. Ottarson, whose dark eyes were sparkling and whose mien denoted extreme perturbation. "I think I can guess a good deal of it. Those two aunts o' yours set you up to it, an' got him to consent. That's 'bout the size o' the whole thing, I reckon. Ain't it, now? . . . Don't cry so. . . . You ain't murdered if you *are* married."

"No, no; you're wrong," cried Olivia through her tears. "*He* wanted it; he asked *me;* his wish — his dying wish — has been behind it all. . . . I — I pitied him, Aunt Thyrza, but it wasn't pity that made me yield. It was something cold and wicked and grossly selfish in me. Yes, that — only that! And now I feel as if I were to be punished for letting that wrong impulse get the best of me. They say he is dying. But he *may* not die. And then . . . think! If he should *not* die! . . . This never even occurred to me till afterward. And when it came it froze my very blood with terror. . . . And now it seems so horrible that I should be waiting his death and *wanting him to die!* It is like one sin begetting another. . . . And yet I must either hope that he *will* die, or else — No, no, no! I haven't been bad enough to be punished so fearfully! Have I, Aunt Thyrza? It would be too cruel, too monstrous — would it not?"

Olivia and Mrs. Ottarson stayed together in Delaplaine's house that night. The room they occupied opened off from the same hall as did that of the invalid. Olivia slept fitfully; Mrs. Ottarson scarcely slept at all. The latter had, so to speak, fully grasped the situation. She had sent for changes of attire to Twenty-Third Street; she had talked with two or three of the servants who had held converse with the nurse on watch at Delaplaine's bedside. If any distinct alteration took place in the condition of the sick man she was to be informed of it. And once or twice, while the hours were very small, she stole out of her own apartment and entered that of Delaplaine, meeting the nurse on its threshold.

He was very ill. There had been no decisive turn for worse or better in his disease. This was all that she could ascertain. By about dawn she sank into a deep, fatigued sleep, and on awakening, she found that the sunny May morning was well advanced, and that Olivia had risen, had dressed, and was now moving about their bed-chamber.

"I could not sleep," said Olivia; "I've been up since quite an early hour. I rang for a servant and inquired after Mr. Delaplaine. The answer was brought back to me that he continues exactly the same."

"Jus' so," mused Mrs. Ottarson. "I s'pose he'll go right off 'fore you can say 'Jack Rob'son.' That's the way a good many 's old 's he is *do* go, 'specially when it's the pneumonia. . . . By the bye, Liv, did the help you saw say anything 'bout our gettin' any breakfast ? "

"It will be served us whenever we want it, Aunt Thyrza."

And not long afterward it was most admirably served them in the dining-room below stairs. What a contrast between this perfect attendance, this gleaming silver and snowy linen, these delicate dishes prepared with nicest art, and the haphazard waiting of Ann and Bridget, the plated forks and nicked china, and the precarious, not to say untrustworthy cooking by which Olivia had for days past been confronted! Two or three of the servants addressed the girl as "Mrs. Delaplaine," and made her cheeks tingle as they did so. In the morning paper, which had been placed upon the breakfast table, she read the announcement of her marriage thus:

DELAPLAINE — VAN RENSSELAER. — On Tuesday, May—, 188—, by the Rev. Dr. Ray Olmstead, SPENCER DELAPLAINE to OLIVIA CLINTON, daughter of the late Houston Clinton Van Rensselaer.

What a queer, impossible look it had! It somehow recalled to her, in an oddly analogous way, a curious

poem which she had somewhere seen, about a ghost
wandering through a graveyard, stumbling over an
old grave and reading his own epitaph upon the crum-
bled tombstone. That ghost could not have under-
gone a more amazed thrill than hers was on reading
those few little lines of divulging print.

"There is nothing for us to do except to wait,"
Olivia said, after they had gone upstairs again and
entered the sitting-room which opened off from the
apartment in which they had slept. "You will stay
with me here to-day, will you not, Aunt Thyrza?"

"Oh, I s'pose so," replied Mrs. Ottarson. It was
not easy for her to give even this partial kind of consent, since no Ida Strang now held a vice-regal position in West Twenty-Third Street, and she could not
look upon the fact of her own absence without visions
of dire domestic topsyturvy-dom. "P'rhaps I can slip
off a little later, when we've heard what the doctors
think. Then I can come back later on still, I guess."

"Oh, do try, please," begged Olivia. "It is so
dreadful for me to feel myself all alone here. And
even if Aunt Letitia and Aunt Augusta do come,
there's somehow such a gulf between them and me!"

"I see," said Mrs. Ottarson, with a grim intonation.
"You jus' want me to kind o' be a bridge *over* the
gulf, don't you? Well, Livvy, that's all right, but
then bridges are *trod on*, an' that's w'at those two
aunts o' yours would like to do to me. Oh, I know
'em. Well, we'll have to fix it so's I'm kep' out o'
their sight, like something with too many claws an'
teeth. I'm perfectly 'greeable to that, I *mus'* say."

Olivia found herself growing bolder as the day
lengthened. She repeatedly moved into the outer

hall and stood there, looking about at the quiet richness of all the appointments. But whenever the lower hall-bell sounded she would disappear frightenedly. This bell began to sound very frequently, it soon occurred to her. Sometimes footsteps would pass her closed door. These, as she conjectured, were physicians coming or departing. By and by there was brought her a request from Mrs. Auchincloss and Mrs. Satterthwaite that she would kindly join them elsewhere.

" I would much rather stay here with you," Olivia said, after she had sent back an affirmative reply. " There is nothing that I have to say to them except the asking of a single question. . . . Well, perhaps they will know how to answer it better than the servants. I suppose Mrs. Satterthwaite has seen him."

" It may be that he wants to see *you*," ventured Mrs. Ottarson.

" Oh, I hope not . . . I hope not!" exclaimed Olivia. " Aunt Thyrza, I should feel so miserably ashamed to stand beside him, having had the — the thoughts about him that you know of. . . . And yet he must have been certain, all the while, of just *why* he prevailed upon me. If I had deceived him, my sense of sinfulness would be ten times worse than it is now!"

Not long after this, Olivia opened the door, preparatory to joining her aunts. But just as her foot touched the threshold of the hall itself, a sound of voices arrested her. The persons who were speaking together could not have been many paces away. Every word of what they said came with the greatest distinctness to her hearing.

"It is a very extraordinary thing, Doctor," declared one voice.

"His vitality," answered another, "is truly marvellous."

"This change in his temperature has astonished me."

"And the marked abatement of congestion — that is even more unusual."

"A superb constitution, Doctor."

"Iron, my dear sir — iron. . . . Well, he has lived a most careful life. It tells now."

"Upon my word, I believe we are going to pull him through."

Then came a laugh, in which both voices participated. "He's going to pull *himself* through," were the next words, in response to those just uttered. "If his pulse and respiration continue as they are now five or six hours longer, he'll throw the whole trouble off as easily as if he were a boy of nineteen."

.    .    .    .    .

Olivia staggered back from the half-closed door. She sank beside the chair on which Mrs. Ottarson was sitting, and hid her head in that lady's lap. Her form quivered, as shudder after shudder passed through it. Mrs. Ottarson was deeply alarmed, but presence of mind stood high among her worthy traits. She suspected that Olivia had overheard something, for she had seen the girl pause in a listening attitude. She stooped down, took Olivia in her arms, and rose, forcing the poor, cowering frame to rise also.

"Now, 'Livia," she began, as the girl's head fell upon her shoulder and the shudders were again manifest, "this aint goin' to do one bit. No, deary, it aint.

W'atever you heard, it don't make any diff'rence. You've *got* to brace up, an' not shame yourself. Come, now, w'at 'd you hear out yonder in the entry? Let me know right straight off!"

Olivia raised her head and whispered these words from colorless lips:

"I heard them say that he was going to get well. They were two doctors, talking together. One of them said that if his pulse and respiration should continue five or six hours longer as favorable as at present, he — he would quite overcome this illness."

Olivia's eyes were as dry in their light as diamonds, and below them lay heavy curves of shadow that her augmented pallor made mournfully plain. A few hours had turned her bloomful girlish face into that of a suffering woman. A desperation had come into it that clad all its features with melancholy maturity. You felt that its beauty would soon vanish if the pain that was wearing at her heart did not lessen.

"I guess I wouldn't see either of my aunts, if I was you," said Mrs. Ottarson, solemnly, while Olivia still clung to her. "If they come up here, that's one thing. I don't think they will, though; I guess I'll act as a scarecrow." And now she permitted herself to add a very imprudent thing. "I'd be one to 'em, sure enough, if they knew what deceit I suspect 'em both of tryin' to practise."

Olivia sprang backward. Her eyes flashed. "Do you mean *that*, Aunt Thyrza? Do you mean they — they *knew* all along he would get well?"

"I mean they jus' played on your belief he *wouldn'* get well. A word from either one of 'em would have made you alter as quick as wink, but they didn't say

it. Not them! They wanted to get you 'way from
me by hook or by crook; an' they wanted you to make
a 'ristocratic match besides, no matter w'ether it left
you widow *or* wife."

"True," murmured Olivia, in her shame, her wretchedness, her growing affright. The homely phraseology of her Aunt Thyrza threw fresh revealing rays
upon all which had passed. She had really been but
a puppet in the hands of two ambitious kinswomen.
She perceived this now, and the realization kindled an
indignant fire in her young soul. She herself had
been blamable enough, but their cunning had dealt
with her faultiness no less coolly than ignobly.

An hour, two hours passed. Olivia had paid no
heed to Mrs. Satterthwaite's request. At last, by
about half-past one o'clock, a second summons came
from the same lady. Would Mrs. Delaplaine have
luncheon served upstairs, or would she take it down
in the dining-room with her two aunts?

Olivia seemed to muse for a moment. Then she
answered the servant that she desired no luncheon
whatever, but that her aunt, Mrs. Ottarson, would be
served upstairs, here, in the sitting-room.

The luncheon was sent up for two, and Mrs. Ottarson forced Olivia to swallow at least a few mouthfuls
of food. She did not like the girl's glassy eyes, her continual startled, nervous motions, and the complete absence of all color in her vigilant, strained, harassed
countenance. The elder woman felt that all consolatory
language must fall ineffective upon the younger one.
That single irrepressible dread had grown into an
anguish of suspense now, and no power except a
certain dark yet distinct piece of information could

alleviate its cogency. Meanwhile, Mrs. Ottarson had misgivings lest some piteous collapse might soon overwhelm Olivia. She was like a being borne in a rudderless and oarless boat at the mercy of a flood which swept her toward an inexorable abyss. If the flood itself would only retard its menacing current, all might still be well with that unhappy, jeopardized life. But if not —! To watch Olivia as she restlessly, almost fiercely waited what she held to be her impending doom, was to comprehend how keen were her spiritual torments.

By about three o'clock there came a knock at the door. Mrs. Ottarson went herself and answered the knock, this time. She admitted Mrs. Satterthwaite, followed by Mrs. Auchincloss. Both gave her a little freezing bow, and passed her without the least apparent concern as to whether she returned it or no.

"My dear," began Mrs. Satterthwaite, as the two ladies approached Olivia, who stood in the centre of the chamber, "since you thought it best not to come to us we have decided it is best we should come to you."

Olivia bowed her head. Both her visitors must have seen the striking pathetic change that had been wrought in her appearance.

"Well," said the girl, coldly and formally, "you have come to tell me that Mr. Delaplaine is . . . recovering, no doubt. I have heard that he will recover. Have I heard correctly?"

The ladies looked at one another.

"Don't speak, please, Letitia," said Mrs. Satterthwaite to her sister, in a low, eager voice. "Let *me* speak."

Olivia caught the two sentences. "Pray do speak at once," she said. "I wish to know my fate."

"You foolish girl!" exclaimed Mrs. Satterthwaite, who had become paler than perhaps she herself guessed. "He *is* surprisingly better. Yes, the doctors now say that with a little careful nursing his life will be spared to his many friends. These will all be so thankful for this miracle. And why should not *you* be as well? You, my child, who now bear his name, and whom he will cherish as his wife with a fondness, an indulgence, that —"

A sharp, harsh cry sounded from Olivia, here. She lifted her hand and clenched it. "You knew — you both knew — that it might turn out like this!" she broke forth, with a voice of accusation, irony, and despair. "You acted with deceit — with cruelty. Oh, you were very diplomatic — very non-committal! There is nothing I can charge you with having said — it is what you did *not* say that now makes me feel how you have acted as my tempters — my enemies! It will kill me — or I hope it will." She swerved sideways, at this moment, and both her hands went to her breast as though she would tear from it something that suffocated her. . . . Again she reeled, and by this time Mrs. Ottarson had darted toward her, past those whom she had thus heatedly addressed.

"If I do die," she went on, with her look still fastened on the faces of her aunts, while she steadied herself, so to speak, in the arms of Mrs. Ottarson, "you — *you* — both of you two cold, heartless women . . . will . . . have to . . . answer for my . . ."

She did not pronounce the word "death," but as her eyes closed, and her breath resolved itself into a few short, resonant gasps, this word was faintly shaped by her lips.

And then her form grew limp and effortless in Mrs. Ottarson's clasp. She had swooned, though the fit of unconsciousness was not a long one. But she awoke from it in delirium. That night her life, and not the life of her husband, was in peril. He had indeed already made wonderful strides toward convalescence. But with Olivia Delaplaine it was just the opposite. The physicians who watched her hourly expected an acute cerebral paralysis, or, if not that, a dementia consequent upon severe nervous shock. Even Mrs. Ottarson (who would not have left her if certain that every boarder in her establishment was to vacate it by the morrow) had not dreamed of how drastic had been the tension laid upon her darling's unprepared brain. As it was, stifling her tears like the brave soul nature had fashioned her, she hovered near Olivia, waiting, hoping, silently praying, but never forgetting capably to prove herself of service as well.

## XIV.

The chronicler of the present history must now record that more than seventeen months have elapsed since Olivia's illness terminated, so fittingly yet so gloomily, the dramatic misfortune of her wedding-day. As the play-bills in the theatres will sometimes have it, our scene changes from grave to mirthful; and one might readily concede that the *café* in Delmonico's, toward about eleven o'clock on a crisp-aired January evening, might supply all desirable elements of mirth.

The large, crowded room certainly looked gay in the extreme. It was not *bariolé* like the lady-haunted restaurant that faced on Fifth Avenue, but its merriment of mingled voices compensated for the absence of festal color. Nearly all the tables were occupied, and at one of these sat Jasper Massereene and as uncongenial an associate as young Aspinwall Satterthwaite.

They had not entered the *café* together, but had met here only a few minutes previously. Aspinwall was now in his graduating year at Columbia, and had long held his manhood to be about as firmly planted a fact in the estimation of a large public as the bluff, gallant, sailor-like bronze statue of Farragut just across the way at the edge of Madison Square. To-night meant a gathering of the fashionable clans, for it was to be marked by the first Patriarch's Ball of the season.

Aspinwall would not for the world have missed airing in the Delmonico rooms upstairs his new coat (just over from London) with the rolling satin collar, his white waistcoat with the gold buttons, and his new cat's-eye stud with the small row of diamonds running round it, of which the young Duke of Dunderhead had condescended to say last summer at one of the Newport Casino balls: "By Jove, now, that's quite neat, isn't it?" Aspinwall's pale, beardless face had lighted up as he strolled into the big, marble-floored room, wrapped in his sable-lined overcoat, and perceived "Cousin Jasper." But the spirits of Massereene momentarily darkened, proof though their usual brightness rendered him against the depression produced by the ordinary bore. Aspinwall was in no sense an ordinary bore. The years that bring wisdom to the sophomore had in his case only inflated with fresh vanities the senior. And the worst of it all, as Massereene may quickly have decided while his young relation flung off the costly outer garment preparatory to sitting down at the same table with himself, lay in the solidity of the worldly backing by which all these vanities were supported. This young Aspinwall Satterthwaite was a nonentity, an ignoramus, just able to acquit himself in his college exercises with decent competency, and yet the amplitude of his father's bank account and the witchery of possessing a family name with a strong patrician aroma diffused from it —here were potent considerations enough to make many a clever young girl, his superior in a hundred ways, feel glad if he would condescend, during the progress of the ball upstairs this evening, to pause even for a few precious minutes at her side.

Alas! we speak with wonder, sometimes, of the days when men like Moore and Sheridan, provided they chose to leave Grub Street and seek the society of the dandies elsewhere, perforce had to cringe hat in hand to my lord this and my lord that, begging the *entrée* to Watier's in Bolton Street, or moving heaven and earth to secure a card for White's. . . . Well, the old order changes, as a poet of our own century phrases it, and yet . . . does it so radically change, after all? "A man's house is his castle," cries the select-souled American of to-day, "and he has a right to ask whom he pleases thither." True; but what if the castle be built with too feudal an architectural touch, good friend, and filled by an assemblage who are lords and ladies in all except the titles that they would break their proud, undemocratic hearts to win? Caste, unless it be founded upon virtue, intellect, or good-breeding, is the foulest fungus in a republican soil. And caste that has none of these claims for its permission to thrive, infests and infects the chief cities of our land at this time. Young Aspinwall Satterthwaite meant and expressed caste of just this baleful character. Where was the difference between his actual hereditary "position" and that of some English, French, German, or Austrian stripling who presumes upon the prestige his own merits never earned him, and of which his follies might very properly dispossess him?

"We have our dukes and marquises and earls here," thought Jasper Massereene as he looked at his cousin, now, across the table of the *café*. "There isn't the same historic romanticism about them; their fields of sway are narrower; they sometimes, though not always, exhibit more vulgarity and less native refinement than

their prototypes do. But their assumption, their mo-
nopoly, their implied arrogance, is after all nearly the
same."

"You won't drink anything more, old chap?" Aspinwall was meanwhile saying. He had just ordered a
brandy-and-soda; he had called for it as a soda-and-
brandy, doubtless with some idea that to reverse the
names of the liquids thus would indicate a more English turn of idiom. He wanted above all imaginable
things to be English; he would rather have been
undissentingly thought *that* by his set than have
received from them any honor their esteem could
devise for him. "I generally drink something before
I go to a big crush like this ball. These affairs are so
brutally common, you know. People break their
necks for tickets. It wasn't so in the old days, when
the town wasn't so large. They hadn't Patriarch balls
at the Fourteenth Street Delmonico's, but they used
to have Assemblies, and then the rush wasn't half what
it is now."

"No," said Massereene amiably, "I suppose not."

He knew nothing with regard to the Fourteenth
Street Delmonico's. He had possibly been at Eton
when its dead-and-gone glories were flourishing, and
as oblivious that it existed as he was conscious of the
old century-battered statue of Henry Sixth in the
quadrangle there, of the sweet, umbrageous elms half
obscuring Windsor's massive towers a few hundred
yards beyond, and of the keen perplexity wrought by
Latin verses upon the undergraduate mind.

But perhaps there may have been a stray reveller
among the talkative company scattered about him this
evening, whose forty or fifty or even sixty years con-

tained vivid reminiscences of that other demolished
and irreparable structure. He may have been as fine
a beau in his day as was Aspinwall Satterthwaite to-
night, while he sat sipping his refection here in the
new Delmonico's, and dreaming of the old. Memory
is a tyrannous optimist on her own ground of retro-
spection. What colors she can paint with, joyous as
well as sombre! This musing individual whom I take
the liberty of fancying, and who may have had no real
identity whatever, would have had to ask his sad soul
after many a dead and loved comrade, many a happy
and treasured reunion.

The wine seethed crisper in the goblet then than it
did to-night, and the laughter of those who quaffed it
rang with a mellower cadence. Where are those
*noctes ambrosianæ* now? Where's Harry with his
wit, Frank with his sporting-talk, Louis with his love-
affairs? What's become of Johnny, with his princely
manners, his exquisitely high-bred face, his early French
education that gave him the least touch of a charming
accent when he spoke English, and his clean, superb
fifty thousand a year? How the girls courted him,
how the mammas beamed on him, how the men
gathered round him! Was ever a life so radiantly
fortunate as his? When he came into the Fourteenth Street Delmonico's, after opera or dinner,
you would somehow always hear the champagne-
corks begin to pop not far away. It seemed like
magic, but it was only tact; a sign, a whisper to
one of the *garçons*, and there we all were, with our
more economical whiskey-and-water spirited off, and
the topaz *Clicquot* or *Verzenay* glistening or simmering
before us. He was so considerate of his friends, so

debonair, so frankly and heartily cordial, was Johnny,
and withal such a natural instinctive aristocrat. . . .
Only a few years later he was met in Broadway with
a faded and rather vacant face, and with his former
laugh, though all the sunshine had gone from it. He
had been very ill somewhere abroad, he said (alas!  we
had heard of the sudden madness that had struck him
down in the midst of Parisian pleasure far too wildly
chased), and they had shut him up for a long time.
It was so good to be out, he added, looking round him
with a dim flash of his once lucid blue eye and a
glimpse of that *bel air* which his mental ailment had
marred pathetically. And not very long after this we
learned of his death, and soon his relations were quarrelling about his money. . . . But others besides poor
Johnny have passed away into the great shadow and
mystery, though he was the star of them all!  How
it would teem with ghosts, that Fourteenth Street
Delmonico's, if it had been left standing as it once
stood, and they had not reared a huge upholstery
store in its place!  I sometimes feel like taking my
hat off to that upholstery store and thanking it for the
painful souvenirs that it spares me. It is like an
immense merciful tomb, hiding a multitude of buried
recollections and suggestions. Better that new-married
couples to-day should go there and buy carpets and
furniture for the flats they have just rented, while
they dream of soon-to-be-sought cradles and of heaven
knows what domestic felicity besides, than that middle-
aged croakers like myself, or the imaginary ruminator
whom I have mentioned, should dine and tipple once
more in the haunt of those dear dead friends. Better
this, indeed, than that we should dance in ball-rooms

where our springing step would now seem a desecration — as though we literally danced on the graves themselves of merry-makers whose blithe feet once kept time so rhythmically to our own!

No doubt most of those who gave the ball this evening would have held Aspinwall Satterthwaite's anticipatory remarks concerning it to be highly impertinent. It was the first large entertainment of a public kind that Massereene had ever witnessed in New York. He had been travelling about the West for many months after his return to these shores. He had wanted to see his country, not the seaboard, metropolitan, ultra-civilized portion of it. He had been everywhere, as a man may say who has roamed from St. Paul to New Orleans and from New York or Boston to San Francisco. At last he had drifted eastward again; and the Satterthwaites, knowing of his return, had sent him a card for the present ball.

Aspinwall accompanied him upstairs, and introduced him, with a flourishing manner which he strongly disliked, to the ladies who "received" in a room not far from the main ball-room. Massereene felt himself a stranger as he passed the threshold of the latter apartment. But Mrs. Satterthwaite, blazing with diamonds, soon saw him and called him to her side. He remembered, then, that he had engaged himself to dance the *cotillon* with Emmeline, and that he had sent this young lady a bouquet in testimony of the honor she was supposed to do him. But Emmeline, who soon paused near him in the promenade that followed every waltz or polka, had by no means forgotten either his engagement or his tribute.

"Thanks so very much for those charming flowers," she said, stopping for a moment at his side, while three gallants who accompanied her opened their eyes uncivilly wide at him. . . . And then Emmeline passed on, and in a little while he saw Elaine, attended with an equal devotion, and not long afterward he had said to Mrs. Satterthwaite:

"Your daughters are enjoying themselves, are they not? It is very pleasant to see how happily their faces beam."

These were commonplace words, and yet Mrs. Satterthwaite turned smilingly to hear them because of their speaker. Several other gentlemen were standing before her; she was one of the matrons who never missed being courteously attended. She was a power in society, and her increasing age was for this reason ignored. The men who wanted to push their way beset her with their suavities, and the men who had already pushed their way and who wanted to remain in her good graces, offered, for the most part, a similar politeness. She never suffered from the neglect experienced by other maturer ladies; she entertained too much for that. Besides, even if it had not been thoroughly well-known that no young gentleman could dine or sup at the delectable Satterthwaite mansion who did not pay his court to "mamma," she possessed the *esprit de salon* which made her at any time a vivacious transient companion.

"Yes," she now said to Massereene, "the girls *are* having a jolly time. They always do, I'm glad to say." And then she tapped him on the shoulder with her jewelled fan. "Come, now," she went on, "you mustn't waste yourself upon a poor old woman like me. You must bear in mind that you are a somebody."

"I a somebody?" replied Massereene.

"Of course you are," pursued Mrs. Satterthwaite. "The idea of your not recognizing it! Lots of people are dying to know you. It's been whispered about *who you are.*"

"I'm the merest nobody, however," returned Massereene.

"*Oh!* are you? Well, they don't think so here. . . . By the way, have you met my sister, Mrs. Auchincloss?"

"Not here — yet," returned Massereene.

"Oh, you mean that you dined there the other day. Yes, I heard that you did. It was quite a large dinner, wasn't it? And Mrs. Delaplaine, my niece, was there, was she not?"

"Yes."

"Did you sit near her?"

"No; at some distance away."

"You were presented, however?"

"Yes; but we had met before."

"I remember — in London. Do you think her handsome?"

Massereene gave a little start at this question. "Who could fail to think so?" he said.

Mrs. Satterthwaite laughed in her metallic "society" way. "I hope you don't say that because she is my niece. You will most probably see her to-night."

He did, a little later. She was standing near her husband; they had just entered the ball-room. She wore white, with a string of large pearls about her throat, and others braided amid the vapory gold of

her hair. A great many eyes were fixed upon her;
she was the belle of the Patriarchs' Ball that evening,
beyond a shadow of dispute. She appeared to be
neither specially ignorant nor conscious of this fact,
but the complete repose of her demeanor may have
meant indifference. She held four or five bouquets of
tea-roses and lilies-of-the-valley, bound together and
making one immense cluster. She was more beautiful
than when we saw her last, though the girlish delicacy
of her face had yielded to the spell of a sweet expan-
sion, like the candor of an unfolded flower after its
half-sheathed bud. But at the same time there was
an expression on her face which had no concern with
its youth and unblemished bloom. Perhaps it was
rather a fitful visitation than an actual expression. It
put, now and then, an icy light into her eyes and her
smile; it seemed to come and go across her brow
darkly, like a shadow; it lived a moment in the tenser-
drawn lines of her lips; it quivered at the edge of her
sensitive nostril, or was conveyed in the transitory
droop of her graceful head. It was intangible, unde-
finable, yet it was there. Was it disappointment,
unwilling toleration of wrong, contempt of self? Was
it either of these, or was it all three subtly commingled
and interblended?

Massereene had just begun to ask his own thoughts
one or two questions of that kind. Olivia Delaplaine's
face had fascinated and haunted him. He knew her
story, or a certain part of it. Who did not know?
Had it not been cried from the house-tops? The
strangeness of her sudden marriage to a man more
than twice her years had caused the widest comment,
and her long subsequent illness had given rise to many

peculiar contradictory reports. But it had never authentically transpired that she had married Spencer Delaplaine with the fixed belief in his immediate death. The world, with all its random uncharitableness, had spared her this distinct charge. It all came to the one result: she had been excessively talked about, but she had chosen a husband of the highest position, and neither gossip nor scandal had cast the least injurious slur upon her own. After everything was said, what had she probably done? Married a man older than herself, answered the babblers in the land, for his money and his station. But then she had had station herself; she was far better born than he; she came of the oldest Knickerbocker lineage. Hundreds of those whom social notoriety of any sort keenly interests, were anxious to see her and know her. It had got abroad that she was to appear in gay circles to-night at the Patriarchs', for the first time since her return from Europe. She had spent last winter at Nice and Cannes and Monte Carlo with her husband, and though they had been home ever since latter August, their life had most successfully eluded publicity. Till late October Mrs. Delaplaine had dwelt in a country-seat on the Hudson, of which her husband had secured a long lease. For a month or so she had been passing her time most obscurely in West Tenth Street, and had not accepted a single invitation until very recently, when she had appeared at a dinner-party given in her honor by her aunt, Mrs. Archibald Auchincloss.

Thus much Massereene and hosts of others had read concerning her in the society columns of the newspapers; for she had remained, as the picturesquely-wedded wife of so eminent a personage as Spencer Delaplaine, just that object of prying curiosity which purveyors of *on dits* and *canards* are forever bent upon jealously observing. Massereene now went up to her and took the hand which she graciously offered him, with a feeling of pity in his large, kindly heart that she should be so mercilessly and speedily beset by the stares of the surrounding throngs.

Spencer Delaplaine, looking, in his evening-dress, a trifle older, but no less elegant and distinguished than when we saw him last, shook hands cordially with Massereene, whom he had met a few days ago at the notable Anchincloss dinner. He was clearly aware of the attention that he and his wife were causing, but he bore himself with a consummate seeming uncon- cern of it. Tall, gray, serene, faultlessly gentle- manlike, he stood beside Olivia, presenting to her loveliness a contrast that was of cruel violence if one were aware of the relationship between them. Some of his old friends asserted of him that he bore himself, since his marriage, in an austerer way, and that he ostensibly cared less for either the notice or the esteem of his kind. Massereene, who rarely permitted himself to dislike people without cause, was repelled by something in his voice, his manner, his gestures and the turns of his phrases. "Bloodless insensibility to all that is most finely human," thought the young man, "was never stamped upon a face with greater emphasis." And then his eyes wandered to Olivia. "What a life he must lead her!" his medi- tations went on. "I somehow can't see in *her* face the reason why she married him, though *his* explains one side of the question perfectly."

Masscreene almost fancied that Mrs. Delaplaine's blue eyes lit for him in a grateful way as he and she soon began conversation. The staring, brief a while as she had been called upon to endure it, must have proved extremely unpleasant. But Spencer Delaplaine's acquaintance was too wide a one for a number of the gentlemen present who desired the honor of knowing his wife not summarily to request that he would introduce them. Olivia's practical triumphs now commenced in vivid earnest. She had never until now felt what has truly been called the intoxication of the ball-room; and where is the woman with brilliant beauty and with her years hardly counting beyond the term of girlhood who ever stops to ask herself whether this heady wine of flattery, admiration and enjoyment that she lifts to her lips be not, after all, a beverage with more sparkle than flavor and with less cheer than enticement? We, who are a little older than Olivia was that night, we of either the *beau sexe* or its opposite, have grown to think this wine a poor and even an acid vintage. But we loved it once, and now our palates are alone to blame. And the wine will always be poured for some glad lips, while other paler and wearier ones refuse it, from satiety, perhaps disgust as well!

Olivia quaffed it very willingly, surprised that the draught should be so agreeable. She had heard a hundred times of the follies that make the impetus and stimulus of society. But the pretty speeches that were now addressed to her had no indication of this aimless quality. Her wit, innate and nimble, exulted in placid contests which it was now called upon to wage. She was not old enough to perceive the

flippancy in such undertaking, and she was sensible
enough keenly and readily to discriminate between
the ball-room bore, so ubiquitous and so intolerable,
and the man of good reason, comparatively rare as he
may be, who occasionally drifts among Delmoniconian
gayeties. Already she had promised to dance the
German with her cousin, Aspinwall Satterthwaite;
this dainty stripling had not been quite sure whether
he had done a discreet thing or no in engaging her at
the Auchincloss dinner, of which he had been one of
the guests. Olivia had accepted his offer, and perhaps the most tasteful and expensive of the bouquets
that she carried had been the one sent by Aspinwall.

Massereene watched her swiftly-growing popularity.
He saw that she not only relished her belleship but
carried it with an air of facile security.

"She is beautiful," he thought; "and young. She
likes to shine, and she deserves to shine. She is unhappy, and this babble affects her like a soothing
elixir. That marble fellow, her husband, is secretly
in love with her. I am mightily mistaken, or he de-
plores while he is proud of the admiration that she
creates."

Delaplaine kept his wife in sight with a vigilance to
justify this belief. Hosts of old friends waited to
shake hands with him, yet he entirely deserted his
former standard of deportment. He ceased to be
the beau of yesterday; he sought no one; his calm
eye observed but did not solicit.

At last, just before supper, Massereene seized a
chance. "You have been besieged," he said to
Olivia. "But have you yet been asked to sup with

any one? I hear that it is the custom here, at these
Patriarch balls, to accept an escort to one of the small
tables below, in the supper-room. Will you accept
me?"

A march was just then struck up by the orchestra;
it meant the march to supper. Mr. J. Remington
Todd had just given his arm to Mrs. Madison Lexington, the richest woman in the room, and the admitted queen of society. He led the way to the
apartment below stairs. The rest of the assemblage prepared to follow Mr. J. Remington Todd,
the arbiter of the Patriarchs', the gentleman who
could by a wave of his little finger "keep out" the
undesirable Miss Smith or "push back" the ineligi-
ble Mr. Jones. There is always a Mr. J. Remington
Todd in all great cities. He is a human expedient
that rises ready at the call of social emergency. He
interests himself with lists; he decides who shall
cross the sacred patrician threshold and who shall
not. He is alert, evasive, dexterous, polite and ap-
propriately frivolous. He has nothing weightier
to do than to make laws of just this petty sort,
and in a country which has the republican right of
despising such laws, he might have something a great
deal wiser to do. Massereene had already heard of
Mr. J. Remington Todd. "Shall we follow the Gen-
eralissimo?" he said, offering his arm to Olivia.

Olivia slipped her own arm into his. But just as
she did so, Aspinwall Satterthwaite rushed up.

"My dear cousin!" he exclaimed. And then seeing Massereene, he drew back. Aspinwall prided
himself upon being always a gentleman of irreversible breeding — among those whom he considered

his equals. "Oh," he said, "I see you have some-
one else, Cousin Olivia."

"Come and join us, won't you?" answered Massereene, shortly. Something made him detest Aspinwall just then. He went downstairs with Mrs.
Delaplaine. Aspinwall followed. There was the
usual great hurry for tables. It happened that
Massereene and Olivia secured one at which the
great Mrs. Lexington and her professional kind of
escort, Mr. Todd, had already seated themselves.
It was not in the order of things that these two
seats at this particular table should be thus occupied.
Mrs. Ogden Van Wagenen was expected; she had
not arrived for some reason. Mrs. Lexington looked
a storm-cloud at Olivia, and then suddenly grew
pleasant. She recognized Olivia as a Van Rensselaer; she had been a Van Twiller herself; it was
so delightful, swiftly mused this great lady, to have
a person of one's own kind near one. She smiled
upon Olivia and promptly began a conversation with
her. She even condescended to introduce herself —
she, the magisterial Mrs. Lexington, a personage
whom even Mrs. Auchincloss would have paid
duteous court to! She spoke to Olivia of her father,
of her husband; she was complaisant, almost garru-
lous. She had a galaxy of the Lexington diamonds
strung about her weirdly thin neck; she was a very
ugly woman, but she was Mrs. Lexington, and so
people bowed down to her. On her other side,
elbowing Mr. Todd, sat a lady named Mrs. Quinby
Spence. The Quinby Spences, husband and wife, had
been desirous of slipping into society for several years
past. Mrs. Quinby Spence, a lady with sharp, thin

face and a pair of nervous black eyes, managed to
get herself seated near the great Mrs. Lexington.
She had contrived to whisper a word or two in the
ear of Mr. Todd. "Introduce me, please, won't you?"
Mrs. Quinby Spence had said. The Quinby Spences
had feasted J. Remington Todd again and again in
their splendid house in Fifty-Seventh Street. But
Mr. Todd now winced notwithstanding. The Quinby
Spences were "in," but they were not so "in" that
they should presume lightly to seek acquaintanceship with a potentate like Mrs. Madison Lexington.
Still, "introduce me, please," had been imperative.
Mr. Todd, with his bland, moonlike face embarrassedly aglow, made the presentation. Mrs. Quinby Spence, talking across the solid shoulder of him
who had thus introduced her, said most volubly and
effusively to the lady whose social *cachet* she desired
to obtain :

"I am so glad to meet you, Mrs. Lexington! It
gives me such *pleasure!* We have entertained so
many mutual friends. I am very fond of entertaining at dinner."

"Really?" murmured the great Mrs. Lexington.

"Yes — very fond. I was thinking over our many
dinner-parties the other day. My husband and I
were trying to recall just how many we had given
this winter. It may seem to *you*, my dear Mrs. Lexington, a rather curious matter to think of at *all*, but
we estimated, my husband and I, that we had entertained, during the last few months, almost a thousand
people."

Mrs. Quinby Spence thought this was all quite
proper to say. So many of the really select peo-

ple had been to her dinner-parties! It had indeed been said of the Quinby Spences that they had "dined themselves" into society.

But the great Mrs. Lexington did not respond. She contented herself with turning to her friend, Mr. Todd, and saying in a tenuously lady-like whisper:

"Good heavens! Does this woman keep a hotel?"

But, all the same, Mrs. Quinby Spence scored a point and succeeded thenceforth in knowing Mrs. Lexington, and thus scaling the last rung of that social ladder which for years she had so assiduously climbed.

Massereene and Olivia were meanwhile at the same table. Olivia had not yet learned the value of social grades. She did not realize how much importance had lain in the civility of the thin, ugly woman who had just been polite to her.

Aspinwall, also, was at that table. He had begun to be very jealous of Massereene. It had vividly occurred to him that Olivia was the belle of the Patriarchs' Ball and he resented the idea of being "cut out" by even so acknowledged a notability as Jasper Massereene.

But meanwhile Olivia had had another most wary and intent observer. This was her husband.

## XV.

Olivia was from that night a reigning success in the fashionable world. The rush and whirl at first pleased her unspeakably; they took her so effectually, for a time, out of herself. And the relief of being thus made in a measure forgetful, during certain moments of the day or night, that she had become the wife of a man whom she abhorred, was deeply welcome. This abhorrence had not been of quick growth with Olivia; it had gradually spread itself through her being with a steadfast, benumbing stealthiness of influence. When her long and dangerous illness terminated, she found herself facing her fate with a resignation that surprised her own spirit. Delaplaine was by this time in his usual health. He entered into his new character as the elderly husband of a youthful bride with steps that were so slow, cautious and discriminating as to awaken Olivia's admiration at his blended diplomacy and kindliness. She could never dream of loving him, but might not the respect which he was in a fair way of both rousing and perpetuating stand hereafter as at least a decorous apology and substitute for love? He had told her that he was dying; but surely, she now reflected, he was not culpable in having failed to die. No one had been culpable except her own miserable, wayward self. As soon as she was strong enough to see Mrs. Auchincloss and Mrs. Satterthwaite, she sent for them, and begged that they would pardon her hasty, hysterical charges. The former accepted her niece's amends with a grieved complaisance, and held it her duty to show as much generosity on the occasion as the sad extent of the injury inflicted would allow.

"Do not say another word about what happened then, my dear Olivia, was Mrs. Auchincloss's highly gracious response. "Of course I felt myself wounded by your words; how *could* it be otherwise? But I hope I am *Christian* enough to forgive them!"

"Oh, Letitia, how magnificent you sometimes are!" thought Mrs. Satterthwaite; but aloud she said to Olivia, with her chin a little in the air, her eyes no softer than if they had been agates, and her voice devoid of the least sympathetic ring:

"Oh, it's all right, my dear, naturally. You were going to be very ill. You didn't know what you were saying. I assure you I should have come to you, just like this, whether you had sent for me or not."

Still later Olivia began to change her opinion regarding the part played by her two aunts in that little matrimonial episode. But whatever certainty of opposite conclusion she may have reached, her future conduct never revealed it to either lady. They had long ago taken the color of their environing world as a partridge takes that of its furrow. And it was a world so full of falsities and treacheries, of sham, meanness and misrepresentation, that one must either accept it as one found it or leave it to its own less critical denizens. To try and improve upon its conglomeration of follies and misdoings would be indeed to try and bail out the sea!

But just now Olivia had not such condemning thoughts about society. It acted like a lulling drug upon her tormented life. Delaplaine had begun wooingly and suavely, but he had soon dropped his mask. Beneath it was the face of a tyrant. Olivia had just made up her mind that to endure him as a husband would not be the misery she had anticipated, when he suddenly appeared before her in a new light. Her health, at this period, was thoroughly restored. They were about to visit Europe together; the season was latter autumn. One day he entered her private sitting-room and found her in converse with Mrs. Ottarson, whose devotion during her sickness had been unparalleled in its noble self-surrender. He had never thus far shown the slightest rudeness toward Mrs. Ottarson, though he had more than once made it clear to his wife that she was not by any means an object of his liking. Moreover, he had paid respect, or something which resembled it, to Olivia's loyal and loving gratitude for all that she now felt she owed her aunt. But to-day his manner was brusque and curt. After Mrs. Ottarson had departed, he said, speaking for the first time with that assertion of command for which the future had so many relentless examples in store : —

"I must tell you, quite candidly, that she sets my teeth on edge, that woman."

Olivia turned pale. "Aunt Thyrza?" she faltered, feeling as if an abrupt knife-stab had entered her flesh.

"Yes, she is insupportable. I hope you mean to drop her as soon as you can. She has been very good as a nurse. But you are now quite strong again. If she had been your hired nurse you would not have done more than give her a handsome salary. I am very willing that you should do that now. You have your allowance; it ought to be equal to rewarding her services in a very nice way. But if it isn't, draw upon me for any reasonable sum — or any unreasonable one, providing your sentiment toward the lady makes you think she deserves notable recompense. Only, I cannot have her continuing to come here and wake the echoes with her frightful sins against grammar and breeding."

Olivia did not reply for several minutes. Then she said, measuring each word: "I think you misunderstand Aunt Thyrza. She would never accept a dollar from me. She would regard it as an insult if I offered her the least payment." After this the young wife's voice broke a little, and she went on, using the name which he had asked her to call him by, and which he had told her that it was most pleasant music to hear from her lips: "It seems as if something had offended or annoyed you this afternoon, Spencer. I hope that I am not to blame for — "

He cut her short with a little impatient toss of the head. "One thing has offended and annoyed me — that woman's ridiculous intimacy with you. If she were a man I should call her a rowdy. It occurs to me, Olivia, that you should rate your position, both as your father's daughter and as my wife, something less cheaply than you do."

He at once left the room after having pronounced these few piercing sentences. To Olivia they meant the infliction of a wholly unforeseen terror. For several weeks past she had been assuring herself that their existence in each other's company was to prove

one of the most unruffled serenity.  The mockery of
their union must inexorably remain.  He was not the
husband of her heart, and she must forever hide from
him spiritual depths of which his inevitable non-pos-
session would forbid all sweeter and holier conditions
of intimacy.  But at least he was going to show himself the gentleman and not the jailer, the indulgent
guardian and not the surly sentinel.  Apart from the
combined farce and sadness of their bonds, they were
no doubt destined to become excellent friends.  Every
new week repeated the comforting disappointment.
Then there were jewels given her, and other costly
gifts as well.  No bride of her years could fail to be
touched by these and like attentions.  Love might lie
as dormant as it pleased, with torch unlit and chaplet
unbraided; but if friendship were going to steal in with
sweet puritan face and a frank willingness to keep the
hearthstone always ruddy through chill weather, why
the days might not lag so sluggishly, after all.

Olivia had in truth made a little hopeful picture of
her own future.  Delaplaine and she were the two
chief figures, of course.  As he would become gradually enfeebled by the multiplication of years, leaving
her still strong and young, she would assume toward
him a more and more aidful and tributary place.
Herein should be the working out of her expiation —
the practical fulfilment of her repentance.  She would
do all that lay in her power to make Spencer Delaplaine bless their marriage.  Her act of selfishness
should be caused to bear sacrificial fruit.  When the
hour came that really laid him upon his death-bed —
not upon that semblance of one which had formed her
past reason for wedding him — perhaps he would take

her hand and tell her that she had been a worthy wife
Such she meant to be, and she now constantly thanked
God that the difficulty of attaining this desired object
would not prove insuperable.

Abruptly the change in her husband shattered aspi-
ration. He was never the same to her from that
afternoon when he showed her his unmantled self.
The passion she had inspired in him had not ceased,
but its primary fervors were diminished. Possibly
the sharp line of division between what he had been
and what he was henceforth to be, drew its extreme
emphasis from a single manifestation of her own.
She refused to obey him in the matter of slighting
her Aunt Thyrza, and most assertively told him so.

"You spoke not long ago," she said, looking at him
with a courage in her glance that did not for a second
flinch, "of my position as my father's daughter and as
your wife. I love poor papa's memory so dearly that
I could not dream of shaming it. If you think I owe
you the concession of discontinuing to know one who
is bound to me by the sweetest and strongest ties both
of blood and gratitude — one I love and respect as a
woman whose great, benevolent heart deserves that I
should do — then I must point out your very serious
mistake."

He started a little, but that was all. "You mean, I
suppose, that you will not drop Mrs. Ottarson?" he
said, with immobility. "She is an irritating vul-
garian, but you persist in keeping her up against my
will?"

"She is the dearest friend I have in the world, and
I shall always treat her as the friend I believe her."

Olivia was prepared to have him reply with fierce

anger, now; but she had not yet followed his imper-
turbable methods. The tenderness he had thus far
disclosed to her had been of about the same depth as
those brittle and curly woofs of lichen that we sometimes find on rocks. She was too wofully destined to
strike against the obdurate silicate that lay below!

"I perceive," he said, with his gray eyes fixed on
her face. "In spite of any orders of mine to the contrary, you will have this person visit you here at my
house."

"No," said Olivia. "It *is* your house. I would
not allow Aunt Thyrza to enter it against your
wishes. Possibly you don't realize or care to realize,
how much she would scorn to do so."

"Ah . . . yes. . . . It will merely be a series of
visits on *your* part?"

"That is what I mean."

"But suppose I forbid you to go there at all."

Olivia firmly shook her head. "I shall not hesitate
to go, all the same," she answered.

He shrugged his shoulders and smiled icily. "Does
this not seem to you a rather bold measure?"

"Not bolder than is justifiable under the circumstances."

He gave her no answer. For hours afterward she
felt like one who has been remorselessly duped. He
was a man of stone; she had thought him so, or very
nearly so, before their marriage, and now the remembrance of this old conviction tauntingly returned to
her. . . .

He proffered no further mention of Mrs. Ottarson.
But almost every succeeding day showed her new
exasperating points in his loveless and cynical dispo-

sition. He soon made up his mind that there was a point with her where his coercion must stop. Some women would have had physical fear of him, if none other. Olivia was so brave, so dauntless in her dealings with him, that he admired her secretly all the more on this account. Still, it would never do, he had assured himself, to go on with that honeymoon pose. He had begun to feel acutely bored by the necessity of maintaining it, and he had concluded that it had best be abolished forthwith. Let Olivia see him once and for all as he was; she might as well get used to him, if she were ever going to be as accommodating as that; she would doubtless have a good deal of his society during the next few years, to judge by the proofs of bodily toughness which he had given the physicians not long ago.

They sailed for Europe a short time afterward. Olivia greeted the event as a source of precious distraction, just as she was greeting the turmoil of New York merriments now, a year later. Adrian Etherege, the handsome young secretary of Delaplaine, surprised Olivia by saying to her, a few days before her departure took place:

"It would give me such delight, Mrs. Delaplaine, if I could only go with you!"

"Go with us, Adrian?" she repeated. She had always called him "Adrian." It had appeared quite natural for her to call him so on taking her rightful place as feminine head of the establishment. Occasionally her husband would permit the lad to dine with them, and once or twice he had done so at his wife's request. Adrian came and went in a most irregular style; it seemed an accepted fact in the

household that he should be exempt from all rules of
punctuality and exactitude. Now and then he would
sleep away from the house in West Tenth Street, and
perhaps not even return thither on the following day.
But no one showed the least concern regarding such
absences, and it was only necessary to look with close-
ness into his fair, star-eyed, poetic face for the least
suspicion that he was of dissipated habits to vanish
completely. His manner toward Olivia had been one
full of exquisite politeness ever since they had first
met after the protracted illness of the latter. At
times it struck her that he might be desirous of oblit-
erating from her memory all retention of the curiously
angry look she had once seen him give her. What
Olivia knew about Adrian Etherege's personal history
and antecedents the youth himself had told her.
Delaplaine had thus far not done more than say in
his wife's hearing:

"Adrian is a good boy, honest-minded and wholly
trustworthy. . . ." On one occasion, just after the
first dinner that the young secretary had taken with
them, Olivia had the fancy that some further information concerning Adrian was to be given her by his
employer. But although Delaplaine then seemed on
the point of volunteering a statement, he refrained
· from doing so, and she did not press him for disclos-
ures, feeling sure that they would be afforded by
other lips.

And they were. Adrian fell into the fashion of
holding little talks with her when he and she met,
in halls, on stairways, or perhaps in the library, to
which he was allowed free access. He pleased Olivia
indescribably. It was not merely his beauty that

attracted her; it was a winsomeness half melancholy
half joyous. He affected her as an individuality that
Nature had shaped for the freest acceptance of all
life's yellowest and richest sunshine, but over whom
circumstance had drawn a kind of shadowy veil. She
had no more thought of being touched by him into an
attachment beyond friendly interest than if his years
had numbered fifteen instead of twenty. This very
concern which he had aroused in her made her question him about his past. She wanted, naturally
enough, to learn whence he had managed to derive
his charming manners. And at length he had made
her acquainted with a little history which she did not
dream of doubting. Why should she so have dreamed?
He gave it, finally, with an air of veracity and simplicity that his lovely brown eyes and his almost ideal
countenance gently seemed to corroborate.

A long time ago, he told her, when he was a small
fellow, Mr. Delaplaine had known his father favorably
as one of the bank-employees. His father had died
suddenly, and he, an orphan, had been recommended
to the charity of the wealthy, powerful banker. Mr.
Delaplaine had been very good, giving him the advantage of a long term of schooling, and then permitting
him to enter the banking-house in a minor capacity.
Afterward the secretaryship had grown from that.
There was really nothing more to narrate. The
school had been a good one — a boarding-school not
far away from town — at Fordham, in fact. If Mrs.
Delaplaine was kind enough to think that he had
fairly cultivated manners, this complimentary opinion
could only be explained by the careful, refined course
of instruction pursued at the suburban school.

Olivia unhesitatingly credited all this. Her heart had so warmed toward Adrian Etherege by the time he made his direct appeal to accompany herself and Delaplaine abroad, that she promptly looked upon such a project with entire acquiescence.

But her husband instantly frowned upon it. His frown was one of unusual sternness, considering his ordinary composure. " Have you lost your senses?" he asked, after she had mentioned to him the wish of Adrian. " I should think you might see the insanity of such an idea."

" Insanity ! " murmured Olivia.

" Certainly." Delaplaine had no reservations from her now. He had cast off all disguises in unrelenting earnest. " An old fellow like me and a good-looking youngster like that ! I'd be a fine fool to let the world talk. No, thank you ! "

Olivia's face crimsoned, and her eyes kindled. " You can't imagine — " she began.

" Imagine ? " he broke in, with a hint of scoff in his tones. " Of course I don't. I'm not troubled with imagination, anyway. I'm what they call an exact thinker. Do you suppose I'm afraid you *care* for the boy? If I did I'd send him packing in no time. Besides, you couldn't care. He's not in your line. I know what *might* be. He isn't. You'd never fall in love with —"

" Stop ! " cried Olivia. " You insult me as your wife ! "

He gave a short, dry laugh. " Do I ? " he retorted. " Oh, no, I don't. I merely show you how I *might*. You would feel insulted all the same if you were fond of poor young Adrian. Women are never so finely

innocent in their assumptions as when they're guilty.
. . . We won't take the boy to Europe, however. I
know it's not a matter of much moment with you
whether we do or not. I keep a closer eye on you
than you perhaps fancy I keep. There may come a
time when you won't be altogether . . . indifferent.
Possibly that time *must* come, as affairs are situated.
But when it does, don't flatter yourself that I shall be
fooled for more than a week. The chances are that I
shall be even wiser from the very beginning than you
are."

He left her, after having spoken these words with
what she held to be an infernal coolness, and he left
her, also, rankling under the infliction of what she
rightly held to be a brutality. But she was yet in her
apprenticeship as regarded the full perception of just
how satanically insolent he could show himself. It
may readily be surmised that he behaved without
provocation during conferences of this sort. He freely
admitted to himself that he did. He was the kind of
man who would have been execrable in all domestic
relations, even if he had married twenty years younger
than at present. The world had been easy enough for
him to get on with. Its points of tangency, so to
speak, were not at all like connubial ones. A very ill-
natured bear in his home-circle may be a popular companion at the clubs. Delaplaine could never have been
called popular anywhere, nor was he at any time a bear;
for in allowing him such a definition as the last, you
would lose sight of his refined rather than blunt modes
of torment, his premeditated rather than impulsive
cruelty. "If I had married an angel from heaven,"
he had said to himself not long before the conversation

just recorded, "I should have found it impossible to get on with her unless we sometimes quarrelled. I don't know what I should have done to get up a quarrel. I think I might have picked the feathers out of her wings while she was asleep."

They went to Europe, leaving Adrian at home. He had grown singularly sad, Olivia observed, during the days that immediately preceded their departure. She wondered whether affection for Delaplaine could possibly explain his altered spirits; it seemed incredible that this should be the case.

"You would like so very much to go to Europe?" she said one day, a little while before they sailed.

"Ah, how I should enjoy it!" he exclaimed, a light seeming to pass across his face and then vanish.

"But some day you will go," said Olivia.

"Some day! Yes — alone!"

"Alone?" she echoed, surprisedly. "Why do you so dread going that way, Adrian?"

And then she saw that he had colored deeply. Thinking his embarrassment might have sprung from a betrayal of the regard which he bore his benefactor, she at once said, with the hope of putting him at his ease:

"But of course you would rejoice in the companionship of one whom you have known so long and so intimately as you have known Mr. Delaplaine. It is always a pleasure to travel with those of whom we are fond."

"Fond of *him — I!*"

The words leapt impetuously from his lips. Olivia saw, hurrying over his face and darkening it, the same fiercely irate expression witnessed there at a previous time. It amazed her that such specks of flame could swim, however momentarily, in the tawny shadow of those peaceful eyes.

"You *don't* like Mr. Delaplaine, then?" she exclaimed.

He burst into the most awkwardly contrite little laugh. "I — I didn't say that," he stammered. "I like him? Why, how could it be otherwise after all that he has done for me? Of course I like him." And then there was another apologetic laugh, lamer than that which had preceded it. "I — I was merely a — a trifle surprised that — that you should be in doubt of how I really felt."

"Oh, I was not in doubt," answered Olivia.

But from that time she became confident of Adrian's keen yet smothered aversion. This knowledge made her somehow set greater value upon the youth's evident regard for her; it forged a new link of congeniality between them. As for her husband's recent words, they wore dyes of deeper insult as she recalled their unprovoked acerbity. . . .

Two days before they took the steamer for Havre, an event occurred which caused her to wonder in an oddly perplexed way. She had gone to make a few purchases in the morning and to speak a loving farewell in the ear of her inalienable friend, Mrs. Ottarson. She returned at about three o'clock in the afternoon, and passed upstairs toward her own apartments. But just as she neared the library, a loud, clear voice, plainly that of a woman, sounded from behind the closed door of that particular room.

"I don't want to have him kicked into a hole, like a dog," cried the voice, "when I'm dead and gone."

"Who cares what you want?" came the answer, loud as well, and most uncharacteristically so, since the new speaker was beyond dispute Delaplaine. "You had no right to come here. You must go at once. And don't ever presume to come again."

Before Olivia had more than just slipped by the door of the library, it was flung open, and a woman crossed its threshold. The woman saw her as she receded, but Olivia caught only the least glimpse of a pale, rather careworn face, lit by dark eyes that were now as rayless as they might once have been radiant.

Then Delaplaine himself appeared, as white as he had looked on the day he was believed to be dying. "Let this be the last time, now!" he cried. "It's no place for you, and by ——, if you forget that again, I'll —."

The woman, who stood then on the upper landing of the stairs, pointed with a sudden gesture and a slight laugh of mockery toward Olivia.

Delaplaine turned, saw his wife, motionless and astonished a yard or two beyond, and gave a terrible start. The woman hastened downstairs, while Delaplaine, more discomfited in manner and speech than Olivia would have thought it possible for him to be, stammeringly began some sort of explanation.

"She is — one — one of those — those beggars who bother me at times for money. They — they come to you with all — all sorts of tales. A person has to be very—very careful, or he runs the chance of getting swindled horridly by them."

The next moment he passed back into the library. Olivia slowly walked on toward her own suite of chambers. Perhaps Delaplaine had spoken the truth,

and it *was* some beggar, who referred to husband, son,
or brother while saying that she did not wish to see
him kicked into a hole, like a dog, after she was dead
and gone. But then Spencer Delaplaine's unquestion-
able agitation . . . why should that have shown
itself?

"Surely," thought Olivia, while her maid was reliev-
ing her of bonnet and wraps, "if the woman had been
one whose presence here should bring shame on him,
he need not have felt the slightest concern on my
account. And as for his really feeling any, it doesn't
at all correspond with his present perfectly undisguised
brutalities . . . *tout au contraire.*"

The traits that she thus uncompromisingly described underwent no diminution after she and Delaplaine sailed for European shores. "I like Paris," he
said to her one day during the early part of their
sojourn in that city. "It is so exquisitely filthy
here."

"Paris is generally thought to be a very clean city,"
said Olivia, quite misunderstanding.

He laughed his raucous little laugh, and leaned
backed in his chair. "Oh, I don't mean her streets;
I mean her morals. Almost every other civilized
nation of the globe has been piling abuse on France
for centuries, and yet we've all such a secret delight
in her. It's too amusing. Whenever I see one of
these highly proper Americans or Englishmen who
shudder at what he calls her 'nastiness' in painting,
novel-writing or the drama, I always feel like sending
a note to that fellow's wife — anonymous, of course —
telling her to have him watched and followed on the
evenings he says he's going to the club for a quiet

rubber of whist and will be home by eleven or a quarter past. . . ."

"Did you ever meet any human being whom you trusted?" Olivia asked him, with a gentle exaspera-tion, at another later period.

"No, not a single being of whom I could say, 'I'll trust him or her through anything that may happen in the way of temptation.' There isn't anybody who *can* be trusted like that. Every one who ever lived has had a price. Sometimes it's large, but then the size depends on the amount of respectability that is to be imperilled."

"Then there is no such thing as conscience."

"No. Emphatically no. Conscience is traditional, and that only. You might have a child, and train him up to believe that looking at the moon was a most horrible sin. All through the rest of his life, no matter how enlightening might be the influences brought to bear upon him, he would never look at the moon without a sense of violation and trespass. You would have established in him what Herbert Spencer would call a line of least resistance for the incident force of fear. Conscience, remorse, scrupulosity, all began with that. . . ." He paused, and watched Olivia with the smile that she had grown to detest. "I re-member I said something of this same sort to you before we were married — and shocked you. Didn't I?"

"You shock me now."

"I know. But I don't mind. I have got you all safe to myself, now; you can't escape me. Can you?"

She saw that he was in one of his waspishly jocular moods, and she rose to leave the room.

"Don't go," he said. "I've something to tell you.

It's about our truly remarkable marriage. For it was remarkable, was it not?"

"Very," she answered, turning pale. She had a sudden curiosity to know what new sting he would inflict. He gave a soft, unctuous chuckle before he went on. "I told you I'd changed my will; I made your aunt Satterthwaite believe I had. But I didn't. I didn't intend to die. I was a little afraid that I might, in spite of my intentions, but still I'd made up my mind not to die if I could help it. It was all a delicious fraud on my part. You can't find many men who have the nerve to scheme like that on what may turn out their death-beds within an hour or two. If I had died before you married me you wouldn't have got a dime. That seeing my lawyer was all a blind — a *ruse de guerre* . . . excuse my bad pronunciation; you know I never could get on with French; I leave that for my young and accomplished wife, who 'had resided abroad for many years previous to becoming the spouse of her eminent banker-husband,' as that silly Franco-American newspaper announced the other day. . . . If I had died after our queer wedding, you'd have got your widow's third — no more." And then he gave another chuckle, and looked out from the window near which he sat, and which commanded a view of the Champs Elysées, bathed in winter sunshine.

Olivia always bore this cat-and-mouse treatment with a solemn, almost a sublime patience. Afterward she would say to herself, thinking over some special dagger-thrust that he had dealt her: "I am glad I made him no answer. I am glad I bore it calmly as I did. It is my punishment."

But now and then, for several days at a time, he would be a model of urbanity and good humor. During intervals like these she could see why he had gained ascendancy with both women and men; his caustic wit spared no person or thing, and yet she comprehended how, with other hearers than herself, it had sounded its discordant notes not too recklessly for the production of a distinct amusement.

When they reached the Riviera all the hotels were packed with visitors, and gayeties reigned imperially at the various Mediterranean-skirting resorts. But Delaplaine would not allow his wife to participate in any festivities whatever. Many of her own country-people sent invitations, but he refused them himself, and vetoed their acceptance on the part of his wife. An occasional luncheon or dinner he permitted; no large gatherings, however, would he sanction, nor any entertainments in which elaborated and magnificent costumes became requisite.

"No," he soon informed Olivia, in his low-voiced, smooth-visaged way, "you shan't, as my wife, cheapen yourself at any of these foreign places. I won't even let you be presented at Court in London. As an American one is incontestably nobody the instant one's foot lands upon transatlantic soil. A good many Americans are constantly forgetting that — more's the pity. I recollect dining once in the *salon* of Delmonico's, and seeing seated next me a party of three palpably raw Westerners, who had come to view the town — a father with a tanned face and a beard down under his chin; a mother with a yellowish fur cape that reached below her waist, and long earrings of gold scroll-work, and a reticule; and finally a son of

about fifteen or so, with enormous front teeth, and his
mouth in a perpetual gape of awe. . . . You know the
kind of rural persons I mean. . . . Well, they seemed
in doubt what they would take. I was dining with a
little party that evening (I believe your aunt Satterthwaite gave the dinner, by the bye), and we fell
into private giggles, all of us, over the absurd hesitancy of father, mother and son. The waiter stood
listening with a resigned air for their decision, and
finally it came. They ordered three pieces of mince
pie and three cups of tea. . . . Well, that, after all,
fairly represents the conduct of the average American
citizen on English or Continental soil. Some Americans do even a great deal worse than that. Others
(people of whom there are a few thousands like you
and me) must suffer in consequence. Socially we are
nothing here, the very best of us, and we need not for
an instant flatter ourselves that we are something.
You might make a great success among the swells
here, but though you would be *in* their throng you
would never really be *of* it; they would always connect you with the species of person that orders a cup
of tea and a plate of mince pie in Delmonico's at the
usual dining hour. It may be hideously unjust all
this . . . who says it isn't? But when you've reached
my age you'll understand the full rarity of justice on
our planet; black swans and white crows are not a
circumstance to it . . . All very well, Olivia, for such
women as Mrs. Brummagem Baker to despair of getting into New York society and go abroad for the
purpose of having an aristocratic stamp put upon
them, that they may come home afterwards with gilt-
edged recommendations to the residents of their own

native metropolis. But you don't require to 'invade
New York' as they used to say Mrs. Brummagem
Baker did, after she'd been received at Marlborough
House and passed a day at Sandringham. No; you
are a Van Rensselaer in the first place, and you're
Mrs. Spencer Delaplaine in the second. That will
have to be enough for one lifetime — or, at least, till
I'm dead and you marry somebody else. Anyhow,
you'd never win anything here but a sort of tinsel
favoritism. They might take you, but they'd take
you with a big pinch of salt — as only an American.
And I won't have you taken that way. . . . We'll
wait until we get home before you try a turn among
the fashionable assemblages. There you're princess,
duchess, and countess all rolled in one. Yes, you are,
thanks to some of the ridiculous shortcomings of our
ridiculous republic — about as great a national failure,
take it all in all, as the records of history can show."

It will now readily be understood why the stay of
Delaplaine and Olivia abroad was not attended by
any except the most meagre social excitements.

## XVI.

DELAPLAINE was of the opinion that America has but a single season whose record is handsome enough to deserve honorable mention in any calendar. This season, he affirmed, was autumn; and on his return to his native land, in August of the following year, he expressed a great desire to see once more the Hudson when its banks were tinted with the summer's prismatic decay. Accordingly he leased a very fine estate not far from Tarrytown, installing Olivia there, by no means against her will. The house was spacious and comfortable; the grounds commanded a noble view of the lordly river near by. Olivia took long walks, long rides and long drives through the delightful surrounding country. She was from early training an excellent equestrian, and the stables were as well stocked with horses as were the halls and chambers of her new abode supplied with drilled and efficient servants. Her husband now and then would spend one or two nights in town, but he always instructed her by letter or telegram of his intended absences, which decidedly did not fill her with inconsolable regret. She was lonely, but not to any despondent degree.. She had books of many sorts to read, and as she kept early hours, slept healthfully, and saw a good deal of the breezy sunshine which was then at its thriftiest, her days hardly dragged more than they could be expected to do amid surroundings of so much undis-

turbed solitude. Besides she had the winter to anticipate. She was to see something of social amusement
then; her husband had promised her that she should
both entertain and be entertained after they returned
to West Tenth Street, and she knew that his pride in
her would make him keep his word, however caprice
might delay him in the ultimate fulfilment of it. She
feared showing too great a desire for distractions of a
social kind; his moods of tantalizing cruelty were
never to be calculated on. She had discovered that
the love he felt for her was one constantly on the alert
to ensheathe itself in the most distressing jealousy.
She had never, as yet, given him the least incentive to
become jealous, but it was plain to her that this trait
in him only waited an opportunity for rapid and
morbid development.

All this time she was very far from being happy.
But, as she told her Aunt Thyrza during several trips
that she made to town, it was not a misery that stood
any chance of shortening her existence.

"He is at times intolerable," she said. "One of the
proofs of just how odious he can make himself, Aunt
Thyrza, is the manner in which he forces me to meet
*you* — either secretly or not at all. I should so love
to have you up there at Greenacre to sniff the country
air, dear old soul, for a week or two, and do just as
you chose with everybody and everything about
you!"

Mrs. Ottarson gave one of her laughs. " *My*, Liv!"
she exclaimed. "I guess I'd have pretty tough work
doin' 's I chose with Mr. Del'plaine round!"

Olivia smiled drearily. "I am afraid any one would,"
she answered.

Mrs. Ottarson took her hand caressingly between her own. "My poor deary! It's all been wrong. No one knows more'n I do jus *how* wrong it's all been. Many's the night, 'Livia, while you was over there 'cross the water, I've laid 'wake in bed thinkin' 'bout it. An' all I can say, Livvy, is that you've stood it splendid ever since you got through that awful illness. You d'serve credit for bein' so brave and womanly."

"I surely deserve no credit at all, Aunt Thyrza," was the answer. "You and I have talked this matter over before now. The marriage may have been fraudulent enough on *his* part; but *I* need not have made it. I believe, now, that I fell a victim to the deceit of more persons than that sick man who lay with so white a face there in that dim chamber. . . . But never mind; it is too late for any good to come of open accusations. Besides, I find no one so hard to pardon, in this matter, as myself. And I don't want to let myself believe, even for an instant, that I was excusable in having taken the downward step I did take. I might begin to waver, then — to lose what courage I possess — to strike back, blow for blow, instead of bearing it all as unflinchingly as I can, because convinced that it is my just recompense, my rightful penalty."

Two or three times Olivia met Adrian Etherege during short visits at the West Tenth Street house, while she was in town for a few hours. A year had made the youth look manlier, though it had robbed him of no beauty. He had a hundred questions to ask his friend concerning the lands and cities embraced by her own and Delaplaine's long absence. But it was not always of foreign travels that Adrian wanted

to talk. He sometimes chose subjects of a far less
material sort.

"You tell me that you are lonely," he once said to
Olivia. "So am I; and I sometimes feel that I shall
continue lonely for the rest of my life."

"Have you no friends, then?" his companion asked.
"I mean — apart from myself," she added sweetly;
for ever since her husband had let fall those memora-
bly sneering words about the project of having Adrian
accompany them abroad last year, she had lost no
chance of showing the young secretary in how much
purely amical regard she held him.

"Few that I care for," said Adrian. "They are
mostly young men of my own age — and they are
devoted to business pursuits; they are at the bank of
Delaplaine and Company, or they are at other banks,
or in brokers' offices. Now, I have no love for the
ideas, the aims and the undertakings that make up the
chief joys of life for persons like these."

"And yet they tell me that you are a clever business man."

Adrian quickly shook his curly golden head. "Oh,
they are wrong — if by 'they' you mean Mr. Delaplaine, as I suppose you do. I haven't my work at
heart; I go through it like an automaton; when it is
over I want to forget it. And there is no one to help
me forget it. That is why I'm so lonely. If I had a
love for books it might be different; but I haven't. I
— I simply like people — the people who amuse
me."

Olivia laughed; she rarely laughed nowadays —
indeed, so rarely that the sound of her own audible mirth woke a little thrill of surprise in her. "You

forget that you also amuse *them.*" She laid her hand on his arm and looked into his adorable eyes, which had never enchanted her more than if they had been those of some woman whom she was fond of and thought singularly fascinating. "But my dear Adrian," she went on, calling him by the name which she had used in addressing him weeks before her departure for Europe, "you have the faculty of being intelligent without the need of books to make you so."

"I am not intelligent, Mrs. Delaplaine," he answered, speaking with excessive earnestness. "I can never do anything in the least remarkable. I can simply like and appreciate those who have gifts and striking qualities above my own. I — I was born to be a background and not a foreground. I'm no talker, as you know; I love to listen — when I may get those to whom I *can* listen without becoming wearied. Let me speak very frankly with you; I don't want you to misunderstand me — to imagine me vain in what I have just said about those mercantile associates. I am far from placing myself above them, but . . . I can't even be a background to *them.* . . . If I had been born above my present position in life, I think I should have made a success of it, as the phrase goes. I should have known persons who interested me — artists, dreamers, poets, men of brains and culture. I should have been their patron, their helper. But now I am nothing. I am simply — agreeable, as you once told me that I was. I'm not of enough importance for the talented beings — wherever they exist in New York, if they exist at all — to seek me out. So I must remain lonely, since

I have no means of meeting or mixing among the spirits with whom I truly sympathize."

Olivia laughed again. "You don't know how you interest me," she said.

Adrian looked at her fixedly for a moment. "Why? Because I declare myself a nonentity?" he asked.

"Absurd! Because you are so much less a nonentity than you imagine. . . . I fancy, from what I have read of the great thinkers, the great poets, the great minds, generally speaking, that it is much more fortunate to be apart from them and admire them than to be one of them and suffer, as their biographies tell us that they nearly all have suffered. . . . But if you really want congenial acquaintanceship, perhaps I shall be able to find it for you."

"To find it for me? You?" Olivia failed to notice just what accent and intonation went into this reply.

"Yes. I shall see a good deal of the world next winter. Mr. Delaplaine" (she rarely spoke of him as "my husband") "has promised me that I shall. And then your chance will come. I prophesy it, Adrian."

A startled, incredulous look responded to her. "Ah, *he* would never allow that!" the young man murmured. "He would never let me even dream that I, his secretary, his servant, was on an equality with *you!* He would forbid the first effort you made."

"Perhaps," said Olivia softly, as if speaking to herself. But suddenly her face brightened. "I would tell him," she proceeded, "that I wanted to secure a wife for you."

"A wife?"

"Yes. . . . Some day you will marry, of course.

Why should you not? And I will carefully look all about me to obtain some charming girl who will be just the proper match for you." Olivia now assumed a humorously grave look. "Let me see: she must, in the first place, be handsome — almost, if not *quite*, as handsome as you are. Secondly, she must be rich — "

"Pray, stop," broke in Adrian. There was a pained, imploring gaze in his eyes as they now lifted themselves to her own, which made Olivia pause and even regret the badinage that she had thus lightly begun. . . .

She had never mentioned to her husband these few interviews which she had held with Adrian. One evening he said to her, amid the almost drowsy dulness following their seven o'clock dinner at Greenacre:

"That boy, Adrian Etherege . . . you remember him?"

"Of course," returned Olivia.

"He had better see to some loose papers which I have been leaving up here, and which need to be filed and labelled. He may come up with me to-morrow night. Do you object to his coming?"

"No," replied Olivia. "Why should I object?"

Adrian came up with Delaplaine the next evening. Dinner was served almost immediately after the arrival of host and guest. Adrian conducted himself, as he always did in the presence of his employer, with repression and comparative reticence.

After dinner he went with Delaplaine into the private study of the latter, and remained there for over two hours. They came out together, and at once joined Olivia, who sat reading near a lamp, in a room that glowed with Japanese decorations.

"I hope to-morrow will be a glorious autumn day," she said smilingly to Adrian, "now it is arranged that you are to stop over at Greenacre for a holiday. We have had so many beautiful days during the past fortnight that it will be a shame if to-morrow is not charming."

"The best plan is never to expect anything good from the weather," said Delaplaine, with his glacial quietude. "Then it *may* agreeably disappoint you —like some few women I have met."

Long ago Olivia had learned to treat the sarcasms of her husband as though they had remained unspoken. "And how do you like this absurdly large house of ours?" she again said to Adrian.

"I am decidedly pleased with it," he answered. "The appointments are all in such taste. You forget both the size and the number of the rooms in their artistic treatment."

"I knew you'd have something to say in praise of Greenacre," replied Olivia. "To-morrow I will show you some of those exquisite views of the river that I mentioned the other day."

Delaplaine had drawn near the log-fire in the big chimney-place; for the evening outside (broken with innumerable voices of crickets and katydids) told chillingly of perished summer. He turned his head a little away from the blaze, though still keeping his slender body bowed and one thin hand crooked like the claw of a bird, with the firelight shining through it and staining it pink. He spoke to his wife:

"Did you see Adrian the other day?" he asked.

"I did," said Olivia. She was sorry that her tongue had slipped. She had not previously referred, before her husband, to these few past meetings with Adrian. If he had asked her whether his secretary were at the house in West Tenth Street when she had presented herself there, she would unhesitatingly have answered " yes." As it was, she had preserved silence regarding the whole affair. Adrian now enjoyed a liberty on which, as the functionary of a man like her husband, he was certainly to be congratulated. Who could tell what sudden restriction might be placed upon his goings and comings, provided Olivia were to state that she had met and talked with him? And so she had held her peace, by no means regretful that Delaplaine had failed to question her.

He moved away from the fire, now. He was looking with fixity at his wife. " You mean in Tenth Street? " he said.

" Yes," returned Olivia, striving to speak with utter carelessness and succeeding. " Adrian happened to be there at the same time with myself."

" Ah . . . indeed," said Delaplaine, with a tone so neutral and colorless as to leave the spirit in which he made this brief response wholly inscrutable for his hearers.

" I am usually in Tenth Street until three in the afternoon," " said Adrian, " when nothing calls me to the bank."

Delaplaine turned and watched him placidly for a moment. " My dear boy," he said, " I know the irreproachable industry of your habits as my secretary. You have no cause to enlighten me upon that point."

Adrian bit his lip. He wondered what displeasure this sudden access of mock politeness foretokened. Almost immediately after this, Delaplaine strolled out of the apartment, and in a few minutes a servant appeared requesting that Adrian would meet his master for a short further talk in the study.

"He is angry," thought Olivia, "at my having presumed to see poor Adrian in Tenth Street without informing him. And he is going to make his anger felt."

She was right. Adrian did not pass the following day at Greenacre. Delaplaine had discovered that there were letters of importance in which he would require his secretary's assistance at the bank. Throughout the remainder of their residence in the country-house, Adrian was permitted to pay them no second visit.

"Is it jealousy?" Olivia asked herself, "or is it only the autocratic protest of a man who searches for some cold-blooded device of annoyance?"

Delaplaine never made her sure just what it was. If he anticipated an expression of disapproval on the part of his wife, no such evidence greeted him. The truth was, Olivia now simply awaited what the coming season in New York would bring forth. If he attempted then to hamper the enjoyment, the relaxation, the self-forgetfulness that she daily grew to crave with stronger yearning, she might have some cards to play in such a cruel victimizing game by which he would be surprised if not repulsed.

Latter October was despoiling the trees about Greenacre of their last leafy brilliancies when Mr. and Mrs. Delaplaine returned to town. The Tenth Street house was most capably prepared for their reception. Servants were in readiness; carriages and horses waited Olivia's order; the air and distinction of the entire household were past cavil. But no one was invited to participate in all this reposeful and flawlessly refined luxury. Olivia had hoped to see Adrian again, but he had seemingly left the abode to return no more. She refrained from questioning her husband with respect to his absence.

November went by. Her two aunts, Mrs. Auchincloss and Mrs. Satterthwaite, had exchanged visits with her. At last came the large Auchincloss dinner, which she was permitted to accept, and which marked the beginning of her career as a woman of society.

The Patriarchs' Ball was of course followed by many others, both public and private, and Olivia went to every one which the marital veto did not exclude. Delaplaine was excessively *commode* about it all. He never danced nowadays, and yet he would sit chatting with the dowagers till the small morning hours, again and again, while his wife shone as a star of the *cotillon*. It began to be declared of him that he would make a model husband. But no one saw his petty domestic tyrannies, or the lynx-like way in which he watched all Olivia's male admirers. It delighted his egotism that she should "succeed" thus brilliantly. He wanted his wife to be not merely a great lady, but also a lady of well-conceded personal charm. For this reason her popularity pleased him. But other points connected with it pricked and irritated him. Like almost every old man who has ever been in love with a young woman, he became susceptible to the sharpest pangs of jealousy; but in his special case they were seizures which all the more clearly indicated how barren and arid was his nature through the aus-

terity of its unrelieved selfishness.  His was the old
dog-in-the-manger feeling: he could not secure
Olivia's heart himself, but he was determined that
no one else should secure it.

Slowly, but with a gathering increase toward their
culmination, his suspicions all assumed a single shape.
The season was now ending; Lent was on the verge
of throwing over the giddy multitude that penitential
nimbus in which it is supposed to conceal its follies
even while still indulging them.  Delaplaine now
felt certain that Jasper Massereene was preferred by
Olivia to all her other devotees.  He privately thought
the young man excellent style, as he himself would
have put it.  What he chiefly liked about Massereene
was the engaging simplicity which went with an intellect of no ordinary calibre.  He had tested that intellect more than once in their talks together, and he had
been astonished at the thoughtfulness, cultivation and
acumen concealed behind manners that were no less
elegant than unpretentious.

The truth was that he failed to see in Jasper Massereene a product of our so-called modern agnosticism
totally opposite from that which he himself represented, and yet in every way as distinctively stamped
by the same peculiar parentage.  Massereene was of
necessity the finer and more thorough scholar of the
two.  His reading had been wider, his outlook was
more educationally sweeping.  But writers and thinkers like Mill, Spencer, Darwin, Buckle, Huxley or
Lecky had stood the mental sponsors of both.  And
yet with Massereene a sincere and thriving optimism
had resulted from precisely the same causes which
had fed and vitalized Delaplaine's implacable pessim-

ism. The contrast between these two individualities could not have been more positive than it was, and yet they had been moulded, so to speak, by one identical philosophic potency.

Delaplaine had asked his own mind, not many weeks ago what could be the inducement which led this English-reared young radical to mix among the frivolities of a fashionable New York winter. He had seen that species of gayety at its most shining stage of London development. Why should he care for so feeble and comparatively provincial a reproduction of it as he encountered here? If he had been a shallow, or even a conventionally mediocre person, it would have altered the case; but he was very far from being either. He might have gone to a few of those entertainments where one meets the meagre literary element of New York society; or he might have dropped in at a few of the Twentieth Century Club reunions, presided over by persons of culture and solid ability, even though their assembled throngs are perhaps not always just the serious auditors to be expected at such momentous gatherings. But to go about night after night, where flippancy reigned undisputed, to dance that mechanical *cotillon*, to send bouquets idly broadcast among silly women, to prefer deliberately the interchange of platitudes for that of ideas — a like course in one so talented and sensible was hard to account for.

Suddenly Delaplaine, with no cheerful sensations, grew confident that he had found a solution of the puzzle. Massereene went out into the merry world because Olivia went. He was more persistently and meaningly attentive to her than any other of her male

friends. The latter were getting, indeed, to pay him
a certain deference of priority when he appeared.
Delaplaine began to watch these demonstrations
with an augmenting inward restlessness. One morning he returned from the bank unexpectedly, and entered the drawing-room to find Olivia seated there
with Jasper Massereene in earnest conversation. A
day or two afterward, having promised Olivia that he
would meet her at a certain large and noteworthy reception, he was exceedingly late in keeping the appointment. Olivia had left the reception with Massereene, having dismissed her carriage a few minutes
beforehand. Delaplaine had the pleasure of seeing
these two, strolling in the most leisurely manner
side by side, from the window of his brougham as
it sped up Madison Avenue.

About a fortnight ago invitations had been sent out
for a great ball at the Satterthwaites' on the day but
one preceding Lent. This ball was regarded as a
most appropriate termination of the winter's mirth-
making. The Satterthwaites were such incontestable
old Knickerbockers that society felt a grateful thrill
to them for thus magnanimously helping to wind up
the season. Then, too, it was so generous of the Satterthwaites; for they had done so much entertaining
in previous years, and their two girls, Emmeline and
Elaine, were still husbandless. "I believe there is a
. . . a . . . Mr. Plunkett who is quite attentive to
the elder of my two cousins," Madeleine Auchincloss
used to say nowadays, with her most innocent smile.
"I don't know much *about* Mr. Plunkett, and of
course the name is not a familiar one, but I think
he has a married sister who goes among artists and

writers and that kind of people. I am not sure but that Mr. Plunkett is a writer himself." These last words were always added with the suggestion of not wanting to be too hard on the young gentleman concerned, and to give him his full right of contradicting what may have been a false accusation.

There was no one conspicuously attentive to Madeleine. But she would never have put up with anybody whose principal recommendations to matrimony were that he possessed gifts either of brains or breeding. Who can guess just how keen a satisfaction it gave her to insinuate that if her cousin Emmeline *should* contract an engagement before very long, it would not be to a person of either station or wealth? As for Madeleine herself, she would never be *à prendre ou à laisser* in the way that some well-born girls allow themselves to become. Not she! Either she would marry advantageously or not at all. Alas! it is just this high and disinterested view of marriage that is yearly filling the ranks of our most select American maidens with cases of inflexible spinsterhood!

A general understanding existed that the Satterthwaite ball was to be given in honor of its hostess's beloved niece, Mrs. Spencer Delaplaine. Olivia's husband, after drawing these conclusions regarding Masscreene of which mention has been made, was now resolved that the intimacy should forthwith end. His wife had, once before, boldly disobeyed him; that revolt had concerned her ceasing longer to know Mrs. Ottarson. But on all other occasions where he had commanded she had acceded, and the meekness with which she had borne his manifold irritations could not have offered any domestic despot more tempting chances of tyranny. There is little doubt that Delaplaine mistook the motives of this former continued meekness when he said to her, only a short time before the much-talked-of ball:

"I suppose you are engaged for the German at the Satterthwaites'?"

"Yes," Olivia replied.

"May I ask to whom?"

"To Mr. Massereene."

"Ah?" murmured Delaplaine. It was about four o'clock in the afternoon, and he had met his wife, clad in a daintily fresh street-costume, at the door of the lower front drawing-room. Her *coupé* waited outside. She was going to pay some visits of etiquette. She had been looking over her cards, and held a little collection of them in her neat-gloved hand. They were the cards of the gentlewomen whose visiting-day happened to be this particular one.

"I have a word to say," Delaplaine now continued, with his usual faultless repose. "Be good enough to let me say it in here, will you?" And he passed immediately into the drawing-room.

Olivia followed him. He had tried her very sorely of late; more than once she had felt her patience giving way beneath his formidable impertinences, his steel-tipped personalities. She knew that her popularity gratified his pride, but she had begun to weary under the incessant goad of slur by which he made her pay for having thus pleased others besides himself.

After they had both cleared the threshold of the outer hall by a good many paces, Delaplaine turned and quietly faced her.

"You are too much seen in the company of that man, Massereene," he said.

"Indeed! You think so?"

"I decidedly think so. It must cease. I allow you to be a woman of fashion for the present, because it suits me that you should show people how my marriage, late in life though it was, has not resulted in my marrying a feminine dullard. You have held your own thus far very well. I did not expect to find it expedient that I should rebuke any imprudence in you. I now find it so. As I said, you see too much of this Massereene. I don't wish you to dance with him the last German of the season. And I will not permit you thus to dance it. You must break your engagement with him for the Satterthwaite ball. . . . Do you understand me?"

"Perfectly," said Olivia. Her eyes had been drooped for several seconds. She now raised them and looked at him as he had never seen her look at him before — not even when she had defied him with relation to cutting Mrs. Ottarson. "Perfectly," she repeated, "and I shall not do as you desire." She paused for a moment, and drew a deep, long breath, her face paling noticeably at the same time. "I am engaged to Mr. Massereene," she continued, "and I shall dance with him on Wednesday night." She took a step or two nearer Delaplaine. A light came flashingly into her blue eyes, and a curl raised her lip so that he could see the white teeth glistening beneath it. "You have asked me," she still went on, "whether I understood *you*. I do understand you, thoroughly. And I refuse — point-blank I refuse — to do as you most unjustly require!"

He stared at her.  He had got out his eyeglasses, and had begun to twirl them by their slender cord over one finger.

"Ah," he said in very low tones; "you . . . you defy me, then?"

Olivia threw back her head, and laughed with a terrible bitterness.  The stored-up misery of months rang in that laugh.  But something else rang in it as well — the desperate challenge of a spirit goaded until resignation was flung quite away.

"I *do* defy you!" she answered.  "You have made me suffer long enough!  Now you shall see me throw off the mask.  Now you shall see just what sort of a woman you married when you made her your wife — made her so by the lies you yourself not long ago acknowledged that you spoke!"

## XVII.

DELAPLAINE drew backward, feeling that he had indeed unloosed a whirlwind. Olivia's face was very pale, now, and its expression was one of blended courage and contempt. She gave her husband no time to reply. She seized upon the swift-passing chance that his own evident amazement afforded her. Her voice was not loud, but its vibrations expressed at once a fierceness and an intrepidity which mere sound could not have more plainly conveyed.

"You have told me how you came to marry *me*. But you have never yet heard how I soiled myself by consenting to marry *you*. My consent had nothing whatever to do with gratitude toward my dead father. I became your wife, in the distressing way that I did so become, because ambitious feelings tempted me — and most unworthily, I admit. . . . You know of my wretched illness after learning that you would live and be my husband. . . . Well, let all that pass . . . I recovered; I *was* your wife, and I faced the fate that I had brought on myself. But how did I face it? Just as if it had been the infliction of a deserved penance; that, indeed, is what I held it to be. You were my yoke — my burden; but I had brought you upon myself, and I determined to bear you bravely. At first your kind treatment was a new reproach to me. I did not merit being thus permitted to endure the consequences of my own misdeeds with so little conse-

quent pain. It seemed only right that I should suffer.
But that came soon enough. You made me suffer.
You cannot say that I flinched often. I am not a
fool; you knew I was not that, when you married me.
I don't know whether you saw or not that I was
simply clenching my teeth and bearing it all as best I
could. I think you did see this, and that it made you
still more cruel in your dealings with me. Meanwhile
I drew upon my own fortitude, and kept my nerves as
steady as the good fortune of my youth could help me
to keep them. If I had been an older woman, I might
have broken down. As it was I did not break down.
'I am taking my punishment,' I said — and I took it.
Once you presumed to dictate terms regarding the
continuance of my friendship with Aunt Thyrza.
There I opposed you, for you passed (and at the very
moment of assuming your real character) beyond the
bounds of either my toleration or my self-control.
But perhaps that little episode gave you my gauge, as
it were; it showed you just how far you could bend
me before I broke. On a hundred different occasions
you have had no cause to complain of my disobedience.
I have never been in the least afraid of you. If I had
been I should have felt fear in taking the stand that I
take now. For I admit that my patience is at last
exhausted. You say that I shall not dance the German with Jasper Massercene at the Satterthwaite ball.
I reply to you with the utmost conceivable defiance,
that I shall so dance. If you try to prevent my going
to the ball, then you must use force — it may be that
you will even use personal violence. I have heard of
husbands like yourself doing just those miserable
things. Very well, then — *tout est dit*. You push the

whole matter into publicity. For myself, I don't care whether you do or no. If they told me afterward that I had any good ground for getting a divorce from you, I am sure that I should sooner or later rejoice very much. I confess my entire *rôle* of hypocrisy to have been a sad failure. I play no longer either the saint or the meek-souled woman. Henceforth I mean to forget that I sinned in marrying you. Or, if I do not forget, I shall consider my expiation accomplished. Your future commands will win from me no more attention than your taunts have done for a year past. You must now either leave me my own mistress or be prepared for my desertion of you. I mean, plainly, that I will go back to Aunt Thyrza. No power on earth can make me live with you against my will, and certainly such power is not represented by either your insolence or your persecution."

Olivia moved past her husband, after this long yet inflexibly sustained speech, with a queen's own *froid-eur* in her face. Heredity is a marvellous fact; you saw, as if by a sudden little burst of revelation, that she was her aunt Letitia's indisputable niece — but with, of course, a vast difference.

She left the room, and he allowed her to do so without volunteering the least reply. He could scarcely have done anything which Olivia would have found more tantalizing.

For a long time, however, he remained there in the drawing-room. He was not angry at his wife. Loving her as, in his curious fashion, he did love her, the audacity of her recent outburst had even placed her ᴗbefore him in a new admired light. But at the same time it had inflamed his jealousy with a wholly new

fire. He assured himself that Jasper Massereene was
at the root of her abrupt rebellion. She had flung
aside all disguise, but not because she was weary and
stung beyond the bounds of patience. A passion had
enveloped her spirit, and she was acting by its imperious dictates. Her swift sentences of accusation and
of explanation had pierced him deeper than he desired
to let any living mortal know — and least of all her
from whose quiver such wounding shafts had sped.
He had always known and felt that she cared nothing
for him; but her announcement that she cared nothing for reputable concealment of her injuries and her
matrimonial heart-burnings, assailed him with an unexpected keenness.

He sat for a long while with his thin hands knotted
together and his gray head most dejectedly drooped.
He had too much power of brain not to perceive the
mournful absurdity of his own position. The love
that he bore Olivia — the love that his acid and repul-
sive temperament could no more express in a gracious
and courtly way than some fountain whose tubes are
mire-clogged can send forth a limpid current to the
sun — this love seemed now objective and apparent
before him, mocking him with its incongruous vitality.
And socially it stood a fair chance of wrecking him.
He had always abhorred the idea of a scandal being
connected with his name. But here, suddenly, he
found himself face to face with a desperate woman —
a woman who had asserted that she would not hesitate
to turn the full glare of publicity upon their past
relations as man and wife.

Still, Delaplaine's agitation, keen as it now was, did
not prevent his lucid mind from working. Almost

instinctively he reviewed Olivia's late conduct, and compared it with the manner in which she had previously behaved to him. Did she not really value her present position? Had she not openly admitted that she had married him solely for reasons of worldliness? Infatuated as she may have become with Massereene, was there not more temporary feminine heat in her late show of recklessness than its apparent sincerity would imply? She had assumed a posture of the most baffling indifference as regarded her present place before the world, but would this dauntless unconcern prove permanent? She had professed herself unregardful of future impoverishment, but would she so bravely meet, after all, the stern, practical test of her boasted hardihood? 'I will try her,' Delaplaine said to himself. And he did try her — believing unchangeably, at the same time, that she was now swayed by an ardent and headlong sentiment for Jasper Massereene.

That same evening they were engaged to be present at one of those great, costly dinners which grow more and more frequent as New York departs farther from early republican ideals. Delaplaine did not again see his wife until he met her in the lower hall, cloaked for the carriage that waited outside. He noted that she was a little paler than usual; otherwise her countenance bore no traces of the tempest that not long ago had stirred and kindled it. A footman opened the front door, and she silently passed out, descending the stoop. Another footman opened the door of the carriage. As Olivia entered the latter she appeared perfectly ignorant that her husband was following her. He seated himself opposite to her, and the

vehicle rolled away. It was dark, and the electric
lights were all aglow. Olivia, leaning back against
soft cushions, let her gaze obliquely fasten itself upon
an unshaded segment of the window nearest her.
They had begun to move at a rapid pace, for their
hosts lived considerably higher up town than West
Tenth Street, and it was now almost the hour (half-
past seven) at which they had been asked to present
themselves. As the carriage was hurried clatteringly
through Fifth Avenue, Olivia watched the various
forms of the passers, outlined with such inky darkness
against the silvery glare all about them. They would
have done, in their weirdness, for a Blake or a Vedder
to have peopled some fanciful hell with. "And yet,"
came her thought, both humorous and grim, "I haven't
a doubt that lots of them would be very unsuited to
infernal surroundings. And I dare say that very few
of them would change fates with me — if they could
look into my heart and see the darkness *there.*"

She had already begun to shudder at the prospect
of Delaplaine's hostility being shown by some act of
vengeful exposure. She was not willing to make the
least retraction of her passionate words, nor did she,
indeed, regret their utterance. But dearly as she
still loved and would always love Mrs. Ottarson, the
mere thought of returning to West Twenty-Third
Street had borrowed from calmer reflection almost
terrifying colors. Still, she would go back there
resignedly if the worst should come. After all, if
her husband refused full surrender, to live with him
longer would be insupportable torment. His jealousy
of young Adrian Etherege had seemed a trifling insult
enough, without this later exposition. It was perhaps

because Jasper Massereene had roused in her feelings where an ardent respect narrowly approached positive reverence, that Delaplaine's last unforeseen fiat, pronounced with relation to him, had marked the absolute limit of her concession. She had still no more dreamed of loving Massareene than she had dreamed of not honoring his intellect, his manliness and his rectitude, or of not finding solace, help and encouragement in his unique companionship. She was a woman whose fervor of sentiment (provided that she, a wife, had realized cherishing it toward any man not her husband) might have burned on in her soul as harmlessly as the fire of a diamond will burn amid its defensive crystal sheath.

The silence that Delaplaine maintained there in the darkness of the carriage began to impress her with the keenest discomfort. What fell intensity of response or of counter action was he reserving behind this stony reticence? The very gloom which enwrapped him added an appreciable dread to his mysteriously speechless policy. And policy was just the word to define his present attitude. He was a man of untold resources. He had doubtless dealt with women before now under circumstances where emotion had arrayed itself against calculation and self-mastery. "And I," thought Olivia, while she continued immovably to stare away from him, through the window of the swift, rumbling carriage, "I have only my heart, my sense of right, my recognition of outrage to guide me, in fighting with his frigid tact, his experienced cruelty."

Suddenly he surprised her by speaking. His voice was just loud enough to be plainly heard.

"You still intend to defy me in that matter of dancing with a certain gentleman?"

She gathered herself together, as it were, on the instant. "Yes," she replied.

"I wouldn't excite myself again, if I were you," he returned, with the same impenetrable undertone. "I can hear you quite as well if you answer me in a lower key. I suppose you don't want to go into dinner looking red in the face and vulgarly flustered. Your appearance was very composed — very reputably so — when I last had the pleasure of seeing you. A quiet question asks only a quiet answer. I'm going to put another question, by the way. Provided you do leave me, as you distinctly threatened, have you weighed the importance of what I could say you stated to be your true reasons for having married me?"

"Have . . . I . . . weighed its importance?" came the somewhat faltered answer. Then, more firmly, she went on: "I have weighed the importance of but one thing — ending the wrongs you have made me suffer from."

"Ah," he murmured. She heard him draw a long breath. "It's rather a serious thing to have said of one that you married an old man on his death-bed for his money — and afterward freely admitted this."

Olivia gave a bleak laugh, unconscious of having done so. "And the old man!" she exclaimed. "Pray don't forget *his* side of the affair. It would scarcely be just."

"Oh, my dear madame, I assure you that I shall entirely forget it. If there is ever any public talk of you and me, the drift of opinion cannot possibly set but one way."

"I understand," she returned; "you will use every means to make it set so that falsehood can supply you with."

"Oh, not at all. My record, you know, is quite unimpeachable. I shall simply make a few state- ments, and people will all believe me. Don't for an instant flatter yourself that they will not. I have been a great many years before New York society. You may think very hard things about me, but New York society thinks exceedingly nice ones. It will say 'Poor Delaplaine! At his age to become the victim of a manœuvring girl like that! What a terribly unprincipled creature she must be!' Some of the people whom you told me you had met in Mrs. Ottarson's boarding-house might sympathize with *you*, after they had heard your side of the story. I don't just know how contented you would feel with that sort of a constituency. But it would be all you could ever secure. Of course if you had money, matters might be different; you could afford, then, to snap your fingers in the faces of your detractors. But as you would now be placed, you would represent two very unpleasant phases of life — poverty and unpopu- larity. You would find that nearly all your friends would drop away from you after you had gone to the Twenty-Third Street boarding-house. It wouldn't be so difficult for them to forget that you are a Van Rensselaer after you had been at pains to remind them that you are also a . . . Jenks. And your slim purse would be no temporary inconvenience, either, provided you really left me. I would get the clever- est lawyers I could find to keep you out of your thirds after you became my widow. I'm not sure but that

desertion would afford rather easy grounds for such
an arrangement. I'm entirely serious about all this,
as I think you must perceive. You might fight my
will, but litigation is expensive."

His words had to Olivia's jarred nerves the sharpness and hardness of knife-edges. "I shall not fight
your will," she said. "If I live longer than you do
I will not touch a dollar of your money except what
you choose lawfully to leave me. As for quitting
your house now, I will only do it if I am driven to it."

"I see. If I don't consent to your dancing the
German with Jasper Massareene." It would be impossible for any spoken sentence to convey satire at once
more caustic and more serene.

Olivia gnawed her lip in the darkness. She had
always detested satire, but when, as she now felt, it
became like a wounding splinter from the stony nature
of him who employed it, her aversion deepened to
loathing.

"Put it that way if you please," she replied. "I
have no objections. What you say is a part, though
far from being all, of the actual truth."

"Precisely," he muttered, with his unalterable repose. "The real cause of war between nations very
often lies wholly outside the excuse for beginning
hostilities."

"I require no excuse," responded Olivia, "and I
have no cause except one — resentment against injury."

Just then the carriage stopped. For the first time
since their entrance into the carriage together, Olivia
saw her husband's face, bathed in the white light that
streamed from an opposite corner. It looked, that
face of Delaplaine's, as though it were cut out of drab

slate. A slight smile flickered about its parted lips.
She had seen that smile hundreds of times before, but
it had never looked so coolly devilish to her as at this
especial time.

"You have another cause," he said. "I mean Jasper Massareene."

"That is untrue," she answered, while her heart
gave one indignant throb.

"You say so in the most virtuously glib way. But
you can prove it by obeying my commands."

"I will not obey them."

"Oh, but you must," he said, looking at her with
eyes that seemed to hold the glint of steel in their dim
pupils.

"I will *not*. What I say to you I say for the last
time, too: *I will not*. Be prepared for any course
you may decide to take. But rely on this: my oppo-
sition meets and matches your tyranny, act for act."

All this passed very quickly between them. In
another moment the footman had swung wide open
the door of the carriage. Delaplaine at once alighted,
and assisted his wife to do the same, with that graceful composure of movement which his years had not
yet destroyed, and which, in his earlier life, had won
him a well-merited repute for courtly and distinguished manners.

It looked, now, like the most momentous sort of
deadlock between them. But circumstance, that
busiest of entanglers and unravellers in her dealings
with the threads of all human destiny, was already
employed on her usual incalculable task after a fashion
that neither could have remotely prophesied.

The Satterthwaite ball never occurred. Not many

hours later, New York society woke to the unpalatable fact that it would be deprived of so festal an
opportunity for crossing the dreary Lenten threshold.

Little Lulu Satterthwaite had been in her gayest
spirits that morning. There was to be a commemora-
tive *cotillon* at dancing-school in the afternoon. The
school continued through Lent, but some of the merry
young folk who' formed its corps of disciples had
induced their preceptors to give them a gala meeting,
as if it were "winding up" an imaginary fashionable
season. Lulu herself had risen the reigning spirit of
the proposed frolic. She had been for days full of
"mamma's ball," and watchful of all its preparatory
details. She knew exactly what her mother and her
two sisters were to wear, and had said to Elaine
several days ago, with her little golden head put sapi-
ently on one side, and a miniature frown of marked
solemnity on her forehead :

"Do you know, Elly, I've been thinking it over
very seriously, and I *do* think nothing will be so
becoming to you, after all, as your blue tulle trimmed
with the forget-me-nots? You've only worn it once
before, you know — at the second of the assemblies —
and you've not a single dress that shows you off half
as well. It's altogether the most fetching thing you
have."

But Elaine had answered snappishly that she would
wear what she pleased, and that such proceedings
were not of a sort to interest little girls. "Besides,
Lulu," her sister added, "if you don't stop using those
slangy phrases which I'm sure that Van Dam boy
teaches you, I'll get papa to make you cease having
anything to do with him."

Lulu tossed her head. "Papa wouldn't," she retorted. "He knows Charlty's a catch; some day he will have lots and lots of money; all the big girls will be setting their caps for him when he grows up. I heard Mrs. Rivington tell her little Eva so the other day, at the dancing-class. Eva is *so* stupid. She wanted to know what kind of a cap, and how it was going to be set. And I explained just what her mother meant. I happened to be passing, on Dickey Van Horn's arm, at the time; and then I heard two or three of the other mammas laugh, and one of them said: '*She'll* hold her own, some day,' meaning— me, of course. Hold my own! I should think I would!" And Lulu gave her slender little body a whirling turn that made her look for an instant not unlike that pirouetting fairy they used to put on the old-fashioned Christmas plum-cakes.

She had been engaged by young Van Dam to lead the *cotillon* with him that afternoon; or rather, she had indicated in a gracious, managerial way that this would be the most advisable plan. Monsieur Duprez, the head of the dancing-school, and his sister, Madame Chantillon, had become Lulu's willing slaves. As her brother Peyster expressed it, "Now, she bosses things, now, Lulu does," and Peyster was assuredly right.

She had even considered with her preceptor all the different figures that were to be led, and her privileged eyes alone had prematurely gazed upon the glowing and tasteful favors after their purchase. She intended to look her very best that day, she had informed the two nurses who would assist her at her toilet. "There won't be many girls there *much* older than I am," she had said, "and I mean to cut them out completely. Oh, dear, how I wish they only would mention *our* affairs in the papers, and describe how *we* were dressed. . . . Well, well, one must have patience; all that is sure to come later, when one really goes out into society."

She had been greatly excited all through the morning; but it chanced to be Saturday, and hence was not a day of study with her. At about eleven o'clock she was handed by one of the servants a bouquet of the rarest roses, with a card attached to it, bearing the name of Mr. Charlton Van Dam. If Elaine's friend, Lord Scarletcoat, could have heard the little scream of pride and pleasure with which Lulu seized this enchanting nosegay, he would hardly have reversed his previous unjust opinion as to there being no children in America.

When the hour came for the child to be dressing, she discovered with dismay that her two sisters and her mother would all be absent. They had visits to pay, or engagements of a similiar sort. Elaine, just before departing, gave Lulu a quizzical look of amazement as she said:

"The idea, Lulu, of your expecting that we would stay in to see your frock put on! It is too absurd. . . . If I only had my way with you, I'd stop all this vanity and nonsense by sending you up to the Park with your nurse, and letting you breathe fresh air and get some healthful exercise."

"Pooh!" cried Lulu, disdainfully. "I see more of the Park than you do, Elly. I rode six or seven miles there yesterday. My riding-school teacher says I'm the bravest and best *young* rider, of my *sex*, that he has."

Emmeline, who was always kinder to her precocious little sister than was Elaine, and who chanced also to be present, just then, here broke into an amused laugh. "Which means, Lulu," she said, "that you ride very well for a little girl. Why are you so afraid of being called a little girl? Some day you'll be sorry nobody can possibly call you one any longer."

Lulu gave a short, self-satisfied nod. "No doubt," she returned. "I want the time to come when I *shall* be sorry; that's all."

"You do too many things," said her mother, who had entered a few minutes ago and had been quietly listening, not far from the doorway. "It's your papa's idea that riding agrees with you; it's not mine. But you've those red spots in your cheeks now, my dear, which show that you are nervous."

"Oh, I'm always nervous," said Lulu, wheeling her tiny figure about. "I'm a nervous constitution."

The three ladies, exchanged glances that showed how comic they thought this admission from so ridiculously youthful an authority; and Lulu swept over all their faces a covert look, revealing the most unchildish self-consciousness. She wanted to see whether she had not said something diverting and extraordinary for one of her years. Among the many faulty features of her unhappy education, was this tendency on the part of her elders to encourage her in the habit of imitating their own forms of phraseology. Eager to be thought "old for her age," she was perpetually having this unwholesome craving fostered instead of repressed by those very observers of it who should have been the first to condemn its indulgence.

Her mother, Emmeline and Elaine soon afterward left her. She was alone with the two nurses at the commencement of her elaborate toilet.

"*Je suis un peu fatiguée,*" she suddenly said to Françoise, her favorite, after the process of frizzing her lovely golden locks had been completed before a large mirror. "*J'ai mal à la tête, Françoise; peut-être c'est une espèce de neuralgie. J'ai rémarqué que maman et mes sœurs souffrent comme ça, de temps en temps. Ce n'est rien; ça passera, j'en suis sûre.*"

But it did not go away. In a short time there came upon the child what she piteously described as a raging headache; she used even in her pain the modes of speech caught from others far older than herself. Her eyes began to shine with a feverishly unnatural light. The two nurses looked at each other in alarm.

"*Mademoiselle se trouve malade,*" murmured one.

"*Vraiement!*" faltered the other.

"I'm not ill," asserted Lulu. She had not yet put on her brilliant beribboned frock. But she went toward it, where it lay, bright as a sunset cloud, upon the bed. "I tell you it's only a headache, and it makes me a little dizzy. I—I had one, something like it, the other day at dancing-school; but it passed off; it didn't last as long as this, and it didn't make me so dizzy. . . . But this will pass off, too. . . . Ah, my dress—my beautiful dress. . . ."

And then, as her voice grew husky, she reeled, while one of the nurses sprang to her. . . .

Mrs. Satterthwaite was the first of the absent ones

to return. She had taken "mamma's *coupé*," and had been shopping a little, and calling a little at the houses of various friends. She had spent money, and talked scandal over more than a single cup of tea, served her in the most delicate of china. She could not have told you in which occupation she found the most enjoyable *désœuvrement*, but spending money, talking scandal and drinking tea were all very pleasurable pastimes.

Her young son, Peyster, met her in the hall as she entered it. His eyes were red with crying. "Oh, mamma!" he exclaimed, and ran toward her, seizing her dress.

But she repulsed him; it was a very handsome dress, and she did not like to have it treated so roughly, even by the son of whom, in her way, she professed to be very fond.

"Peystey, what *are* you doing?" she cried. And then she saw what the dimness of the hall had not yet allowed her to see. "You're crying? What has happened?"

"Oh, mamma! *Lulu!* Now, she's, now . . ."

The poor boy could say no more for his tears.

## XVIII.

During the next half hour or so, Bleecker Satterthwaite and his daughters, Emmeline and Elaine, all three returned. They were all going to dine out somewhere; they had calculated their time for dressing. Emmeline was going to one dinner-party, Elaine to a second, and Mr. and Mrs. Satterthwaite had a similar engagement which necessitated their keeping it in one another's company. As for Aspinwall, he had not returned at all. It was nearly always thus with the members of this mundane and insatiably pleasure-seeking household. Domesticity was unknown to them. Theirs was a home without a single home-like trait. They were a family who resembled some fanatical priesthood all passionately employed in various offices of pagan worship. Their temple was that of fashion, and their rites were performed with a truly sacerdotal zeal. It is doubtful whether they reaped much enjoyment from the whole senseless cult — so doubly and signally senseless amid a government that professes to be lifted on republican bases above the Old World claims and protestations of caste.

What charities were undertaken by Mrs. Satterthwaite or by either of her daughters bore relation solely to the kind of co-patrons who would appear on the same lists with themselves. Mrs. Auchincloss and Madeleine literally, on many occasions, would

seek the slums of the city, personally acting as the
teachers and agents of mission-schools and various
other institutions. They were snobs, but snobs with
a religion, and as far as their religion went, its ethical
effects were salutary. Their trouble was the old
pharisaical one; they penetrated into the most doleful purlieus of the "East side," but it was known in
Fifth Avenue that they did so, and their pilgrimages
were not solitary; they always made them in the society of ladies who, whether young or old, were incontestably *dans le monde.* In fact, neither Mrs. Auchincloss nor Madeleine would have thought herself quite
as socially secure without her charities as with them.
They were a part of "duty," and not to have a code
of duty which you practically and rigorously respected
was, in their belief, not to be crowned with the best
sort of gentility. The root of the whole impulse —
religious, no less than eleemosynary — may have lain
in that one word, gentility. I am by no means sure
that the chief recommendation of godliness in the eyes
of Madeleine and her mother was not the highly
respectable odor which they considered to pervade
it. They prided themselves, too, upon being devo-
tional thinkers. They were always, in spite of their
avowed and seemingly adamantine faith, reading some
book of the many which our curious age now pro-
duces, wherein the defence of faith and its diligent
support from metaphysical sources, were made the
subject of numberless eloquent chapters. This month
they would be "oh, so *much* interested" in "that enchanting volume," "Science as the Confirmation of
Scripture," and next month they would own to an
equal admiration for "that wonderfully comforting

series of essays," "Modern Thought as the Hand-
maid of Revelation." Mr. Auchincloss and the
blameless Chichester would appear to share their
esteem for works of this description. Mrs. Auchincloss would now and then say: "My husband has
been so absorbed, lately, in the delightful book," or
Madeleine would declare: "My brother, Chichester,
tells me that he has never read anything at once so
logical and so cheering."

With the Satterthwaites it had all been markedly
different. Their world was not the world of books,
and they would as soon have occupied their superficial,
butterfly existences with the evidences of Christian
creeds, from Methodism to the last decision of the
Œcumenical Council, as they would have questioned
the advisability of mounting a tantivy coach or the
wisdom of playing lawn-tennis. They accepted both
modes of diversion, just as they accepted the rather
tiresome but wholly proper occupation of aristocratic
almsgiving. They lived solely for personal enjoyment; but since others, who lived just as they did,
had conceded that it was "the thing" to show some
heed for those disagreeable hundreds of thousands
who made up the lower strata of society, they treated
such a popular drift of taste as though it had been a
new shade in bonnet-strings or a prevalent caprice in
the tying of them.

They were all keenly shocked on discovering the
illness of Lulu. Mr. Satterthwaite and his daughters
entered the little girl's chamber to find her mother,
the nurses and two physicians grouped about the bedside, while Poyster, with an awed look on his dull,
hobbledehoyish face, sat quite still in one corner.

Lulu was fearfully ill; it soon become apparent to the whole family that this was the case. Her trouble was a brain congestion of sharp violence. The physicians were loth to administer narcotics except in the smallest quantities, and these appeared thus far to accelerate rather than retard her disorder. There was no doubt that she now grew hourly worse. Fits of coma would be succeeded by bursts of delirium, in which her lips, hot with sudden fever, would let fall pell-mell sentences of the most pathetic mania.

And it all bore incessant reference to the unnaturally strained, gay, frivolous life that she had been permitted to live!

"Mamma," she would suddenly cry, seeking to lift herself from the bed, with glassy, staring eyes and a face flushed crimson amid her yellow wealth of hair — "Mamma, I *shall* be late for the dancing-class! And you *know* I'm to lead the *cotillon* — I've told you so fifty times! . . . Who's that girl in my dress? Make her take it off! *Is* it Sally Van Dam?" (Then a wild, shrill laugh that pierced her hearers.) "Oh, if it's only Sally, I don't care. She is Charlty's sister. . . . But none of the other girls shall dance with Charlty. . . . He and I are to lead together. On horseback, too! Isn't it nice and queer? A German in the Park — on horseback! Yes, Monsieur Duprez said it was all right. . . ." (Then a shivering moan of terror and a glare of untold affright from the poor, dilated eyes.) "Oh, look! look! One of the horses is dancing all wrong. He's — he's gone mad. . . . It's Peystey's black pony; he wants to kill Bessie Ludlow. . . . He'll trample her to death. . . . Peystey! Can't you manage him! *Can't you!* Ah!

it's all over! He's killed her!" (And then plaintive shrieks, these ending in convulsions that gave the frail limbs an almost unearthly strength.)

By about ten o'clock that night she woke from one of her stupors, calling out: "Oh, I'm blind! I'm blind!"

It was true. There had been some suffusion of the visual nerve-centres, and from that moment sight was hopelessly paralyzed.

And then a most bitter thing happened. Mrs. Satterthwaite, trembling with distress, bent down and clasped the terrified child in her arms. "Lulu!" she cried, perhaps addressing her little girl with the first true motherly accent that she had ever yet heard from maternal lips: "Lulu! Don't be frightened! I'm here. Mamma's here. Don't you know mamma?"

But the child pushed her away, and rose up from the bed with both arms gropingly outstretched, as though her lost sight were hiding from her somewhere near by and she sought to regain it. The mother's embrace of consolation and protection was futile and meaningless to her. What did she, poor sufferer, know of such love as that? A pat on the cheek, or a stroke of the curls, now and then — a nod, a smile, or a laugh, when she delivered any of her bold, shrewd, quaint sayings — an occasional frown, lifted finger or biting word of reprimand — this child knew her mother by these and similar tokens, but by these alone. And now, in the ordeal of horror and pain, there was no sweet magic and magnetism of affection to claim her instinctive response. The arms that leaned to clasp her had no familiar feeling; the bosom that would have pillowed her head bore no recollected warmth.

"It must be that I'm dying!" she shrieked. "The darkness must be that! Oh, I don't want to die! I want to live! It's horrible to die, and turn all white and stiff, and be put in a dark grave! And I love so to dance, and to ride on horseback, and to wear nice clothes! . . . What is it that makes me blind? Oh, can't somebody tear the blackness out of my eyes? . . ."

Poignant as was all this for those who observed it, mercy at least lay in the fact of its not lasting very long. A swoon followed what had perhaps been the most agonizing of Lulu's outbursts, and for a long time she lay so pale and still that her watchers anticipated death at any instant. But just before death, came re-awakened consciousness, and while a shudder ran through the group at the bedside because they feared a repetition of the lamentable scenes just enacted, Lulu opened her still sightless eyes and began to babble fragmentary sentences that soon told their own dreamy and sombre story. . . . She was at dancing-school — at the grand *fête* that afternoon, from which, hours ago, a messenger had been hurried with dismay, to learn what detained herself and her brother. . . . Now she sat beside Charlty Van Dam and smelled the bouquet he had sent her, and told him how lovely she thought the flowers, and how kind it was for him to send her such a real *grown-up* bouquet. . . . Again, she would be in the mazes of a *cotillon*-figure, prompting some fellow-dancer who was more dull of wit than herself, or less nimble of foot. . . . And at last she would seem to be in soft wonder and perplexity why the *fête* had not begun. "Everything is ready, Monsieur Duprez," she would murmur. . . .

"Where's the music? We are all here in our places. . . . Why don't the musicians play for us?"

But the musicians *had* played, poor little absentee, and you were not there to hear them! The lights have all gone out; the ball-room is silent and deserted; the children are home and in bed. They missed you very much. They heard with surprised and startled looks that you were ill and could not come. But they did not even fancy that you would never come again, with your eyes that danced as gayly as your pretty beribboned toes did, and your face as old and thoughtful in one way as it was young and bloomy in another!

Somewhere near midnight, Lulu's babblings grew fainter and fainter, like those of a brook that has lost its path among alien pebbles and can trill but in the thinnest of voices what melody it has borne from its urn up among the hills. No complaint about her own blindness had fallen from her lips for a long time. She was very peaceable, with the cool white cloths laid and re-laid against the temples that had burned and throbbed so. But they did not burn or throb now. For many minutes she would not speak at all, and then the words that sounded from her would seem to have no more significance than the tender cooings of a pigeon by its cote. But when the end was very close at hand indeed, a smile broke like light about her lips, and a dim flash came into the blind eyes just before they dropped their lids in rest forever. All who stood at her bedside could plainly hear what she then said.

"Oh, *now* we're going to begin. . . . There's the music! How merry it sounds!" Perhaps she caught the strains of a finer music than earthly flutes and

viols can make. But if truly she had heard such
harmonies, her spirit went nearer to where they soared
and floated, not ever returning to the small, placid
little body whence it had flown on its far-away adven-
ture and quest. No one was ever to know what Lulu
had vanished to find. Though the great city where
she had lived her brief span of days might crumble
into the time-spurned ruin of another Thebes, through
all its multitudinous morrows the light that she had
seen and the music to which she had hearkened would
remain as two more drops of gloom in the vast ocean
of secresy we name death! For, every life that the
mighty shadow takes into itself is bathed by an equal
dusk, and one same dignity of mystery clings about all
who have sunk into its unsurrendering tides — the
pure as the sinful, the lofty as the lowly, the old,
white with years, and the young, yet scathless under
their goads!

After all was over, the family met, one by one, in
the large drawing-rooms below stairs ; but two of its
members remained absent — Aspinwall, who had not
yet come home, and Peyster, whose sobs the nurses
were seeking to quiet, and whom everybody save
these had forgotten. The drawing-rooms were per-
vaded with preparations for the never-to-be-held Satterthwaite ball. It would have occurred on Monday ;
to-morrow would be Sunday, and as such work, for
so-called holy reasons, must cease even in this secular
household, arrangements had been fully completed
before dark on Saturday evening. The floors were
neatly covered with glossy linen " crash " for dancing;
the furniture had been set close to the wall or else
removed altogether; the mantels were stripped both

of drapery and ornament, waiting their burdens of bedded flowers. The apartments were not brightly lit; they had a ghostly, staring, comfortless look; and to the people who now gathered in them their aspect was horrible. As for Mr. and Mrs. Satterthwaite, Emmeline and Elaine, they sat and gazed at one another, above the pale glare of those wide, long floors, in a senseless, blank, stupefied way. You might have detected a kind of irritated *hauteur*, too, in the expressions of their faces — noticeably in that of Bleecker Satterthwaite himself. Perhaps it seemed to this family as if death had smitten them with an unwonted insolence in thus at all abruptly afflicting them. As for grief, they did not appear to know how one should show it. Possibly they were too stunned, just yet, to realize its existence in their souls. They had never given much heed to the question of souls. There had always been something brassy and flaunting about the completeness of their materialism. They had thought considerably more concerning the welfare of horses than that of their fellow-creatures. They had always found a stable more congenial quarters than a library — this being as true of "papa" and Aspinwall as it was of the two grown-up girls.

Aspinwall had not been home since luncheon time, and might very possibly have drifted into some gay company of college-friends. Nobody had known where to find him; he had left no orders with his valet; and there were certain rare occasions when even one with whom dress was so much a *faible* as with Aspinwall Satterthwaite, did not feel himself compelled to attire himself for dinner.

Midnight had sounded some little time ago. They

all had tacitly conceded, while sitting there in the big
shadowy room, that they were waiting for "Aspy" to
come home. Mr. Satterthwaite had begun to pace
the long apartments with hands clasped behind him
and lowered head. Emmeline cried a little, now and
then. Her sister Elaine would turn and look at her
very seriously as she wiped her eyes and drew shortened, sobbing breaths. Elaine did not feel like crying.
Her tears had never flowed except for selfish causes,
and seldom even for those. It was not that she failed
to mourn, but rather that a dazed and clouded sensation had come upon her faculties. Such a calamitous
event as this which had befallen herself and her kindred arrived in the guise of so bewildering a novelty!
Death had always been to her a possibility clad with
remoteness. Of course it might enter their house one
day. But it would give premonitory rumors of its
hateful advance. There was so much time in which
to become prepared for that; and meanwhile there
were all the pleasurable pursuits, with inestimable
bodily health added, to sum up, to adorn, to merrily
intensify life. Elaine had not dreamed of scanning
the whole problem deeper. To her it was not a problem at all, but a festivity. She had thus far had her
choice of cultivating or ignoring its guests. This
black one, thrusting itself into her notice and insisting
that it should not be treated *de haut en bas*, thrilled
her with an unprecedented terror.

Mrs. Satterthwaite remained motionless in her chair.
She realized more piercingly this night that she was a
mother than the worst pains of child birth had ever
taught her to realize before. Her thoughts had flown
to Aspinwall, her eldest son, loved beyond all her

other children by a heart which too often had let her only vaguely know that she in reality loved any of them overmuch. At intervals she would lift her head, as if listening for a sound in the outer hall. The sound for which she listened was the turning of a latch-key in the lock of the front door.

At last she felt sure that she heard it, and suddenly rose. Her husband paused in his monotonous walk. She glided toward the large main doorway of the drawing-rooms.

"That is Aspy, now," the others heard her say; and then she disappeared into the hall. Frigid woman of the world as she had always been, her spirit of motherhood now yearned with an immense longing to clasp her favorite boy against her breast and be the first who should break the tidings of his little sister's death.

A minute or so later they who were in the drawing-room heard a faint cry. All three, in an instant, gathered at the threshold of the door.

They saw Aspinwall standing in the hall with a shamed leer on his face and a sagging laxity of posture that swiftly told its brutal tale.

Mrs. Satterthwaite, pale and convulsed, motioned with one hand for them to leave her alone beside her son. The father and the two sisters drew backward. There was a potency of appeal in the look of that wife and mother which neither of them could resist.

Still, while he receded, an oath of exasperation broke from Bleecker Satterthwaite.

But Emmeline, whom they had been wont to laugh at in other days for her moods of so-termed sentimentality, sprang toward her father now.

"Papa," she cried, "don't judge him too harshly! Remember how we, who are all older than he is, have never taught him to feel the disgrace of it as we should have done! And *you*, papa — would you have cared so much, after all, if it had not been . . . *to-night?*"

Satterthwaite did not alone hear these words. His wife, there in the near hall, heard them as well. Who shall say what an arrow of reproach they became, to cleave the conscience of either blameful parent?

The news of little Lulu's death gave a sharp shock to hundreds of the Satterthwaites' friends. But it may be said to have acted most tellingly upon the very destiny of Olivia and her husband. Still, it is supposable, on general principles of deduction, that Delaplaine would finally have yielded. But he would not have done so until, as the phrase goes, the last gun had been fired. He would have waited for concession from Olivia, knowing how radically her present assumptive position would be weakened the moment she betrayed fear of consequences.

As it was, Delaplaine hailed the non-occurrence of the Satterthwaite ball for a priceless piece of luck. He was now enabled to maintain his reputation as an unflinching opponent of contumacy. But a few days after Lulu's death had changed everything, Olivia surprised him by saying:

"I wish to have a full understanding with you on the subject of Mr. Massereene." Her tones were all steadiness and self-command; her blue eyes met his with an unfaltering fixity.

"Ah," he said, preparing himself. Almost any other

man would have started with an irrepressible embarrassment. Delaplaine only delivered himself of this ruminative "Ah," and leaned farther back in the big leathern chair of his study, where Olivia had found him. "I imagined that we had reached a full understanding on that subject already," he coolly went on.

"Then you were mistaken," returned Olivia.

"Mistaken?" He did start, now, although his not doing so was merely pretension. "I assure you I had entirely made up my mind to the contrary. I had told you my wishes; you had very hotly refused to follow them. But I had not the least fear that you *would not* follow them when the time came."

Olivia threw back her head a little. The damask slipped up into her cheeks, and a glitter pricked its rays through the calm of her eyes.

"In that case," she replied, with plain scorn, "it may have been just as well for your peace of mind that the time did *not* come."

"You mean that you would have disobeyed me?"

"I would have disobeyed you, as you are pleased to put it. There is not the faintest doubt on that point."

He stroked his chin, smiling in a frozen way. "Your determination, courage, firmness — whatever you choose to call it, my dear Olivia — might have failed you at the last moment."

"It would not have failed me."

"Ah, you tell me so *now*," he drawled.

She was silent for a little space, standing there at his side. He saw with the corner of his eye that she was biting her underlip, and it gave him a pang of malicious delight to perceive that he had irritated her honest, brave nature anew.

"Do you wish me to drop Mr. Massereene's acquaintance?" she presently asked. "Because if you do there had best be an immediate understanding between us. I—"

But Delaplaine had now sat up in his chair, lifted both shoulders, then lifted both hands, and, turning toward his wife, had shown her a countenance possessed by so much vivid surprise that she involuntarily became silent with surprise correspondent.

Ever since receiving intelligence that there would be no ball at the Satterthwaites', he had felt certain that his own sanction of Massereene's further acquaintance with his wife must become a question at issue between them. His jealousy was now much stronger than it had been; the rebellion of Olivia had fed it into full-grown, viperish thrift. He believed that his wife loved Massereene, and all the wiliest duplicities of which he was inwardly master found themselves on a sudden summoned together by the most imperative little roll-call. He would never have forbidden Olivia to dance the German with her friend if he had been as jealous then as he was jealous now — if he had wanted then to discover what he now wanted to discover. At present he was bent upon watching every slightest feature of their intercourse. No detail should be trivial enough to escape him; *l'âme se mêle à tout.* Once empowered with proof of her infatuation, he would be able to control Olivia as he desired. She might brave him to-day, but if to-morrow she were detected in a compromising attachment, he was confident of knowing her character too well not to anticipate as a certainty her pliant and alarmed humiliation. "She would never take the foolish plunge that some

women take," he reflected. "She might look over the
edge of the precipice, but she wouldn't jump. I understand her too thoroughly not to be sure of that."

The truth was, his tingling, senile-savored jealousy
prevented in him the least lucid judgment of what she
might or might not do. Olivia moved before him,
daily and hourly, as spotless as ever wife could be,
and morally incapable of even dreaming the misdeeds
that his inflamed fancy needed but a mild incentive to
lay at her door. She was obdurate, unswerving, in
her new course of action — that and that only. She
would either live her life beneath his roof as a gentlewoman whose honor rose above aspersion, whose decent social privileges resented vulgar molestation, or
she would seek refuge and freedom elsewhere. She
was implacably unwilling to give up the right of receiving Jasper Massereene whenever he might care to
visit her. If Delaplaine meant to push his objections
beyond that boundary at which circumstance had
lately compelled him to pause, she desired enlightenment concerning his intentions; and for this reason
she had quietly, intrepidly, sought the interview now
in progress.

Its new turn, on her husband's part, astonished her
as she observed and followed it.

"Do *I* wish you to drop Mr. Massereene's acquaintance?" he gently cried, repeating her own words.
"Pray, have I ever given you the least excuse for
thinking that I wanted you to do anything of this
preposterous kind? Can't you see the difference between behaving civilly to a nice, gentlemanlike fellow,
as I admit Mr. Massereene to be, and allowing the
idiocy of gossip to connect your name unpleasantly

with his? Now that Lent has come, and all the
lime-light glare of society has been extinguished
until another season sets it blazing again, I haven't,
of course, the vaguest objection to your receiving the
man as often as you please." Here Delaplaine took
off his eyeglasses and began to polish them with
leisurely touches. "God bless my soul, Olivia!
what *do* you take me for? An Othello? Ask
Massereene to dinner, some day, if you like. I can't
conceive why you shouldn't. He's excessively clever.
We don't agree on some points, but I haven't met
any one in an age who impressed me with being a
better thinker or a more interesting talker. . . ."

Olivia left her husband's study that afternoon with
a distinct sense of victory and an indistinct sense of
adroit deception. But she shook the latter feeling off.
She told herself that she should be thankful for any
sort of respectable armistice. It chanced that on the
next afternoon Massereene paid her a visit. While
they sat and talked together in the drawing-room,
Delaplaine entered. His greeting of Massereene was
faultlessly courteous, and he sank into a chair after
having extended it, while saying with his most gracious air :

"So you have reconciled yourself to the repose of
Lent, my friend?"

"Yes, and most willingly," answered Massereene.
"But it has begun gloomily, as Mrs. Delaplaine and
I were just telling one another."

"In what way?" Delaplaine asked.

"We were speaking of poor little Lulu's funeral
yesterday," said Olivia.

Her husband broke into one of his most cynical

laughs. It was doubtless true he had of late grown
more unconventionally daring both as to the bitter
things he uttered and as to how he uttered them.
" I should scarcely call the death of a child important enough to affect a community. Anybody's death,
for that matter, is really a thousandfold less important
than it gets the credit of being."

" I am with you there," smiled Massereene. " We
mortals magnify our own pettiness. But the Satterthwaites are what would be called an influential family, and so their loss appears larger to those immediately about them."

" And a fine sermon could be preached from such a
text," said Delaplaine. " I suppose none of the fashionable ministers dare touch the event, however discreetly. It would be an excellent thing if they
exchanged one of their ordinary dull discourses for
one with a subject like that. The little girl perished
from sheer neglect in a home crowded with luxuries.
Nobody had time to think of her; they were all occupied with trying to make themselves believe they
were enjoying themselves. And poor little Lulu,
with the constitution and nerves of a fairy, watched
her elders, and thought it a capital idea to do as they
were doing. She did, and it killed her. The Satterthwaites are pleasant enough people to meet,
but . . ."

" Be careful," interrupted Olivia at this point.
" They are Mr. Massereene's cousins."

" Which does not prevent my agreeing with Mr.
Delaplaine," hurried Massereene, " as far as he has
gone. I am sure that he knows the family much
better than I do."

"I know them very well indeed," said Delaplaine. "They make the unhappy mistake, I think, of living solely for outside appearances. They have brains, but they never dream of using them, and for the reason that most of their acquaintances are brainless. Hence they are at times keenly bored, though their loyalty to a fixed aristocratic principle remains extreme. If they were a foreign family, with a historic name, such desire for ascendancy might be forgiven them. But we are all commoners here, and intense American self-valuation, whether because of money or birth, is apt to recoil in ridicule upon those who profess it." He paused now, and gave Massereene a glance of direct scrutiny. "This nonsense of caste in New York must have surprised you considerably. Or had you heard of it before you came across?"

"I had not heard of it," replied Massereene; "and it did not merely surprise, it grieved me."

"Ah, you're patriotic, then?"

"I hope so."

"I was, at your age — or I fancied I was."

"Perhaps you now only fancy you are not," Massereene said.

"Oh, no, I don't; I'm sure that patriotism is merely a grandiose form of selfishness. It's astonishing how 'self' can be found at the root of all human exploits, performances, and even so-termed ideals, if we only search deep enough."

Olivia started and looked at Massereene. He somehow returned her look, and Delaplaine did not miss the interchange.

"She has told him of my cold-bloodedness," passed through the mind of Olivia's husband. "It is the

next thing to her telling him she detests me. Perhaps it even went with some such pretty disclosure,
as a sort of confirming embellishment."

Almost at once Masscreene said : " The one supreme patriotism is, of course, philanthropy. All
our widest modern thinkers recognize this truth.
But to serve one's country while living, and to die
for her when occasion demands, is obviously, I should
judge, the nearest that modern civilization will permit
us to approach lofty self-sacrifice."

"Right, indeed!" exclaimed Olivia. The eager approbation in her tones dealt Delaplaine a sting. He
smiled as he now placidly watched Massereene, quite
ignoring his wife's quick, impulsive comment.

"You make me suspect you of enthusiasm," he
responded, with his voice like an audible sneer,
though his demeanor failed to betray the least touch
of incivility. "I am always exceedingly timid when
an enthusiasm pops up at me. I know I shouldn't
stand the faintest chance against one while discuss-
ing such a question as this. I confess I've regarded
it from a very matter-of-fact standpoint. The soldier
who defends his country is just as apt as not to receive wages for defending an abominable cruelty or
injustice. In thousands of cases he doesn't care; he
is too ignorant to care, and too intimately a part of
that huge mechanism, an army. When he does care,
and is an officer, he nearly always has to go dancing
about as the puppet of statesmen and politicians, on a
wire long enough to reach from their closets to his
own battlefield."

Massercene shook his head : "Patriotism is not war,
though it must too often use war's weapons."

" And be thrashed by them, as well."

" Washington was not thrashed."

" He came near being hanged."

" And the elevation he reached is a good many times higher than the highest scaffold," said Massereene, with his sunny look and smile.

This rapid retort, with its not infelicitous turn, seemed to pique Delaplaine. " And perhaps a good many times higher than he deserved," the latter said, in tart semitone.

" Deserved?" Massereene echoed. And then, with a most serious intonation, he went on : " Such words as these have indeed a strange sound in America, Can you possibly mean that Washington is not worthy of great honor for purity as for bravery? "

Delaplaine began to polish his eyeglasses. " Oh, come," he said ; " that's quite too leading. There are still some subjects on which a man is compelled to think with the big crowd. Otherwise he runs a chance of being mobbed or lynched. Liberty of thought has here reached that superfine degree of development. . . ."

At this moment Olivia rose to receive another visitor, and not long afterward Massereene found occasion to say, with lowered voice, in her ear : " Is there anything or anybody *not* liable to the sneers of your husband? "

She looked at him surprisedly, and saw that he was annoyed. " I am sure I cannot tell you," she replied, almost stammering, and with still greater consternation. She had got to know him quite well, and he had never before made the least adverse allusion to her husband. It somehow shocked her that he should

do so now. But she quickly recovered her former
equipoise. After all, why should he not speak like
that? Was it not natural, she mused, for one of
Jasper Massereene's healthful and hopeful temperament to resent the positively mephitic and mildewed
sentiments of Delaplaine? . . .

Weeks went by. Lent passed, and Spring, having
first converted our New York streets into rivers of
slush, froze them one day so that they glittered like
glass, thawed them again the next, dried them up
with irrelevant repentance after a few more morrows,
and finally devoted herself to decorating some of the
trees in the parks with buds that it was uncertain
whether she would nip and blight before another
twenty-four hours.

Meanwhile, Massereene had repeatedly visited the
house in West Tenth Street and had often, if by no
means invariably, met Delaplaine on these occasions.
Olivia still drew only perplexity from her husband's
politeness. She was yet waiting to ascertain what
occult meaning, if any, lurked behind his hospitable deportment. Omens were somehow in the air,
and yet she could gather from these no palpable
prophecy.

In an unforeseen way she was fated shortly to arrive
at much more satisfying conclusions. The veil of her
uncertainty was destined soon to be rent with consequences of revelation no less definite than sudden.

## XIX.

The Satterthwaites would have been both amazed and incensed if they could have heard the harsh criticisms that Delaplaine had passed upon them. They had for years looked upon the bachelor banker of West Tenth Street as a staunch ally and supporter; and now that he had become the husband of their kinswoman, they took it for granted that he was bound to them with still firmer ties. Delaplaine's contemptuous opinion of their daily habits and doings, however, in no manner concerned the open homage that he was willing always to extend them. When, some time in May, he learned that Emmeline was engaged to Mr. Arthur Plunkett, he said to his wife:
"We must give the girl a dinner. She's your cousin, and the Satterthwaites are all in mourning; so we'd better make it a family affair and invite those soporific Auchinclosses. We will fill up all deficiencies with outsiders, however, so as to give a Jill to every Jack. It ought, by the way, to be a rather handsome dinner, because I hear that Emmeline is marrying badly."

In one sense Emmeline Satterthwaite was marrying remarkably well. Her *fiancé* was a gentleman, both in manners and aspect. What caused numberless pairs of eyebrows to be lifted when the engagement became known, was the distressing fact that Mr. Plunkett did not belong to a family of the slightest note, and yet presented no gilded apology for this shortcoming by being able to rank himself a millionaire. Indeed, if he had been a little less prosperous than he was he would have been actually poor. Society thought it a magnificent thing for him, but sighed that a Satterthwaite should so have lowered her standard. It chanced that young Plunkett was a man of considerable intellect, a rising star in the legal profession, and possessed of literary taste in no small degree. But these minor features of the alliance were naturally ignored. He wasn't a swell and he wasn't rich, and one of the Satterthwaite girls had consented to throw herself away on him — *voilà tout.* Intellect? Literary taste? " Bah! " would have cried that charming goddess of caste and cultivation who presides over the holy inner circles of New York. " You can find plenty of that anywhere; it grows on trees." Meanwhile, Emmeline carried herself with as grand an air as if she had just become engaged to young Lord Scarletcoat, whom Elaine had been tempting into cis-Atlantic matrimony with her most winsome smiles, but who had recently sailed for his paternal estates, whither, it was whispered, a sharp letter from his anxious ducal father had hastily summoned him.

"I'm going to marry Arthur Plunkett," Emmeline had boldly said to her cousin Madeleine, one day, "and I know very well that people assert it's not a good match. But upon my word, I should like to know why. If Arthur were a baker or a grocer, I could at once give him position by marrying him. And as for money, papa's promised us the interest on four hundred thousand dollars — twenty thousand a year. Then Arthur has about six thousand a year, and that will make twenty-six thousand. Nothing very wonderful, of course, but then it isn't precisely poverty when you bear in mind that we shall be guests of papa and mamma at Newport in the summer, for as long as we please. We can rent a small house on Fifth or Madison Avenue, and have two or three carriages and about four horses, and a butler besides the coachman, and a man to assist the butler, while at the same time going out alongside of the coachman and also acting as Arthur's valet, morning and evening, and a maid for me, and then about five other servants. But all of the other servants must be women. We can't afford a *chef*. Arthur and I have been figuring it all down, and we've decided that a *chef* is impossible. It grieves me to think of this, but the line *must* be drawn. It will be plain, genteel living, you see, but it distinctly will *not* be poverty, and I should be *very* glad, *really*, Lina, if you would contradict any reports you may hear circulated about papa having objected to the marriage, and his not intending to help us a particle."

" I certainly will," replied Madeleine. " It must be so satisfactory," she went on, " to marry just as your heart prompts, whether *he's* rich or poor, high or low."

' If there ever *was* a falsehood,' thought Emmeline, ' she's telling it now ; for she thinks nothing of the sort.' But aloud, with the most amiable smile : " My dear, there's *no* such happiness — *none!* And I do hope you'll find it soon, for you've waited long enough to deserve it."

" *Waited!* " faltered Madeleine.

" Well, then, only *expected*," said Emmeline, making matters a little worse instead of better between them, as one young lady nearly always contrived to do with the other, during those urbane verbal fencings which they held together under the guise of pleasant conversation.

The dinner-party given to Emmeline by the Delaplaines was of sumptuous quality as regarded the repast itself. But it brought conflicting elements into real if not stormy commotion, and lacked, for this reason, all the better traits of a congratulatory reunion. The Satterthwaites had fallen under the secret disapprobation of the Auchinclosses through their conduct since little Lulu's death. They had not conducted themselves with a sufficient attention to "duty" as mourners for persons of their own race and name. They had done nothing in strikingly bad taste, but they had hovered upon the edge of such violation. And to-night it seemed to the Auchinclosses that their bereaved cousins were all much too gay. Olivia observed the whole series of demonstrations, and secretly smiled at them. Mrs. Auchincloss looked reproachfully at her sister whenever she laughed aloud. She had told Olivia, not long ago, that she had noticed a "softening effect, at first, upon Sister Augusta, caused by the loss of little Lulu, though it had unfortunately been one quite too soon obliterated." Mrs. Satterthwaite, who might still have had her depressed moments, evidently took pleasure in maltreating Mrs. Auchincloss's nerves this evening, by continuous exhibitions of mirthful spirits. Emmeline and Madeleine tossed bitter but sugared little pills at one another, across the table, Elaine now and then abetting her sister. Chichester Auchincloss attempted to patronize his cousin, Aspinwall Satter-

thwaite, on the subject of too profound a fondness for
horses and horse-racing, and received from the heir of
his uncle certain sarcasms which labored under the
disadvantage of an ill-tempered crudeness. The majestic Mr. Archibald Auchincloss came augustly to the
rescue of his son, and was met by his brother-in-law,
Bleecker Satterthwaite, with so much veiled yet manifest belligerence as to make Arthur Plunkett, Massereene and two or three other guests uncomfortably
stare at their knives and forks. But the contest
passed away in a travesty of genial reconciliation,
like the ending of many similar engagements. Mr.
Auchincloss had managed, however, before peace was
restored, to say several caustic things about the Metropolitan Club, and Mr. Satterthwaite had held his
own by vigorously deriding the Centennial.

"What an unfortunate dinner it was!" Olivia said
laughingly to Massereene, when they met, a day or
two later. "I never heard so many disgreeable
remarks in the space of two hours. And Mr. Delaplaine," she added, perhaps unconsciously changing
her tones from levity to gravity, "was all the time
astonishingly good-natured."

"Does that happen so seldom?" asked Massereene.
He had again and again asked himself whether Olivia
would ever consent to speak without reserve on the
subject of her extraordinary marriage.

She colored a little, now. "You are beginning to
know him quite well," she replied. "Judge for yourself.

"Oh, he is always civil enough with me."

"But he is terribly pessimistic," said Olivia, looking
at her companion as though she wanted him either to

confirm or deny this view. "It seems to me that he grows worse and worse as time passes. But that may only be my imagination."

"He *is* a pessimist," returned Massereene. "And perhaps you're right about his 'growing worse.' *L'appétit vient en mangeant.*"

"A short time ago I did not even know what the word 'pessimist' meant," she exclaimed, with a rueful accent on each word and a troubled light beginning to shine in her eyes, which made their blue like that of shadowed water. "I had never heard of such people as pessimists. I might easily have been persuaded they were a kind of mineral."

"They're thought to be of the earth, earthy. . . . But you had heard about Diogenes?"

"Oh, yes. But it never occurred to me that the kind of things he said were worth listening to. I believed that all the darkness in the world was the natural shadow cast by the brightness."

"And I hope you haven't changed your creed. Have you?"

She shook her head very dubiously. "In a little while," she murmured, "I have had so much material for a totally new species of thought thrust upon my mind! I used to accept all the arrangements of life as functions of one perfect system. Those who were charitable, self-disciplined, kindly of spirit, received their reward not merely hereafter, but very often here as well. The selfish and cruel and wicked people were punished in the same way. . . . I do not feel my faith waver at all on the subject of a 'hereafter,' but as for 'here,' . . . well, it seems to me as if those who get the most out of life are those who can serve their own

interests with the greatest dexterity and craft." At
this point Olivia paused, and laughed a little flutteredly.
"That sounds as if I were turning pessimist, myself,
in good earnest; does it not?"

"It sounds as if you had been . . . disappointed."
He lingered over the last word before pronouncing it,
and as though he were on the verge of choosing
another.

"I *have* been disappointed," said Olivia, drooping
her eyes. "In myself," she added.

"Ah . . . Who is not?"

"I did a wilful, reckless thing, not long ago, and I
am suffering for having done it."

"Was it a selfish thing?" asked Massereene.

"Yes — miserably so.".

"There," he said gently. "See how a minute has
made you contradict yourself. You *have* served your
own interest, by your own confession. But you have
*not* found it 'getting the most out of life.'"

"You misunderstand. I meant those who began
very young and lived that way in everything."

"I see. The crustaceous persons. But you are not
one of those. The people of such hard prose as that
resemble the poets in a single respect at least — they
are born and not made."

Olivia looked fixedly at the speaker for a moment.
In her full gaze there had always been to Massereene
a blending of courage and sweetness which made her
face wholly different from that of any other woman he
had met. "No," she said, slowly and thoughtfully,
"I was never born to deafen and blind myself
thus."

"Never," Massereene repeated, with fervor. "And

this fault . . . do you mind telling me what it is —
or was?"

"Oh, it still *is*. . . . Its results are an incessant reminder. . . . No, I will not tell you *what* it is. I
don't doubt that you have more than half guessed
already. *Rien n'est plus facile.*"

The long spring afternoon, which had been somewhat chilly out of doors, filled the luxurious room
where they sat with a light at once drowsy and cheerful; what came to them was bright enough sunshine,
but folds of lace and velvet obstructed its too glaring
ingress. A fire snapped and sparkled on the silver-
grated hearth, sending little reddish floods of lustre to
the big leaves of a tropic plant not far away, and making it appear as if visited by wizard memories of its
own equatorial heats. As Olivia sat in one corner of
a satin couch, with her feet on a carpet of richest
texture and an arm resting upon the most costly of
embroidered cushions, Massereene could not but feel
how much irony of contrast lay between the luxuries
of her environment and that discontent, that self-scorn,
of which he had long ago guessed her to be the victim.

He leaned a little nearer to her, and said: "You
mean — your marriage?"

She nodded, and looked about her with a sudden
alarmed expression, as though an eavesdropper might
be lurking behind one of the screens or arm-chairs.
But this fancy, if indeed it had come to her, possibly
caused the dim, sad smile that edged her lips as she
now said:

"Of course that is what I mean. I do not doubt
you have heard many strange statements regarding my
marriage."

"Well . . . frankly . . . I have heard it criticised."

"And with little charity?"

"Not always, perhaps, in the kindest manner."

"I have often felt," she softly exclaimed, "that it deserved the worst odium."

He seemed not to know just what interrogatory ventures on his part would transgress delicacy. With some hesitation he asked:

"Was not Mr. Delaplaine very ill when you married him?"

"Yes. Dying, I *thought*." Her head drooped, and he watched the rosy color bathe the cheek nearer him. "If ever shame stained a woman's cheek," he thought, "it is staining hers now." "He says that he deceived me," she went on; and here, as though swayed by a thoroughly new impetus of feeling, she raised her head, and he saw that her eyes were most spiritedly enkindled. "He admits that he *meant* to live if he possibly could manage it. But I had received only his entreaties as a dying man; I knew nothing of the hope which he had of his own recovery. He used my father's name in imploring me to become his wife; he offered their long friendship of the past as a reason for my present consent; he —"

"Why, this completely exonerates you!" Massereene broke in. His face grew radiant to Olivia as he thus spoke. "I dared actually to blame you," he hurried on, with excited tones, and an expression in his eyes full of self-accusing ardor. "Yes, I, who had no earthly right, presumed to say that you had acted in a way unworthy of your better nature. I must ask your pardon for it. After having confessed thus much, I must beg you for absolution."

"But you were right," said Olivia, firmly, measuredly, and with a look of unflinching resolve on her face. "I *did* violate my better nature —"

"But he deceived you; he —"

"He never once clouded my mind to the fact that I would be aiding my own fortunes in marrying him. There lies all my self-humiliation. I don't see how I can ever pardon myself for making *what I believed a death-bed marriage, yet one which I knew would prove greatly to my own worldly advantage.*"

"And you would like to be pardoned this fault by your own conscience?"

"Yes."

Massereene clasped his knee with both hands, and bowed his head musingly; the attitude would have been called, in some men, objectionably unconventional; but he was always as graceful as he was natural in his movements, and for this reason took liberties with taste while managing not to offend it. "Pray what do you call your conscience?" he questioned. "Give me another name for it."

"I will," said Olivia; "God."

"Ah! . . . you mean that your religious sense cries out against what you hold as the commission of a grave fault."

"Yes, because with me all sense of right is religious sense. I cannot think of good without I think also of God."

"And you believe God is offended with you for having . . . married as you did?"

She nodded a sombre little affirmative. Then, seeing a slow smile creep about his mouth, she exclaimed protestingly: "I know it seems absurd enough to you,

who have thought and studied it all, and could probably write a book upon it, to-morrow, of which I
would not be able to understand more than an occasional chapter. But neither can you understand my
faith ; " and as she pronounced that final word Massereene seemed to see what he would almost have defined as an expression of holiness flash across her
face.

"I cannot understand your faith," he said, "but I
am by no means without a faith of my own."

"You are an agnostic," said Olivia ; "I heard you
tell my husband so."

"I told him, yes. It is true."

"But you and he are so different! He is an agnostic, too, or so he would claim. But he always seems to
be saying: 'Well, if this insoluble mystery that baffles
me were really solved, I think we should find nothing-
ness behind it.' You, on the other hand, seem at times
to have chosen a hope for yourself that is enough like
faith to be her twin sister . . . I like to hear you talk
with my husband on these terribly important themes.
He never conquers you, though he is supple and adroit
and a combatant to feel in dread of. And the reason,
I am assured, is simply this: you have a divine conviction, and the power of presenting and advancing it.
All his strategies of pessimism and cynicism cannot
argue *that* away."

"I sometimes think that I acquit myself very un-
philosophically in those discussions," replied Massereene. "For conviction, however it may secretly
comfort its possessor, will be apt to make him a sorry
ally in debate."

"I have not seen it prove so in your case," said

Olivia, with earnestness. "Your points always appear admirably taken. Whenever you have talked with my husband I have felt as if I might come to your rescue provided you were in danger of defeat; but I have never yet seen you even moderately jeopardized. And surely that is fortunate, is it not?"

"By no means," he returned, smiling. "I should enjoy being so honorably reinforced. . . . But this trouble of yours?" he pursued. "Since you are capable of imagining to yourself a definite individual God, I should fancy that you might gain comfort from the thought of making this Deity some atonement — some " . . .

"Ah," Olivia here broke in. "That is just what I have sought to do!"

"And successfully? I mean, with satisfaction to your own wounded conscience?"

"No. I have failed — wretchedly failed."

"Failed!" he repeated.

She had averted her face, but she now turned it again toward his own, and laid her hand, as she did so, lightly and briefly on his arm. The instant she spoke he perceived that her voice was filled with the tears which had begun to swim and glitter in her eyes.

"I — I can't tell you just now what I mean," she faltered. "Perhaps some other time I *will* tell you. I — I would like your help — your counsel. But not now. Let it be enough, at present, for me to answer you by saying that I *have* failed — that the God in whom I believe fervently now seems angry with me, as with one who has not profited by the gifts of fortitude and self-control that he gave me in the past. And yet I somehow cannot take up the task where I have let it fall. Or, if I were willing so to take it up, there might be reasons against its resumption as before . . ."

"I understand you," began Massereene. You have — "

"Never mind what I have done!" Olivia broke in, rising. "We will speak of all this again, no doubt, though I — I can't promise you at just what hour such another talk will suit my humor." She looked down at him with a faint smile on her trembling lips and a starry plaintiveness in her moistened eyes. . . . But the next minute she had drawn out a pretty little bediamonded watch and glanced at it. "You came to take me to the Academy of Design," she went on, with an immediate alteration of tone. "It is already past four, and I shall need at least ten minutes to put on my bonnet and wraps. It will be nearly five by the time that we get down there . . . well, I hope you will not think I have quite spoiled our afternoon's project with my aimless commonplaces."

"I have heard no commonplaces," Massereene answered; "and I should dislike to call what you have said to me aimless, because, as I pray you will not forget, a sort of engagement results from it."

"An engagement?" she repeated, puzzledly. . . . "Ah, yes, I remember But don't treat it as anything like a compact between us, or I may never be able, through sheer nervous reluctance, to speak again of the melancholy matter."

"I hope you will be able — and soon," he said.

Olivia had glided toward the door. She stood for a moment looking at him over one shoulder. "Why?" she asked.

"Because I *might* offer some bit of advice not wholly despicable — that's all."

She left the room without a word of reply. Massereene paced the floor until she returned. He had never so vividly seen as now what a mockery and misery her life with Spencer Delaplaine had proved. If she ever gave him the right to counsel her, this young man knew (or he now passionately told himself that he knew) just what form such advocacy would take. He had seen enough of the Delaplaine *ménage* to comprehend how a sensitive and high-strung woman daily suffered under the lash of persecutions that her own large-mindedness alone kept her from resenting. He was alive to the painful delicacy of his own position, should any real question arise of urging Olivia to avail herself of a certain expedient; for nothing, as he clearly realized, could exceed the difficulty of enacting this rôle with due tact and grace, when a little emotion of too lightly-bridled a quality might reveal more than the friendly spirit of intercession which he solely desired to exhibit.

"She is the most charming woman in the world," Massereene now somewhat excitedly mused, "and one of the most spotless. In spite of what she believes the sin of her marriage, she would have made him the loveliest of wives, if the old satyr had but permitted. . . . Live? He may live twenty years yet; and meanwhile, age will not wither nor custom stale his infinite hatefulness. . . . If she allows me to speak ten words of guidance to her hereafter, I know what those words will be."

Olivia reappeared about a quarter of an hour later, dressed for the visit to the Academy of Design. They

walked from West Tenth Street up Fifth Avenue,
talking on subjects that seemed to Massereene the
airiest of trifles after that discussion which had preceded them. The day was brilliant and salubrious;
the Avenue rang with the hollow clatter of high-stepping horses, and from open carriages Olivia and Massereene received more than one smiling bow. Mrs.
Delaplaine's career during the past season had been
marked by so much·enviable notability that a bow
from her was no less eagerly sought than, in most
cases, it was beamingly given. Among those who
saluted Olivia and her companion, were Mrs. Satterthwaite and Elaine. Mother and daughter were being
driven out to the Park for an airing in the prettiest
and most *chic* of landaus. They were both in mourning, of course, and the coachman and footman were in
mourning also. The whole effect was very imposing
in its general suggestion of strict family adherence to
propriety, decorum and the *usage du monde*. But
Olivia did not repress a sad smile as the carriage of
her aunt and cousin rolled by.

"Poor little Lulu!" she said. "Such majesty of
mourning seems like an overwhelming tribute when
one recollects what a tiny childish life it commemo-
rates." . . . Then she bit her lip and added, soberly
enough, "It would not seem so, I suppose, if any of
them really cared. But I half believe they have
almost, if not quite, forgotten " . . .

The Academy of Design caused Massereene to burst
into an amused laugh as they approached it. "I find
it so ridiculously like and yet *unlike*," he said, "the
Venetian palace it is copied from in miniature."

Olivia smiled. "I am afraid we are not going to

see anything half as artistically worth our notice *inside*," she said.

" Is it an inferior exhibition ?" he asked.

" Oh, I suppose it will be tame enough. And yet I have no reason to anticipate mediocrity. I have not even taken the trouble to read the newspaper notices upon it; did you ?"

" No. It is surely time that we had some good art in this country. And, indeed, I am sure that we have, Since my arrival I have met several American artists, and have visited their studios. They showed me excellent work, though it was mostly in landscape. They complain bitterly of the national tendency to do just what you have done."

" And what have I done?" asked Olivia, as they ascended the handsome marble steps leading into the *suite* of lofty and elegant apartments beyond.

" You have unconsciously fallen into the popular vein of detraction. Before even getting a glimpse of what you come to examine as the production of your country-people, you have assumed that it is to strike you unfavorably."

Olivia paused at the centre of the last stairway. " You are right," she affirmed, with vehemence. " I deserve to be both reproached and repressed for my unjust and unwarrantable prejudice."

" I meant nothing so severe."

" Yes, you did, and I thank you for it. I can so easily understand that good American artists should groan under the burden of indifference which constantly oppresses them. Is it such a very heavy one ? Before we go to look at these pictures, tell me what their ground of complaint truly is. Do they not say that they are forced to struggle against foreign competition to a disheartening degree?"

"That *is* their complaint," replied Massereene, interested by the swift repentance that he had awakened, and mentally matching it with other tendencies in Olivia's character which he had before marked as setting toward a humane and kindly estimate of her fellow-creatures. "They claim," he continued, "that the foreign craze of nearly all American buyers cruelly stands in the way of their own fair appreciation as painters. Mediocre canvases, bearing European names, are sold here for prices far above any which the best native effort may hope to secure. They state that the American spirit in art is a servile worshipper of imported labor. They admit that their cause has been defended by certain friendly journalistic pens; but it has been so defended, they declare, without avail. No one seems to deny the wrong inflicted upon them; but the great public here is like the Chancellor in Tennyson's poem, "who dallied with his golden chain, and smiling put the question by." It does not even trouble itself to contradict the fact that Smith and Jones, in their studios yonder on Fourth Avenue, or just across the street in the Young Men's Christian Association Building, can paint remarkably well. But it prefers to decorate its drawing-rooms, all the same, with the paintings of Germans and Frenchmen."

"And this protest?" said Olivia, thoughtfully, as though Massereene's words had impressed her with no slight force. "Do *you* consider it founded upon a legitimate grievance?"

"Generally speaking, I do. Of course there are the incompetent grumblers; but then they always skulk at the skirts of any reformatory movement. Not that this should be called one. The contempt in which good American artists are held by those who should aid and support them is not, like our lack of all Copyright Law, a subject for progressive legislation. There is a kind of ethical equity which cannot be secured either at Albany or Washington. On the chance of ultimately gaining this (for their descendants if not for themselves) our painters must base all future hopes."

Olivia woke herself from a little revery. "Come," she said, ascending the last few steps that remained to be taken; "let us look at everything we find here, with thoroughly impartial eyes. Let us *mettre les points sur les i's* like the most careful and incorruptible critics."

"You *are* a critic, then?" asked Massereene.

"Yes; why not? I have opinions. Is not a critic a man or woman who has opinions?"

"That would make all the world a critic."

"So it is. Is not everybody forever delivering an opinion on somebody else? If it is not expressed about the picture you paint, the poem you write, or the house you build, it is made to concern the man you did marry, the woman you didn't marry, the beauty of your wife, the solvency of your husband." She broke into a gay laugh, and waved her catalogue to and fro. "A critic? Of course I'm one. I don't *really* know any more about painting than astronomy; but that doesn't ever prevent me from saying fearlessly what I think. Do you hold that to be unpardonably impudent?"

"No — for an excellent reason."

" What reason ? "

" Being confessedly ignorant, you only *say* what you think; you don't *print* it, as so many similar critics do."

But Olivia misrepresented her own taste and knowledge in an equal degree. With her father, in past years, she had visited many of the most famous galleries abroad. She had acquired that power to seize upon the best attributes in a good picture or the superior ones in a picture of slender merit, which is less purely instinctive than resultant from early familiarity with superfine models.

The various halls, opening one into another, contained groups of people scattered over their floors, with an occasional pair, such as Olivia and her escort, but nowhere the least semblance of a multitude. Three or four weeks had elapsed since the Academy had once again flung back its doors to the public, and that, for a city whose artistic perceptions are as languid as those of New York, meant quite a protracted interval. Olivia had been betrayed, as she herself frankly conceded, into three or four little bursts of eulogy, and she was moving onward with her companion from one of the large chambers into a second still more spacious, when she suddenly became aware of a gentleman, catalogue in hand, who advanced directly toward herself and Massereene. The next instant she had seen that this gentleman was her husband.

Such a meeting might have been the most accidental circumstance conceivable, and it might have been prearranged with vigilant adroitness. The latter explanation of it now shot through Olivia's mind. She had nothing to be in the least ashamed of or embarrassed at, and yet while she stood beside Massereene and waited for her husband to approach still nearer, she could feel the deepening flush of crimson heat her cheeks.

## XX.

It was a confusion, a loss of *savoir faire*, that she hated herself for experiencing. She feared that Massereene would observe it, and she knew that her husband would infallibly do so. In another minute, or less time than that, she perceived that he had done so. On his own part there was not the faintest revelation of surprise. He came to the spot where she had paused, with a tranquillity as unruffled as any that she had ever seen him show. He shook hands most composedly with Massereene, but Olivia was conscious of his cold, undeserting gray eye, fixed upon her flushed cheek with what her fluttered nerves readily construed into relentless exultation.

"Have you come here to look at these amateurish pictures?" he said. "How odd that we should have hit on the same day! It speaks plainly for the dulness of the season, does it not? I hardly know any mode of amusement that I should not have preferred."

"We were just deciding," said Massereene, "that we had hit upon a very agreeable one."

Delaplaine, as he had heard this, lifted his eyebrows a little. "What? Truly?" he murmured. Then he became at once his serene self again. "Oh, they are not *all* daubs, of course. But so many of them are, that one loses sight of the few creditable things."

Olivia had striven with her detested agitation, by this time, and conquered it. She felt certain that her

color was receding, and on that account she trusted
her voice.

"The word 'daub' is such a very harsh one," she
hazarded. Then, satisfied that the tones just used
were firm as she wanted them to be, notwithstanding
those more rapid heart-beats which continued to annoy
her, she boldly went on: "We have only seen, thus
far, the contents of this one room. But, for my part,
I like several paintings very much. I did not suppose that American art was in half so flourishing a
condition."

Delaplaine had on his glasses: he lifted one hand
and re-arranged them by the daintiest of movements;
then he stared all about him, with a smile breaking
through the hueless edges of his lips.

"American art?" he queried with undisguised superciliousness. "I don't discover the vaguest evidence of any. There is a picture of some negroes
grouped round a stove, grinning at one another, in the
next room, which possibly might merit that name.
But it is a bit of mongrel crudity, with horrors of
coloring and the most precarious draughtsmanship.
Whenever you light on anything good here, it strikes
you as being so simply because it is not as bad an
imitation of modern European masters as its ambitious but inefficient author might have made it." He
ceased to speak for a moment, and his dry laugh
sounded as shrill as the crackling of fagots in a quick
breeze. "American art, indeed! Why, the whole
affair is like the work of a lot of pupils in some *atelier*
of France or Germany. Even the clever landscape
men are irritating copyists. I should like to discover
a single original brush-stroke among them all."

Olivia, without reply, passed slowly into the next apartment, whose threshold was but a few yards away. Delaplaine and Massereene followed. She went from picture to picture, gradually collecting herself and feeling the unpalatable certainty augment within her that this abrupt appearance on her husband's part had been the sly *sequitur* of some deliberate ambuscade.

Soon she heard her husband speaking again, and seemingly close at hand. He was no doubt answering some remark which Massereene had just addressed to him.

"Some thinkers deny that there ever *can* be anything like an American literature, and they're most probably right. Nations cannot be expected to have a literature of their own without having a language of their own. What literature has Switzerland or Belgium? As long as the same language is spoken in London and New York, Liverpool and San Francisco. our Letters will deserve but a single name — colonial, I don't see how any one who isn't quite besotted with patriotic prejudice can refuse to grant this. Why, some of the Greek poems and plays were written in such un-Attic Greek that it would almost have puzzled an Athenian; and yet the whole collection was called Greek literature; no one ever dreamed of calling it anything else. But as regards American art, that is a wholly different affair. We simply want to assert ourselves, to be representative, to be American, if there *is* anything artistically American to *be!*"

"And you are inclined to think there is not," said Massereene. In his voice Olivia could detect only dispassionate inquiry, without the vaguest ring of either approval or censure.

"I can't see any evidence, from present indications, that such an element exists. And if it does, it is abominably neglected. Take the figure-painting here. It is all — even the strongest of it — weak as the struggles of tyros always are. Here we have an academy of tyros; I dare say that some of them are gray-beards, and have 'been at it' for an age; but they're tyros, all the same."

"I wonder," now thought Olivia, "that he dares talk like this. He may be overheard, but even if he is not, how can he know that Jasper Massereene doesn't secretly regard him as a person with whom the *mauvaise langue* is a mere mania? I have never known him so recklessly bitter as he has shown himself of late."

And then a little thrill of dread passed through Olivia. What if his mind were beset by some malady of which these intemperate condemnations formed the discordant prelude? Her life with him sane had been one of enough aggravation and dreariness. To what depth of distress might not this life sink if he should develop some cerebral distemper, fraught with new ordeal to herself, while at the same time exempted from the usual restrictions demanded by violence?

She now turned and joined her husband and Massereene, just as the latter was saying:

"Your disrelish, Mr. Delaplaine, is a besom that sweeps away everything before it. For myself, I find some good painting here, though some that is both tentative and irrational."

Delaplaine gave one of his bleak little laughs. "Every man who presumes to paint the human form should remember that though genius may not be teachable, anatomy is. Look at that Carlovingian princess, yonder, praying to her barbarous conqueror. You find yourself astonished that she should have so little feminine vanity as to pray with such abnormal finger-joints. No true woman would have done it. She'd have seen her captive lord lose his head first."

"That depends upon the captive lord's previous use of his head," Olivia could not resist saying, as she peered at one of the smaller pictures in a slightly stooped posture. Before her husband could answer — if he had had such an inclination — Massereene began :

"Allow that there are faulty figure-pieces. The landscapes ——"

But at once he was interrupted. "They're mostly either slavish in their copying of renowned landscape men abroad, or so finical and detailed that they suggest a new kind of nature, known and cherished only by their photographic portrayers of it."

"I do not at all agree with you," remarked Massereene, with quiet firmness. "There, for instance, is a landscape by——," and he named a painter of more talent than fame, whose canvas fronted them. "Those autumnal tints are to be found nowhere in Europe; this man has drawn his inspiration from the woods and fields of his own country. That mist upon the distant hills, that brooding smoky color in the leafy valley, that cluster of frosted foliage pluming the foreground — they are all American beyond dispute, and all treated with a lavish poetical spirit . . . At least *I* think so," finished Massereene, who scarcely ever permitted himself to be downright, even when convinced that he held the ruling side of a discussion. ·

"Ah, yes," responded Delaplaine, with a blunt

asperity that struck a most unhabitual note in his
wonted composure, "'I think so.' That is the usual
arbitration of the judge who has no better critical
resources. 'I think so.' . . . Yes, yes, no doubt."

This narrowly bordered upon impertinence, and its
recipient answered it with a look full of gentle yet
assertive dignity. But somehow, a moment later, he
caught Olivia's eye, and saw there a kind of worried
pleading which caused him speedily to forget her husband's unmannerly rebuff.

"He is full of hatred toward Jasper Massareene,"
Olivia was then telling herself. "I am almost certain,
now, that he *has* spied upon us. Behind all this scorn
of American painting lies a mood whose harshness I
shall feel the brunt of hereafter."

They soon began, all three, to move onward, and
for quite a long time there was no perceptible abatement of Delaplaine's inclement verdicts. Every new
work that he condescended to notice at all he made a
target for his most unmerciful raillery and disdain.
There was often so much truth mingled with his savagery, that if some adept at shorthand could have
taken down all that he said, and printed it *verbatim*
in a newspaper, it would have served excellently for
an example of the "brilliant," "slashing" or "fear-
less" criticism of our period. In other words, it was
wholly uncharitable, and marked by a perspicacity that
reserved its keenest discernments for the worst errors
of the artist. Meanwhile, however, he contrived to
blend with all his acerbity a vein of clear conciliation toward Massareene. It soon became apparent
that he desired to express regret, if nothing like contrition; and they had not finished their tour of the

five or six apartments before he had courteously asked Massareene whether he would not find it agreeable to give Mrs. Delaplaine and himself the pleasure of his company at dinner that evening.

Massereene acquiesced. The young man may be said never to have formulated his own feelings as regarded the exact terms of his acquaintanceship with Olivia Delaplaine. But it is certainly well within the bounds of probability that he should have indulged a little self-introspection as to why he so coolly and unalarmedly confronted the prospect of a dinner at the board of her Rhadamanthine husband. As it was, he gave up a partial engagement to dine with an Englishman at Delmonico's that same evening. He softened his own compunction, after saying *au revoir* to Olivia on the outer steps of the Academy, by assuring himself that the Englishman was a pushing fellow whom he had always thought third-rate in nearly everything, and that he had not by any means promised his own presence as an unfailing certainty. For the rest, a memory dwelt with him of Mrs. Delaplaine's last look, and so dispelled all further conscientious qualms. The look had seemed to say: "Do not disappoint; your coming may save me untold discomfort." Still, this was the mere haphazard interpretation of a most dubious intuition. Mrs. Delaplaine (as Massereene soon afterward informed his own thoughts) might have intended to do no more than look polite sanction of her husband's hospitality.

Delaplaine's brougham was waiting for him outside the Academy. Massereene had already left them when husband and wife set foot upon the lower pavements. Olivia had by this time seen the brougham.

"I shall walk down home," she announced, very placidly.

"There is not time for you to do so," he replied, pulling out his watch and giving it a glance. "It is nearly six now, and if you wish to dress for dinner —"

"I don't wish to dress for dinner," she interrupted, moving away. "I shall not be late — and I prefer walking."

She passed right on toward Madison Avenue without offering another word or waiting to hear one. The thought of being driven home at Delaplaine's side had become execrable to her; she did not know what thrilling insult might leave those unmerciful lips of his after he and she were once in the carriage together. She felt glad that Massercene had hurried off up town, to dress, as he had told them, for dinner; otherwise her husband might have construed her present course into some design of seeing the young man again between now and dinner-time. "I will not look at one of the carriages that go past me in the avenue," Olivia mutely determined; and she did not. If her homeward progress was being scrutinized by a pair of pursuant marital eyes, she therefore remained ignorant of it. As for Delaplaine's late cordialty to Massereene, she had grown almost convinced that this had been founded upon sham. But why the employment of sham? Why the invitation to dinner? Had her anxiety but conjured empty spectres after all? It may even have been that the meeting in the Academy of Design *was* accidental. Olivia tried to soothe her own troubled sensations by asking herself if she had possibly allowed mere nervous misgiving to cast a fantastic or hobgoblin light over the commonplace.

She went immediately to her room, on reaching home a little before seven. The changes that she had decided to make in her toilet were slight; she had completed them when a servant knocked at her door, informing her that Mr. Massereene was in the drawing-room and that dinner was served. But she had scarcely gone out into the hall before she perceived her husband coming toward her from an opposite direction ; like herself, he was approaching the staircase that led below.

" You are in time for dinner after all," he surprised her by most amiably saying.

" Oh, yes," she answered, making her tones extremely affable, and beginning to descend as she spoke; " I was sure that I should be."

" I suppose it quite astonished you to find me there, at the Academy."

" Well, it seemed a little strange, as you said, that we should both have hit on the same day — especially as you had not mentioned going. But no doubt you go every year; do you not ? "

He did not answer, and a minute later they both stood in the lower hall. Suddenly, she saw a look of great moroseness and acrimony possess his face, and it seemed to her that a cold, bluish light leaped electrically from his angered eyes.

" You know very well," he said hissingly to her, " that I went there because *you and he went* — because I saw you from my carriage as I drove along — because I had a most natural curiosity to . . . to learn how this very friendly intimacy was developing."

The plain sneer in his last words lost its point for

Olivia, because of the suppressed fury that accompanied it.  She had become so used to his sneering
under conditions of the most entire immobility that
this unusual evidence of exasperation, and perhaps of
burning jealousy as well, at once gave a weapon to
her dauntless young spirit.  She had never feared
Delaplaine, as we know.  She regarded him now
with a look full of that rebuke which a larger nature
can sometimes visually, inexplainably, and in a trice,
as it were, communicate to a smaller one.

"What admirable taste!" she said, under her breath.
"But I might have been prepared for it in you."  She
pointed to the closed door of the drawing-room, near
which they both stood.  "Why ask here, to dine with
you, a gentleman upon whose acts you have played
the spy?"

He made an enraged gesture.  "Do you want me to
speak out what I think," he said, "before him? — before you both?"

Her eyes flashed.  "If you insulted him, he would
know how to resent it," she answered.  "If you insulted me in his presence, you would be lowering
yourself more than a man of your social prudence
would be at all apt to do."

Her retort was vibrant with the most challenging
scorn.  She at once went forward to the closed door.
As she placed her hand upon its knob, she heard him
say, in tones replete with agitation and menace:
"Take care — take care."

But she waited to hear no more.  She felt desper-
ately goaded and stung.  In another moment she had
glided into the drawing-room.  Massereene was there,
and rose as she entered.  She left the door open, ex-

pecting that her husband would follow her. But he did not, and she seated herself, indicating by a slight motion that Massereene should do the same.

"You seem excited," he murmured to her, as he dropped upon the sofa at her side.

"I am," she could not help acknowledging. "Something has happened — something most distressing. I am not sure — " and then she paused, with a break in her voice that her paleness accentuated to him while he waited for her to speak again. "My husband may make matters unpleasant," she went on, much more evenly and calmly. "I have just been greatly annoyed by certain words that he has addressed to me. There are limits to one's patience. I confess that I would not speak thus if I had not a fear — an actual fear — lest he may seriously embarrass us both by — "

But Delaplaine now crossed the threshold of the drawing-room. He looked perfectly collected and host-like. In another minute he had shaken hands with Massereene, and almost jovially congratulated his guest upon the virtue of punctuality.

"I believe dinner is served," he continued, with his best bow — the bow that had long ago helped to establish him as a favorite in the *haute volée* of a now dead-and-gone epoch. "Will you give your arm to my wife, Mr. Massereene?" he continued, with a little burst of laughter. "I will walk unaccompanied behind you. I will imagine that I have on my arm the most delightful and charming lady in town *except* our hostess. . . . Now, *there's* a compliment to my wife, Massereene; isn't it? And rather creditable for an old fellow past sixty, eh? What do

you think of it for a proof that I'm the shining type
of a model husband ? "

Olivia slipped her hand into Massereene's proffered
arm.   The hand trembled and she could not but be
aware that he was conscious of this betrayal.   "What
*does* it all mean ? " she was silently questioning herself.   "Will some horrid thing soon occur, or does he
only wish to torture me in a new way, after having
tortured me in the old one for so many months."

But as the dinner proceeded, Delaplaine gave no
signs of adopting any such painful course.   It was
not long, however, before he had turned the conversation between Massereene and himself into a somewhat philosophic channel.   And by degrees his
materialistic views clouded his discourse more and
more darkly, till Massereene, accustomed to all
forms of argument among his English university
friends, could not help exclaiming ;

"You denounce as autocratic those who insist
upon that 'one far-off divine event to which the
whole creation moves.'   But why are they more
daringly *à priori* than those who affirm the direct
contrary, granting that both sides dispense with revelation as a kind of supernatural support ?   Is it
not, when all has been said, dogma for dogma?
Only, have not the optimists the best of the dispute?   For my part, I maintain that they have —
immeasurably."

"Ah," replied Delaplaine, with a shrug of the
shoulders, "if you have the remotest intention of
beginning to justify and account for the whole absurd
series of phenomena we call life on grounds of trans-
cendentalism, you will find me a rather tough contest-

ant. You might as well quote Bishop Butler or Paley to me, and have done with it."

"I have no intention of quoting either author," replied Massereene. "My belief is something quite apart from their elaborate efforts to prove a personal Divinity."

"You mean — your belief *in* a personal Divinity?"

"No; I neither believe nor disbelieve, there."

"Ah, of course. From the purely agnostic vantage-ground I should speak in the same consistent terms of formula. But a minute ago you mentioned your belief. Am I to understand by this word your faith in the posthumous continuity of all human life, with results that throw satisfying light upon every present mystery? or, conversely, your denial that all is futility, with blind forces flung accidentally together to create consciousness at the beginning, and the disruption of these forces, with annihilation of consciousness, at the end?"

"You are certainly to understand my denial," declared Massereene, "that life is any such terrible travesty as this. A hundred signs point oppositely."

"Give me one," said Delaplaine, while he selected a plump Spanish olive and began to nibble it.

"The existence of mind as an apex, a terminus, of nature's many grades and degrees of performance. Man's possibility of progression is boundless. His divine destiny cannot be misinterpreted. He has but to speak, to think, to feel, and he has suggested his own heirship to eternity."

Delaplaine smiled, while he still made little bites at his olive with his white, well-preserved teeth, holding it in a gingerly way between thumb and finger.

" Bah, my dear fellow, you talk like a poet. Candidly, if I had my say, I should render all people who were tried and found guilty of being poets, unable either to inherit or purchase property, besides taking away their privileges at the polls. The truth is simply this: for about five thousand years past, man has been ceaselessly endeavoring to find out whence he came, whither he is going, and why he is here at all."

" He has probably been doing it for a much longer time than five thousand years."

"Oh, we'll say two or three millions, if you please. I dare say it took a very great while longer for the ape to reach even the rudimentary human biped. But we *know* that man's inquiries as to the whence and whither of his fate have certainly been going on for about that period of five thousand years. And in all the monstrous interval thus employed, what has he learned? Nothing. He has prostrated himself before the gods of many and many a separate theogony. He has spilled seas of blood in the defence of his different creeds. But to-day the sphinx holds the secret just as firmly as ever. Now, in this nineteenth century, we are beginning to make up our minds that there is no secret at all. We are concerning ourselves with matter, and we are gradually arriving at the rational conclusion that matter begins everything and ends everything."

" Do you imply, then, that we are approaching atheism ?"

" Yes."

" Oh," cried Olivia, " that is horrible even to think of ! "

Delaplaine took no notice of her exclamation.  " All

the great modern thinkers," he went on, addressing
Massereene, "are atheists at heart. They pretend
that they are not, but science is their gospel; and
science, the more facts that she gathers, grows the
more certain of how many picturesque falsehoods
have been circulated in the name of metaphysics."

"Science pauses at the unknowable," said Massereene, "but she does not presume to postulate beyond
it. She leaves the spiritual part of the question alone,
and rightly. But she does not, for this reason, assert
that no vast realm of marvellous supervision lies outside
her powers of perception or analysis. I remember no
instance among the writings of these thinkers to whom
you have alluded where they can be credited with
stating that a supreme Providence fails to overlook
and direct the whole inscrutable plan."

"No, they don't state it, but what do they infer?
Far more than that, what does the immense misery
and sorrow inflicted upon the race at large infer? It
is when we take a broad view of this "inscrutable
plan" that we discern how faint, how feeble is the
testimony it furnishes of an intelligence in the least
concerned with its welfare. Millions of people are
now staggering, throughout the globe under a yoke
of drudgery. A few are prosperous and comparatively happy in all lands. Disease fastens upon those
whom affection guards, dragging them to untimely
death. Nature, the inveterate enemy of mankind,
destroys by earthquake, cyclone, malarial infection,
pest, shipwreck and the numberless ills through which
she is ever proving to us that the sentimentalists have
lied about her sympathy and her kindliness. Science
conquers her dumb, stolid enmity in the steamship,

the railway, the telegraph, the telephone. But Nature, still an unlaid foe, inflicts her innumerable ills upon the race. Meanwhile, prayers and hymns of worship go up from the churches, and what answer do they receive? None. We find in ourselves the sole remedy for the enormous misfortune of existence. And it is a very meagre one. Our hospitals and asylums keep from us, in centres of civilization, the full sadness and horror. Our prisons aid too, for they hide the moral maladies as well as they can. Something perpetually compels man to hope, to bear up — to eat his dinner, when he can get it, and not fix too acute a gaze upon the general wretchedness of his lot. He is really a captive, cursed with a durance that has clutched him for the crime of having been born. But he is more than a mere captive, since he is one continually under sentence of death. And those whom he loves are under a like sentence; at any moment they may be torn from him, making his custody still more like the caprice of a tyrant. When he sees the whole despotism in its darkest hues and has the boldness to affirm life the unsolicited oppression that it is, he receives the condescending commiseration of those who wilfully darken their sight and stuff their ears. He is called 'morbid,' and 'unhealthy,' and 'a brooder.' By shibboleths like these he is denounced and silenced. Poets foam at the mouth before him in their illogical epilepsies which they call 'divination.' Religion tries to crush him with its tomes of 'revealed truth.' He is only a poor wretch of a pessimist. He can't hear the music of the spheres, or the choruses of the seraphim. He can hear other sounds, however — very earthly ones, like groans and sobs and cries for help. He is

compelled to cloak his 'morbidness,' or his most influential friends will cut him, and that may be a question
of his bread-and-butter. But all the while, poor fellow,
he has only told the truth about life. It's a king with
a coffin for a throne, death herself for a queen-consort,
despair for a prime minister, and religion for a court-
jester. . . . There's poetry for you, Massereene, as
you seem to be fond of the muse."

It would be impossible to convey the real effect of
these sentences as they fell from Delaplaine's lips, each
one being spoken with an air of indifference, if not
positive languor. His voice never once rose above the
most ordinary conversational pitch; and, delivered
with a glacial disregard of all rhetorical parade, every
phrase he uttered seemed to acquire a new pungency.

"I am fond enough of poetry," returned Massereene,
"but not of that kind — one which reminds me of a
certain French poetic school that prides itself upon
wholly ignoring the spiritual side of life. I confess
that I cannot honestly contradict anything you have
said; but there is to me proof of the infinite meaning
and potency of life in the thought that two diverse
lines of vision may touch it in such totally varying
ways. The unhappiness that afflicts humanity is
broken by gleams and flashes of the most exquisite
joy and contentment. Scarcely a single man has ever
lived who cannot truthfully assert this of his mortal
career. But when he lives unselfishly, when he nur-
tures within his own soul impulses of generous concern
with the misfortunes and misdeeds of his fellows, then,
in proportion as he grows less occupied by personal
fears and hopes, the more does he realize how magnificent may be the incumbency which before has seemed

so doom-like and so dispiriting. The finer agnosticism, then, offers him beautiful rewards for perished ortho- dox faith. He comprehends that to live duteously, sacrificially, cannot be to live in vain. He finds that even though the farther side of the grave may hold an eternal void and blank, this side of it teems with a potential godliness. Reason may repulse with its insuperable bounds, but the deeper that he probes the sources of philanthropy the more clearly he becomes aware from what sacred fountain-heads these have sprung. Where one may discern such riches of spirituality as those manifest in a chaste, altruistic life here on earth, it does not seem hard to let imagi- nation do reason's work, and point to some statelier disembodied condition. Still, evolution, from the marvels it has already shown us, may mean so glo- rious a rise, for the race if not for the individual, that in the mighty pulse and push of this great energy alone may lie our sole attainable heaven."

"You are laudably cautious," loitered Delaplaine, watching the almost rapt look that had overspread his wife's face while Massereene had spoken — her parted lips, her glistening eyes, and the tender tremor of either nostril — though Olivia was herself quite una- ware of having provoked his attention. "You outline a Paradise for the race and not for the individual. And evolution is to bring about all that millennial state of things, eh? How about *dissolution*, then? This relatively small sun and tiny earth of ours will sooner or later, according to the very law you instance, be two cinders whirling through space. Astronomy as- sures us that many a solar system has burned itself out, and that the mementos of these are dark and

frozen worlds, which swing round their dark and
frozen luminaries in the most ghastly way conceivable.
Here is the priceless lesson that evolution teaches us!
I fail to see the necessity of progression and ameliora-
tion, if it brings us a heaven based on such perishable
foundations."

"I am far from believing that the individual is cut
off from all entity after death," Massereene replied,
while a shade of annoyance crossed his face at being,
as it struck him, maliciously misconstrued. "How
can one touch these subjects except he does so in a
speculative fashion? If I were to put my creed in a
few words, I should say that I am an agnostic, but a
very reverential and idealistic one. No tidings may
yet have reached us, but on this account we should by
no means be comfortless."

"Comfortless!" cried Olivia, wholly forgetting herself and stretching forth one hand until it rested on
Massereene's wrist; "*I* am not comfortless, but ah,
how miserable it would make me if I thought no tidings *had* reached us!" She paused, and with flushing
cheek drew her hand away; she had caught her husband's eye, and its cloudy look had made her guiltily
conscious of what was, after all, the most harmless bit
of friendliness.

"We three," said Massereene, somewhat with the
air of a person who wishes to fill an awkward pause,
"represent three separate forms of mental growth."

"Decidedly separate — in my wife's case," muttered
Delaplaine, with a stinging dryness. "But women
would be lost without religion, I suppose. I can't
recall any who did not possess it and were not more
or less depraved." He now rose from the table;

dessert had been served; Olivia was prepared to have him propose a cigar with Massereene upstairs in the library. But, to her surprise, he said:

"I have an engagement which will detain me for two hours or so. I must be among a lot of financial fellows by nine o'clock to discuss the advisability of a government loan which I have already made up my mind not to be advisable. I would much prefer to remain here and talk with you of less tangible and mundane matters — in my materialistic way." He shot a furtive look at Olivia while ending the last sentence. She understood (or believed that she understood) this look, as signifying that his own side of the conversation with Massereene had been visibly if silently disapproved by her. And indeed, she had loathed both to watch and to listen while he vented what she considered his odious ideas and theories. It had occurred to her, once or twice, that he might have some desire to show Massereene in a worsted and humiliated plight, stricken by the lances of the Delaplaine logic. But it would have taken a whole arsenal of such weapons, each one wielded by a most brilliant adept in their use, to have made Olivia's firm faith waver or tremble.

Her husband now went on, still addressing Massereene: "I must apologize for this summary exit; but probably you won't mind letting Mrs. Delaplaine have your society for the next hour or so." (Those last few words were, for Olivia, fairly steeped in the most acrid sarcasm.) "I am sure my wife will not object to your smoking; but my library, if you will allow me to say it, is the pleasanter room for that. . . . Edward" (to the butler) "you know where my cigars are to be found. . . . It is possible that I may return before you depart. But in case I do not, I will say good evening now. . . ."

Olivia was not at all averse to ascending with Massereene into her husband's library. Delaplaine's proposition that she should do so astonished her almost as much as his sudden withdrawal from the dinner-table. But his appearance in the Academy of Design and his invitation to her companion afterward had both been astonishing. This third little *coup de théâtre,* as she could not help secretly thinking it, was productive of a still greater amazement.

"I doubt if he has any engagement whatever," she now said to her own thoughts. "He wishes to mystify, to bewilder me by a little train of eccentricities. Perhaps he has seen that he cannot wrangle successfully with Massereene and not become merely insolent, so concludes to retire and brood over some new means of provoking my future irritation."

"You have never seen this room?" she said with a forced lightness to Massereene, after they had entered the library. "It is pretty, is it not?"

"Exceedingly pretty," her guest answered. The shaded lamp, and one or two dim-lit gas-jets in the chandelier above it, threw just the requisite illumination upon rich-toned walls, low book-cases, infrequent yet rare objects of ornament, and carpet, rugs, table-cloth and tapestries of the most admirably harmonious hues. Across a wide doorway at some distance from the commodious chairs in which Olivia and Massereene now seated themselves hung a heavy curtain of velvet on rings attached to a gilded rod. Beyond this curtain, lay Delaplaine's own *suite* of apartments. Olivia

had not the faintest suspicion that her husband had
not already left the house. She and Massereene had
talked together in the dining-room over their fruit and
coffee for at least a quarter of an hour after Delaplaine
had disappeared. They had said very ordinary things
to one another, and now, when the man at her side
made reference to their brief colloquy just before
dinner, his quiet but serious change of subject affected
her with a startling sense of abruptness.

"You spoke there, in the drawing-room," he began,
"of a certain fear that seemed to bear upon your
husband's forthcoming behavior. . . . Well, you were
agreeably disappointed, were you not? He did not
make matters unpleasant, after all — unless one takes
into consideration your dislike of his cheerless tenets
and canons."

"Those chill me whenever I am obliged to hear
them," she answered. "But no it was not to them
that I alluded. He had been saying——" But now
her voice sank, while the color slowly dyed her face.
"Well, I can't tell it," she broke off impetuously.
"Never mind what he said or did — or threatened."

"Threatened?" Massereene repeated very sharply,
and with an unmistakable note of query in his tones.

She gazed steadily into his dark, manful face. How
capable he looked of bravely defending one for whom
he cared! But she drooped her eyes a moment afterward.

"Threatened, I mean, to — to distress me in your
presence. No matter how." Here she again lifted
her eyes and gave a little perturbed laugh. "Dear,
dear, I am always wanting to talk of 'something else'
with you lately, am I not?"

"I should like to talk of something else," said Masse-reene, staring down at the ruby end of the cigar which she had herself lighted for him not long ago. "I wonder though if you will think now a time for it. Perhaps you will not. I shall remember that you promised me your confidence, but I shall not seek to force from you, however gently, its expression. *Entre l'arbre et l'écorce ne mettez pas le doigt.*"

"You mean about how I strove to atone for my fault — the fault of my marriage — and how I failed?"

"Yes," he answered.

There was quite a long pause between them now. Olivia had lowered her eyes again, and somehow it seemed to him who watched her as if their glance had fallen upon the wedding-ring that shone, among others, from the small white knot which her clasped hands were making in her lap. And presently she began to speak, without altering either her attitude or her countenance.

"I told myself that I had committed a sin by marrying as I did. But I had bowed my head under the yoke, and I must wear that yoke with fortitude until death — his death, most probably — disburdened me of it. I would endure the full consequences of my own sordid piece of ambition; I would neither flinch nor murmur. . . . At first it seemed as if God had already forgiven me. . . . (You see, I *cannot* speak of God in *your* way; when I think of *Him* at all He is a living, breathing presence to me, and in all sympathetic sense as human as He is in other senses divine.) But soon I discovered how greatly I had erred. A very hard task was before me." She now spoke on for many minutes, describing the humilia-

tion, impertinence, and generally deplorable treatment
to which, during months and months after their marriage, Spencer Delaplaine had subjected her.

"But at last," she pursued, "I — I broke down; I
gave way. I could stand it no longer. There is no
need of my telling you just why this miserable collapse of mine occurred. But it did occur, and with the
*débâcle* of my strong self-scourging resolves, I grew
desperate and disdainful. I amazed him by the heat
and intensity of my revolt. I poured out my re-
proaches upon him; I warned him that except on
certain conditions I would not live under his roof,
but would go to my aunt, Mrs. Ottarson. . . . Well,
circumstances arranged so that a particular demand
which he had made of me and which I had refused to
grant, could neither be enforced nor disregarded. A
kind of compromise has been the result. There are
times, however, when his treatment makes me dread
a recurrence of those former piercing aggravations.
. . . And I *cannot* suffer them to be resumed without
resenting them . . . I have told you all that I — I
deem it best to tell regarding his methods of render-
ing me unhappy. If they are resumed, do you not
think it would be wiser for me to leave him?"

"To leave him?" echoed Massereene in a meditat-
ing tone . . . "Yes!" he suddenly burst forth, his
voice ringing as if a transport of passionate pity had
seized him. "By all means, yes!"

"This is your advice to me?"

"It is my advice."

"You do not think it would be unpardonable weakness in me, after having entered into such a marriage
of my own free will, to——"

"Oh, absurdity!" cried Massereene, springing to his feet. "Your own free will ? Why, has not your own story made it as plain as day to me that you were deceived, played upon, absolutely bedevilled by that man and your two heartless aunts? You, almost a child! I don't think you understand the strength of the influence that they exerted. I believe there is hardly a girl living who would not have yielded under the stress of such persuasion as that brought to bear upon you then! I —— "

He paused, for Olivia had given a quick, shrill cry, and risen. She was looking toward the large velvet curtain at the farther end of the chamber. It had been partially withdrawn, and with his face showing very pale indeed against its dusky background. Spencer Delaplaine was standing just in front of it. He had heard every word of the recent conversation between Olivia and Massereene.

## XXI.

During about as long a time as it would take for
any one in a leisurely manner to count ten, there
reigned complete silence in the library. Neither
Olivia nor Massereene was at all sure that the master
of the house had been playing eavesdropper. But his
extreme pallor, mixed with an accusative tension of
the lips and a slight but distinct clouding of the brows,
gradually rendered this conclusion almost a certainty.
And while both were making up their minds how it
would be best to break a silence every new instant of
which was growing more severely painful, Delaplaine
himself spoke, with the huskiness of an ungovernable
wrath.

He advanced toward Massereene, raising one hand
rather with denunciation than with any hint of assault.

"So you dare, sir," he cried, "to advise my wife
that she shall leave me? Is this what you call being
a gentleman? I'm, of course, no match for you in
strength, but by G—— if you do not leave this house
at once, rascally prig and charlatan that you've shown
yourself, I'll . . ."

Massereene, pale from the shock of insult, here uttered a suppressed cry; but his doing so was not the
reason for Delaplaine having paused. The latter had
just lifted one hand to his throat as though assailed
by a fit of choking. In another instant his eyes

closed, and then rapidly re-opened, with a dilated and glassy stare. These changes had taken so little time that Massereene, through some oblique effect of the light, and no doubt because of his indignation as well, had not perceived them. He was even about to frame a retort that would have told his anger most unsparingly, when he saw the form of Delaplaine sway and then fall with piteous heaviness to the floor. . . .

He was unconscious when uplifted, and he had sustained an abrasion of one side of the head near the temple, which bled profusely and distressingly, and which had, in the opinion of at least one physician who attended him, saved his life after the violent apoplectic stroke imperilled it.

Olivia had no recollection of parting from Jasper Massereene that night. She was in a state of pathetic turmoil; it seemed to her that if her husband died she would be steeped in shame for the rest of her lifetime. They had carried him upstairs, and she stood half the night listening at the door of his chamber, in tremors lest the announcement that he *had* died should freeze her already palpitating nerves. If she had wantonly violated those marriage vows taken in that same room near which she now kept eager vigil — and taken there with such uncanny gloom of accompaniment! — she could not have been more despondently the prey of remorse.

"Mine is indeed an heirship of misfortune," she declared to herself while she waited in the dimness of the outer hall, kept by a sluggish horror at the heart from entering the room where he lay and assuming there the post or duties of an ordinary wife. "I begin to think that Jasper Massereene may have been right

— that I *was* dragged into that marriage. And then all the sorrow and struggle that has followed it! And now this new torment of having been implicated in his death! For even although he survives the present attack, I shall always feel as if his life may have been shortened by *me!*"

He did survive the present attack, and of course Olivia's desolation of spirit did not abide by any means as darksome as while the shadow of death hung most menacingly over her husband. But the self-rebuking, penitential mood had not departed. For a fortnight her husband lay quite speechless, and only conscious at intervals. During this period (at any minute of which he might suddenly have ceased to live) Olivia bestowed upon him her most devoted attention. The ice once broken, in so far as concerned her appearance at his bedside, she left no effort untried to preserve a life for whose extinction she felt that she would be at least partially culpable. But this impression began to vanish after a while; it was expelled from her mind, so to speak, by the salutary forces of health, just as foreign element is cast out from the flesh by pure blood. Olivia was herself too healthy to brood long over an entirely imaginary fault. In all her relations with Jasper Massereene, she had been thoroughly guiltless, and this fact could not but thrust its knowledge, like some vivid beacon-ray of encouragement, through the tempest of her trouble.

Still, she refused to receive Massereene, though he came again and again to see her. At last she wrote him. The letter was extremely difficult of composition, because her avowed reasons for desiring to break their friendship once and for all, played about prov-

inces of mutual relationship describable only in terms
that repelled her by an undue warmth. "I cannot tell
him," she mused, "that his society has for weeks past
been so dear to me as now to make our separation a
positive trial." . . . And yet she did write very much
in this strain. But her refusal to meet him again was
absolute. "Our intimacy," she wrote, "must end for
the present. If I were to put in words just why it
cannot now be resumed, I should run one of two risks:
I might wound you by too bluntly dealing with a
friendly regard of which I have had such ample proof;
or, still worse, I might soil in your eyes those gossamer
things, my womanly delicacy and dignity, by reference
to impediments both needlessly and cruelly reared."

It was a good fortnight longer before Delaplaine
was pronounced out of danger. He now spoke, choosing his words, at first, with so much hesitancy and
deliberation that aphasia (most deplorable of infirmi-
ties) became dreaded by his watchers. But this threat
passed away, and it was soon found that the invalid
could speak quite as intelligently and fluently as ever.

A little while afterward, indeed, he began speaking
to Olivia, and showed that none of his old cynicism
had left him. He was still exceedingly feeble, and
could not move about unassisted, one arm and one leg
being partially paralyzed.

A great many of Olivia's new fashionable friends
now paid her visits of etiquette, but for very few did
she permit herself to be "at home." Of course, when
the Auchinclosses or Satterthwaites called, she was
obliged to see them — or, rather she chose, however
inwardly disinclined, to pay the sisters of her dead
father this courteous tribute. And yet the presence of

either lady was a stringent reminder to her of that strange episode from which a certain amount of hollow splendor and a very great deal of solid, remorseful misery had been born. Mrs. Auchincloss. came with Madeleine, just as Mrs. Satterthwaite afterward came with Emmeline. There was something almost super-human to Olivia in the deceit of self (if that were really the proper name for what she was often tempted to call quackery and mealy-mouthedness) which her Aunt Letitia and that formal precisian, Miss Madeleine, were capable of exhibiting. They both had not the slightest suspicion that Spencer Delaplaine's death would cause sorrow to his wife. They were indeed both very safely confident that such an event would produce relief rather than regret. Nevertheless, Mrs. Auchincloss announced, with her head put a little sideways, and her tones adjusted in precisely the right commiserating key:

"Madeleine and I want you to feel, my dear, that in this hour of bitter trial you can command our services just as you *know* that you *do* command our sym-pathies."

"Yes, Cousin Olivia," supplemented Madeleine, with her ascetic smile. "If ever one's blood relations should feel it their duty to be near one, it is at just such times of suffering as these."

Olivia looked into her aunt's eyes until they fell, as she responded: "It is not so much a question of suffer-ing as of suspense."

"Oh, yes," said Mrs. Auchincloss, glad to seize on any pretext for airing (what she would have thought you a most horrible person if you had refused to be-lieve) her "humanity"; "the suspense must be really

frightful. And do the doctors give you any *decided*
hope that he will recover?"

This was during the first few days after Delaplaine's
seizure, when the doctors had given very little "hope."
Mrs. Satterthwaite and Emmeline paid their visit
somewhat later. The contrast between themselves
and their kinswomen had in it a degree of real re-
freshment to Olivia. They were so politely and non-
committally brutal on the subject of Delaplaine's illness. Perhaps little Lulu's death had had its
permanently softening influence upon Mrs. Satterthwaite, but if this were true, she did not in the
least reveal any such *attendrissement* to the world
at large. The facets of her personality remained as
hard and clean cut as ever. Already no one in the
family ever spoke of Lulu; it was such a painful
subject. Emmeline had occasionally referred to her
dead little sister, but both her mother and Elaine had
assured her that every time she did so it sent through
them a kind of nervous chill. Aspinwall's unhappy
return to the home of his parents, late on the night
that Lulu breathed her last, formed doubtless, a reason for this excessive sensitiveness. If Augusta Satterthwaite had any love in her soul it was for the son
who had come reeling into the house of death that
night; and there was a ghastly enough melancholy
to her about this entire incident for its recollection
to prove both abiding and acute. Still, "Aspy" had
been forgiven not long afterward. His father held
out the most obdurately of any one — a circumstance
doubly annoying to the young gentleman, because it
involved not merely a plethora of disapprobation but
a dearth of pocket-money. Mrs. Satterthwaite ulti-

mately talked her husband, however, into a more
indulgent frame of mind, and Aspinwall gave his
mother a drawled-out promise that he "wouldn't
touch any spirits, don't you know, for a whole
year." He kept this oath of penance exactly two
weeks. But it was quite late when he came from
Delmonico's on the night that he broke it. Nobody ·
saw him or heard him enter the house ; they were all
sleeping almost as soundly in their warm, wide beds
as poor little Lulu was sleeping in her cold and narrow one. After a short time his violation of his word
transpired among them. And when it did, nobody
thought Aspy had committed so very dreadful an
offence. Even his father, who had been so severe
with him at first, was finally heard to say : " Poor
young rascal, I hardly see how he could get along
without taking an occasional drink. I suppose that
ass of a Chichey Auchincloss could ; but thank God,
Aspy isn't cut after *his* pattern."

Mrs. Satterthwaite, to whom these remarks were
chiefly addressed, answered them in a tone that
evinced regret for the lie of her son, however she
may have felt willing to condone his vinous habit
on grounds of easy, fashionable indulgence among
youths of Aspinwall's age. " But the boy was only
asked that his promise should relate to spirituous
*liquors*," she said. " It allowed him still to drink
*wine* whenever he pleased."

" I know," replied Bleecker Satterthwaite dryly.
" If it had forbidden the first and permitted the last
I dare say he'd have been just as much tempted to
break it. There is one glory of claret, another of
champagne, and another of brandy-and-soda," he

added. "We must only hope that the boy will in time learn *how to drink*, as I did."

And meanwhile, as in thousands of similar cases, it was an affair of the merest chance whether or not "the boy" drank himself into his grave before he had reached five-and-thirty. Every gentle yet subtle restrictive educational force had been denied him; all his early training had been a haphazard flinging away of salaries upon modish but incompetent masters; he had been "crammed" in order to enter college, and had pursued his studies there with the audacious aid of "ponies," just escaping graduation at the foot of his class. The laurels of scholarship; the honor of the intellectual life; the fine, sweet wage that after years of toil is due a faithful political servant; even the rectitude and probity crowning a long and useful commercial career — these gains he had not been taught, in plain black-and-white, to despise, but he had never been taught to respect either the qualities that could win them or the prizes themselves when attained. Fashion; pretension; cultivation so cultivated that it had become vulgarity; the un-American malady of caste that has crept into. Americanism and may one day leave it a mass of mere democratic wreckage; Anglomania — which means the servile licking of England's hand, not the brotherly grasping of it — these, and a hundred other items of perverse instruction, had formed a part of his practical daily tuition, while above the whole noxious collection of precepts, one fixed and deep-founded article of faith towered proudly paramount — the worship of money as the be-all and end-all of earthly precedence, valuation and *prestige*.

"I suppose you have no . . . er . . . expectation that he will ever be much better?" said Mrs. Satterthwaite to Olivia, during this visit of hers with Emmeline. "I mean, he'll continue an invalid, even if he doesn't . . . er . . . die?"

"That is about what the doctors now appear to think," said Olivia. "But he may become so little of an invalid as to dispense with attendance, to go out alone, and all that."

"How perfectly horrible," said Emmeline, "to have him *not* get any better and yet not . . ." She paused, but by no means embarrassedly, leaving her meaning to be understood, as she was wholly confident it would be.

"Oh, perfectly agonizing," struck in her mother. "His . . . er . . . death would be *far* preferable, of course." And then its hardest note got into this lady's voice as she looked about the room and proceeded: "Especially, my dear Olivia, when he leaves you *so* comfortable."

"He hasn't left me yet," answered Olivia. There was no one in the world whom she would have answered in just that curt way except Augusta Satterthwaite, the woman whom she knew to have schemed, not long ago, against her maiden content, as also against her maiden integrity of principle. Her bluntness now resembled that which some accomplice in a crime might have used at an after period to him who had shared his guilt. Even Emmeline, sitting broad-shouldered, high-colored and robustly handsome at her mother's side, looked somewhat astonished. Then the girl gave a laugh of cold amusement, as she said :

"Well, Cousin Olivia, you don't speak as though you were to be exactly shattered by such a bereavement."

"Shattered?" said Mrs. Satterthwaite, looking at her daughter. "What an odd word to use, Em! I fancy that if Olivia *is*, she'll manage to collect her fragments and re-exist with them." Then, turning to Olivia : "Shall you not, my dear?" . . .

It was not very long after this that young Aspinwall Satterthwaite presented himself in the drawing-room of Olivia. Deplorable as she thought him in many respects, he was nevertheless her cousin, and he was making an evident call of condolence : so she saw him. But scarcely had Aspinwall begun to talk, in his blended strain of pomposity and fatigue, when a card was handed to Olivia bearing the name of Chichester Auchincloss. " *Que faire?* " she questioned of herself, and then promptly decided. They were both equally related to her by blood, arch foes sworn though she knew them to be. Their detestation of each other might prove diverting under the circumstances. She briefly instructed the servant who had brought in the card, and presently either of the two young men was producing a bomb-shell effect upon the other. They shook hands, and then surveyed each other with a mutual scorn, veiled under what was at least the similitude of politeness.

"The old gentleman 's no better, then, Olivia," inquired Aspinwall, playing with a stick that he carried, superbly mounted in silver.

"No," Olivia said.

"Does Aspinwall allude to *your husband ?* " asked Chichester.

"I imagine he does,".replied Olivia.  "Don't you, Aspinwall?"

"Certainly," said Aspinwall.  He half turned, and scanned Chichester with the corner of each eye; his steep collar would not permit much greater laxity of movement, unless he shifted his entire position.  Chichester, clad in the darkest and most simple garb, offered the sharpest contrast to his cousin, whose gloves were bright yellow, whose hat was of cinnamon-brown, whose necktie was of sky-blue satin, whose waistcoat was blue with a kind of yellowish sprig in it, and whose trousers were of a flaring check pattern, red, black, white, and perhaps a few more colors beside.

"What's the matter with 'old gentleman'?" said Aspinwall.  "Don't you like it?"

"No," emphatically answered his cousin.  "Used in reference to Olivia's husband it savors painfully of slang.  It is evidently employed in the same spirit as the 'old gentleman' which very many young men apply with such dreadful taste to their own fathers."

Aspinwall laughed rather coarsely, and then looked at Olivia with a glance that expressed unfathomable contempt of his kinsman.  But Olivia pretended not to see the glance.

"I always call my dad 'old gentleman,'" said Aspinwall, in a provocative and highly satirical voice; "that is, when I don't call him 'dad.'  Sorry you think it such bad form."

"Aspinwall," exclaimed Chichester,."you know we seldom do agree."  This was meant to silence Aspinwall.  "*Pray* tell me something of Mr. Delaplaine's case," the young gentleman continued, leaning toward

Olivia and bending upon her his very closest attention; "I've read a little upon neurological subjects
myself, and—"

"Jiminy!" scoffed Aspinwall. He put up one
yellow-gloved hand and hollowed it behind his ear.
"Let's hear that big word again," he cried. "Where
did you get it from, Chichy?"

Chichester coughed a little, and threw back his head
a little, and crossed his own dark-gloved hands in his
lap, with a piqued, snappish manner which his sister
Madeleine sometimes rather tellingly adopted, but
which with him had the effect of an almost old-maidish
effeminacy.

"I got that word, Aspinwall," he replied, "from a
book you've not seen much more than the outside of.
I mean—the dictionary." Then he laughed titter-
ingly and looked at his hostess. "He's probably as
wise now as he was before; don't you think so,
Olivia?" But Olivia merely smiled in a neutral way.
She had no intention of arraying herself on the side of
either Montague or Capulet.

Chichester at once proceeded, speaking to Olivia as
though he were so oblivious of Aspinwall's presence
that he had no longer the faintest remembrance of it;
"I should not have used the word 'neurological' with
reference to your husband's case. It is one of apo-
plexy, as I understand. Now, unless past inquiry into
this subject quite escapes me, cerebral hemorrhage
may be divided into four separate kinds."

"Good Lord!" ejaculated Aspinwall, under his
breath, falling back into his chair. "What are we
going to have next?"

But Chichester, with magnificent self-possession,

pursued his monologue, keeping his gaze fixed, all the
while, upon Olivia's courteously disposed visage. "The
first on the list is the case in which two or three or more
bleedings rapidly succeed one another. The second is
where death occurs inside twenty-four hours, and
where the temperature falls at first, though it afterward greatly increases. The third is where illness
terminates in a few days after the attack; and here
the temperature diminishes, but is followed by a sta-
tionary period in which, after its physiological standard has been regained, the body of the patient is
beset by oscillations above and below this point. And
the fourth is that stage in which the patient recovers.
There is then —"

"Houpla!" exulted Aspinwall, with his head absurdly far back on the cushion of the lounge he
occupied, and a cigarette between the thumb and
finger of his right hand. "May I smoke, Cousin
Olivia? Yes, I know you'll let me. I couldn't stand
this medical lecture if you didn't."

"No, Aspy," said Olivia. " *You can't* smoke here,
and you ought not to think of doing so."

" There is, fourthly," continued Chichester, still
haughtily ignoring his male cousin, "that happy case
in which they say the patient stands an excellent
chance of recovery. The temperature then falls, as in
other serious attacks, but it is followed by a temporary
rise, and later the normal standard so clearly asserts
itself that —"

"Oh, look here!" interrupted Aspinwall, pulling
himself up from his semi-recumbent position and
frowning serio-comically upon the speaker. "We don't
want to know about the chances of the old chap getting

well. We'd rather hear your highfalutin remarks on
the subject of his quietly doing the other thing. . . .
Eh, Olivia?"

As the last word left Aspinwall, Olivia turned her
eyes on him. "You are impertinent to me," she said,
"and inhuman to my husband."

Aspinwall sprang from his chair. He was one of
the young New York gallants who pride themselves
upon being gentlemen, without the dimmest real conception of those quieter occasions and intervals when
high breeding should make itself smoothly and accept-
ably evident. "By Jove!" he exclaimed, "I hope I
haven't bored you the least in the world! *Have* I?
Now, do tell me if I have, and I'll get right down on
my knees, don't you know, to beg your pardon!"

"Oh, you need not do anything so humble," said
Olivia, smiling amicably, and at the same time telling
herself how all indignation must be thrown away
on such wearying fatuity as this cousin of hers
represented! "The only apology I shall exact from
you," she continued, "will be the civil treatment
of our cousin Chichester's rather learned medical
treatise."

"Oh, he got it all from some book before he came
here. Didn't you, Chi?" exclaimed Aspinwall.

Chichester drew himself up. "I have never in my
life before been called 'Chi,'" he said, with the edges
of his lips, as it were, "and I really wish you would
never again, Aspinwall, address me by such an unpleasant diminutive."

Aspinwall shrugged his shoulders and toyed with
the cigarette which Olivia had forbidden him to light.
"All right," he replied, and at the same time assured

himself that nature had never, no, never, created such a thorough ass as his cousin.

When her two visitors had gone, Olivia went up-stairs again to the sick-room of her husband. He was then still so weak both in mind and body that he could scarcely address a coherent word to her.

But in a short time he became strong enough to deliver himself of many words, and often excessively bitter ones. As he grew convalescent his venomous remarks increased, each day adding to their malignancy. Olivia was in just the repentant state to endure them silently. She had lost all her old rebellious impulse. She was still often haunted by the idea that she had pushed him into his present sickness, and the chief comfort she obtained with regard to this question of her culpability was secured from Mrs. Ottarson, whose friendship and loyalty strengthened in time of trouble.

"Let him talk," 'Livia," asseverated her aunt. "You know jus' w'at he says that's false an' jus' w'at isn't. Make believe you don't care. He's sick. You've got to stand it. Goodness me! If you only had some o' *my* troubles! Deary, I'm glad 'nough you haven't got 'em. Mr. Spillington an' his wife have both left me, an' there's that thirty-five dollar suit of 'partments empty. An' w'y? 'Cause Amelia Sugby, the authoress, wouldn't stand bein' browbeat. That woman's full o' spunk. I s'pose it comes from scribblin' those stories that curl people's hair. An' she got, oh *so* cantankerous! An' I guess she was 'bout right, after all. He jus' laid himself out one evenin' at dinner. He told her she was *panderin'* in her writin's. That's the word he used, though I kind o' forget how he said

she *was* panderin'. But she didn't like the word, an'
neither did I. An' she says to me, one mornin':
'Either he goes, Mrs. Ott'son, or else I go. Now
w'ich is it to be?' 'Well,' I says, 'Livia, 'fair
play's fair play, an' I won't see any boarder o' mine
unjustly attackted.' An' then it came out that he'd
called her a penny-a-liner one afternoon when I wasn't
round. That *was* bad, 'specially as she gets a sight
more'n a penny a line for that stuff she writes, though
I *do* think it's the worst trash I ever tried to read. So
she said she'd quit if Spillington didn't, an' she's good
pay, an' she's lately got an order from the *Weekly
Evening Lamp*, or some paper like that, which'll bring
her in four thousand dollars. Now, Spillington owed
me over a hundred dollars, an' I was 'fraid to tell him
he must go, on that account. Still, I asked him to
'pologize to Mrs. Sugby. *'Pologize!* I wish you'd
seen him! He jus' cleared that throat o' his an' began
to talk so you'd almost heard him in 'Leventh Avenue.
So I got mad, an' I says 'Go.' Well, he went, an'
the hundred dollars went too. I don't believe I'll ever
see a cent of it, an' I needed it. Still, I can scrape
along, I guess, without it."

Olivia drew out her purse and pushed it into her
aunt's hand. "Here are two hundred dollars, Aunt
Thyrza," she said. "I've no earthly use for the
money. I've been simply carrying it about with me
for an age. There, now, kiss me and take it. Don't
say a word. You know how I love you. And
remember all you did for me in those days when poor
papa was dying!"

Toward the end of June, Delaplaine showed marked
signs of recovery. The physicians recommended a

change of air. Greenacre was waiting, and a body-
guard of servants also was waiting to conduct him
thither. Olivia offered no objection whatever. She
asked herself whether Jasper Massereene would hear
of their departure or no. Yes, she concluded, since
it was sure to transpire in the newspapers. Of late
the dark, composed, virile face of Massereene had
repeatedly shone upon her in her dreams. She loved
him, and fully realized that she loved him. But her
soul was so unstained, so helped by a faith in a God
of immeasurable goodness, so convinced that this God
would befriend her through all possible trials, that she
found unspeakable comfort in prayer and in medita-
tions no less holy. Her life became more and more
penetrated with the most earnest belief. She reviewed
her past temptations, and remembered them unceas-
ingly in her prayers. She prayed not only for herself but for Massereene. After they had arrived at
Greenacre she devoted herself to Delaplaine with all
the nursing arts that it lay in her power to exhibit.
He incessantly made her the butt of his bitter wit, his
torturing satire. As his health augmented, his cruelty
kept pace with it. He referred to Massereene both
openly and by the most hateful innuendo. But no
matter what sinister things he said, Olivia maintained
her post unflinchingly at his side.

His cynicism revealed new depths that she had not
dreamed of before. One day, while she accompanied
him in a walk about the grounds (he moving with the
paralytic step that plainly betrayed his wretched disease), she read to him a sad note from a friend in
town who had recently lost a young child.

"Bah!" he said. "How much absurd sentiment

is poured upon the question of parental affection! What, after all, is a mother's or a father's love except the most utter selfishness? And the children them-selves — what is really lovable about them? You can always buy a child's affection with a few sweets. I have often thought that all the badness of humanity is to be found in the undeveloped male or female biped. Where can you see more detestable traits of bullying coarseness than are to be met with in a boy? I have always abominated boys. They are like young Neros and Caligulas. They delight in the meanest and wickedest deeds. Fortunately for the race, they unlearn some of these by the time they have become men. Among the numerous inanities for which ro-mance is responsible, a glorification of childhood and children stands foremost. Such writers as Victor Hugo (whom, by the way, I have for years believed to be a lunatic) do much toward popularizing such rubbish as that children are angelic. Satanic would be a far more suitable term for lots of them."

He appeared to understand the new power which he had gained over his wife. It was evident to his shrewd mind that she had become possessed with the remorseful idea of having caused his perilous illness. He had no intention of altering the will which he had made on recovery to health after his singular mar-riage, and in which he had left Olivia mistress of his entire large property. Nevertheless, he delighted in having his lawyers visit him at Greenacre, and in remaining closeted with them for an hour or two at a time. Afterward he would devour his wife with a prolonged stare behind his glittering glasses, and say at length, with a little malicious writhing of his

pale lips, while he fumbled nervelessly among the
documents that covered his desk:

"It's a great bother, this re-arrangement of one's
money affairs — a *great* bother. Still, there's no telling just when I may pop off now, and if I do I shan't
be fool enough to have all my money fill another
man's pockets — not I!"

Olivia's face would flush at times like these, and
she would gnaw her lips in agony of spirit. But not
a word of retort left her. As for her husband's
money, there were moments, even hours, nowadays,
when she longed that he would bequeath her nothing.
She wrote as much in a letter to her Aunt Thyrza,
wherein she poured out her soul, telling of the exquisite pain he was inflicting upon her. "His allusions
to Mr. Massereene," she wrote, "sting me more than
all others; for that name now points, as it were, to
the very high-tide mark of his tyranny and my own
complete innocence."

Meanwhile he exulted over the thought that he was
possibly filling her with the sharpest alarm regarding
those lawyers and their mysterious departures and
appearances. In reality some few changes of invest-
ment were all that were meant by the latter; but he
constantly would inquire of both gentlemen, with an
expression and a tone which indicated sharp avidity
for the exact truth: "Did Mrs. Delaplaine say a
word, when you met her down-stairs, this morning,
about *why* you had run up from town!" Or again:
"My wife, by the way . . . has she asked you at any
time *what was the object* of your coming up here from
the city? Now think, please." . . . And he would put
one of his tremulous hands upon the shoulder of the

gentleman addressed. "I beg that you will try accurately to recollect. I have an especial motive in presenting to you this question." But neither of the lawyers had the slightest gratifying information to impart. Olivia had made no inquiries of them; and though quite unconscious that her reticence had the most irritant effect upon Delaplaine, she was none the less punishing him through it with about as much stringency as if she had employed some skilfully deliberate method.

"You appear to be losing your looks," he said one day, in his inhuman sort of mutter, to which she had grown so forlornly accustomed. "Are you not well?"

"I am not precisely ill," she answered, "though I have felt better."

"Ah, I see. Greenacre is boring you. You had expected Newport this summer, with a pleasant touch of Lenox in the autumn. Long drives on Ocean Avenue, long rambles over the hazy Berkshire hills, with" . . . . He paused, and she knew that he was watching her face, to see whether the color mounted to it or no. "Why don't you ask Massereene up here?" he presently said, in a darting, stabbing way.

She bent her eyes a little closer on the book that she was reading. "I should not know where to find him," she said.

"Oh, are you sure of that?" he asked, with a mocking insolence of distrust that she had long ago become more used to than she herself realized.

"Yes," she replied. "Perfectly sure."

He remained silent for quite a little interval. They had been sitting on the piazza. It was a day full of summer's brightest and most dulcet fascinations. The

sky had not a cloud in it, and the south wind was
pulsing incessantly among the leaves, making their
vibrant greenery sing like hundreds of voices heard
in a dream.

"Perhaps it *is* a trifle dull here," said Delaplaine,
breaking the silence. "When Adrian comes up you
may find it less so."

"Adrian?" echoed Olivia, laying down her book.
"Have you decided to ask him here?"

"Yes. But not as a guest. I must have a secretary, now that I've begun really to interest myself
again in the conduct of my business affairs."

"The doctors in New York said that you should
not touch business affairs for at least six months
longer," Olivia said. She thought it her duty to
remind him of this injunction, and did so.

He nodded, and gave that dry laugh of his, which
had made Olivia feel, while in a fanciful mood of
criticism, the other day, that there were withered
laughs, just as there were withered leaves.

"How enchanting of you to take so much care of
me!" he answered. "One would imagine that you
were really anxious that I should get well!"

## XXII.

OLIVIA was charmed by the plan of having Adrian at Greenacre. But on meeting him she was instantly struck with surprise, and of by no means the most agreeable nature. The sweetness, the pensiveness, the winsome femininity had all gone from Adrian. It seemed incredible that a few months could have so radically altered any one's personality. His brown eyes had hardened and brightened into a colder, more crystalline lustre. He carried his fine figure with an assertiveness that made it almost look martial. He had never lacked suavity and ease of manner; but a virile element was blended with his grace that gave it the most unexpected tinge of worldly-wise gallantry. Olivia found herself greatly interested in the lad's development, if it were worthy of so large a name; after watching it a little she had a sense that perhaps it was worthy of being called only a pathetic effacement. To her husband's eyes there had been no metamorphosis at all, or else one which he had already observed. He showed perfect indifference, now, to all interviews between Adrian and his wife. He treated his secretary with a civil enough bearing, and made no attempt whatever to interfere with Adrian's hours of leisure. These were not few. Olivia no longer rode, and drove only in the company of her husband when he expressed a desire that she should do so. She soon found herself wondering at the perfectly polite and yet marked repression in Adrian's manner toward herself. She had never had any but the most cordial feelings of friendship for him, and his coolness, however decorously he chose to mask it, roused in her a natural pique. It was all very well to make allowances for a swiftly disclosed maturity in Adrian, but this ceremonious waiving away on his part of their once frank and easy intimacy must be accounted for by other reasons. What were these reasons? Olivia was too generous to dream of enforcing an explanation by any such magisterial means as those to which her semi-proprietorship at Greenacre would have entitled her. She resolved to break the ice with a very sharp blow as soon as occasion served; and it did serve within a few days after Adrian's arrival.

It was about two o'clock in the afternoon. Luncheon was just over. Delaplaine had gone upstairs to take his daily sleep of at least two hours' duration. Olivia had passed forth on the broad-sweeping piazza that lay just outside the low windows of the dining-room. She had been asking Adrian whether or no he thought that Mr. Delaplaine's health was being retarded by his dictation of financial correspondence during the morning. Adrian had answered negatively, adding:

"The occupation is, I think, more of an amusement than a task. He merely gives me the roughest outline of what he wishes said, and I frame it in the kind of epistolary English that I know he prefers."

"And with great skill, I am sure," said Olivia, smiling graciously if but transiently.

" No ; it is nothing except the result of long habit.
I've become quite used to the kind of work he de-
sires."

" And you have made up your mind to remain there
at the Bank for a long time yet ? "

Olivia artfully put this question just as she was
stepping across the threshold of one of the windows.
He was obliged to follow her out upon the piazza, or
else to appear unpermissibly rude. She was almost
certain that he would not have quitted the dining-
room with her unless that much urbanity had become
obligatory. But he bowed, as it was, to the necessity
of acquiescence. There were several wicker-work chairs
scattered about, and Olivia sank into one of them. He
stood at her side, with his hands meeting behind him,
a figure full of the most happy symmetries and crowned
by a face and head which it struck her that some of
the famed marbles have not surpassed.

" I expect to continue at the Bank," he answered,
" If Mr. Delaplaine will not object to my doing so ;
and I suppose he will not."

" But if anything should happen to Mr. Delaplaine ? "
questioned Olivia, looking up at him from where she
was now seated.

" Then there would still remain two other partners,
as you doubtless know. I am on good terms with
both of them."

" You should be a partner there some day yourself,
Adrian," she said to him very sweetly. " I wish it
with all my heart. I think you deserve it."

He colored, bit his lip, and half turned away. She
stretched out her hand and caught his coat-sleeve,
detainingly, between thumb and finger, pulling at it

with a hearty good will, as if she were well in earnest on the subject of his not leaving her just yet.

As if suddenly conscience-stricken, he veered round and faced her. "Oh, Mrs. Delaplaine," he exclaimed softly, "how good of you! But you were always good to me."

Olivia burst out laughing. "It's pleasant to receive that bit of intelligence from you, Mr. Etherege, at a time when I have been wondering what precise bee you've lately allowed to buzz in that bonnet of yours. Once or twice I've been on the verge of asking you if you would not, *de bonne grâce* tell me what I had possibly done to offend you — to put you on your 'high horse,' in this perplexing manner. But no; I concluded that I'd wait and dexterously drop my handkerchief so that you'd have to pick it up, with a grand Louis Quatorze bow; and then, while receiving it, I'd inform you how beautiful your new manners were, and ask you whether you'd purchased them expressly to wear up here at Greenacre."

Adrian dropped into a chair at her side. "That would have been cruel — and consequently very unlike yourself."

"I can be terribly cruel when I believe people deserve it," she said.

He shook his head, pointing upward. "There is somebody in this house from whom I am beginning to see that you are *bearing* cruelties angelically."

She gave a little start. "Oh, say philosophically," she replied coloring. "But never mind *him*, Adrian. Why have you treated me like so thorough a stranger?"

He had drooped his eyes while she intently watched

him. "I almost dreaded to meet you again." And now he turned upon her the full, mild brown splendors of his eyes, and she saw that they were moist if not really tearful. "I — I *knew* it was best that I should not come here. And yet something drew me ; I may say dragged me! I had made up my mind that I would not come — that I would invent some excuse — that even if it enraged him, even if he discharged me angrily because of it, I would still avoid coming. But at the last moment I weakly yielded. I — "

He impetuously caught her hand in both his own, and was lifting it to his lips, when she tore it away and rose from her chair. She had become pale, and her eyes were shining ; but otherwise there was not the least sign of agitation in her manner.

"You are so irritating in your folly," she murmured. "Do you suppose I will permit you to stay here now?" A little scornful laugh ran rippling through her next sentence. "I am not the least anxious to wound your feelings — of which you have just given me so astonishing, so regrettable an evidence. But I have now only this to tell you : If, by the day after to-morrow, you have not found some excuse for leaving Greenacre, I must inform Mr. Delaplaine that you have been guilty of a very great discourtesy to me. . . . Do you understand?" she went on with much of sad appeal in her eyes and lips, while she put out both hands toward him, anxiously, compassionately, to withdraw them again in an instant. "I have understood *you*. . . . I am very, very sorry. But it cannot be arranged otherwise."

Then she hurried indoors, without his making the least effort to detain her, and reached her own room.

There she sat for a long time, staring at the huge silver
serpent of the Hudson beyond, and telling herself that
this whole affair was miserably unfortunate. In her
solitude, broken as it was only by such unpalatable
companionship as that of her husband, she had felt a
soft little thrill of real joy to learn that she would
soon be shaking hands with Adrian Etherege. She
had never comprehended until then how sisterly had
been her regard for the lad, how severe was her annoyance at the separation Delaplaine had forced upon
them, and by how many acts of helpful friendship she
would have been willing to prove her attachment.
The festivities of fashion, crowding upon her as they
had done with new demands both upon consciousness
and memory, had never made her forget Adrian
Etherege. Not even Jasper Massereene had made
her forget him.

Perhaps it was Jasper Massereene's influence upon
her now — the recollection of his unfailing humanity,
his power not only to feel *for* but *with* suffering fellow-
creatures — that gradually changed the whole current
of her thought and intention.

"How can I be sure," she mused, "that I have not
behaved blamably in my dealings with Adrian? His
nature is impressionable, ardent; it may be that I
(mentally older than he was, if not so in years) did *not*
use toward him the discretion he merited."

When they next met, Olivia said, as soon as opportunity favored: "I hope you are willing to assist me
in forgetting what passed not long ago. I spoke too
hastily, and apologize. You also spoke hastily; it
may be that you will consent to ask my pardon. If
you do I will readily grant it." She put out her hand
as she finished speaking.

He caught it, looked at her steadily first, and then lifted it to his lips. But she had studied his eyes and let him do so, this time.

"I behaved myself like a — a ruffian," he faltered. "How few good women there are, good enough to forgive me!" . . .

After that they were the best of friends again. And yet they were not friends in the same way as before. She had learned his secret.

Adrian's company formed her sole social pastime. "There are a few people about us," she said to him, during one of their talks, "who have shown a desire to be more intimate with me this summer;" and she mentioned the names of several neighboring families. "But I have pleaded Mr. Delaplaine's illness as an excuse."

"He is so much better, however," said Adrian.

"Yes. But nothing restrains him from those bursts of bitterness and of personality — the latter always directed, as you know, at myself. He prefers we should live quietly, and I think it is fortunate he does. I had hoped your presence might have some effect; but he pours forth his streams of cynicism just as freely as before you came. I suppose they sometimes make you inwardly shudder, as they do me."

"I bear them better, much better than I did," replied Adrian, with a touch of mysticism in his air.

"How is that?"

"Shall I tell you?"

"Why not?"

"I do not see why not," he returned, with sudden impetuosity. "In those other days when you and he and I were together I believed him —"

"Well?" questioned Olivia, as the young man paused.

"I believed him — my father."

She made a gesture of surprise.

"And now?"

"I know to the contrary."

"You know?"

"Yes."

"He has told you?"

"No."

"Who, then?"

"My mother."

"Your mother? Ah, I see. And you asked her if such a thing were true?"

"No. But she saw how I hated him, and how my hate grew. The suspicion that he was my father had entered my head several months before you and I ever met. It made me hate you, at first, because I believed that I could compel him to right by marriage the wrong which he had done my mother."

"That look you gave me — that look of positive savagery — on the day I became his wife," Olivia murmured. "I understand it now."

He indistinctly caught her words, and said: "To what look do you refer?" He searched her face with eagerness while he thus spoke.

"Never mind," Olivia returned. . . . "And your mother has told you . . . ?"

"That I am *not* his son. It has lifted a great load from my heart."

"But she — your mother — how was it that she induced him to aid you as he has done?"

"She would not tell me that. Some day I hope to

know. But my mother and he were never — well, you understand. It has been a great relief to me."

"Poor boy!" thought Olivia. "I don't doubt that his mother has told him a merciful falsehood."

She soon got away from Adrian. These revelations had affected her in a singular way, and she wanted to be alone to brood on them.

What she had heard made her regard her husband with a fresh, uncontrollable antipathy. . . . That night, at dinner, he was in one of his most cheerless and biting moods. He appeared in the dining-room with a card which he had just lighted on in the hall.

"General and Mrs. Swartwout," he read from the card. "The General was never in but one action during his life, and on that occasion he was slightly wounded. . . . Where? Some people said it was in the left breast, just above the region of the heart. A faithful friend and comrade of the General's, however, who chanced to be in the same action with him, used to deny this statement. He said that there was no wound in the General's left breast at all, as the bullet had stopped before getting there. 'What stopped it?' asked some one innocently. 'His shoulder-blade,' replied that kind-hearted friend." . . . Here Delaplaine laughed to himself in a smothered chuckle, as though he did not expect either Olivia or Adrian Etherege to join him. . . . "Ah," he presently went on, beginning to sip his soup, "of all honorable occupations there is none to which society, feather-headed society, so bows down as the profession of *killing.* The moment you are a killer extraordinary of your fellow-creatures, like a general or a colonel, you are more or less worshipped. The clergy is simply nowhere in comparison. There have been more monuments reared to the men who have killed successfully than to all the painters, sculptors, philosophers and reformers combined. You see, I leave out poets, not thinking them worthy of a moment's concern. They're merely melodious liars; they'll lie prettily on anything, from life, death, or the so-termed human soul, to a glove, a ribbon, or a rosebud. . . . Well, Olivia, did you see the General and his wife?"

"No," said Olivia; "I was not at home."

"You mean . . . in a poetical way."

"I had gone for a little walk."

"Um-m-m. And to gather a little sunburn. I wouldn't. It's horribly unbecoming."

"Why, Mrs. Delaplaine does not seem in the least sunburned to *me*, sir," said Adrian.

"That's because a young stripling like you thinks half the milk-maids that he meets are goddesses."

"Well," said Olivia, laughing, and at the same time hoping to turn the talk, if she might, into pleasanter channels, "*I'm* certainly no milk-maid."

"You!" scoffed Delaplaine. "I should say not — in the sense of pure-mindedness."

Adrian colored and started. These thrusts had for him a sacrilegious atrocity. He looked straight at Mr. Delaplaine, and spoke with an accent of the deepest sincerity and a sudden sparkling out of his old youthful demeanor:

"I should say, sir, that your wife had as much pure-mindedness as any woman that ever lived."

"Ho, ho!" laughed Delaplaine. "Much *you* know about the matter! Take care, or she'll be twisting you round her finger in fine style. She's craftier than when you knew her last; she's had a season of New York deviltries to practise on."

"In most of which you were my companion," Olivia either could not or simply did not resist now saying, although she had but lately shot Adrian a look that enjoined silence upon him.

"I'm not so sure of that," he answered, and gave his laugh again.

Olivia had trangressed her usual rule in having shown the faintest resentment toward her husband. She now regretted this fact, and immediately turned to Adrian, with a second pitiful attempt to alter the conversational current.

"This General Swartwout," she said, "has *such* a pretty daughter. I should like, some time, to present you."

But Delaplaine was unpropitiable to-night. "Why on earth," he asked, "would you present Adrian? She's an airy girl, with a great idea of marrying a bigger swell than she is herself."

"Oh," said Olivia, with a smile at Adrian, "we will not mind the marrying part, will we?"

"No, indeed," said Adrian, "I'm not at all ambitious to marry."

"Still," struck in Delaplaine, "you'd like to marry ambitiously; there's a difference."

"There is no difference for me, sir," Adrian replied.

"Stuff!" Delaplaine said. "Every man or woman, unless made a fool of by the mental distemper named love, always wants, if it be possible, to fly the matrimonial kite high. . . . I have very rarely seen an extremely rich man who did not marry a beautiful wife.

They have the pick of the market, as it were; any one whom they choose to ask is delighted to accept."

Adrian shook his head. "You yourself admit, sir, that the mental distemper named love, exists after all."

"It doesn't stand the dimmest chance against money, once in a thousand times. Not the dimmest. Let the young capitalist appear on the scene and Phyllis will begin to smirk at him over Corydon's very shoulder. And presently she gets up and waltzes toward the new-comer, leaving poor Corydon her crook, perhaps, for consolation. She won't need it any more; she's going to be too fine a lady."

"Corydon ought to take up the crook," laughed Adrian, "and lay it over the millionaire's back."

"Much good if he did. There'd be a lawsuit, and the millionaire, having money enough to supply himself with the highest legal intelligence in the land, would handsomely win the day. And Phyllis would be sure to call her old swain a horrid rough wretch and to declare herself *so* glad she didn't marry him, while she gazed down at the glittering engagement-ring somebody else had just given her."

Adrian again shook his head, but this time with a melancholy emphasis. "I hope, sir, the world isn't quite so black as you paint it!" he exclaimed.

"It's a good deal blacker, in many cases."

"But I'd rather not — at my age — think it so," cried Adrian. "I want to think that it holds many good women and noble men."

Delaplaine pointed across the table at his wife. As he did this, a light thrill shot through Olivia's blood. What new insult was he about to perpetrate? Every week his outward integument of gentlemanliness appeared to lose a layer or so of its density. He was perpetually sinking lower and lower toward a brutality of which his extreme physical weakness alone prevented Olivia from dreading a still more gross deterioration. She had begun to tell herself that there was nothing his irritated and semi-diseased brain might not prompt him to say, for there are some maladies which intensify and reduplicate the worst and most prominent faults of just such a nature as his. But the chances of his doing her any bodily harm were slight enough, since his own muscular feebleness, if no other cause, would have prevented this crowning outrage.

His finger still pointed at her. On his face was a smile of infernal derision.

"Many good men and noble women?" he said, with a mockery that to Olivia had in it the flickering of a snake's forked tongue. "There sits one of the latter. She's a noble woman; I suppose you think so; eh, Adrian?"

"I do!" exclaimed Adrian, with a nervous break in his voice, as though he too were fearful of some insult specially violent.

"Well, then, she married me on what she believed was my death-bed, and just for my money. No other reason. She thought I wouldn't live three hours. There's nobility for you. Eh, Adrian?"

He fell back into his chair, laughing shrilly, while his finger still pointed at his wife.

Olivia shuddered as she saw the butler and footman smile and turn away. She rose staggeringly from the table; she was pale and gasped a little; every instant it seemed to her as if she might swoon; the room whirled round with her; but pricking through all other sensations with an intolerable poignancy, was her exquisite shame!

The next-instant she saw Adrian spring toward her husband and stand over him with lifted arm and blazing eyes.

"You scoundrel!" Adrian cried, every influence of past authority swept away in this one overwhelming moment of passionate championship. "It's only your weakness that keeps me from ——"

"Adrian!" Olivia screamed. "No, no!" But before she had reached his side the young man had folded his arms on his breast. There was a sneer on his lips and a look of scathing scorn still in his beautiful eyes.

"Do not be afraid," he said to Olivia. "I shall not touch him."

"Puppy!" Delaplaine hissed. He had drawn himself so far back into his chair and he was so bloodlessly pale that he looked ten years older than his actual age. "Leave my house, and never dare to ask a dollar of me again!" he went on, huskily.

"I will leave your house this night," said Adrian. "I should feel degraded by every hour longer that I remained there." He was breathing hard, with set teeth, as he turned toward Olivia. "Good bye," he muttered, looking into her eyes. Then he strode out of the room, and she followed him.

"Adrian," she pleaded, stopping him in the hall, "do not go to-night."

"Yes — yes," he said. "There is a train I can catch. If not, I can sleep in the village till morning."

"But you must make up with him — you *must.*
Think : what will become of you if you are suddenly
discharged from the bank? What will become of your
mother, who, as you have told me, depends upon you
for support ? "

Adrian smiled. "There are twenty houses, at least,
that I know of, willing to give me a corresponding
position as clerk. Do not fear on that account." He
watched her with a chivalrously tender look growing
in his gaze. "*You* are far more to be pitied than I
am, since you are a woman and must live on comparatively alone with *him.*"

Olivia shuddered: Suddenly she put both hands up
to her face. The whirling feeling had come into her
head again. She uncovered her face and reeled toward
Adrian, who caught her. "My God!" she gasped.
"I feel as if I were dying. I — I hope it *is* death!
I —"

And then a night put its blackness into her brain.
But what seemed to her possible death was only the
briefest of fainting-fits. She awoke to find herself on
a lounge in the sitting-room, with one of the woman-
servants bathing her temples. As soon as she felt
sufficiently strong and collected to go in search of
Adrian, she found that he had left Greenacre. He
had gathered only a few articles of apparel together,
had taken these with him in a portmanteau, and had
informed a domestic that he would send for the
others. . . .

Olivia had a sense of absolute loathing now, as she
prepared once more to enter the presence of her husband. She conquered such reluctance all the more
easily, however, on recalling her new and positive

determination.   She meant to leave on the morrow
for New York and her Aunt Thyrza.   It need not be
a permanent absence ; she would be willing to return
if certain promises were afterward given her.   The
self-accusative feeling had not yet left her.   She could
not rid herself of its occasional spell.   But for the
confession that she had made to Jasper Masserceene,
her husband would perhaps have escaped the stroke
to which a great deal of his later abuses and imposi-
tions might be attributable.   In truth Olivia now bore
herself with a martyr-like loveliness, where many another woman would have pursued a course either of
lamentation or rebellion.   Yet she had been taxing
too severely her forces both of endurance and resignation.   A spiritual fatigue had resulted — perhaps she
did not dream how cogent a one.   But she was destined soon to learn, and in a way which it would
have appalled her with horror could she have soberly
foreseen.

Her husband had by this time gone, as she supposed,
to his library upstairs.   But on entering that room
Olivia found it vacant.   She next tried his bedcham-
ber, but as she approached the latter she was met by
Delaplaine's valet.

"I do not think Mr. Delaplaine is at all well,
ma'am," said the man.

"Is he lying down?" asked Olivia, pointing to the
apartment which the man had just quitted.

"Yes, ma'am.   He says he's in a good deal of pain."

"Pain?"

"Yes, ma'am . . . I wasn't with him when he had
those fits of internal gout, but from what he tells me
I'm afraid it's another attack."

"Did you send for a doctor?"

"I haven't yet, ma'am. Mr. Delaplaine said 'twas best to wait and see if the pain got worse . . ."

Here the man paused. A heavy groan sounded from the near chamber.

The pain was already worse, and a doctor was immediately sent for. Lulled through many months into submission and quietude, with its right of possession usurped, as one might have believed, by another wholly different disorder, the man's old foe, gout, had suddenly leaped upon him and begun to inflict its keenest pangs. The attack was a terrible one, and Delaplaine fainted two or three times during its first most agonizing seizures. By about twelve o'clock on the following day his regular physician arrived from New York. He remained about three hours at Greenacre, carefully watching the patient. "There is nothing for me to do," he told Olivia, "which the physician whom I found in attendance cannot do as well. We have consulted together, and our views entirely agree. This sudden access of hot weather is certainly against Mr. Delaplaine. He has rallied before from similar attacks, but he was not then, as now, weakened by the results of hemiplegy. Still, unless the internal gout should again manifest itself, I see no reason for further anxiety."

The practitioner from L——, near by, stayed with Delaplaine until about nine o'clock that evening. The patient was then seemingly better, though very weak. He slept at intervals, awaking after dozes of ten or fifteen minutes' duration, and complaining of extreme thirst. It was not thought advisable to give him any means of gratifying this thirst except minutely-cracked ice, which he disliked and protested against as insufficient to relieve his needs.

The night had become oppressively hot. A full moon flooded the lawns of Greenacre and showed the great river beyond them in a scimetar-like curve of brilliance. All the windows had been opened. Olivia supposed that the servants would close the house below stairs when the regular time came for doing so; she had not given this question the least thought; she had had too many other thoughts of over-towering import with which to concern herself.

Just after the doctor from the village had gone, she said'to the woman who watched at Delaplaine's bedside:

"You may go and lie down, now, Martha. I will stay here for two or three hours. When I grow very tired — if I do grow so — I will go upstairs to your room and call you. Then you can relieve me."

"Yes, ma'am," said Martha. "Do you know about the medicine, ma'am?"

"Yes."

They were standing just at the threshold of Delaplaine's dim room, where the yellow glow of a shaded lamp blent with the silver rays drifting in through two broad windows.

"He is to have a tea-spoon of that medicine in the large glass — the aconite — every hour, provided he awakes," continued Olivia.

"That's it, ma'am," said Martha. "But we're to be careful, you know."

"Careful?"

"Yes, ma'am. The doctor said it was so dangerous . . . don't you remember, ma'am?"

"Oh, yes," answered Olivia, really remembering. "You mean he might drink it if he reached out his hand, or anything like that. . . . Yes, I recollect what the doctor said. But he seems to be sleeping quietly, now; and besides, Martha, it's not on the table by the bedside; it's there on the bureau. . . . Oh, I'll be very careful."

Every syllable of her own and Martha's words appeared so completely unimportant, then. But every syllable returned to her memory with so frightful a distinctness, not very long afterward!

Martha went upstairs to bed. Olivia stood at the door-sill of her husband's room for a slight while. His breathing was quite regular; he seemed in a wholly placid sleep. She passed into the room adjoining.

It was the library, and here, too, the light had been turned somewhat low. But three windows, opened to their fullest extent, showed the magnificent pearly glamour of the moonlight, whose quality, for some reason belonging to the dead sultriness of the atmosphere, revealed a kind of milky, brooding thickness as the night advanced.

Olivia seated herself near one of the windows. If her husband should wake and utter the least sound she knew that she could instantly hear him.

She brushed the hair with both hands back from her heated temples, and leaned out as far as the window-ledge would let her.

She was thinking: "How horrible my life has been of late! What if its wretchedness *should* end to-night, or soon after to-night? Do I hope that it will? Have I power quite to crush down such a hope? Let me try — let me try with all my soul! . . . I used to have

those wicked impulses in the old days of the *pension*
abroad. I thought I had conquered them, when I
came back for the last time with papa. . . . How poor
papa used to laugh at them! . . . I wonder if he is
where he can know about me now, and be sorry that
he ever *did* laugh. For it was one of those impulses
that made me—Olivia Delaplaine. Yes, it was all
my fault. Neither Aunt Augusta nor Aunt Letitia
was to blame, but I, only I!"

Then she thought of Massereene, as she sometimes
could not help but think. "Where is he now? Has
he forgotten me? If anything *should* happen, would
he——?"

But she forced herself to banish him from her mind,
as she had done a hundred times before now. The
exorcism cost her a struggle, however. To-night the
failure to effect it seemed fraught with a peculiar
unduteousness. "He is so good and high himself!"
she pursued, rising amid the vagueness of the moonlit
chamber. "He would respect me more if he knew
that I had striven to——"

At this point a sound broke upon her ears. She
knew on the instant whence it proceeded. Her husband had waked and uttered it. She glided without
delay into the next chamber where he was lying.

## XXIII.

"Did you call?' she asked, pausing at Delaplaine's bedside.

He was wide-awake. A beam of moonlight had shot in from one of the windows, and spread its ice-like pallor across his colorless face. He looked like a living corpse.

Olivia waited beside him. Some change in his expression (she could not have told just what) made her perceive that he recognized her.

"Yes, I called," he said, presently. His eyes had begun to wander from point to point in her costume, as a child's might do, pausing once more at her face. And then, in the dimness, Olivia saw that a new expression filled them. It was vulpine to her, and she recoiled from it. But as she did so, he reached out a hand and clutched hers. The grasp was not a strong one; she could easily have cast it off. But she did not. If it had been less weak, she would have done so; but as it was, she did not.

"I shouldn't be surprised if it were all up with me, this time," he said to her, in a voice not greatly above a whisper. "I feel as if it were going to be that way." His voice sank, and it seemed to her that the eyes with which he now fixedly stared into her own had become two spots of fiery, molten gray. She could never afterward quite be sure whether this effect was born of her own disturbed state or whether some actual basilisk-like change of the sort really took place.

"I hate to go," he said, "and not take you with me. Ah! if I only could have you die when I died ! If I only could! You witch, you, that made me care for you in my old age, what shall I do without you if there *should* be any after-life? . . . Eh? what shall I do without you? If I were only strong enough to kill you just when I'd got sure of dying myself! Then we 'd go together — *together*. That's what I want. It's horrible to think of going like this, and leaving you with all that youth to live out, and all that love in you, too, that you never gave me the tiniest part of! It's horrible, I say, Olivia, and . . . "

But she snatched her hand away from him, here. He had leaned a little forward, but he now fell back upon the pillows, laughing hoarsely and faintly to himself.

She felt certain, by this time, that his brain was afflicted with some serious lesion, even if she had truly doubted it during many weeks before. Shivers were passing through all her nerves, though she still forced herself to remain at the bedside. He roused in her an abhorrence that strangely blent with pity. She loathed and shrank from him, and yet she could not but feel now that the ravage of his disorder had been stealthier than she herself had appreciated, and that his present almost infantile demeanor showed a brain of no common order pitiably wrecked. Then, too, the thought shot through her mind: 'If I had more persistently kept before me this fact of his mental decay, might not many of the distressing things he has done have lost their chief power to wound?'

Still, almost simultaneously, these last words of his were ringing through recollection with a frightful mockery. Could it be possible that he really desired her to die with him, in case he himself died? His clutch upon her wrist had affected her as though its coldness and clamminess had been those of the dead. She felt its pressure yet, and furtively rubbed the wrist against one side of her gown as she at length said:

"It is time for your medicine. I must give it to you now."

He made her no answer, and she went to the mantel where the medicine was placed. She brought it to him. The glass which contained it was almost full. He watched it with a greed in his gaze.

"I'm thirsty," he said.

Olivia was stirring the liquid in the glass with a spoon. But she now stopped, and looked down at the small table placed close beside the bed. "There is your ice," she answered.

"I hate that horrid, slippery ice. It doesn't quench my thirst; it only aggravates it by leaving those little drops of water in my mouth when I don't want drops of water at all — when I want a whole glassful, like that you have in your hand."

"This!" exclaimed Olivia, starting, while both the doctor's and Martha's words came back to her. "Why, this is deadly poison."

"And you're going to give it to me!" he said grimly, as she stooped down toward him with a teaspoonful of it.

"Only a small dose at a time," she answered. "It is aconite, you know."

He let her place the spoon between his lips. "I didn't know," he muttered, "and I don't much care."

Immediately after he had taken the medicine he uttered a little sound of exasperation, and as she looked inquiringly into his face she saw that he was again staring into her own.

"Don't be too sure," he began in a voice as husky as it was meaning.

"Too sure?" she repeated.

"Yes. That I *am* going to die this time. Perhaps I'm not. Remember how I fooled you once before. Threatened men, you know . . . . Don't be too sure, that's all."

Olivia repressed a shudder. "It is all in God's hands," she said.

"God's hands," he grumbled; "yes. When medicine goes out of the sick room by one door, religion's invited to come in by the other. . . . I wish you'd turn that light down lower. It keeps me from sleeping. I believe it's that; it must be that."

Olivia at once obeyed him, turning the lamp down until it made but a vague star in the moonlight as vague. Her hand trembled so while she performed this little task that but for the gloom he might easily have remarked the agitation he had produced in her. To have him read, like this, emotions that she had sought to hide even from her own intelligence! There was a kind of crucial wizardry in it that made her want to fly from the chamber where he lay. She knew that his belief as to his not sleeping was wholly a delusion, and that he would soon have dropped into another slumber like that from which he had lately awakened. Slipping from his room, she gained the one adjoining it. Here the moonlight was much ampler of volume, and a great silvery medallion, wrought by it, lay upon the carpet. She had a calmer sensation, somehow as soon as she was in this other apartment. . . . Why had he taunted her with those last words of his, that had pierced like one of the sharpest shafts which conscience itself can forge?

She *had* been anticipating his death. She could not help doing so. But if by any preventive act she could possibly keep him alive, would she not perform such act with all willingness and promptitude?

A wave of new nervous dread swept over her as she reflected upon what he had just said. This extraordinary fondness of his, which appeared to borrow its modes of exhibition from antipathy rather than affection, might perpetuate itself through many future years. And if it did, how hateful must be her lot! Men with his vitality lived sometimes until ninety, and past that age. And she, if this prolongation of his life occurred, would still be young by contrast with his afflicting, burdening decrepitude. What fresh funds of patience and self-control must she draw upon to meet the continuance of all this martyrizing bondship? Where and from whom should she seek the needful fortitude? In the sore straits of weariness, exhaustion, disgust, whence to draw added courage? *À quelle porte frapper?*

Suddenly, after perhaps five good minutes had passed, while she stood there in the moonlight, terrified at the potential future that had piled its masses of gloom before her mental vision, she recollected something, and a sharp little gasp left her lips.

She had omitted to replace the glass of aconite upon

the mantel. It was there, now, on the table at her husband's bedside!

She flew to the threshold of the doorway that led into his room. And then, almost as abruptly as if some palpable hand had set upon her its detaining contact, she paused.

Paused. . . but why? She knew, and yet her brain had begun to whirl in a chaotic way.

Why did she not go to him and take the glass of poison from where he could so easily reach it? She kept asking herself this question, dumbly, insistently, and yet . . she still remained immovable.

With a frightful panoramic vividness, occurrence after occurrence of her past life had begun to rush before her inward vision. She saw herself at the *pension*, beset again and again by those malign attacks of evil tendency at which her father had afterwards laughed so lightly but of whose pregnant meaning she was herself far better aware than he. Bursts of mischief as they had been, they had preluded that larger temptation, that more momentous fall, which had made her the wife of Spencer Delaplaine.

And now? She had only to leave the glass there a little longer. If he drank of it she would not be giving him to drink of it. He might reach out his hand, and lift it to his lips, in the craving of his thirst. It would kill him, no doubt, before they could get the doctor to his bedside. . . Well; and if it did kill him?

"Wait here just a few more minutes," a voice had begun piercingly to whisper. "You've a right to wait here if you chose. And should he reach out for that glass and drink what it contains, imagining this to be water, how should such an act at all incriminate *you?*

The chances are that he will *not* drink; for he does not even know that the glass is there. How should he know? He asked you to make the room darker, and you did so. He has most probably fallen into another doze. . . *Still, wait here a little while longer.* You have a perfect right to do so. *Wait.* There; the time is passing on, on, even now. Before you fairly know it, fifteen, twenty minutes will have elapsed. *So much may happen in fifteen or twenty minutes.*"

Olivia's eyes, all this time, were riveted upon the window through which the misty silver of the moon was passing. She·lived through many a new moon before the beams of it had become to her anything else than a ghastly reminder of that fateful interval. The lawns went sloping off into nebulous dreams of their own spaciousness; and, beyond, glittered the huge river. It had the sparkle of diamonds, of wealth; it was shaped like a curving sword as it lay along the shadowed lands, and a sword·symbolled power. But though power was good, liberty was more what Olivia longed for. Perhaps the contour of the sword meant that too — the severance of bonds that were both an agony and a horror! These wholly idle fancies, rushing with gloomier and weightier thoughts through her brain, as light foam-wreaths will cling to dark throngs of on-rolling surges and be borne whither they hurry, came back to Olivia with a fearful definiteness during after reflections.

She did not turn from the sophistries of that voice. She let it speak still further; she listened to it. Her heart had got beating so violently that its strokes sounded like hammer-blows in her ears. She realized

that this baneful force, though a mere pranksome imp
of old, had grown a devil now, and had silently but
jeeringly challenged her to wrestle with him and overcome him. What a contrast between this demon and
that of her girlhood! What a contrast, and yet how
traceable, how authentic a similarity!

But a full conception of her own resistant power at
last broke upon Olivia. She sprang aloof, as it were,
from the sorcery of temptation enmeshing her. She
spoke to her own soul in that clarion way which it
cannot but hear. Truth itself seemed to leap up her
ally, and to help her destoy this enslaving spell, as the
breeze might help a taintless flower to shake from its
petals the brackish water that some froward chance
had spilled upon it.

"Free?" she faintly sobbed to herself, recollecting
the fancy that the sword-shaped glory of the river
had given her. "I am free *now!* Thank God for
saving me!"

But abruptly a new thought darted through her
mind. A certain length of time had intervened between the beginning of that miserable struggle and
the present moment. How long had it been? Say ten,
twelve, even twenty minutes.

What if —?

But she would not let herself think the thought out.
She sped through the little passage-way leading into her
husband's room. It was just as dim as she had left it.
She stood with her foot on the threshold, listening.
At first she told herself that she could hear him
breathe with the regularity of one who sleeps tranquilly. But soon she had become otherwise convinced;
he was breathing in an odd and very uncertain way.

And then, making her strained nerves tingle, he gave, without any warning, a heavy and most painful groan.

Olivia hurried to the lamp and turned it up. Then her glance shot toward the little table at the side of the bed.

The glass was there, but it was empty.

She would not believe her own senses at first. She went nearer to the table and peered down at the glass. Yes! Empty!

Still clinging to a last frail hope that her eyesight had tricked her, she raised the glass in her hand. But it fell from her effete fingers to the floor.

She did not attempt to pick it up, or even to ascertain whether it had been broken or no. She had turned her look upon her husband's face. He had closed his eyes, and lay upon his back. He appeared to be quite unconscious. She leaned over him and grasped his shoulder, slightly shaking his form once or twice. He seemed either in a state of sluggish coma, or else dead. Which was it?

She rang the bell violently several times. Then she sank down on her knees at his bedside. Her face was hueless, her hands were clasped tightly together, her eyes were dilated, as though she were undergoing some intense physical torture.

## XXIV.

AFTERWARD she felt as if she were in a dream — as if .the servants who came hastening into the room were visionary shapes — as if the voice with which she addressed them and that with which they answered her were heard through deadening folds of fog. The poison had begun speedily to work upon Delaplaine, as aconite nearly always does, and his sufferings became acute. He complained of a wretched giddiness, of a peculiar tingling in his arms and hands, of pain in the abdomen, of an almost asphyxiating heaviness about the heart. Then followed spasms of the most racking nausea, with other symptoms no less deplorable. Believing that her husband would die, it was a relief to Olivia when he at length ceased staring at her and entirely lost consciousness. Until the arrival of the doctor she joined the servants in leaving scarcely an effort at restoration untried. From the first she had not hesitated to tell them, one and all, the cause of this unexpected attack. If she had failed to do so she would have seemed to herself like a veritable murderess concealing her crime. And, as it was, she had already told herself, with pangs of remorse which made her heart feel as if it were being cut in twain, that Delaplaine's death, if this really occurred, would be a result of those few minutes wherein she had so weakly, ignobly lingered and demurred.

"Mr. Delaplaine must have drank his medicine," she said, "for I found the glass empty on returning to his room after being away from it only a little while."

And then to her own soul she mutely added: "Though they arrest me and put me in prison as his assassin, I *will* speak the truth. God knows, if I did not do that I should then despise myself even more than now?"

When the doctor at last came she told him in a clear and perfectly sustained manner just how her husband's illness had been brought about. "I may have been careless in leaving the glass of medicine on the table at his bedside," she finished, "but it could not have remained there more than twenty minutes at the utmost, and the room had been darkened through Mr. Delaplaine's desire, as he said that he wished to sleep and could not do so otherwise."

"Mr. Delaplaine did not know that the medicine was on the table, I suppose," said the physician. He was watching, as he spoke, the few faint convulsions that of late had assailed the sick man. He had already concluded that there was no chance whatever of saving his patient's life; the dose had been too heavy a one, and too much precious time had been lost before he had been enabled to reach Greenacre.

"I think that he knew nothing of the medicine being there," answered Olivia. "I imagine that he gave this point no heed at all, however, and simply drank the first liquid that he could find."

"Strange," murmured the doctor."

"Do you consider it strange?" Olivia asked, with controlled voice and a self-possession that surprised her while she assumed it.

"Yes," came the reply.  This country doctor was a quaint man, replete with bony angles, and having two dark, bluish streaks under his eyes that gave to his long, haggard face a look no less lugubrious than sincere.  You had only to glance at him in order to see what a terribly serious matter with him was the rising of each day's sun, and also the going down thereof.  He had instantly begun to blame himself for having left so large a dose of the deadly aconite in Delaplaine's apartment, and for not having sufficiently warned those who surrounded the invalid concerning just how baneful a preparation it was.  He was a person, this Dr. Matthew Gleason, who rather morbidly blamed himself a great deal for a great many things.

"Yes," he now repeated.  "If, as you say, the room was dark and no one was here to hand it to him, why, his taking it at all was certainly strange."

The color flew to Olivia's cheeks.  But for a brief period, at least, her sensations were not guilty ones.  It gave her, indeed, a certain hectic gladness to speak the next words, which fell from her lips with a little accent of indignation :

"No one could have been here *to hand* it to him.  I hardly understand your meaning, Dr. Gleason.  One would suppose— "

But the doctor did not hear her.  He was bending over Delaplaine, in whom the first struggles of death were beginning.  Assiduously, spurred by an energy that seemed determined to leave no conceivable resource unused, this sombre man worked on and on, for an hour or more, with remedy and antidote.  But at length he failed, as he had been almost convinced beforehand that he must fail. Perhaps the anticipation of how much he was hereafter to have on his brooding and sensitive conscience through the dreary and lonely nights of the coming winter, stimulated him now into making the prospective burden as light as possible.

The sultry summer dawn was just breaking when Spencer Delaplaine died. He had been breathing almost imperceptibly for some little while, when without a hint of premonition his frame was disturbed by two or three light, swift shivers.

Dr. Gleason stooped down, with a ducking gesture whose infinite awkwardness could not escape Olivia, notwithstanding her perturbed state. He placed one of his large ears just below the left breast of the prostrate man, and appeared for several minutes to be listening intently.

When he raised his head, he at once turned toward Olivia. She silently bowed, wondering at her own thorough calmness. There was no mistaking the new gravity that had gathered upon the doctor's habitually mournful face.

"Dead?" she murmured.

"Yes," he answered below his breath, and she fancied that he shot at her, from his doleful eyes, a look of irrepressible reproach and accusation. . . .

But she was mistaken here. In about half an hour Dr. Gleason had asked her to give him a few moments of private conversation. They went together into the room adjoining that where Delaplaine had lately expired. The moonlight had given place to the dawn, and Dr. Gleason's countenance, illumined by the whitish glimmer that struck upon it, confronted Olivia with an unearthly ugliness.

"Is he going to charge me with having killed my husband?" she asked herself, as she stood before him in statue-like composure.

But Dr. Gleason had not the remotest intention of playing any such grim part. On the contrary, he broke the silence by saying, with tones full of conscience-stricken disarray:

"Mrs. Delaplaine, this unhappy accident has occurred, and — and it must (I feel *sure* that it must) reflect very unfortunately upon — upon myself as a medical man. If possible, I would endeavor to have the real facts hidden. But that cannot be. Too many people are already acquainted with them. . . . As for my culpability, I — I don't know just how other physicians — those who practice in the great centres like New York — will regard my — my share in the mistake. There is no doubt that I *might* have left a smaller portion of the dilution. But as it was, I gave clear warning in the matter of its noxious quality. And just now I am hard-worked in the village. It has been an unhealthy summer. I feared lest I might not reach Mr. Delaplaine again until to-morrow — I should say *this* afternoon. And therefore I acted as seemed to me most wise and prudent. But I have apparently committed a — a most grievous professional error. I acknowledge this; I feel that it is my duty to make such acknowledgment, both before you and—— "

But here Olivia broke in. "I cannot see where your error lies," she said. "Blame, if there is any blame, should belong to those with whom you left the dangerous drug, after having so explicitly warned them." And now she rested one hand upon Dr.

Gleason's big, angular arm. "I shall tell everybody," she went on, "that you deserve the fullest exoneration." Her voice almost failed her, for a few seconds, and then she again continued, with a fresh repose and serenity : "I shall tell everybody — I promise you this most faithfully — that my husband's death has been due to my own neglect in leaving that glass of aconite near him, even for the short space of time that I did so leave it."

Dr. Gleason stretched forth one of his large-knuckled hands and clasped one of her own with it.

"Oh, Mrs Delaplaine, I thank you! I thank you so much! You — you haven't just taken the load from my mind, but you've — you've *eased* me wonderfully!" . . .

Olivia kept her word. From the morrow, as might be said, she faced the whole world unflinchingly with the truth. Or, if not the real truth, with enough of it to make everybody believe that she had kept nothing in reserve. The former gossip concerning her peculiar marriage was now revived, and perhaps a few cruel things were said in connection with that and the almost equally peculiar manner of her husband's death. But these comments were spared Olivia. And, yet, for that matter, she heard them in imagination ; for this was a period of her life when those receptivities that mean in us the dealing of deep and incessant wounds were with Olivia most briskly operative. Night followed night, after Delaplaine's death, and not an instant of sleep came to her. It was the sort of insomnia that has no briefer moods of mercy. "I shall go mad," she had begun to gasp in the dead night-watches, sitting up in bed and hearing the clock

tick and the very darkness itself seem to flow about
her in whirls and counter-currents. But she had the
vigor of youth, as yet, for this vampire of distempers
to draw upon. An increased pallor was the sole
change in her that, during several days, any of those
whom circumstances called upon most closely to
observe her remarked.

Meanwhile Delaplaine's body had been brought to
West Tenth Street, and his funeral had been held at
Grace Church with that preponderance of black coats
which invariably will mark such ceremonials when they
take place in the middle of the summer season. The
Auchinclosses had felt it their "duty" to come into
town, notwithstanding the extreme discomfort of the
heat, but the Satterthwaites had remained at Newport
and written Olivia a note of "condolence." That is,
Emmeline (who had secret misgivings lest her future
wedding-present, when she married Arthur Plunkett
in the autumn, might suffer as to size and general
expensiveness) volunteered to represent her family by
the composition of such a note. She began it with a
yawn and ended it with one. "Oh, dear," she said,
after two sheets of her mourning-rimmed paper had
been covered, "what monstrous fibs I have told! The
idea of alluding to Olivia's 'painful affliction,' when
we all know, and she knows we all know, that if she
has any feeling at all regarding the affair, it must be
one of pure delight."

"Delight?" echoed her sister, Elaine, lazily. "Oh,
*Em!* isn't that too strong?"

"Not a bit," returned Emmeline, "provided his
Will is found to leave her everything."

"It has somehow got around," said Elaine, with a

note of conviction in her voice, "that he has left her very little. They say he got to perfectly detest her for some time before he died. How horrible if he left her *poor!*"

"Oh, *don't!*" remonstrated Emmeline, as if the possibility were too harrowing a one for serious contemplation.

But Spencer Delaplaine left his wife all his very large property, without reservation or stipulation of any sort. Olivia was keenly surprised when she learned this fact; she had expected (when thinking at all on the subject) a legacy as great as the law itself apportioned her and not a dime greater. She was now an exceedingly rich young widow; but during those days of feverish inward turmoil and outward tranquillity, she found herself constantly forgetting that this was the case.

The lawyers, however, soon began most pertinaciously to remind her of it. "I guess, 'Livia, they'll worry an' pester you a good deal 'fore you're through with 'em," said Mrs. Ottarson, who was sitting with her one day, and whom Olivia liked to have at the West Tenth Street house as often as that lady could spare the time for coming.

"There would be no worriment at all, Aunt Thyrza," she replied, "if—if . . . ." She paused, and lifted her hands to her eyes, rubbing them almost as a sleepy child might do. "Well," she finished, with a little laugh as faint as it was discordant, "if I were only feeling more . . . more as I used to feel, somehow."

The last words were spoken with the saddest of tremors, and then a forced brightening of demeanor followed them.

Mrs. Ottarson gave a little start, and afterward let her black eyes dwell very fixedly indeed upon Olivia, while the latter bent her head over a legal document which the servant had recently handed her.

Presently Mrs. Ottarson rose from her chair. Olivia did not seem to be aware that she had done so until the lady's hand touched her shoulder.

"'Livia?"

"Well, aunt?"

"Look here, 'Livia."

Down sat Mrs. Ottarson, after that, and close to her niece's side. She caught one of Olivia's hands and held it pressed tight in her own.

"Now, 'Livia," she recommenced, "I want you jus' t' look right straight *at* me. No droppin' your eyes like that, deary: I ain't 'fraid t' meet *your* eyes . . . . There; that's it. . . . Now, 'Livia, you're jus' *mis'ra-ble!* I've seen it ever since you sent for me t' come here. I've watched you pretty smart, too, all the while we've been t'gether, an' I'm ready to swear somethin' 's half settin' you crazy."

"Oh, no, Aunt Thyrza . . ."

"Oh, *yes*, Aunt Thyrzy! Come, now, you can't fool me like that. I *will* jus' know w'at 't is. Out with it, now, 'Livia. I ain't to be bluffed off."

"I — I sleep badly," murmured Olivia. She had lifted her eyes but now she had again drooped them. "The truth is, if you will know, that I — I don't sleep *at all*."

"Don't sleep at all?"

She shook her head. "I haven't had a minute's sleep, since — "

"I understand. Since that night. You're worryin'

'bout his drinkin' that med'cine. 'S if you could a helped it ! "

" I *could* have helped it."

She whispered the words. Mrs. Ottarson barely caught them. " *Could* ? " she repeated. . . . And then the color died quite out of her olive cheeks. " 'Livia, you don't mean w'at you're sayin'! No, you don't ! " Suddenly lowering her tones, she pursued: " W'atever you *do* mean, tell me! Don't be 'fraid. Tell *me!* "

She dropped Olivia's hand. She put forth both arms and threw them round her companion's form, through which shivers had begun to pass in quick, alarming succession.

" I will tell you," Olivia cried, while her head fell upon her aunt's shoulder. " I will tell you, though you should hate and loathe me after you've heard ! " Then her voice fell almost to a whisper. " I — I left the medicine there by mistake. He wanted the lamp turned down, and I turned it. All that is true. Everything you've heard me say is true. But . . . there is something else."

" Something else ? Well, what? "

" This ! " she answered, in a choked, hoarse way. And now for perhaps five minutes, with her head still on Mrs. Ottarson's shoulder, she spoke, agitatedly, brokenly, but not once with the least sign of tears. Her ending sentence was: " There, I have confessed to you just what a guilty creature I am, and how little sympathy I deserve from any living fellow-creature except those as much steeped in sin as myself! "

For a few seconds there was no response to this

hopelessly mournful outburst. Then Olivia felt her
aunt's arms tightening about her frame.

"You great goose!" exclaimed Mrs. Ottarson.
"'Xcuse me, 'Livia, but I can't help it! W'y w'at on
earth *did* you do? You jus' stood there in that dark
room, an' had a few evil thoughts. Who mightn't a
had 'em, if they'd been through all you'd been through?
An' then you conquered 'em, as you was certain to
conquer 'em, an' rushed in t' where he was layin'.
*My!* is *that* all?"

Olivia raised her head, and stared supplicatingly,
childishly, passionately, at the speaker.

"Oh, Aunt Thyrza, *are* you in earnest? Don't
deceive me! It means so much to me if you think—
if you *really* think—that I. . . " She could say no
more, and just as her lips were trembling incapably
her aunt placed a heavy and hearty kiss upon
them.

"Who's dreampt o' deceivin' you, Livvy? W'y it's
all sheer nonsense f' you to go on so 'bout nothin' 't
all. Ev'rybody has spells o' badness like that. It's
the way the devil tries to catch his own, I s'pose.
Gracious! I've had 'em fifty times. An' la sakes
alives, what did you *do*, after all? 'Livia, 'f you really
felt well you wouldn't care a snap for such rubbishy
fancies. . . . You ain't well, an' you mus' see a doctor.
. . . I'm glad you're cryin'; 't will do you good.
'T ain't the first time, is it, Liv, you've cried on this
old shoulder o' mine?"

Olivia's tears came in a tempest. Perhaps they
saved her reason. That night she slept profoundly,
and far on into the next morning. Physically she was
well enough afterward. But nevertheless a certain

reaction succeeded the supreme burst of thankfulness and exultation which Mrs. Ottarson's comforting words had invoked. Olivia soon found herself looking at her own behavior in what she could not but assure her own moral sense was the properly judicial light. She had been so far from actually causing the death of her husband that to accuse herself of having played such a hideous part was clear absurdity. Her temptation had amounted to this: She had remained passive for a certain number of minutes when passivity might have meant fatal neglect of duty. She had resisted the impulse to continue away from Delaplaine's bedside — stoutly and successfully resisted it. But success had not come until a certain time had gone; and during that time the death-dealing potion had been lifted to the invalid's lips. Had she staid near him, she, his voluntary nurse — had she been a sentinel at her post and not one who did worse than to desert it — she might easily enough have saved his life.

"It all lies there," Olivia afterward ruminated: — "in the fact that I allowed those minutes to pass before I had put that hateful feeling away from me! I shall never pardon myself for that hesitation. I shall never cease to blame myself because of it. I shall always think of myself as different from the fellow-creatures whom I daily meet and talk with. Even though I may not have committed a positive crime, the shadow of one has fallen upon me. Amid that shadow my spirit must dwell, alone and apart, from now until I die."

In the second or third week of the autumn following Delaplaine's death, Jasper Massereene called upon Olivia. She had heard that he had been in Newport all summer, and had dreaded lest he should present himself in West Tenth Street on his return. For it belonged to the gloom of that "shadow" in which through the rest of her days she must be bathed, not to permit any but terms of the most distant future acquaintanceship between herself and Massereene.

But for once, at least, she resolved to see him. Thereafter she would avoid doing so as far as lay in her power. She had silently rehearsed their meeting a hundred times, but when it took the guise of reality it was so diametrically different from what she had expected! They shook hands with the most ordinary kind of collectedness on both sides. They fell to talking of Newport in tones and terms that might have been employed by two persons without a single true common interest.

"They tell me it is a very delightful place," Olivia said.

"Oh, very. You have never been there?"

"No. . . . Were you quite gay while there?"

"Not gay at all. I did not see many people. I had pleasant rooms, and I read a good deal, drove or rode a good deal, and occasionally dined with friends, though not oftener than twice a week."

"You selected a rather fashionable spot to be quiet in."

"That, I found, is the charm of Newport. You can be as retired in the midst of all the merrymaking as though you were a hundred miles off." He hesitated, and looked with a sudden meaning animation at Olivia. In an instant, as it were, she realized that her ordeal had begun.

"Besides," he added, "I had no choice for amusement — no choice and no heart. You may perhaps guess why."

" I may guess?" she asked, making her voice neutral, except for its faint, conventional shading of surprise.

He ignored this composed answer, "I came in town for . . . the funeral," he said. "I wanted to call upon you afterward, but thought it best not to do so. I suppose that was the wiser plan; was it not?

" I was quite unwell for some time afterward," she said.

"Naturally. The shock must have affected you.".

"It did."

" But you have recovered by this, I hope."

" Oh, yes."

There was a silence. She felt rather than saw his eyes restlessly sweep her face. "May I say to you," he began, "that I trust my coming this afternoon has not been at all . . . inopportune?"

She bit her lips. "Inopportune?" she repeated.

He made an impatient gesture, and leaned nearer toward her. "You are receiving me with a terrible coldness," he exclaimed. "What have I done to deserve it?"

" You have done nothing; you are always blameless," Olivia answered, with a little defiant, hollow, embarrassed laugh that she immediately regretted. "It is I," she added, with a less artificial air and just the hint of a break in her voice, "I who continually am making myself culpable."

" You imagine that you are," he said, with an instant kindness. "Surely you had done nothing, in former days, to feel so grievously guilty about; it had all been done to you. And yet you dwelt in a perpet-

ual atmosphere of self-arraignment . . . And now —
well, I have not caught even a rumor of what your
true spirits are, but I will engage they are dark with
remorse and repentance."

He had ended smilingly, but she almost snatched
the words from his lips, while her face was whitening.
"Remorse — repentance?" she cried. "What *do* you
mean? Why — why should I feel either?"

"You look as if you might have been a sufferer from
both," said Massereene, shaking his head while the
smile deepened on his lips. "Ah, I was sure of it!
That mistake about the medicine would, I knew,
plunge you in agonies of contrition. You cannot
forgive yourself. You are not just sure how it happens
that your fault is so black, but you are no less confident
of its blackness."

His playful satire, so completely unsuspicious of the
real truth, had by this time become apparent to his
listener. He had thought manifold thoughts regarding Olivia Delaplaine since their separation, and among
these could conspicuously be placed the deduction that
she was the victim of an excessively tender conscience.
In referring to the matter of the draught of aconite,
he merely mentioned what had of course become a
theme for current discussion during at least two or
three weeks after Delaplaine's death. Olivia felt that
he was indeed carelessly laying his hands upon wounds
which the least rough touch might make betrayingly
bleed. She managed to speak with a fair amount of
quietude as she said:

"I suppose that the story of the medicine got about
everywhere. . . . Did they say ill-natured things of
me?"

"None that I heard." He laughed. "What could they say except the merest *bêtises?*"

"Even those are waspish, now and then; they carry stings."

"Only for very sensitive persons. . . . But you have a right to be sensitive — to have a hundred trifles 'give you some nerves,' as I once heard a Frenchman say while he floundered in English. You have been through untold trials. But now all that is past. Your liberty has come again. You are still younger than many a girl who has not yet thought much about marriage. Everything should point to your perfect happiness, and no one hopes for it with greater sincerity than I do!"

He was the Masscreene of old to her while he thus spoke; she surrendered herself to the rich sweetness of his voice and let herself enjoy the candid sparkle of his gaze. . . . Then, abruptly, came the chilling recollection of that "set gray life and apathetic end" with which she had resolved that her future should be unalterably associated.

"I thank you," she said, in tones grave enough thoroughly to suit the mourning attire which he had expected to see her wear, and yet which had seemed to keep her unduly removed from him ever since they had met this afternoon. "I begin to think there is no such thing as happiness in the sense you evidently mean. But I hope to secure the contentment that comes of charitable work toward my fellow-creatures. In this way I shall achieve that self-forgetfulness which is, after all, perhaps, the one most desirable aim. . . . My life is to be a busy and yet a very quiet one. I shall quite give up the world. Poor dear Aunt Thyrza will be about the only friend whom I shall retain — though for that matter, I was without friends here when I came back from Europe for the last time, and —— "

"You have made none since!" broke in Massereene. His brow had clouded both perplexedly and angrily. "*I* am doubtless not your friend! You wish to toss me aside — you have done with me!"

"I — I did not say that," answered Olivia, sitting pale before him, with drooped eyes.

He sprang to his feet. "But you meant it — you wanted to convey that meaning. You came down to meet me with the fixed intention of sending me away from you, if you could do so in a peaceable way, forever. . . . You, at your age, and after the dog's life that Delaplaine led you, to talk of 'that self-forgetfulness which is the one most desirable aim.' Good heavens, woman! you have your life to live, healthfully and sensibly! No one objects to your being as charitable as you please. Give thousands to the poor, if you like. But an ascetic — you! The very idea is preposterous! . . . There," he ended, half turning away, "I have incensed you; I see it in your face."

"You have not incensed me," Olivia replied. "But you have not changed my resolution of wholly forsaking the world — or at least that part of it called society. I can't fully explain to you my determination. But it exists — it exists unchangeably; and if you neither approve it nor respect it, you can still recognize its permanence."

He turned his back upon her, and she saw him bow his head; but in another minute he had faced her once more; and with tones through which vibrated an unmistakable despair, he cried :

"I love you! I want you to be my wife!"

"No, no," she said, rising and moving away from him.

But he hurried close to her, then. "I can't give you up like this — I can't and I won't! There is no reason why I should, unless you care nothing for me. Tell me on your word of honor that you *do* care nothing!"

"I — I care for that other life," she faltered. "I do not mean that it shall be the life of an ascetic. But I am resolved to live it, and I have no other answer than this."

"And this is no answer! At least, it is none if you love me. When, before *his* death, you forbade me even to know you, and wrote me that most repelling of letters, I said to myself that I would bide my time — that I would wait until that dead wall of circumstance no longer lifted its hard, chill bulk between us. I *have* waited, and now you inflict upon me this cruel sorrow without the least rational cause!"

Olivia felt herself begin to tremble. She slipped toward the door, which chanced not to be far away. "I gave you no cause, in those other days," she said, "to believe that I ever meant to become your wife."

"I thought then that you loved me. I think still that you love me. This should be cause enough, surely!"

"But — if you were wrong?" she asked, with a sort of haughty exasperation. "If you were wrong then, and if you are wrong now?"

He took several steps in her direction. His eyes

were glowing — the eyes that she loved, that she had seen gazing at her through the mist of a hundred dreams, that had nearly always made her heart beat quicker if she had looked into them deeply or without warning.

"I am not wrong, Olivia," he said. "Your soul tells you that. . . . Don't let any mad fancy, caprice, theory, come between us. The stars in their courses should be with two hearts that love as ours do." He stretched out his arms and opened them.

For one swift instant she longed to bound toward him — to lay her head on his breast — to tell him everything — to accept the forgiveness that he was certain of extending her, and to let such forgiveness stand in the place of what she would have called God's.

But her longing died under the stress of another; it was one that she held to be far holier and higher. She receded to the very threshold of the room, all the while looking straight at Massereene.

"I hope," she said, without a quiver in her voice, "that we shall never see one another again on this earth. I hope it most earnestly, devoutly. I may write you — I am not sure. But if I do not, take my good-bye now and here." Then she saw his face through her rushing tears, and as it seemed to come nearer, she turned, hastening from the room.

"Olivia!" she heard him cry. . . . For days afterward that sound echoed through her reveries, and now and then she would tell herself that it must so echo until the one last silence made it forever cease.

But for two or three hours after disappearing from

the presence of Massereene, she remained in the most supplicatory and entranced mood of prayer. She poured forth thanks to God for having enabled her to resist the happiness offered her in place of that life-long expiation by which she could at least partially annul the atrocity of her sin. She prayed for strength, hereafter to discipline every desire which bore upon self-gratification; and having thus prayed for strength, she arose, like the majority of those whom an ecstasy of personal prostration and abasement has intoxicated, believing that she was already vastly stronger.

But she met with no further temptation from Jasper Massereene. In about three weeks' time she learned through the Satterthwaites that he contemplated recrossing the ocean . . .

Spencer Delaplaine's will had required that his widow's share of the banking-business should, as soon as possible, become completely null. Her fortune was to be withdrawn from the house, and subsequently re-invested elsewhere. All such operations as these took time, and were attended with not a few legal complications as well. Olivia had many a prosy term of converse to undergo, and some of the proceedings explained to her were by no means as lucid after explanation as she might have wished. Suddenly, one day, the thought of Adrian Etherege flashed through her mind. How materially he could have aided her in the clearer understanding of these perplexing details! And why had she not remembered him before?

The truth was, she had absolutely forgotten him for weeks. "How ungrateful of me!" she reflected. "And after he defended me so bravely at Greenacre that evening! He must have felt bitterly toward me all this time. No doubt he has been waiting for me to summon him. What harm can there be in my doing so at once?"

Still, she feared the questions he might ask her regarding that fateful night. Massereene's reference to it had caused her many a memorial shudder. What if Adrian had refrained from seeking her again because he suspected her of greater guilt than that with which she already charged her own unhappy self?

A few hours later one of the employees at the Bank — a gentleman with whom she had already held more than a single rather wearisome parley — presented himself at her house. After not a little hesitation, she made up her mind to inquire concerning Adrian.

"Etherege?" was the reply. "Oh, we have not seen him at the Bank for certainly six weeks. They say he is quite ill. I don't know what the trouble is. We have paid him his salary as usual. Once or twice his mother — a tall, solemn-faced, elderly lady — has appeared and received the money in person. I myself had no conversation with her, but I believe she said her son was seriously ill with a fever. Several of the clerks called at Etherege's house, but I don't think any of them succeeded in seeing him. Mrs. Etherege always received the visitors, if I am not mistaken, and gave them the same answer — that her son was too ill to have any one enter his room. . . . I've no idea how his sickness will terminate, but it is beginning to be whispered, down at the Bank, that he is in a very dangerous condition. You knew him well, I suppose, Mrs. Delaplaine, when your husband was alive?"

"Yes," Olivia said. "I knew him very well. His illness is a great surprise to me — and a shock also. Can you give me his address?"

"I can have it sent to you," came the answer.

"Please do so, then, immediately."

On the following day Olivia received the address. It was considerably up-town, in one of the easterly side-streets, not far from Second Avenue. That afternoon she had herself driven there in her own private carriage.

She felt convinced that the woman whom she would now most probably meet was the same whom she had seen for a brief minute or two at the head of the stairway on a certain afternoon, not very long ago, while Delaplaine's curt words of dismissal had rung out with such astonishing harshness. And this woman — the mother of Adrian — had no doubt once been the mistress of Delaplaine. All indications, as presented by Adrian himself, had tended toward such a belief on Olivia's part. It was not pleasant to seek her friend with the prospect of being accosted by Mrs. Etherege at the very outset of the search. Still, the gloomy character of the tidings Olivia had heard left her no alternative. In the way of sacrificing her own inclinations or prejudices, much more than she now contemplated doing would have cheerfully enough been undertaken by her for reasons like the present.

The house at which her carriage finally drew up was one of those small, third-rate red-brick buildings that contribute so multitudinously toward the re- nowned ugliness of the metropolis. Here dwelt Mrs. Etherege, renting the house and sub-renting all floors of it but one. This was the first, or "parlor" floor, and in its front apartment she received Olivia, amid surroundings of a shabby-genteel quality. Effects here and there suggested the taste or influence of Adrian; but the *ensemble* was in the main both dreary and threadbare.

Mrs. Etherege looked indisputably the first if not the last. Olivia recognized her at once. And the solemn lines on her worn face did not grow a grade more cheerful after she had been told her visitor's name. Indeed, Olivia noticed the lines about her mouth tighten ominously as she said :

"You called, ma'am, to inquire about my son?"

"I called to see him, if I could. I hope he is well enough to see me. I—"

"He never sees anybody," was the interruption, hard as a blow.

"I am very sorry," said Olivia, sweetly. "Is he then so exceedingly ill?"

"Yes. He's pretty sick."

"Dangerously, do you mean?"

"Yes."

"Will you let me ask you what his trouble is?" ·

Mrs. Etherege did not seem at all disposed to tell. She was occupying a straight-backed chair in front of the easier one into which Olivia had sunk. She had drooped her eyes and was scanning the carpet with them. It appeared quite possible to Olivia that she might raise them any minute, and show them glittering with most inhospitable beams. It was evident that the woman did not like her boldness in coming thither, but also that she had motives for not making this disapproval too palpable. Meanwhile, notwith. standing the grimness and bleakness of her visage,

Olivia could detect in it a strong though covert resemblance to Adrian's; one might almost have said that its beauty had become insultingly flouted by trouble and disappointment — two as malevolent vitriol-throwers, in their way, as any that ever prowled.

" He's affected strangely," she at length said, raising her eyes. " He *had* typhoid. But that's gone now, and he's . . . well, he's very weak." All expression of animosity died on a sudden from her face, and one of excessive worriment succeeded it. " I'm very often afraid he's going crazy!" she exclaimed.

" Ah! how dreadful!" Olivia cried. " But perhaps it's only the *result* of the fever. It may wear off when he gets back his physical strength. Such cases are happening all the time."

Nothing could have sounded more spontaneous, more sympathetic, than these words of the visitor's, uttered in her dulcet voice and with softly sparkling eyes. They perceptibly softened Mrs. Etherege, who gazed long and earnestly at her companion, and then said :

•" Adrian's mind is in a very curious state. He lies without speaking, for hours. Then he'll begin to murmur to himself in a most incoherent manner. It seems as if he were hiding something from me — something that he's heard or done in former days — and yet as if this were preying so on his mind that he *must* sooner or later disclose it. . . . He's often spoken of you, ma'am. . . ."

" Of me!" exclaimed Olivia, a pang of self-reproach passing through her heart.

" . . . And I must acknowledge that lately," pursued Mrs. Etherege, as if she had made up her mind

to have it all out while her own propitious mood lasted,
" he's been begging that I would send for you."

"And why did you not?"

Mrs. Etherege began to gnaw her lips. "Well,"
she said, " there were reasons. Mr. Delaplaine, as you
know, was very good to Adrian. For quite a while
he almost adopted him. There was nothing very remarkable in his doing so. Adrian was a handsome
boy, and I . . . er . . . I was a relation of Mr. Delaplaine's. I don't know if he has ever mentioned this
fact to you or not."

"No," said Olivia, "my husband never mentioned
it to me. At least, not that I recollect." She had
become somehow most promptly convinced that Mrs.
Etherege's latter statement was a premeditated falsehood. All in all, however, she was rather glad that
this coolly audacious way had been adopted of dealing
with the whole awkward and unsavory subject. If
Adrian's mother had ever sought to convince Delaplaine that he was the father of her son, she must signally have failed after the lad reached any appreciable
age, since he bore no vaguest trace of such fatherhood.
Whatever Delaplaine had subsequently done for Adrian
must either have been prompted by some lingering
shadow of sentiment for his mother (which, as Olivia
had seen, that lady was inclined too daringly to count
upon), or by the mingled comeliness and capability
which the boy himself presented.

"Yes, oh, yes," proceeded Mrs. Etherege, with a
slow, decisive nod at Olivia. "I'm surprised he
didn't speak of the relationship. *Adrian* knew
nothing about it; I never told him." Here she
coughed, as though to give herself time for fresh

inventions. "I thought he might refer to it on some occasion when Mr. Delaplaine was not in the best of humors — you understand?"

"Yes," acceded Olivia mechanically. She thought she understood very well indeed.

"Now I was *more* than astonished," went on Mrs. Etherege, "I was *grieved* when I heard that Mr. Delaplaine had not even remembered me by as much as a small legacy." She paused, and drew a long breath, and Olivia wondered whether, during these few minutes of intercourse, she could not read her character somewhat clearly. Was she not a woman who had started life on a large stock of good looks and a moderate amount of principle, and who, having found the resources of both insufficient to keep her prosperously afloat, had mixed herself up in a hundred petty duplicities, remaining now, at a rather advanced age, wholly dissatisfied with the successful diplomacy of any?

"If, as you tell me, you are a relation of Mr. Delaplaine's," Olivia at once answered, "I shall be glad to make some amends for my husband's neglect." She said this, thinking of Adrian, and hoping that she could thus turn a little golden key in the doorway of obstruction between himself and her.

Mrs. Etherege smiled, and the smile seemed to astonish her sombre, *fade* face; you might have fancied that certain little muscles used in the process had grown stiff from lack of exercise.

"Oh, thank you, ma'am — thank you very much. We're *not* in the best of circumstances, and one or two of my boarders think of leaving me. If Adrian's salary at the Bank should be stopped, it would be very hard on us. The truth is, as I can tell *you*, my up-

stairs drainage isn't what it ought to be, and people
don't stay with me long, even if they come.   But I've
a three-years' lease of the house, so I *must* stay here
and try to make both ends meet."

" Well," said Olivia, smiling, " I will help you to do
that.   Trust me."   She was anxious to see Adrian at
once, and would have made almost any kind of promise, just then, in order to secure his mother's good
will.

" It was because I felt so hurt about Mr. Delaplaine's
forgetting me altogether," now pursued this lady,
" that I — well, I didn't think it was best to send for
you, no matter how hard Adrian begged."

"And he *did* beg hard?" exclaimed Olivia.   " Ah,
I hope you would have relented soon and sent for
me ! "

"Well, I dare say I would," she replied, looking
down with an uneasy roll of the eyeball ; and her
hearer almost concluded that she would have been
cruel enough to delay the summons perhaps many
days.

But Olivia now made an eager request to see Adrian.
Mrs. Etherege presently rose and left the room, after
saying that she would ascertain if such a plan were
feasible.   Her return was awaited most impatiently.
But not until twenty good minutes afterward did she
again appear.

" He is very weak to-day," she said.   " I had to tell
him in the most cautious way that you were here."

" And it gratified him to know?" asked Olivia.

"It — shocked him.   He's in a state when so little
*will* shock him.   But he seems very glad now.   He
is waiting to see you with a kind of new look in his

face. . . . . Please do not let him excite himself any more than you can help."

" I will do my utmost to soothe, to quiet him," Olivia answered.

" Very well. He wants me to leave you alone with him for a half an hour. . . . That is rather a long time, considering how ill he is. . . . But I shall be within call, if you should want me. It's only two rooms off. Will you come with me now ? "

Olivia rose, following Mrs. Etherege. Very soon, after that, she was standing in a neat, plainly-appointed room, near the bedside of Adrian.

## XXV.

His face, as she cast her eyes upon it, sent a thrill of horror through her nerves. Its beauty of contour and proportion was not so altered that she could not recognize it at once; and yet the change, the pallor, the attenuation! . . . Olivia did her best to conceal a visible tremor, and succeeded. She went nearer to the bed and took the hand that Adrian stretched out to her. Its clasp was burningly feverish. His exquisite brown eyes seemed to devour her face as she paused close beside him.

"Leave me here with Mrs. Delaplaine, mother," he said, suddenly making this appeal. "Remember your agreement."

"Yes, Adrian," was the reply. Without another word Mrs. Etherege passed from the room.

There was a chair quite near Olivia. She took it, and then, amid the silence that ensued after Adrian's mother had departed, she said, with her voice full of the tenderest solicitude:

"I had no idea until yesterday that you were ill."

"No?" he responded. His eyes dwelt upon hers as though some fascination compelled the searching intensity of their survey. "I wanted mother to send for you; I wanted it *so* much! But she kept putting me off. At length I made up my mind to do a certain thing, for I had lost all patience, and I suspected that she was deceiving me with false promises. If she did

not send for you this very day I had determined to
give her a fright — for she loves me, notwithstanding
her tame and gloomy way of showing it."

"A fright, Adrian?" asked Olivia. "You mean —?"
"I'd have told her the blunt truth — that I'm dying,
and that if she kept us apart any further length of
time she would be merely hastening the end for me."

"No, no, no," Olivia murmured. "You cannot
mean *that*, Adrian!" She laughed as cheerily as she
could, though her heart had begun to beat in a sicken-
ing way.

"Yes, it is true. I made the doctor tell me yesterday. He is a clever man, Dr. Wallace; he saw that
I was in earnest, and that no prevarication would
avail with me. Mother thinks that because my mind
wanders, now and then, while I'm lying here as weak
as a little child, it's my brain. But it is not. It's my
heart. Dr. Wallace says so. There's no hope for me;
it's what they call an atrophy, a wasting away. It
followed the fever; I had typhoid, you know, for
months. . . . Isn't it strange that I should die from
that? — a heart that is starving! I used to feel as if
my heart were starving when I looked at you in those
other days."

"Oh, Adrian!" Olivia faltered, drooping her head.
"I did. But all that is past, now. I had resolved
not to speak of it when you came. You knew that I
loved you. It was torture for me to see *him* treat you
as he did. I shall never forget that last evening at
dinner. When I left you, a little later, after you had
fainted, you believed (did you not?) that I had left
for town?"

"Yes."

"It was not true. I staid in the village all the next day. The next night I went back to Greenacre. My thoughts all day had been horrible. It seemed to me at times as if your very life were in peril from *him*. As I said, the next night I went back to Greenacre."

He appeared purposely to emphasize that last iterated sentence. He spoke in a low voice — almost too low for his mother, if she had chosen the part of eavesdropper, to have heard him. Speaking doubtless fatigued him, and at times a glassy light would replace the richer and sweeter lustre of his eyes. He was too sick a man to talk as much as this. Olivia was about to tell him so, and gently bid him to exert himself less, when his repetition of those words, "the next night I went back to Greenacre," somehow made her forget her designed injunction.

"Do you mean that you went there and asked for me?" she inquired.

Adrian closed his eyes for a moment, and a smile of the most ironical sadness broke from his lips and slowly faded there.

"No; I did not ask for you. I asked for no one. It was some time after dark. The night was very warm, as you perhaps remember."

"I do remember," Olivia said, with a slight inward thrill.

"The front doors were open; the light from the hall shone out across the piazza upon the lawn, where it joined the full, splendid moonlight. I did not know of Delaplaine's illness, but I felt sure I would not encounter him, as a closer view of the piazza told me he was not there, and I had observed that since his state had become so enfeebled he moved about very little. But I believed that I might see you, and I wanted very much to see you. I had been racked by the most forcible pity for you. I longed to press your hand in farewell, and assure you that if you needed my presence hereafter you had only to telegraph me and I would obey the call without an instant of delay. . . . All looked lonely and deserted as I ascended the piazza. If I had met a servant I would have sent a message to you. But even after passing into the hall I met no one whatever. Then the idea occurred to me of going upstairs to your sitting-room. Perhaps you would be there alone, and on such a warm night your door might be open. That would be better, I speedily decided, than to ring the bell for a servant, and send up my name to you, thus risking the fact of my presence being made known to *him*. . . . Well, so I mounted the stairs and soon found myself in the upper hall. As I passed your husband's bed-room the door was slightly ajar. You were speaking with an attendant, and before I had realized it I had heard all you said and all she said. I even caught a glimpse, too, of the man who lay there, and understood clearly that he must be very ill. . . . The woman soon left the room, and by the time that she had done so, going straight upstairs, I had withdrawn into a corner of the dim-lit hall. If she had turned and discovered me, I suppose she would have screamed and taken me for a robber . . . and then I should not have done the thing that freed you from him forever."

"What thing?" questioned Olivia, with her breath coming in gasps. A terror had begun to creep icily through her veins, but it was a terror somehow mixed with wild gladness.

"Can't you guess?" he answered. "You went out of the room, and I was going to follow along the hall and enter the other room where you were. But something held me back. I was thinking of the poison in that glass; I was thinking of how it could rid you of him forever."

"Adrian!"

"Presently he called you. You went in to him again. I heard those horrible words he spoke to you about wanting to have you die when he died. I was on the verge of rushing in when he grasped your hand like that; but I stood still outside there, instead, and felt my hate of him and my compassion for you mingle and surge through my veins. . . . Then he spoke of his thirst and of how he wanted a glassful of water as large as that of the medicine you were giving him. You told him it was a deadly poison, and after he had taken a spoonful of it you left the glass on the table at his side, because you were most probably agitated by those other words of his, warning you not to be too sure that he would die, after all — you who would not have retarded his detestable life by one second for all the wealth of all the world! . . . Then he told you to turn down the light, and you did, and left him. . . . And then my mind was made up, and I waited my chance."

"Your chance?"

"It came almost at once. He said, presently, in a husky voice, which you were too far off to hear, 'Oh, how thirsty I am!' . . . And then I did not wait any longer. I went into the dark room, softly, on tiptoe. He did not see me enter. I glided up toward the head of the bed, too much beyond him for him to have seen me, even if the room had not been in such thick shadow. I reached for the glass on the little table. 'Here's water,' I said, and the voice I spoke in startled me; it was very faint, but it was so shrewd a copy of just the way you would have spoken those two words. He put out his hand in the gloom, and I gave him the glass. I heard him begin to drink, with the sound a very thirsty child might give. . . . And then I did not stop even to see if he would put the glass back on the table or let it fall. . . . I shot away, and no one saw me dart downstairs and hurry out upon the lawn again. The news of his death came to me here in town. . . . I dare say the illness would have attacked me anyway. . . . I don't know. But I began to suffer fearfully for what I had done, and — and when the news also reached me that you had admitted his death was owing to your own carelessness in leaving the medicine so near him, I had a sick sort of dread lest you might — might be reproaching yourself with — the — thought —"

These latter words were broken painfully, and uttered with a difficulty that seemed to indicate the approach of death itself. But extreme exhaustion, not death, was now at work with Adrian. In another moment his eyes had closed, and his ghastly face, turned a little sideways on the pillow, revealed his complete loss of consciousness. . . .

Olivia rose from her chair. For a slight space of time she forgot even to cry out and summon the assistance of Mrs. Etherege. A single thought dominated her being. She was not guilty, after all! Heavy bonds were falling from her spirit, and as if with the audible noise of shattered chains. Darkness was flying away from her, struck into a hundred cloudy frag-

ments by shafts of poignant, enrapturing sunshine!
"Thank God! — thank God!" broke from her lips,
and as the words escaped her she seemed to gaze upon
the very face of Massereene, as though it had become
visible in the flesh close at her side. But she discerned
it through a blur of besieging tears; and when, a little
later, she hurried to find Adrian's mother, these tears
were streaming down her cheeks as though the bitter-
est grief and not the most impassioned joy had caused
them.

A few hours later she sat alone in her own room.
An open letter lay before her, sheet after sheet, with
the ink scarcely dry on the last one. It was to Massereene. It told him everything — the entire story of
her temptation, her self-loathing, her renunciation of
all future individual delights — and it confessed that
the love she bore him was chief and paramount among
those delights. Then it recorded the meeting with
Adrian Etherege and the new, dizzying revelation that
had come to her from his lips.

"Even if I should never see you again — and that
is now for you to decide — " the letter here went on,
"I implore you to keep as an absolute secret what I
have just written. But I know your merciful heart
— and Adrian is a dying man! His sin has been
terrible; I feel that I can judge somewhat of its
magnitude by the anguish that its consequences have
cost *me*. There is no other living soul except yourself
to whom I would have told his unhappy story. I
wonder if it is selfish of me to feel that you *must*
know the whole truth — that it is only justice to myself for such completeness of knowledge to be given

you. . . . As I said, Adrian Etherege will not live long; you already may read on his face that he is doomed. Explain it as you will, but I cannot help a feeling of infinite gratitude toward him. Still, in any case I would have promised his mother very liberal help, both before his death and afterward. . . ."

Olivia directed her letter, sealed it, and sent it to the hotel at which Massereene always lived when in New York.

"Will he come to me?" she asked herself.

Massereene, seated in his own room at the hotel, received two letters. He took them both carelessly, opened one and read in it that the particular state-room which he desired on a certain steamer sailing a few days from then would be reserved for him. . . . Then he glanced at the other envelope and gave a great start. His recognition of the handwriting set him in a quiver of excitement. . . . About fifteen minutes afterward he came downstairs with unwonted speed, almost threw himself into a cab, and gave orders to be driven to West Tenth Street. . . .

"Foolish child!" he said to Olivia, afer the first and almost silent ecstasy of their meeting had passed; "why should you not have told me your trouble before, when it was tormenting your soul? I would have convinced you that your sin (no matter what may have been its result) was far less unpardonable than you believed."

"Nothing could have so convinced me," said Olivia. She drew away from him with a little shiver, though his encircling arms would not let her recede far. "I have misgivings even now," she went on, "that I am absolving myself much too easily."

"Oh, don't bother, then, about absolving yourself at all," smiled Massereene. "Leave it all to me. Make me the keeper of your conscience."

"You've enough that is mine to take care of already," said Olivia, looking deep into his eyes and answering his smile.

. "I've your heart," he said. "Do you mean that?"

"Yes."

He laughed. "Well, I'll own to the responsibility, my dearest, and not be too ambitious about increasing it."

Olivia drew a long sigh. "Responsibility?" she murmured. "My sense of a great one will never cease while I live; for I shall always see reproachful proofs of my weakness in the strength which ought to have made it self-control."

"And I," he replied, still playfully, "shall always hope for strength to grapple with your hardiest metaphysics, and repress them when they take too morbid an outlook."

But she shook her head forbiddingly at this lighter mood of his, even while she drooped closer to him and let his arms more fondly enwrap her; for with all her ever-to-be-endured regret, she could not but love the levity that his happiness forced from him, — and as naturally as the dawn itself will force a dewy glitter from those grasses that its first beams have bathed!